PRAISE FOR THE LANE WINSLOW MYSTERIES

"The 'find of the year'... With the feel of Louise Penny's Three Pines, the independence and quick wit of Kerry Greenwood's Phryne Fisher and the intelligence of Jacqueline Winspear's Maisie Dobbs, this mystery series has it all!"—Murder by the Book, Texas

"Whishaw nicely captures the rhythms and dynamics of small-town life while maintaining suspense. Maisie Dobbs and Phryne Fisher fans will be pleased." —*Publishers Weekly*

"Relentlessly exciting from start to finish." —*Kirkus Reviews*

"There are days when nothing suits a reader like a good old-fashioned classic cozy with a puzzle plot, a country setting and some nice slight characters. When that urge strikes, Iona Whishaw's delightful BC series featuring Lane Winslow and, now, husband, Inspector Darling of the King's Cove constabulary, are just the ticket." —*Globe and Mail*

"There's no question you should read it—it's excellent." —*Toronto Star*

"In the vein of Louise Penny... a compelling series that combines a cozy setting, spy intrigue storylines, and police procedural elements—not an easy task, but one that Whishaw pulls off."—Reviewing the Evidence

"Whishaw's writing is worthy of taking its place alongside the works of Agatha Chr
deftly crafted and briskl
of *The Dressmaker's Gift*

PRAISE FOR THE LANE WINSLOW MYSTERIES

"Think a young Katharine Hepburn—beautiful, smart and beyond capable. Winslow is an example of the kind of woman who emerged after the war, a confident female who had worked in factories building tanks and guns, a woman who hadn't yet been suffocated by the 1950s—perfect housewife ideal." —*Vancouver Sun*

"I absolutely love the modern sensibility of these novels, of their feminism, sense of justice, their anti-racism, their progressiveness, which somehow never seems out of place in a tiny BC hamlet in 1948." —Kerry Clare, author of *Waiting for a Star to Fall* and editor of 49th Shelf

"An intriguing mix of character, plot, time, and place. Highly recommended." —Ian Hamilton, author of the Ava Lee novels

"Fantastic... readers will stand up and cheer." —Anna Lee Huber, author of the Lady Darby Mysteries and the Verity Kent Mysteries

"Richly conjured... deftly plotted... this series just keeps getting better!" —Catriona McPherson, award-winning author of the Dandy Gilver series

"Complex, suspenseful, and deeply felt, this is a smart series for the ages." —Francine Mathews, author of the Nantucket Mysteries

A SORROWFUL SANCTUARY

THE LANE WINSLOW MYSTERY SERIES

A Killer in King's Cove (#1)
Death in a Darkening Mist (#2)
An Old, Cold Grave (#3)
It Begins in Betrayal (#4)
A Sorrowful Sanctuary (#5)
A Deceptive Devotion (#6)
A Match Made for Murder (#7)
A Lethal Lesson (#8)
Framed in Fire (#9)
To Track a Traitor (#10)

IONA WHISHAW

A SORROWFUL SANCTUARY

A LANE WINSLOW MYSTERY

TouchWood Editions
touchwoodeditions.com

Edited by Claire Philipson
Cover illustration by Margaret Hanson

CATALOGUING DATA AVAILABLE FROM LIBRARY AND ARCHIVES CANADA
ISBN 9781771512893 (softcover)
ISBN 9781771512909 (e-book)
ISBN 9781771513746 (audiobook)

TouchWood Editions acknowledges that the land on which we live and work is within the traditional territories of the Lkwungen (Esquimalt and Songhees), Malahat, Pacheedaht, Scia'new, T'Sou-ke and W̱SÁNEĆ (Pauquachin, Tsartlip, Tsawout, Tseycum) peoples.

We gratefully acknowledge the financial support of the Government of Canada through the Canada Book Fund, the Canada Council for the Arts, and the Province of British Columbia through the British Columbia Arts Council and the Book Publishing Tax Credit.

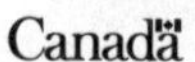

PRINTED IN CANADA AT FRIESENS

27 26 25 24 23 3 4 5

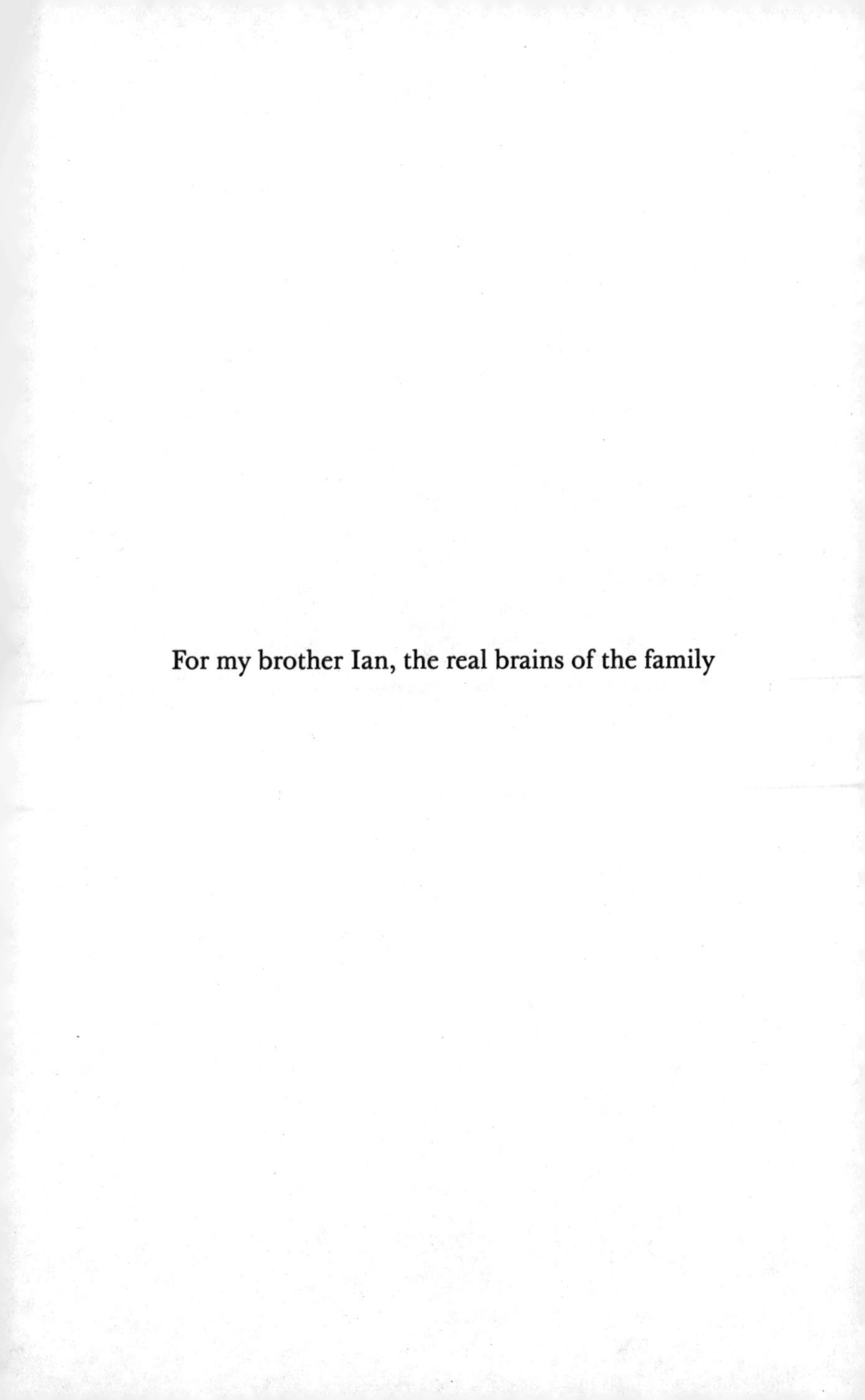

For my brother Ian, the real brains of the family

CHAPTER ONE

Friday, July 18, 1947

WHEN THE SHOT CAME IT deafened him. He fell backwards, down, down, until he lay rocking, facing the night sky, wondering who had been hit. Above him stars whirled like a carousel in the moonless dark, and he felt himself smile at their antics. There was the Great Bear, its north-pointing star, still in the maelstrom, a sign for him. He closed his eyes but felt the rain on his face, wet, falling, as he was. How had he mistaken the rain for stars? He opened his eyes, trying to will the stars back, trying to hear something besides the din reverberating in his skull. He did not hear the urgent whispers or the pounding of running feet, nor was he aware of the man hiding in the water under the pier, shivering with cold and terror because he had seen it all. He could not remember any moment in his life before this one had engulfed him.

Saturday, July 19

"HOW LONG HAS it been?" O'Brien said into the telephone. It was first thing Saturday morning, and the desk sergeant at the Nelson police station was having a difficult time with a caller. He was leaning heavily on the counter, prepared to take notes but already impatient at the woman's unnecessarily panicked tone. Young men rarely went missing. Gadding about, more likely.

"He went to work yesterday and he hasn't been back. It's not like him. If he's planning to stay away, he always tells me. He writes down the phone number if there is one, and tells me exactly when he'll be back."

"How old is he, ma'am?" O'Brien wrote *Friday* in his notebook and underlined it.

"He's twenty. And he never misses work. Mr. Van Eyck at the garage has no idea where he is."

"Are you sure he hasn't gone on a bender with some friends, or gone off to see a girl?"

There was a longish silence. "Are you going to help or not? I want to talk to somebody else." The woman sounded desperate and angry.

"I'll put you through to the inspector," O'Brien said. Let him deal with it. It was time he got back into the swing of things after his little holiday in London.

Darling was at his desk reading through the notes about an affray at the local hotel bar the day before. Both men had spent the night in jail and had been released that morning, rumpled and smelling of stale beer. They'd fought over a woman. A bigger cliché was difficult to imagine, he thought. He earnestly hoped she would drop them both. The phone's ring triggered a hope that some real meaty case was in the offing, or better yet, that it was Lane Winslow calling.

"That fellow I was talking to is a useless lump! Are you going to help me or not?"

Not Lane, then. "If I can, madam. Tell me what's happened."

"My son, Carl, is missing is what's happened. He went off yesterday. He comes home from the garage at noon every day for his meal, only he never came back at all, and he's not been seen since. As I told that imbecile a minute ago, it is not like Carl. I'm his mother. I should at least know what is and is not like him, and this is not."

Darling was sympathetic. In his experience people not behaving like themselves was something to pay attention to.

"Can you tell me your name and where you live?"

"Vanessa Castle, and I live near Balfour. We have a poultry farm. My husband is dead, no surprise, and I'm running the farm. Carl works at the garage. He left in the morning, like usual, put on his hat, and went to work. Only he didn't, because Van Eyck doesn't know where he is. He was quite offensive. He asked why I thought he should have seen him."

"And how old is he?"

Barely containing her impatience, Mrs. Castle snapped, "Twenty."

"You're worried something has happened to him," Darling said, wanting to get away from the barrage of questions.

"Look, he's always been a good, straight boy. Doesn't drink, even after he signed up near the end of the war and was with those other fellows in training. He used to come home on his leave and tell me some hair-raising stories about how they all behaved. He never did go overseas, but he liked the work on the vehicles and got a job at the garage. I called one of his friends from school, but he's gone up north to some mining camp. You have to believe me—what's your name again?"

"Inspector Darling."

"You have to believe me, Inspector Darling, when I tell you Carl would never go off and not tell me. He was none too happy with his dad's treatment of me, and he's kind of tried to make up for it."

"I imagine you've contacted anyone he knows?"

"That's not a long list. I had to wrestle the name of the mining outfit from his friend's mother, but I finally got through to him and he hasn't seen or heard from Carl."

"His friend's mother was not willing to tell you where her son was?"

"No, she was not. Kept telling me she didn't want her son involved."

That's odd as well, Darling thought. "Did she say involved with what?"

She hesitated. "I asked her what she meant, and she said something about it being better that her boy got away from all that. The war is over, she tells me. Best leave things be, she tells me. Then she rang off. The idea that Carl is 'involved' with anything is ridiculous."

Darling noted her hesitation. "Did he belong to a club, go to a legion or anything?"

"He went into town sometimes, after work, but he isn't a drinker. He'd always come home early."

There was that insistence again that he didn't drink. "And you've checked the hospital?"

"They don't have him. I wanted to be relieved when they told me that, but I'm more frightened than ever."

"Did he go off in a car?"

"Yes, his dad's old Chevrolet. Yellow, about ten years old. Are you going to find him?"

"I'll need the licence number if you have it. Then I can get on to my colleagues in the RCMP, and my constable and I will come out to see you, if we may, to look at his room and so on. Please don't tidy up or touch anything till we get there."

"I don't know the licence plate. I'll look for it." She didn't sound hopeful.

Darling took down her address, resisted being reassuring, called down the hall to Constable Ames, and was rewarded by silence.

"Where's Ames gone?" he asked O'Brien irritably, picking up the phone.

O'Brien shook his head at the phone receiver. "You said he could have the morning off, sir. He's helping his mother move some furniture."

"Why can't she get moving men like normal people?" It was a rhetorical question, but O'Brien seemed to feel it wanted an answer.

"Because that's what sons do for their moms."

Darling thought about sons and their mothers. He never had opportunity to do much for his own mother. She had died an agonizing death from cancer when he was sixteen. To this day he couldn't think clearly about what that had meant to him. The shock of her suffering and the finality of her absence had seared itself into his young mind, and he had stored the memory, tightly sealed and unexamined, in the farthest recesses of his consciousness. His father had once called one of his high school friends a "mama's boy" and had made an unflattering observation that at least he, Darling, had been saved from that by his mother's death. All he felt he'd been saved from was understanding women, and perhaps—he thought of Lane Winslow and swallowed—giving himself freely to a relationship without fearing that it would all be taken away.

Glancing at his watch, he saw that the morning was nearly over, and he was feeling a little hungry. He'd have to wait for Ames anyway. "I'm going next door for a quick sandwich. Tell Ames to meet me there." O'Brien saluted and got back to the crossword puzzle he kept under the files he was meant to be working on.

"Good morning, Inspector. No trusty sidekick today?" the waitress at the counter said. Darling knew April because Ames had gotten into a lot of trouble with her the year before when he dropped her for his current flame.

"He's helping his mother move some things. I expect him here soon, though, so get your game face ready."

"A regular fair-haired boy, then. Honestly, I stopped being mad a long time ago. I just love to get his goat."

"Me too. I admire your technique."

April beamed engagingly. "What can I get you?"

"A grilled ham and cheese and—" The sound of the door opening caused him to turn. Ames was taking off his hat and advancing cautiously to where Darling was sitting. "And whatever he's having. Make sure he gets the bill."

"THE INTERESTING THING to me is what his friend's mother said. That business of not wanting to get involved," Darling said. They were third in line for the ferry ride across the lake. Both had their windows wound down to combat the heat of the day, and Ames had one arm dangling out his window. He hoped they would be able to keep the windows open, but the weather had been dry and the dust kicked up by cars ahead of them on the road could be bad.

"How much trouble would it be for someone to sling a bridge across here?" Ames asked impatiently.

Darling turned and looked with surprise at his constable, who was tapping nervously on the steering wheel of the maroon Ford that served as their police vehicle. "You're not your usual sunny self, Ames. What's going on? And let me caution you that if it's your usual troubles with women, I'd prefer to be kept in the dark."

"You act like it's nothing, sir, but you wait till something happens with Miss Winslow and see if you think it's nothing!" This shocking outburst was accompanied by an angry slap of the palm on the steering wheel and then almost immediately by an apology. "I'm sorry, sir. I was out of line. Oh, thank God!" This was because the ferry had arrived and put down the gate to disgorge the two cars coming into town.

"You certainly were," said Darling, wondering if he was too dismissive of Ames. Perhaps Ames didn't have anyone to confide in. And considering the anxieties he himself confronted in his newly minted relationship with Lane Winslow, he ought to be more sympathetic. He wanted Ames to go to Vancouver in late August to take the sergeant's training, and hoped nothing would interfere with that.

"She's a nice girl, Violet," said Ames, driving onto the ferry deck.

"She puts up with you," agreed Darling.

"But today I was helping my mother, and Mom suddenly said that she wondered if Vi was the right girl for me."

Darling frowned. "I thought it was normal for parents to disapprove of their children's choices."

"Not my mom. She's never said anything about any girl I've dated. She's very cautious, which is why it stood out. And maybe I could have ignored it, except Vi and I had a fight over children a couple of days ago, believe it or not."

"Good God, Ames, you're not—"

"Really, sir! No. I was talking about that case with that kid who robbed the cash out of the register at that grocery store at the bottom of the road, and Vi says, 'I'd give him a good thrashing. Kids need to know who's boss.' I pointed out that the kid was only eleven years old, and she says, 'There you are, then,' like it was the answer."

"It's a pretty normal response. Most children get a spanking once in a while, don't they?" He had.

Ames was silent until they were on the road. The two cars ahead of them had both turned off the road almost immediately, so they were able to keep the windows down.

"I don't believe in it, sir. That boy was thrashed most of his life by his drunken father. How do we know that wasn't what caused the problem? My father generally didn't go in for it, but a couple of times he felt he had to, and I don't think it improved me much. You go on about my 'sunny temperament,' and I think I got that because generally my parents didn't believe spanking me would do much good. I think there's enough suffering in the world without parents hitting their children. It's not fair, apart from anything else. They're smaller than us. When my mother said that about Vi, I asked her why, and she said something like, 'She's a nice girl, I can see that, but she's not like you.' And I have to say, at that moment I got worried that she was right."

"So the long and the short of it is that you're in this lousy mood because you're thinking you'll have to break it off." Darling offered this in a sympathetic manner.

"I was close to thinking about popping the question. Now I don't know, but I think she's expecting it. She's been hinting quite a bit. I feel backed against a wall."

"Well," said Darling, rubbing his chin thoughtfully, "I don't have much experience with these things, but I wouldn't recommend marrying when you aren't sure. It's bad enough having the town swimming in your angry ex-girlfriends. Fill the place with angry ex-wives and you'll have to join the Mounties and go up north somewhere. I'm not paying for you to get your training so you can take it to Prince George."

Ames knew his boss was right and appreciated the real concern being cloaked by Darling's mockery, but in a way that made it all the worse. If he admitted to himself that he couldn't marry Vi, then he would have to face that putting it off wasn't going to be the answer, and hiding out in Vancouver while he took his training would only delay things. He had no idea what to do. To his relief Darling took up the subject of the missing man.

"This boy's mother is entirely certain he would not go off without a word. Is she right, or has he been keeping secrets from her?"

Knowing this to be Darling thinking out loud, Ames did not answer. He would have said mothers often lived in the dark, but his own mother's astute observation had rattled him.

"I've told her to leave his bedroom alone. I hope she has. She seems very fond of her son. If she finds something disagreeable, she could get rid of it, and we'd probably be missing a crucial bit of evidence. Of course, we could get there and find he's safely at home telling her comforting lies about where he's been."

"Is this where we turn?" Ames asked, slowing down. He'd been watching the odometer, and they were about a mile past the turnoff to the Balfour store. Getting a nod from Darling, Ames turned right onto a road that bumped down toward the lake. It ended in front of a small house, neatly painted and fenced, flanked on both sides by a large kitchen garden. They parked where they assumed the yellow Chevy the missing man had gone off in would normally be parked and got out of the car. They could see behind the house fenced-off outbuildings from which a gentle chorus of clucking emanated. It was clear immediately that the young man had not come home. The minute Ames turned off the engine a distraught woman appeared at the top of the stairs. She was waving a piece of paper.

"God. She's been through his room," Darling said. "The very thing I told her not to do."

CHAPTER TWO

LANE DREW BACK HER ARM and cast her line in an arc, hearing the gentle plop of the lead weight on her line hit the water below. A violent rain during the night had woken her as it slashed in waves against her bedroom window, but now the sky was a transcendent blue. Despite the coolness in the shade of the trees, the afternoon had become hot and dense. She relished the warm smell of the carpet of pine needles that came from the forest at the edge of the rocky point, rising some ten feet above the water where she stood. She could hear Kenny Armstrong conferring quietly with Angela Bertolli behind her. Angela had tried fishing once or twice but was taking advantage of Kenny's expert advice now, though Lane could see she was only partly attentive because Angela's three boys, Philip, Rolfie, and Rafe, were below them on the beach making a good deal of noise. Lane, smiling, gave a little shake of the head. She was certain all that racket would scare off any nearby fish. The would-be anglers had chosen Saturday, when they would not be interrupted by the steamer coming into dock at the wharf just south of the point. They had hoped to set off in the morning, but any enterprise involving three children, Lane learned, was bound to be delayed, in this case until nearly three in the afternoon.

"Got it!" she heard Angela say. "I'll try it, but I warn you, I'll be hopeless!"

Lane fell into a reverie about the strangeness of life. Angela was her second real friend. She thought about what went into making a friendship. Until Angela, she would have said it was shared hardship.

Her first true friend was Yvonne Bernard, whom she had met through Yvonne's work in the French resistance. Their bond had been formed in the extreme conditions of war—constant danger, loyalty, secrecy, and the imminent fear of capture or death. And now here was Angela, like a woman from another universe, American, sunny, effusive, and intelligent. It occurred to Lane now that it was possible to have a friendship based solely on proximity and cheerfulness. Lane's mind wandered happily along the path that had brought her to this moment, including her new-found and completely unexpected happiness in her relationship with Inspector Darling, who was no doubt fighting crime from the police station in Nelson.

She smiled. It was a perfect day. The lake was still and almost glassy after the torrential rains of the night before, the only other signs of life a rowboat far out on the water. "I wonder if they're having better luck out on the lake?" she said.

What Kenny might have thought about this was lost in what happened next.

Rafe Bertolli, pointing toward the bottom of the point, shouted, "Look! A rowboat! There's no one in it!"

The boys by this time had gone up onto the end of the wharf and had been jumping noisily into the water. They swam like fish, Lane knew, but she could see that Angela kept one eye on them all the time. The shout, and a thud below her in the water, brought Lane back to the present. Rafe was not pointing at the boat out on the water, as she expected, but directly below where she stood on the rocky outcrop of McEwen Point. Frowning, she leaned forward, trying to see, but the slight overhang made it hard to see properly. Putting aside her fishing rod she scrambled down the slope toward the beach until the area below the point was visible.

"Can you see it?" Kenny asked, coming along behind her, followed by Angela.

"Now who would let their rowboat off the leash? It's drifted here from somewhere. It's lying pretty low and has one oar dangling off the edge as well. It's obviously been taking on water." Lane looked out across the lake, wondering what direction the boat could have come from. Then she heard a hoarse groan. "There's someone in it!" she cried.

She bolted the rest of the way down the rocks to the beach, tore off her shoes and sweater, and splashed into the water, an involuntary gasp escaping her at the sudden cold. She swam along the edge of the rocks to where the small green rowboat was banging gently against the edge of the cliff. A frayed rope hung off a metal ring at the prow, trailing into the water. She needed to pull the boat to the beach.

"Horrors!" Angela exclaimed. "Is he alive? Children, up to the car, right now." By this time the children had seen, from their vantage point above the water, that there was indeed someone in the boat.

"He's bleeding!" Philip shouted. "I bet he's dead!"

"Now!" barked Angela, pointing at where she'd parked the car near the apple shed at the top of the wharf. She had reached the wharf by this time and was herding the boys toward the car.

"I've got you!" Lane called out to the person in the boat. She had heard one more soft groan as she had approached it. Now there was only silence.

Lane pulled at the boat, heavy with water, with one hand, and swam toward the shore, relief flooding her when her feet met the ground. Kenny waded toward her, grabbing at the rope Lane was pulling. He pulled the oar out of the oarlock and threw it onto the beach, and between them they dragged the rowboat onto the shore, the wooden keel scraping along the pebbles and sand.

"Oh my word," Kenny exclaimed, his hand momentarily over his mouth.

Lying awkwardly with his head thrust uncomfortably forward by the wooden slat it rested against was a young man, his arms at his sides, his head flopping with the movement of the boat. The deep wash of bilge water was dyed red and soaked his clothes so that he looked like he was floating helplessly in his own blood.

CHAPTER THREE

THE MAN'S LIPS MOVED SLIGHTLY. They were a ghastly shade of blue.

"He's alive," Lane said quietly. "He's freezing. Can you see if Angela has anything in the car to cover him with?"

Lane put her hand gently on the man's shoulder, saying quietly, "We'll have you out of here in a moment." He was so young, she thought. She'd seen this before, she remembered with a start, when she'd approached a safe house where she was to make contact during a drop in France and found three men shot to death. One of them had barely been twenty, and she'd been struck by how much younger he looked in death. Where was all that blood coming from?

Kenny turned without a word and clambered back up to the wharf. He and Angela came back with a blanket and a tarpaulin. The boys, who were confined to the car, had their faces pressed to the window.

Lane reached in to take his hand, and then saw it: the blood-soaked mess in his abdominal area.

"I've found where that blood is coming from," Lane said to them. "He seems to have been stabbed or shot in the stomach."

Kenny peered forward. "Unlucky fellow. That's a bad kind of accident."

"What do you think? He needs to come out of there. I'm worried about aggravating that wound, but he can't lie in the water like that," Lane said to them. The young man's hand remained nearly frozen in hers. "He's icy, and there's barely a pulse." Lane considered for a moment. Kenny's truck was also on the wharf, and she thought about sending him to call for the ambulance and the police. "As soon as we get him out of there, can you drive home to call for help? Angela and I will try to keep him warm."

They laid out the blanket, and Lane was relieved to see that Angela had also brought the large Thermos of tea she had made.

As carefully as they could, Kenny holding the young man under the arms, Lane taking his feet, and Angela trying to support the middle of his body, they pulled him awkwardly from the boat. He was a dead weight, and the boat tipped as they pulled him free, spilling the blood-soaked water onto the rescuers.

They laid him on the blanket, and Kenny said, "Here are the keys. You'll be faster than me. Take my truck and phone for help. And then bring Eleanor. She was a nurse in the Great War. I think she even has some stuff in a bag."

"Hurry!" said Angela. She was already folding the blanket tightly over the man's body.

Back up the hill at her house, soaking and shivering, with the acrid metallic smell of blood in her nose, Lane turned the crank on her phone and waited impatiently for the operator at the exchange in the little shop on Balfour Road to answer. "Nelson police station, please." She tried to put quiet urgency into her voice. The phone went dead. Cursing volubly, she hung up and tried the whole procedure again. Again she got the exchange.

"What happened?" the operator asked.

"Bloody phone died. Can you put me through? It's an emergency."

Lane waited tensely, worried that the phone would die again. She knew she should replace it. It was all very well thinking this ridiculous old phone was charming, but you had to be able to count on a telephone! At long last the desk sergeant picked up on the other end. "Inspector Darling, please," said Lane. "It's urgent. Is he there?"

"As it happens, he just got in from a call up the lake. One moment."

Another wait.

"Inspector Darling." The crisp business-like voice of the man she loved.

"Darling, it's Lane. You've got to get an ambulance out here immediately. Tell them to drive down to the wharf. We have a young man with a bad abdominal wound. He's lost a lot of blood. He was floating in a rowboat, which he's probably been in most of the night. He's barely alive."

Darling, who initially had been delighted at the sound of her voice, now shouted out to his constable in the next office. "Ames! An ambulance to King's Cove, down to the wharf!" He was rewarded by hearing Ames shout, "Sir!"

"We'll be out as soon as we can. Do you recognize him?" he asked Lane.

"No. He's young. I'd say under twenty-five."

"Do you have an idea about the origin of the wound?"

"I can't tell. His clothes are completely soaked in blood. It looks like he was speared by something. Or shot," she added unhappily. She was beginning to feel her teeth chattering. Cold and shock, she thought. She waited for an answer, but there was only silence. The phone again! She slammed the receiver onto its hook.

"Damn!" said Darling. He heard the word "shot" and then the phone went dead. "We're on our way," he said into the dead receiver. He wanted to add, "You sound cold." Well, he had what he needed. He seized his hat off the rack in his meticulously tidy office and shouted, "Let's go!"

EXHAUSTED, LANE LEANED against the wall for a moment. The reek of her clothes was almost unbearable. She hurried down the hall to her front door and peeled off her wet garments outside. She couldn't bear to have the smell in the house, but she didn't have time to do anything but throw on something dry.

Warmly dressed, she considered what she ought to take down to the beach. The ambulance would not arrive for some forty minutes if all went well. It would depend on which side of the lake the Nelson ferry was on. If it was on the wrong side, there would be a delay of another ten minutes. She grabbed another blanket, a small pillow, and a dry pair of pants for Angela, in case she was going to be stubborn and stay. Lane planned to tell her to take the children home the minute she got back to the wharf.

Throwing the things she'd collected into the truck, she pulled out of her driveway and drove the hundred yards to the Armstrongs' house. Eleanor was in the front garden and looked up with first a smile and then a puzzled frown when Lane jumped out of the cab. Eleanor pushed herself off her knees and hurried toward Lane.

"What's happened?"

"We've found some poor young man half dead in a nearly submerged rowboat. He has a huge wound in his abdomen. Well, it might not be huge, but there is plenty of blood. Angela and Kenny are with him, and he said you might be able to help. The ambulance won't be here for nearly an hour."

Eleanor took off her gardening gloves decisively. "Stay there." She rushed into the house and came out carrying a small leather bag. "I was a nurse in the Great War, after all. I'll remember something in a pinch."

"What's in that bag?" Lane asked, backing and turning the truck. She was not used to the gearshift and made it scrape in protest as she put it into reverse. "Sorry, Kenny."

"It's my old kit. A tourniquet and bandages, mainly, vials of iodine, which may still be good. I don't know how long it keeps. A bottle of alcohol. That was still okay a year ago when I cut myself with the garden shears. Tell me about his wound."

Lane described it as well as she could. They were turning onto the Nelson road, which they would cross before navigating the curving and narrow rutted road down to the wharf. She hoped the ambulance could manage it.

"Why would a man with that kind of injury be adrift in a rowboat?" Eleanor asked incredulously. "He's lost a lot of blood?"

"Judging by the boat, he's lucky if he has a drop left in him." Lane shuddered involuntarily at the memory of the bloodied water sloshing out of the bottom of the boat onto them.

She drove the truck onto the wharf and parked it in front of the packing shed. She could see the scene farther along on the beach. The sun was glinting off the water. That would dry them at least, Lane thought. Kenny was sitting on a rock, and Angela had the young man's head on her lap and was holding the top of the Thermos up to his lips. Kenny got up slowly, stretched his back, and made his way along the pebbled beach toward the wharf. The children were still watching from the windows of Angela's car. Now that Eleanor was here, Angela should take them home, Lane thought.

"Young fellow is holding on, but just," Kenny said. He offered his hand to his wife, as the path down to the beach from the wharf was rocky and narrow. "I don't know that you'll be able to do much for him," he added, eyeing her bag.

"Has he warmed up at all? We have another blanket."

"Not much," Angela said quietly. "But more warmth will be good."

Lane spread her blanket over him and carefully tucked it around his body. "He hasn't spoken?" It was a faint hope, but she wanted to know why a young man would be wounded and adrift in a leaky rowboat.

"No. He is barely breathing. I think some of the tea has gone down, but I don't know. He hasn't taken much."

Eleanor was on her knees and feeling the pulse in his neck. "It is very weak." She looked at the watch she always kept pinned to her dress, as if in unconscious memory of her time in that earlier war. "I'm going to take a quick peek at his injury in case it's still bleeding, but the medics should come in the next twenty-five minutes. Then I think we should try to keep him warm and drinking tea till they get here."

Carefully Eleanor peeled away the two layers of blanket to reveal the torn and bloodied shirt. With utmost gentleness, she tried to peel away the shreds of cloth. At the nursing stations in France she had seen injuries where bits of clothing had been driven into the wounds, increasing the risk of complication and the chance of infection. The young man was wearing a stained and torn singlet, and a wool plaid shirt that had soaked up a good deal of blood, and as she lifted it gently away from his body, she could see what looked for all the world like a gunshot wound.

"There's a lot of damage," she muttered. "And I would say it is a gunshot wound. Can you pass me the scissors and some of the gauze in the bag, please?" She held out her hand but did not take her eyes off the wound. Lane fished frantically in the bag and found a brown paper parcel that felt like it might contain gauze, and tore it open.

"Here. How much?"

"Yes, that will do. He's no longer bleeding heavily," said Eleanor. She used the scissors to cut away as much cloth as she could to try to expose the wound. The flesh gaped, and with the singlet pulled away, blood began to pool in the gash. "I'll put this over the wound to keep it clean and I'll just have to keep up some pressure to prevent more blood loss, not that there appears to be much left. Can you find more gauze in there?"

Lane fished again and found what was needed. Eleanor wanted to cut the whole length of the singlet to keep the area clear, but knowing the ambulance would be there soon, she decided to focus on keeping him warm. She folded the blankets back over him. "That will have to do. I hope they come soon. It is hot out here, and I'm worried about infection. It's difficult to know what to do. He seems to have hypothermia, so we have to keep him warm, but I don't want that wound getting warmer."

Angela, still holding the Thermos, had been standing to one side watching Eleanor with amazement. In no way could she square the prim, elderly, white-haired postmistress and baker of lemon oatmeal cookies with this woman who apparently knew her way around bloodied and broken men.

"Gosh," she said finally.

"Angela, why don't you take the boys home? They're being very good, staying in the car, but it is hardly suitable," Lane said. The boys were sitting now, playing a game of slapsies, having found that the adults huddled on the beach around an invisible man had failed to sustain their interest.

Angela nodded, relinquishing the Thermos to Eleanor and looking anxiously toward where her children were still incarcerated in the car.

"He's still alive, tell them, and we've sent for help," Lane said.

"Are you sure?" Angela asked. "I don't want to leave you in the lurch."

"Certainly, my dear," said Eleanor. "We can handle it from here."

Gratefully, Angela hurried up to the car. The people on the beach could hear the chorus of questions floating out of the car windows as Angela drove her brood back up the hill and away from the awful scene of carnage. Lane wondered if they would have nightmares. She wondered if she would. Since the war she had had them in waves, sometimes going for weeks without one and then suddenly having her nights shattered by shuddering and images of fire.

While Eleanor and Kenny worked on trying to keep the patient warm, Lane walked over to the edge of the water where the boat lay tipped, the one oar beside it. Much of the water had drained out, but there were still the remains of the bloodied water, now turning a darker colour. She was about to turn away when a metallic glint caught her eye. There, mostly submerged in the gory water, was a revolver. She frowned. She reached toward the weapon and then drew back. The police, she thought, can deal with that.

She turned. Eleanor was leaning forward. "No, no. Hold on. An ambulance is coming."

Lane hurried back to where Eleanor was standing, looking anxiously at the young man, who lay as if dead.

"Is he . . .?" Lane asked.

Eleanor shook her head and turned away from him. "He said something but he was slurring so badly I could scarcely catch it. It sounded like 'Just let me die.'"

CHAPTER FOUR

"BEFORE YOU START, THIS ONE is still alive," Darling said. "Can you hurry it along?" They were stuck behind a logging truck that was struggling up a steep section of the road. Darling was referring to the fact that in his relatively short acquaintance with Lane Winslow, she seemed to be responsible for the bulk of his work because of her habit of finding bodies.

"The medics got out ahead of us, anyway." Ames leaned impatiently to the left, hoping he could pass the truck that was not only holding them up but also throwing up a whirlwind of dust. Why couldn't someone oil the roads out here, he wondered. "Hurrah!" Ames revved up and bolted past the truck, whose driver had waved them on. Putting his hand out the window in thanks, Ames settled back in the seat. "I can't believe we're doing this twice in one day."

"How are you getting on with your studies?"

"Middling, sir. How will you get around while I'm gone to Vancouver? It's a six-week course."'

"I can drive, Ames. See you don't botch it up. I must have been mad to suggest a promotion."

Ames smiled. "It was a weak moment on your part, sir, I grant you. You were no doubt relieved to be home and relieved that Miss Winslow came back and did not stay on in England. What did happen while you were in the old country?" Ames glanced at the inspector, who was staring moodily ahead. He'd been a peculiar combination of moodier and more cheerful lately. The moodiness Ames was used to, the cheerfulness he hoped came from Darling's growing attachment to the beautiful and intelligent Miss Winslow. Sadly, the inspector was no more forthcoming about his personal life than usual.

Darling sighed. What he told people was that he'd gone to London to sort out some bureaucratic details regarding the crash in '43 of the bomber he'd piloted, followed by a short holiday in Scotland. What truly happened was more along the lines of being jailed and nearly hanged for a wartime crime he did not commit. At this moment, on the way to a possible crime scene, he did not want to think about the peculiar complication his sense of gratitude to Lane Winslow had imparted to his abiding love for her. Nothing about their relationship fit any of the narratives he was familiar with, though admittedly, those came mostly from fiction. His one brush with romance during the war had been an embarrassing and unmitigated disaster, a circumstance that both freed him and at the same time filled him with an underlying anxiety about where the whole thing was going.

"Sir?" Ames's voice penetrated Darling's rumination.

"What?"

"Did she say what the wound was from?"

"Gunshot was all I heard. Her ridiculous phone went dead after that."

"Who would shoot a fellow and put him adrift in a rowboat?"

"That, Amesy, is why she called us. We are the police. In case you've forgotten, our mission is not to drive up the lake to gaze at Miss Winslow, but to solve yet another crime she has discovered."

"That's hardly fair, sir. It's hard not to think that the guy is Carl Castle. I mean, it can't be a coincidence. I feel sorry for his mother."

"Just what I was thinking."

They were on the downhill from the little general store and gas pump at the top of the Balfour hill, below them the great curve of the cove from which King's Cove took its name. They'd had to slow down as they approached the store because a black Lab lay in the middle of the road and only reluctantly got up and trundled toward the store. A man had come out of the store and shouted at the dog, and waved as the maroon Ford sped up.

It was clear when they had bumped down the winding and narrow road to the wharf that the ambulance van had arrived only moments before them. Ames pulled the car onto the wharf that now seemed crowded with the red pick-up truck he recognized as belonging to Kenny Armstrong, who ran the post office with his wife, and the van, its rear doors gaping open, waiting for the hapless patient it must bear back to the hospital in town. The medics were only just hurrying down the sandy slope from the wharf to the beach, carrying a stretcher. The heat of the afternoon seemed to have intensified, so Darling left his jacket on the seat and positioned his hat to cut down the glare of the sun glinting off the water.

Lane, who had been kneeling by the wounded man, got up at the sound of the emergency vehicles rumbling onto the wharf. Eleanor and Kenny were standing nervously by the young man. Both looked exhausted, as if the vigil of hoping he would not die had been a physical feat. The medics hurried to the victim, and Ames and Darling followed them down onto the beach.

"Inspector. I'm sorry about this. You remember Kenny and Eleanor Armstrong. Eleanor was a nursing sister in the Great War and has done what she could."

Darling nodded at them and then looked at the young man's face. His pallor made him look nearly dead, but Darling could see the tiniest movement as breath passed painfully in and out of his blue lips. The medic was bent over him, removing blankets. Could this be the missing man? He cursed himself for having left the picture he had taken from the mother in his office. The photo had showed a vigorous, laughing young man in a light jacket, his hands in his trouser pockets, feigning nonchalance for the camera. Darling could see nothing familiar in this drained shadow of a human.

The ambulance medic had assessed the situation and looked around at the small crowd assembled in silence, watching. "Who did this bandaging?"

"I did," said Eleanor. "I had a bit of stuff in my kit from the war. I wanted to keep it clean and covered."

The medic nodded and waved his hand at the stretcher-bearers. "Try to jostle him as little as possible." Then he turned back to Eleanor. "Good work. You found him here, like this?"

"No, sorry, I should have clarified," Lane said. "He was adrift in that boat. We took him out as carefully as we could because his legs were immersed in cold water and we thought we'd better risk getting him out to try to warm him. He was absolutely icy." She pointed to where the boat sat crookedly on the beach, the water lapping gently against its stern. It was tipped toward them, and what normally would be a tranquil lakeside scene was rendered chilling by the bloody water still visible in the bottom of the boat.

"It's a bad wound. His insides will be a mess. It's hard to know if it was made worse by the move, but you were probably right to get him out of the cold. Come on, fellows. Let's get him out of here." When the man had been carefully borne up the hill and put in the ambulance, the others turned unconsciously toward the boat.

"I saw this after we'd taken him out," Lane said, pointing into the centre of the boat where one seat partially covered what seemed to be an overly large revolver.

"A Smith and Wesson," Darling said, frowning. "I'm going to leave things for a moment and get Ames to take some pictures." He stepped back and looked out across the lake. "Tell me again how you found him."

"We were up there, fishing." Lane pointed up toward the rocky peak of the point rising above them. "The point is rocky, and the lake is low today. From where we were it would have been difficult to see down directly below us to the water. One of Angela's children spotted the boat from where they were playing at the end of the wharf just as we heard it knock against the base of the cliff. I thought at first that it was an unmoored rowboat till I heard that unearthly groan. I swam around and pulled the boat to shore by that rope."

"And how was he positioned in the boat?"

"Lying with his head at this end, slightly elevated by this seat thing, and the lower half of his body was nearly submerged. The boat had been taking on water, and it was collected here at the stern end."

Darling looked now at the length of rope, perhaps four feet long, hanging off the prow. He carefully lifted the end. It was frayed and worn. It could have come loose from whatever it had been tied to in even a mild storm, but when he looked closer he saw that some of the strands of rope showed signs of having been cut. "Someone's cut this." He looked out at the lake, as though it might reveal the sequence of events. "Could the gun be his? He was planning to attack someone or was being attacked and didn't get it out in time. If he was shot by someone else, why leave the gun? If you were going to cut a boat loose to drift, besides that being an inefficient way to get rid of a body, you wouldn't provide oars, would you?"

"The whole thing is a pretty awkward carry-on in a rowboat," Lane said.

The ambulance finally began its laboured ascent of the narrow winding road back to the Nelson road. Ames, who had been looking along the water's edge near the boat, was coming toward them on the beach. Darling waved him back.

"Camera, Ames. I want photos of this. There's a Smith and Wesson in the boat I want snapped in situ. Get photos of the end of the rope there as well." Ames gave the tiniest nod and turned back toward the wharf.

Eleanor and Kenny were folding up the tarp and the two blankets. Regretfully Kenny said, "I don't guess you need us, so we'll drive back up to the house. There's tea if anyone needs it."

Darling looked at Eleanor. "You dressed the wound. Gunshot?"

"Yes. I've seen plenty of them. I'm surprised by the location. Shooters are going to aim higher if possible, are they not? Though gunshot wounds can be all over the place. If you're close enough with something like a bayonet, this is more like what you get. With a bayonet, you stab at the nearest thing, often straight at the middle of the torso. This looked something like that." Eleanor could hear herself speaking, could feel the years fall away. She had the sudden visceral memory of reporting to the doctor in charge at the station in France. Kenny was looking at her with raised eyebrows and a slight smile that suggested he admired this rarely seen side of his wife.

"If I may, I'd like to come up when we've finished here and take some notes. We'll probably be glad of the cup of tea, as well." Thus gently and tactfully dismissed, the Armstrongs made their way back to the truck and followed the ambulance, which had gained the Nelson road and was speeding to the hospital.

"Remarkable woman," Darling said. "You see only a dear old thing with white hair who looks as mild as a buttercup, and she starts talking about the best way to bayonet someone." He looked at the point. "Can you show me exactly where you were standing?"

While Ames, who was back with his camera, took pictures, Lane and Darling climbed back along the rocks to the point. From the promontory the long sweep of the north end of the lake was visible, as well as the curve of the bay to the south.

"You didn't see it floating about before it fetched up at the base of this?" Darling asked.

"No. The first I heard of it was Rafe shouting. I tried to lean over to see it, but it's nearly impossible to see the base of the point from this angle without going into the drink."

Darling smiled slightly for the first time. "That would have complicated the whole scene," he observed.

As if to emphasize the activities of the afternoon, Darling, walking toward the north side of the point, tripped over Kenny's fishing basket, which had been abandoned as they'd hurried to rescue the man in the boat.

"I'd better get that back to Kenny," Lane said, collecting the basket. She picked up the fishing rods, winding the line back onto the reels of each of them. "I'm sure he was devastated to leave. He's an avid secret detective. He is agog with fascination about every aspect of investigative procedures." Kenny had proved to be a very eager armchair detective on earlier cases Darling and Ames had been called upon to solve.

"How long would you have been here before you heard the rowboat?" Darling asked.

"Thirty minutes, perhaps?" Lane ventured. "Are you wondering how long it was there?"

“Well, that and where it came from, and how long it was on the lake. The way it took on water it could have been bobbing about all night. There was a storm last night. I wonder if that is why it took on so much water?”

“Sir!” Ames’s voice carried up to where they were standing.

Darling walked back to where he could overlook the scene on the beach just below. “What is it?”

“There’s a bag here, sir, jammed under the seat at the back. A sort of small military kit bag. I’ve photographed it. Permission to take it out?”

“I’m on my way down.” Darling turned to where Lane was juggling the rods and basket. “Can I help?” he asked.

Lane smiled for the first time since the drama of the wounded man had begun. “I think I can manage, thanks. Ames needs you more than I do.”

Darling’s eyes lingered for a brief moment on Lane’s face and then, with a slight upturn of the lip, he wheeled around and descended by jumps to where Ames was wrinkling his nose at the prospect of extracting a bloody-water-soaked bag out of the boat.

Lane tried not to think of the momentary smile reflected in Darling’s charcoal eyes as she went down the rocks to the beach behind him. It was most unseemly to think about them in the middle of this sorry drama.

Darling watched with his hands in his pockets while Ames rolled up his shirt sleeves and leaned into the boat to pull out the thick canvas bag. “Don’t drop it,” advised Darling levelly.

Lane smiled again at the scene of Darling tormenting his second-in-command and then turned to go back up to the wharf to drop the fishing gear in the apple hut.

"I'm wondering where the boat could have come from," Darling said. "I can't help thinking it came from up the lake from the Kaslo end. Or even from the other side."

Lane was crunching back along the beach toward them. "Was it windy out here last night?" Darling asked her.

"It was indeed. And very rainy. I'm not surprised the boat is so full of water. I woke up at about one in the morning and the rain was hammering down. What's over there?" Lane asked.

"Ainsworth, Kaslo, and on the other side, Riondel is up that way," Ames said. "Tiny place. Practically abandoned mining town."

"I wondered about the current of the river running through the lake, but that runs from south to north. Would a rowboat, even with the help of some wind, float south against a current like that?" Darling asked.

"According to Kenny Armstrong, the Duncan River comes down the north arm of the lake in this direction and meets up with the Kootenay River, and then they both go off to Nelson along the west arm and points south," replied Lane. "He was telling me about it this morning when we were up on the point. I imagine the boat could definitely have floated from up Kaslo way."

Ames had managed to get the bag out of the boat and had placed it on a canvas sheet next to the revolver, where it lay exuding water that ran down the folds of the canvas and sank into the gravelly beach. He was holding his hands away from his body as if he'd rather not know them, and then he went to the edge of the lake and shook them vigorously in the clean water at the shoreline.

"Poor Ames always gets the dirty jobs," Lane said to Darling.

"Nonsense. It's good for him. Builds character. Anyway, I won't make him get into that bag until we have it back to the station," Darling said. He turned to Ames. "Could you get onto the wharf and go down to the end of it and take some shots of the point from there? I don't know if they'll give us much information, but you never know." He turned back to Lane. "We've had a call out about a missing young man. A widow named Mrs. Castle. I very much fear this could be her son."

"Oh, dear," said Lane. "Can she be the woman who sometimes has eggs at the Balfour store? How beastly for her. Even if it is not him, the injured man belongs to some other poor unfortunate family."

"She does have a chicken farm," Darling said. "Have you met her?"

Lane was walking back toward the boat. "No, but I sometimes stop at the store at Balfour for eggs if Gladys has run out." Gladys was the imperious mother of Gwen and Mabel, two spinster sisters in their fifties who lived up the hill from the post office and presided over the most spectacular gardens Lane had ever seen. Lane stopped near the boat, trying not to breathe deeply. The smell of blood seemed to have settled permanently into her nose. "One oar. That's interesting. It's illogical that someone trying to kill him would provide oars, unless he's fleeing after being wounded and tries to row away. One oar falls out of the lock and he's too weak to continue. Or, what if it is a suicide attempt? Does he get into his boat, cut the rope, and then trust to the tides to carry him away to somewhere he can shoot himself? He's made a poor job of it, if that's the case. If he's going to do that, why get into a boat at all? And he's got a bag. If I want to kill myself and spare my loved ones the trouble and cleanup when they find me, I might row out up the lake, either to the middle or to some hidden and wild bit of shore. But why am I taking a bag?"

Darling turned to her. "Why do you think it might be a suicide attempt?"

"Oh, yes, I forgot to say. Eleanor said he whispered, 'Let me die.' He slurred his words terribly, but she was pretty sure that's what he said. Doesn't that suggest a suicide? Perhaps he brings the gun to kill himself but bungles it, and then hopes to bleed to death."

Darling shrugged. "Hmm. Possible I suppose. If it's our missing man, according to his mother he's as cheerful and well balanced as can be."

"Or that's what he wanted his mother to think," Lane observed.

Darling, his mood darkened suddenly by the number of things his policing life had shown him were kept secret from loved ones, saw that Ames had finished with the pictures and was making his way back to the car.

"Let's go get that tea."

CHAPTER FIVE

IN THE BACK SEAT OF the police car, Lane felt wrung out, as if she were recovering from a bad night of sleep.

"This is hardly the day I had planned. I wanted to enjoy the benefits of the peaceful country life. Sitting in the sun, learning to fish. Instead it's been all blood and mayhem," she said, watching the verdant wall of trees that lined the road to the post office, their leaves reflecting sun and shadow, a cheerful contrast to the grim turn of the afternoon.

Darling turned to look at her and then said with such kindness that her heart constricted, "You've had a beastly day. Should we drop you at home?"

"What, and miss more revelations from the hitherto blameless and mild Eleanor Armstrong? Not on your life!"

"Besides," said Ames, who had heard the soft tone of Darling's voice and rejoiced at it for Lane's sake, "you seem to like being involved. I don't think it's too much to say that you've been helpful in the past. Wouldn't you agree, sir?" Darling merely harrumphed in reply.

Lane had received a letter from Yvonne only last week wondering at her involvement with police investigations. She had answered this query with "Really, I don't try, and I don't particularly want to. It's just happened somehow. I suppose if I were honest, I would say that I find the challenge intriguing. I can't stand a question being unanswered." After this afternoon she was beginning to feel that she attracted crime. The feeling was in no way a comforting one.

Revived by the tea Eleanor offered in so domestic a manner that her earlier revelations of her wartime work seemed like mere fantasy, Darling and Ames took their leave. Ames had taken proper notes of the observations Eleanor had already made, and Darling was anxious to get along to the unfortunate Mrs. Castle about her missing son.

"Drive to the farm. We had better collect Mrs. Castle. I very much fear this could be her boy."

"I wonder if it could relate to that paper she found?" Ames said.

Mrs. Castle had presented the notice she'd found in her son's room in a triumphant manner that suggested it proved something was definitely amiss. Trying to disregard the fact that he had specifically told her not to touch anything in her son's room, Darling had taken the paper, an announcement, read it, and passed it without comment to Ames.

"Well?" Mrs. Castle had demanded.

"It suggests that someone wanted him to go to this meeting," said Darling. The note, scribbled in pencil said, "Should be good" and had the signature "H." "What kind of meeting, I wonder. 'A Greater Dominion.' Do you know what this was about?"

"No, I do not," replied the woman. "He wasn't the sort to go to meetings."

"Would he belong to something and not tell you? A club or society of some sort?"

Mrs. Castle had looked down and shaken her head. "I told you, he wasn't the type. And he didn't keep secrets." She had said this defiantly, as if to reassure herself as well as the police.

"Do you know who 'H' might be? Is it the friend whose mother you called?"

"No, and I know of no friend whose name begins with the letter *H*. He would have told me."

This mother's absolute certainty about her son's movements and his habits had taken on a new complexion for Darling in that moment.

"I have to confess that after meeting her I came away with the feeling that if I were her son, I'd want to disappear too," Darling said.

"I know what you mean. A bit too much in his life, as it were. He is, after all, twenty."

"If the rowboat man is her son, then she was right, and I will have to learn to be a less judgmental policeman," Darling added.

He was feeling unsettled, cursing himself quietly for being so dismissive about the paper she'd found in her son's room. Such an oversight was not like Darling. He believed that every bit of evidence, however trivial, was important. Why had he dismissed this woman's feelings so out of hand?

"I can't agree with you there, sir. I don't think you were being judgmental. I think you were being cautious. You saw a woman who, fair enough, was all in a panic about her son, and you were trying to calm her. As if to say, 'Let's not get worked up. This may be nothing.'"

"Thank you for the vote of confidence. But the point, Ames, is that it may be something."

"Depends on whether someone just handed him that announcement and whether he even went. I don't think it's necessarily significant that the mother didn't seem to know who the note was from. I have friends my mother has never met."

Darling sat in silence, thinking about how upended he was feeling. Not only about this case, he knew. Since he'd left the Royal Air Force, he had been gradually settling into the comfortable role of dour and reliable police inspector. He had not seen marriage in his future, or any disruption to a life as a respectable small-town inspector. But meeting Lane had forced him out of himself, forced him to question how he had been taught to see the world. His recent experience of being accused of a horrendous wartime crime had made him realize how vulnerable he, or anyone, was to error or the machinations of some power beyond anyone's control. Without Lane, he might be sitting in some ghastly cell waiting for the hangman. This powerlessness disturbed his sense of the world he had believed in, a world where crime could be fought and justice administered fairly. It disturbed him that Lane had come from a world where power and justice were defined by such unseen forces and slipped and slid like snakes on a rock.

"Sir. We're here."

Chastising himself for the overdramatic imagery, Darling pulled himself back to the problem at hand, preparing for what was going to be a very sad and difficult task indeed.

AFTER THE POLICE car had disappeared up the road, Lane did not indulge in introspection, though she had felt a wistful and unfulfilled longing to kiss Darling before he left. But they were on business, and gruesome business at that. She hoped the young man would not die, whomever he belonged to. She went into the house, got her car keys, and drove back down to the wharf.

Now, with all the traffic gone, it hardly seemed possible that such horror had been visited on this quiet beach. Only the rowboat remained, still tipped on its side. She got out of the car and stood with her hands on her hips, looking at it. It should be emptied and pulled somewhere safe. The children would want to come back and play here and eat hot dogs by the fire as they always did. It wouldn't do to have the rather gory relic of that afternoon where they would see it.

Going down onto the beach, Lane felt her stomach turn at the sight of the remnants of the bloody water. She held her breath, heaved the boat over to drain, and looked around to see where she could stow it. Under the wharf, she decided, as close to the end of it as possible so it would be well hidden from the beach. The children would probably go have a look next time they were down, but overturned the boat would provide little interest, and they'd go back to their usual pursuits.

She turned the boat upright and was about to attempt to drag it up to the base of the wharf when she noticed a very new looking chip just on the inside of the frame. She peered at it. Judging by its location, she knew the chip was not something she'd done while turning the boat over. It looked as though it had been hit with a hammer, causing the wood to chip along the grain. Had Ames seen it and photographed it? Perhaps it was nothing, except that it was so clearly fresh. The wood was almost white under the damaged blue paint of the frame. Only one oar in the boat. The second oar could have banged it as it slipped out of its lock. Or, what if there was only ever one oar in the boat and the other was still on a dock, and someone had used it to shove the boat away from the shore, into the lake to drift. But that would have involved pushing on the outside of the boat. This chip was on the inside of the frame. The gun? It was heavy and could have caused the damage. Had the man tried to swing it to shoot his assailant and had it knocked out of his hand when he banged the rim?

It turned out to be somewhat easier than she imagined to drag a medium-sized rowboat on its keel up a pebbled sandy beach. When she got to the base of the wharf she shoved the boat under and turned it over, stepping back out into the sun and stretching her hands to get the feeling back into them. She didn't know if what she'd seen was important and wondered whether she should even bother the police with it, but then remembered how Darling felt about the importance of every piece of information, something she'd learned at the very beginning of their acquaintance. It was hard to believe it was only a little over a year ago that he had arrested her when she and Robin Harris, Kenny's cousin, had found a body in her creek. As angry as Lane had been at being jailed, she had understood how all the available information had led to her. She'd learned that no information was trivial and that facts, however inconvenient or ill fitting, must be considered equally and impartially.

Back on her own porch with a glass of iced tea, Lane looked out at the lake way below her and at the blue rim of mountains that held and shaped it on the other side. She thought of the scene that might have led to this afternoon. The young man is angry, throws his gun into the boat, and then gets in himself, cutting the rope because he can't be bothered to cope with untying it. Is he already wounded, or is he taking himself off to commit suicide? Is someone pursuing him, perhaps? Suicide suddenly seemed doubtful. There was the bag, after all. He throws his gun and bag into the boat, cuts the rope, and pushes as hard as he can away from his pursuer, and then rows as hard as he can till loss of blood exhausts him. He lets an oar slip away and gives up, passing out.

Well, if he cut the rope, why was there no knife in the boat? And if he shot himself, why did he make such a bad job of it? But if someone else shot him, why was the gun in the boat? Perhaps the wounded man was shot by a different gun. If he had been running from someone, had he got a shot off at whoever was after him? And there was still the possibility that the chip in the frame had been done before and had no bearing at all. She looked at her watch and decided she would call the station toward evening when they might be back from visiting the worried mother. In the meantime, her garden, which had been mostly planted by her kind neighbours while she'd been away in England, needed weeding.

DURING THE TRIP to the hospital, Mrs. Castle sat in the back of the car saying over and over, "I knew something was wrong, I knew it."

Darling had avoided being specific about the injuries to the young man in order not to further disturb her and could think of nothing reassuring to say. They drove up the hill to the hospital, and he told Ames to get back to the station on foot. Mrs. Castle, in a jacket that was too warm for the weather and a bedraggled, rimmed black hat, was clutching her handbag and shivering as they approached the main desk.

Darling showed his identity card and said quietly, "We'll need to see the young man that was brought in a couple of hours ago by ambulance."

"I don't know, sir. I . . . I'll call Dr. Robles."

Fearful of what new development the receptionist's hesitation might mean, he looked back at where Mrs. Castle sat on the edge of her chair staring at the swinging doors into the hospital wards, her face a combination of brittleness, determination, and fear. He thought of all the mothers and fathers who'd sat just like that waiting for news of their sons missing or wounded overseas. Indeed, some still were.

"Inspector Darling?"

Darling turned and nodded at the doctor. "Yes. We are hoping to get an identification on the young man. This may be his mother. Will it be possible?"

"He's still unconscious. We're getting ready to roll him down to surgery to see if we can deal with the mess inside. His internal organs will have been badly damaged. Whoever shot him was very close. There is a risk of infection at this point, and he's lost a lot of blood." He stopped and looked at Mrs. Castle. "He's still in the hallway on a gurney. We can have her wear a mask, and one of my nurses can take her to have a quick look. I imagine it will be better to know who he is if we can, in case he doesn't make it."

Mrs. Castle stood up. "I want to see my boy," she said, in a voice that brooked no denial.

"Dr. Robles, this is Mrs. Castle," Darling said.

"So, Mrs. Castle, I'm going to ask Nurse Powell here to give you a mask and take you to where you may look at the patient. I should caution you that you must not touch him. He is in a delicate state, and we are taking him to surgery."

She nodded. "Yes, yes. I understand. Can I see him now?"

She had lied, she knew, to the inspector. She wondered, terrified, if this was the moment in which she would pay for the lie. She had relived so many times the scene of two weeks ago when the whole life she had tried to salvage from the wreck of her marriage had come crashing down. It had been late on a Saturday night, past midnight, and Carl had not come home yet. She was sitting in the kitchen staring into the dark when she heard the car at last. He had staggered in, looking angry and confused, and clearly drunk.

"Look at the state of you!" she'd said.

"Leave it, Mother." Carl had thrown his jacket on the table, knocking over a glass. Ash from his cigarette had fallen on his chest, and he'd used the flat of his hand to brush off his shirt. “Sorry,” he’d muttered, and started for his room.

“You’ve been drinking.” She’d stopped him in the hallway. The sheer choking familiarity of this scene terrified her, even now.

“What of it? It’s not against the law, and it’s Saturday night. What am I supposed to do? Stay in here with you?” He’d glared at her with what? Loathing? “I’m tired.”

And then she’d pulled at his sleeve, making him stumble. “Don’t you see what’s happening? It’s your father all over again.”

Wheeling on her, Carl had pushed her violently to get her to let go of him. “Do not compare me to him! I am nothing like him!” On the floor, stunned and rubbing her back where it had struck the edge of the table, she had watched him shake his head, as if trying to clear it, trying perhaps to shed the guilt he felt. She’d seen that too, from his father. Then, most terrifying of all, the look of rage, the look of his father back from the grave.

“You have no right!” he’d shouted. “You need to stay in your place!”

The next morning he’d promised he would never get drunk again. She knew he’d promised it with all his heart.

DARLING STOOD LOOKING out the window of the foyer. The hospital was situated on a curving rise above the main road into the centre of town, and from his position he had a partial view of the lake and the mountain beyond. What Ames unpacked from the bag would be of interest. Like Lane, Darling wondered how the man had come to be there. The bag and the gun suggested he was off somewhere, on the run maybe, away from his mother, or fearful of someone, either the law or . . .

The swinging door banged against the wall and Darling turned. Mrs. Castle had burst into the foyer and now stood sobbing, holding onto the reception desk with one hand. A nurse was offering her a glass of water.

She caught sight of Darling approaching her and looked up, her face screwed up in the effort not to cry. "It's not him!" she cried.

CHAPTER SIX

AMES CARRIED THE CANVAS-WRAPPED BAG and revolver to one of the interview rooms and dropped them on the small wooden table. There was no point in smelling up his office. He contemplated starting immediately but realized he was starving. It was past five, and he hadn't eaten since the morning. "I'm going for a bite. Don't touch that stuff I put in the interview room. When I get back I'll need you to take notes." He said this to O'Brien, who manned the desk and was now perched on his stool, leaning on the counter looking at the local paper.

"It's like his nibs never came back," muttered O'Brien, looking up from his reading. While Darling had been away in England, Ames had briefly been in charge of proceedings at the Nelson police station, a circumstance that only slightly rankled the good-natured O'Brien, who outranked Ames but was near retirement and very content with his current role. "Do you see this garbage in the paper? 'Nelson police have been unable to solve the string of burglaries in the Nelson area.' Makes us look incompetent."

"You know what reporters are like. They see the crime and look for the solution. They have no idea what we do every day to solve cases. Their ignorance makes them think we do nothing. Do you want anything?"

"No, thanks. I ate my lunch at noon like a proper Christian."

Ames pushed open the door into the café next door, wanting to think about the possibility that the wounded man and the missing man might or might not be the same person, but finding his mind turning to the problem of Violet. Because it was not quite dinnertime, he did not have to squeeze in at the counter and instead found a seat by the window where he could look out on the street.

He had his usual, a ham sandwich and a Coke, delivered to the table by the now-friendly April. He'd heard a rumour that she was happily engaged to an up-and-comer at an insurance office. He knew he should be thinking about poor Mrs. Castle, about to see her severely injured son, but instead, having thanked April, he turned his mind to whether Violet should be engaged to an up-and-comer at the local police station. He was up and coming. He was studying for his detective sergeant licence. She had every expectation that he would produce a ring. Lord knew, she had begun a campaign of hinting at it. After all, they'd been going steady for the better part of a year. She'd gone back to work at the bank but had suggested more than once, with a wink, that she could see herself in a frilly apron preparing his dinner when he came home, a role now performed by his mother, who had suddenly and infuriatingly begun to express misgivings about Violet. He had wanted to brush off his mother's doubts, but his conversation about children with Violet had unnerved him. As a policeman he'd seen more than his share of unhappy marriages, and he always congratulated himself in advance that he'd never be in that situation.

The trouble was, he thought ruefully, wadding his napkin up and dropping it onto his plate, he had met Miss Winslow. Here was a woman unlike any he'd ever known. Too fancy for him, to be sure, and perfect for the inspector, who at last, it appeared, had gotten off his behind and made a move. But she had opened up a new world to him of women who were deeper and more interesting than the ones he knew here. No, that wasn't right. Maybe the women he knew were perfectly deep, but he hadn't figured out how to have a more—here he lost his way—personal? intellectual? relationship. Intellectual wasn't like him, but he admired whatever seemed to be going on between Lane Winslow and the inspector. They bantered constantly in a way that suggested some hidden depths of connection he did not think he'd ever attained with any of his girlfriends, though he had liked them all well enough. He had thought the fun and cheerfulness involved in stepping out with them would suffice, but the conversation with Vi about the boy needing a thrashing had also suggested hidden depths in which he might find himself married to someone with whom he fundamentally disagreed on real-life issues.

A figure outside the window caused him to come back to the moment. It was Darling, whose pantomime suggested Ames should get back to the station right sharply. Rising hastily, he threw some money on the counter and smiled regretfully at April when she said, "Nabbed, eh?"

"Back, sir? Is that fellow Carl Castle?"

"He is not. So we now have a missing man and a second, completely unrelated, nameless and wounded man."

"How was Mrs. Castle when you dropped her off?" Ames had not been unhappy to be dismissed and made to walk back to the station from the hospital to get on with looking into the bag while his boss had driven Mrs. Castle home. He knew he should have started on the bag and was aware now how squeamish he was being about the whole thing. "I know. The bag. I'll go now."

"Good man," said Darling. "So quick on the uptake." They started back to the station and Darling filled him in. "I was able to glean more from Mrs. Castle, who didn't know whether she should be relieved or more frightened. She seems very confident that her son would not go off somewhere and start a new life. It began, I think, to dawn on her as she spoke that he had started to change in small ways. He'd always been docile, but of late had begun to talk about himself as the man of the house. Apparently, a couple of days ago he said something like, 'Father wouldn't have put up with that.' She said she was surprised and maybe even a little frightened. Her husband was abusive to both of them, apparently."

"You mentioned that she had no idea who H is. Perhaps he, or she, is behind it."

"Maybe. How about you get into that bag and we'll have a look, and then you can catalogue it while I go home and put my feet up. It's been a long day."

"Sir," said Ames, half smiling. He'd never known the inspector to go home before him, and he knew he wouldn't now.

IT WAS STILL light, though in mid-July the sun was already setting a little closer to nine than ten. Lane decided to avoid the slight melancholy that always came over her as the sky began its turn toward night by going over to the Armstrongs'. She hoped they had eaten so it didn't look as though she was coming over to mooch. She had dined on bread and cheese but felt a slight envy at what she assumed must be the proper dinners Eleanor prepared for the two of them. They'd certainly been good the few times Lane had been over for an evening meal. Usually it was lunch or tea when she visited.

"Come in!" cried Kenny, swinging open the screen door enthusiastically. He was holding a tea towel.

"Doing the washing up?" she asked.

"Someone has to while Madam lounges with the papers."

Inside, Eleanor Armstrong had put her nursing bag on the table and was beginning to pull things out of it. "I'm not lounging, I'm taking stock. If we're going to be flooded with injuries, I thought I'd better have a good look."

Kenny, putting a plate up on the sunny green open shelves next to the sink, said, "I wouldn't call one person a flood, would you?" He winked at Lane and bobbed his head toward her favourite chair.

"Not yet," Eleanor said. "But none of us is getting any younger. Robin could keel over off that tractor any day and run himself over. Gladys could impale herself with a trowel. One ought to be prepared. The nearest doctor is that old coot at the hot springs, Dr. Whatshisname."

"Truscott," said Lane. "He's all right. But after what I've seen today, if I cut myself chopping kindling, I'll be very comforted knowing you are nearby with your little kit. Weren't you amazed at your wife's display of sang-froid today?"

"Ha!" Kenny heartily exclaimed. "She's full of surprises. Surprised me right from the start by falling for me. You come to expect just about anything from a woman who can do that."

This is why I come over, Lane thought. To be enveloped in the affection between these two.

"I saw the picture of you in the other room, with the other nursing sisters at the front. I never thought much about it till you pulled out your bag of tricks this morning. I don't think you've ever mentioned it."

Eleanor looked up and smiled. "It doesn't do to talk about it, does it, dear? You know that. But it can be useful. I ought to be prepared. I mean, it's been over thirty years, but I can still slap a dressing on a wound till proper help gets here. What I'm wondering is, ought I to go into town and get some more things from the drugstore? Mercurochrome, iodine, some bandages. Make it a sort of first aid kit. I honestly can't believe I haven't needed it much before now."

"I think it's a splendid idea! I'll drive you, and I'll take you to lunch at Lorenzo's. It's the least you deserve after today's heroics!" Lane accepted a cup of hot cocoa from Kenny, who'd been preparing it before Lane arrived. "Tell me, if it's not being too nosey, how did you two meet?"

"We met first in 1910, I think it was," said Kenny. "John and I were absolute savages. We were made to put on good clothes and go along to some gawd-help-us church bazaar up the lake to please Mother, and there was Eleanor. She'd come over to visit an aunt. She was drinking tea and chatting with a little West Highland terrier. Someone introduced us and I shuffled about like a yokel. I knew she'd never be interested in a rough specimen like me."

"I was smitten straight away," said Eleanor, "because he ignored me and crouched down to play with the dog. I knew there was a lot of good in a man like that. It took some work, but I got him to propose before I was scheduled to ship back. I spent the whole war engaged to him. I never told my aunt, and Kenny never told his mother. But the minute it was over I came back. A much sadder time. John died in France and Robin was missing."

"Mother was pretty cut up about John, you know. I was down in the dumps as well, because I felt guilty that I hadn't signed up. It should have been me, I always thought." Kenny took a deep breath and opened the stove to poke at the burning wood. "Anyway, much to my amazement Eleanor came shooting back after the war, apparently still determined to marry me. Can you beat that?"

"Secretly engaged all that time! But I understand her perfectly," Lane said, smiling. "But what a difficult time for you." She'd seen the silver-framed picture of Kenny's brother John, looking resplendent in uniform, in pride of place in the sitting room.

Kenny looked at his wife and shook his head, smiling at her. "She cheered Mother up, I can tell you. Mum had lost any hope for me and was sure no woman of good sense would come back just for me. I think it helped that Eleanor was able to talk about the war. It helped Mum get through it. You go on, don't you? At first I felt like he was here every day, and finally she persuaded me that we should let the poor boy go to his peaceful reward."

There was a long silence. The fire crackled and Eleanor's cup clinked softly against the saucer as she picked it up.

"Do you know, I've had a call from that Mrs. Enderby up at the mansion. They've got a new litter," she said.

"Oh, lovely," cried Lane. "Will you get a puppy? I've been thinking of getting one myself. I need something small enough to sit in my lap and big enough to annoy Robin."

"I've seen that look in Eleanor's eyes before," sighed Kenny. "I'm guessing we're getting a new puppy. You'll want something a little bigger if you want to annoy Robin. We should keep our eyes peeled."

Robin, Kenny's curmudgeonly cousin, lived down near the turnoff from the Nelson road and had land and orchards adjacent to Lane's. He seemed, she often thought, to live in constant irritated anticipation that she'd one day get a dog that would stray onto his land.

"Have you heard anything about that poor man?" asked Eleanor, surveying her kit, now laid out in two rows. Vials of something, brown packets of bandages, scissors, a tourniquet, a couple of slings, and a little palm-sized and well-thumbed book of medical terms.

Lane wanted to ask what was in the vials but instead looked at her watch. "Goodness. I should get back. I sometimes get a call around now." She could feel herself blushing. Of course, they might have guessed that things were on a different footing with the inspector, but she hadn't talked about it. "I haven't heard about the young man, but perhaps I'll get word. He didn't look too well, did he? But I bet if he's still alive, it's down to you."

"Of course," said Eleanor. "That nice inspector. I'm glad. Though I'm afraid my little bandage would not have kept that poor man from death's door. I fear only Providence can help him. In any case, do let us know. We don't go to bed till after ten thirty. I'll feel better knowing."

Promising to call no matter what, Lane sped back across the gully and through the little glade of birch trees that separated her white Victorian house, once that of Kenny's mother, Lady Armstrong, from the post office. The phone began to ring as soon as she came through the door. As if he knew, she thought. She pulled the receiver off its hook and prayed it would not conk out on her. "KC 431, Lane Winslow speaking," she said into the horn.

"Hello, darling," said Darling, his voice soft. "Why do you sound out of breath?"

"I've just dashed over from the Armstrongs'. Eleanor was showing me the contents of her nursing kit. I feel much safer now, I can tell you. She knows how to use everything in it. She wonders how the young man is."

"Clinging to life. We found something very interesting in his kit bag. But you left a message at the station about something you saw in the boat."

Lane leaned against the wall feeling slightly guilty that she was so happy to be talking to Darling when some poor man lay close to death. "I don't think it was much. Only a gouge in the rim, as though someone had hit it with something sharp or heavy, like a hammer, or, as seems more likely, that heavy revolver. It may be nothing, but it looked new."

"Well, nothing is what we have a lot of right now. The young man did not belong to the woman with the missing son, and nothing in his bag indicated who he is."

"What was in the bag? You said you had something interesting. Has poor Ames recovered from handling it?"

"Ames is no doubt being fussed over by his mother, or out with that sharpish girl of his, though things seem a bit wobbly there. The bag looked like a bag of shopping and provisions. Some new clothes, socks, underwear, a couple of shirts, a few cans of beans, and a wallet with five dollars in it, but nothing else, no identification. The interesting thing is the last page of a letter from the Red Cross. The key sentence is this: 'The paperwork shows that Henry and Julia Fischer and two children were shipped to Poland on December fourth, 1940. We regret that the news could not have been better. Please accept our condolences.' It was followed by an unreadable signature. We only know it's from the Red Cross because of the logotype on the bottom of the paper."

"Oh, God! I wonder if they were relatives and ended up in one of those hideous death camps? Were they Jewish? Fischer could, I suppose, be a Jewish name. That poor man!"

"And is he called Fischer? There must be thousands of people like him trying to find lost relations after that beastly war," Darling said.

"If so, it is a circumstance that suggests the idea that he could have been trying to commit suicide. But I'm surprised at the shopping and no identity in the wallet. If he was distraught about the letter, why would he remove his identity? On the other hand, if he was attacked, the attacker could have decided that rather than trying to get rid of the body somehow, they would rid the body of its identity. The attacker could have thought he was dead. And," she added, "is that awful letter related to what happened, or just another circumstance in a life gone awry?"

"Awry is right," Darling said. "I have to go talk to the man who hired the missing boy, Carl Castle, but I'll come out and have another look at the boat before it floats off, and we can get Ames to fingerprint the oar."

"Oh. No, that's all right. I moved the boat off the beach to under the base of the wharf, and the oar with it, but I held it by the paddle. Mind you, Kenny pulled the oar loose and put it on the beach, so there might be a couple of his prints."

"I would like to kiss you," Darling said.

"For that? I shall work even harder to keep my fingerprints off evidence from now on."

"For that, and for agreeing to love me."

"That I do," Lane said. When she hung up, she rang through to Ken and Eleanor with the news that the boy was barely hanging on and that the contents of the kit bag were inconclusive, including the last page of the letter.

"The Red Cross?" asked Eleanor.

"Yes. Have you some thoughts about that?"

Eleanor was silent on the other end of the line for a moment. "I feel a bit melancholy at the thought of it, I suppose. The Red Cross was the chief way families searched for missing men. Some of the nursing sisters I worked with had beaux that went missing. More often than not a letter from the Red Cross had only bad news. I suppose in this war it was much the same. I wonder if he was searching for some family member? Poor fellow. Perhaps it drove him to suicide. Well, he's not dead, so no need for despair yet."

Lane felt Eleanor's melancholy. She poured herself a small Scotch and put on her pyjamas. The window was up and the curtains were open. A warm night breeze lifted and furled them gently. She held the glass in her hands and looked out into the dark, trying to imagine what sort of troubles the young man had had before he became a nameless patient, clinging to life. He's depressed and cannot face going on. He throws his bag and a gun—his, leftover from the war?—in the boat, and cuts the rope and rows into the lake where he shoots himself and then waits for death. But no . . . no one shoots themselves in the abdomen. The head most likely, or maybe the heart. Could he have tried and the gun slipped?

But what if he was attacked by someone else outside the boat? He's shot and dumped in. He must have been near the boat to start with. Is it his boat? They, the murderer or murderers, think he's dead. Do they push the boat off into the lake and an oar slips off?

The letter is completely relevant in one scenario and completely irrelevant in the second. She drank back the Scotch and thought how unsuitable scrutinizing the whole business was as a pre-sleep activity, and turned instead to her book. Lord Emsworth was being tormented with guests when all he wanted to do was spend time with his prize pig. Somewhat uplifted by the Wodehousian nonsense, Lane turned out her lamp and closed her eyes. But her last seconds before sleep were filled with the smell of the blood.

CHAPTER SEVEN

"ONE AND ONLY ONE," ADMONISHED Kenny, standing by the ash pile with his shovel.

"Don't be silly. We're going to buy first aid supplies," Eleanor said, pulling on her gloves and snapping open her handbag to make sure she had everything she needed. She was wearing a small, dark blue straw hat with a white flower on the side that had long ago surrendered any pretence of being a recognizable species. She'd pulled out her best pale green summer dress and had run a brush over her brown shoes before she laced them up.

Kenny shook his head, smiling at her retreating back. "God knows what those two will get up to," he said out loud. He knew perfectly well that Eleanor would not be able to resist stopping at the mansion to have a look at the litter of West Highlands, and the truth was, he was happy at the thought that she might bring one home.

"Those ashes won't shovel themselves!" Eleanor said over her shoulder.

The morning was still and beautiful. It would be hot again, and Lane waited by her car, surveying her garden. She'd have to water when she got back and look into the matter of the pond under the weeping willow. It would be cooling and lovely to have a pond sparkling in the dappled light coming through the drapery of the willow. She could put her two deck chairs and a small table there and sit in the afternoon, reading. She smiled. She always leaped to the final scene of one of these garden-improvement schemes, where she was lounging about with a book and some lemonade, now with the addition of Darling. There'd be some work in between.

She turned when she heard Eleanor hallooing as she came across the footbridge. "You look lovely. I don't think I've ever seen that hat. Hop in." Lane herself wore a turquoise skirt and a white blouse, and a turquoise sweater on her shoulders. Her auburn hair was tied back with a yellow ribbon.

"This poor hat! It should never be seen, but one has to have something if one is going to luncheon. Kenny's over there as envious as a schoolgirl! And you, my dear, look good enough to eat. Do you think we'll see the inspector?"

"I'm sure he's busy solving crime. Today we're doing what you want to do." Lane wouldn't have minded seeing the inspector but could think of no excuse to stop by the police station.

"Well, I've never been in the station before, and I'd like to know how that boy is doing," Eleanor said, very nearly winking. More seriously she added, "Would you mind awfully if we stopped at the mansion just outside of town? Mrs. Enderby—she's the daughter of old Mrs. Franklin—is the one who called me about the litter. She said there's a great deal of interest, but she'd make sure I got first pick. If I wanted one, that is."

"Stop to look at puppies? I don't know how this day could get any better! You bet."

LANE PULLED INTO the drive and stopped, gazing at the house. It was a mock Tudor confection set back on a sweep of lawn surrounded with a nearly perfect landscaping of trees and exotic bushes. "Wow. You know someone who lives here? They must have very expensive gardeners."

"Mining interests," said Eleanor. "Come along. No one need by wowed by Mrs. Enderby." They walked up the driveway and around the back, where Eleanor knocked on a door that was ajar. "Halloo!"

A sturdy woman in her late forties, encased in a tweed skirt and wearing wellington boots, came to the door. "Dear Eleanor! Good for you! You've come right away. Hello, dear, I'm Graciela Enderby." She moved a bucket from her right hand to her left so she could shake hands with Lane. "You're even lovelier than I'd heard! Well, we'd best get a move on. Councillor Lorimer is already here nosing about in the kennels. It's a grand batch of puppies"

Wondering how the energetic Mrs. Enderby had heard about her at all, Lane followed the two women along a gravelled path to the kennels, which proved to be adjacent to some stables. There was room for five horses, but only two watched them curiously over the gates as they walked past.

"How gorgeous!" Lane exclaimed. She would have liked to stop and nuzzle one of the horses, but Mrs. Enderby was striding on. Lane could already hear the little yips of the puppies. The three women turned into a barn-like structure and encountered the man Lane presumed was Councillor Lorimer. He was leaning over a wooden barrier, gazing at the family of terriers. Lane guessed he was in his mid-forties, and he had a moustache and thick brown hair swept back off his forehead. For the briefest moment it crossed her mind that he looked like someone pretending to be a grown-up, and then he straightened and favoured them with a charming smile. He was wearing a deep blue ascot. No wonder he's in elected office, Lane thought, he must turn that multi-watt smile on everyone.

"Mrs. Enderby, you've outdone yourself!" he exclaimed. "And who are these lovely ladies?"

"This is Mrs. Armstrong, who has first dibs, mind you, and her friend Miss Winslow, from up King's Cove way. Councillor Lorimer. Running for mayor in the fall, if I'm not mistaken?"

"For my sins," said the councillor, smiling. "A quixotic bid, I'm afraid, but I thought it would be fun to try." The councillor shook Eleanor's hand and then lingered momentarily with Lane's. "Mrs. Armstrong. Charmed. Miss Winslow. I don't think I've seen you before?" Lane smiled politely. A puppy is just the thing to charm the voters, she thought uncharitably.

Eleanor had moved to look at the puppies, something Lane now longed to do. "I don't get up to town much," she said.

"But you're English! How delightful. My mother, God rest her soul, was from Norwich. Married my dad after the Boer War and came out here. Have you come to get one of these beauties?"

Pushing back an instinct to dislike the councillor, Lane smiled. He could, after all, be considered Darling's boss if he was on the Nelson council. "No. Mrs. Armstrong is. But they are lovely. Very tempting, aren't they?" She moved to where Eleanor was leaning over and petting the wiggling mass.

"They're completely endearing when they're puppies. It seems unfair to break them up," Eleanor said.

"Kenny wouldn't object to two, would he?" Lane asked, wondering how she herself would resist buying one.

"I'm under the strictest orders. We've only ever had one. We are never away so he would never be lonely. They are terribly loyal and think they are one of your children."

"I've got my eye on one, Mrs. Armstrong. I'm crossing my fingers that it is not the same one that interests you," Lorimer said jovially, making Lane jump a little because he was suddenly so near her, leaning in to look at the litter.

As it happened, Eleanor was gazing at a puppy that was looking back at her as if she were its long-lost mother.

"Ah!" exclaimed Mrs. Enderby. "That nice little bitch. I think she's much the most intelligent. Look at those eyes. She already seems to know what you're thinking! Will I keep her back for you?"

"I think she's the one. You hadn't got your eye on her, had you, Councillor Lorimer?"

"My dear lady, how perfect! I'm after that little fellow

there." Lorimer pointed at a puppy who was batting happily at one of his brother's ears.

"Wonderful. They're ready to go. I've got some baskets here. I'll need them back, mind."

Eleanor sighed contentedly. "Can you keep little Alexandra till we are on the way home? I've got to pick some things up, and Miss Winslow is taking me to luncheon at Lorenzo's."

Lorimer, who had scooped up his puppy and was nuzzling it, looked up at them, smiling. "Ah. That dago restaurant. Good choice. They do food so well, don't they, if you like that sort of thing. I haven't been in since the war, but forgive and forget, eh? Might be time to go back."

ARRANGEMENTS HAVING BEEN made to pick up the grandly named Alexandra, Lane and Eleanor were back on the road to Nelson. Lane was forcing herself to be happy about the new Armstrong family member but was quietly fuming about Lorimer's casual offensiveness. Poor Lorenzo. Did he have to put up with a lot of that sort of thing? It reminded her of the worst of her insular, prejudiced species. "In spite of all temptations, to belong to other nations, he is an Englishman." Of course, Gilbert and Sullivan were being slyly funny. Englishmen, she thought, generally had no temptation of that kind at all. Certainly not this councillor.

"Alexandra is perfectly enchanting," Lane said, "though I couldn't help wishing your eye had landed on the one that dreadful man wanted."

Eleanor laughed. "I agree. That would have given some satisfaction. He's in the papers all the time. Always cutting ribbons and smiling with businessmen. I'm not surprised he's bucking for mayor."

"Well, then, I'm glad I don't take the paper. I've been able to avoid reading about him. Presumably he's not going for the Italian vote."

"Oh, that. Well, I'm afraid that sort of attitude is not uncommon around here. There's a general distrust of 'foreigners.' He certainly had his eye on you!" Eleanor added.

"Surely not. There must be a Mrs. Lorimer."

"There is. She appears from time to time standing next to him, gazing at him adoringly. But I bet when the camera is gone she's anything but adoring. He has a bit of a reputation of being a man for the ladies. I don't think having a missus would stop him, do you?"

"What does he do, besides being a councillor?" If he has a business, I'll make a point of avoiding it, Lane thought.

"He inherited a small machinery factory and has been buying up other businesses as their owners retire or they look like they're going belly up," Eleanor said. "I mean, I only get this from the paper. I think the war was good to him."

I bet it was, Lane thought. "A man like that ought to pay more attention to his jacket. There were some threads pulled out of his lapel. You'd think he'd have a man of some sort to attend to that. Well, enough about him. He's brought out the worst of my absolute pettiness. What do you want to do first, stop at the station or go to the pharmacy?"

"Oh, do let's stop at the station first. I'd love to see it, and I want to know about that young man."

O'Brien greeted them affably. It was still a bit difficult for him to shake the memory of Lane having been a prisoner at the station the summer before, but she was a looker and he supposed she must be all right, because she seemed familiar with the inspector. He was on the phone to let the inspector know they were at the desk, but this thought about Lane and the inspector caused him to look up at her with sudden interest. Could they . . .? "Righty-o, sir." He hung up the phone. "Inspector Darling will be right down."

Darling led them to his office, where he'd placed a third chair, purloined from Ames's office next door.

"So this is where you do all your brilliant police work!" Eleanor said. "Kenny will be beside himself that I have seen the inner sanctum!"

"Police work is more drudgery than brilliance, I'm afraid, Mrs. Armstrong," Darling said, pulling the chair out for her. Could Lane look more provokingly beautiful? he wondered. "Miss Winslow." He held her chair, longing to touch her, and then went around to his side of the desk.

"We don't want to take any of your time, Inspector, but I am wondering about the young man. Miss Winslow did call me last night after she spoke with you and said he was still hanging on."

"I haven't heard otherwise. We're hoping he will be able to speak to us soon. We need to find out how he got into that state." So as not to alarm Mrs. Armstrong, he resisted talking about a murderous individual still being at large.

"I'm so glad. I am being taken to lunch at an Italian place, and I shall be able to enjoy my lunch so much better now. We are celebrating. I have just bought a new West Highland puppy. We'll be picking her up on the way back."

"How splendid," Darling said, imagining a domestic scene with himself and Lane, and a West Highland, whatever that was, romping around on her lawn. "Lorenzo will certainly be happy to see you," he added, turning to Lane.

"I'll give him your best," Lane said. "Anyway, it's you he truly loves."

"Everybody seems to love Miss Winslow," Eleanor said. "You should have seen that smarmy councillor ogling her at the mansion."

"What smarmy councillor was that?" Darling asked, smiling brightly.

"You know, that Lorimer man. It's a bit disturbing that he's a fellow West Highland fancier, I can't help thinking."

"Is he indeed?" Darling asked evenly, looking at Lane with raised eyebrows. He would have liked to comment, but didn't feel he could in front of Mrs. Armstrong, that he did indeed know of Lorimer and had more than once wondered how close to the lines he coloured in his business interests.

"I imagine he does very well by his constituents. He has a most charming smile," Lane said. "And an ascot. Now I think we'd best be off. Eleanor is replenishing her first aid kit, and it's getting on for lunchtime."

LORENZO, WHOSE RESTAURANT was near the bottom of the hill sloping down to the railway station, was delighted to see Lane coming through the door. "Miss Winslow! *Benvenuto* to you and this lovely lady. If you wait only one moment, I will prepare this table by the window for you." A quiet babble of conversation came from the other diners, a mixture of men from the railway and local mills, and office workers from town. Lorenzo's had been virtually shunned during the war because of anti-Italian feeling, but business had since picked up.

"Good afternoon, Lorenzo. May I present Mrs. Armstrong? She has heard me talk so much about your wonderful restaurant that I thought I'd better bring her along."

"Dear lady, I hope you will not be disappointed," Lorenzo said. "*Un momento*."

"It smells lovely," said Eleanor, while Lorenzo put a new tablecloth on the table by the window.

"It is lovely. And if he is true to form, you mustn't expect to get a menu. His wife always has some daily special, and she's a divine cook. He's very keen on Inspector Darling. Treats him like royalty."

"He's clearly very keen on you," Eleanor commented.

"It's just being in Darling's wake. I've been here a few times with him. Oh, no! Now what is he doing here?" What caused this exclamation of dismay was seeing Councillor Lorimer approaching the restaurant with a young man in a suit and an expensive hat. Lorimer pushed open the door and looked critically around the restaurant, and then focused on Lane and Eleanor.

"Well, I never. Twice in one day! Ladies, how are we?" Without waiting for an answer, he turned to his companion and said, "Go bag that table would you? I want to talk to these ladies for a moment."

With rising anger, Lane watched as the young man moved through the restaurant and pulled out a chair at the table Lorenzo had prepared for them. She was about to say something when she heard Lorenzo remonstrating with the young man.

"No, no, signor. Excuse me, please. This table is already taken. It is for these ladies, you see. I have another table over there, yes?" He pointed across the room to a table in the corner. Other diners had begun to notice and were now watching.

"They can sit there, then," the young man said, removing his hat and throwing it onto the middle of the table. He pushed the chair back onto two legs and looked out the window, as if Lorenzo would disappear if he stopped looking at him.

Lorenzo, unsure of how to move forward without causing a further scene, looked flummoxed.

As if he had only just that moment understood what the problem was, Lorimer exclaimed, "Oh, dear. I am sorry, ladies. I assumed you were on your way out. But of course, you must have your table! I shall ask my secretary to move this instant." He wove a path through the other diners, smiling and nodding, and leaned in to say something to the young man. The chair thumped down and the younger man took up his hat, a momentary flash of anger distorting his face.

"Beg pardon, ladies," he said with a pasted-on smile as he passed them on the way to the table by the wall. Lane was sure she just caught his muttered "Bloody Itie" as he took his seat.

Lorenzo gave his head the tiniest shake when Eleanor and Lane were seated. Smiling, he leaned forward as if to take their order. "My country was full of these men. It is why we left," he whispered. "Certainly, right away," he said out loud.

"Well," said Eleanor, "I never."

Lorenzo had gone into the kitchen and returned with two menus, which he took to Lorimer's table. He winked as he passed Lane. She watched him conferring with Lorimer and the young man, nodding and writing something on his note pad. Lorenzo glanced back toward the window table and nodded.

"The gentlemen would like to offer you wine as an apology for the table mix-up. I could open the most expensive bottle I have. It would give me great pleasure."

"So kind," Lane murmured. She looked toward the two men and smiled. "Do thank them so much, but I should drive back up the lake immediately after lunch."

"And I don't drink," Eleanor said, not being entirely truthful.

A bell sounded from the kitchen. Lorenzo disappeared and returned with two large shallow bowls of something intoxicating. "It is bigoli with duck. A traditional dish of the Veneto. My wife is from there. By a miracle there were two servings left!"

"Miracle indeed," said Eleanor with a giggle when Lorenzo had retired.

CHAPTER EIGHT

"RIGHT, AMESY, SADDLE UP. I told Miss Winslow we'd be out this afternoon to have another look at that rowboat, and I'd like to stop and talk to that Van Eyck who owns the garage Carl Castle works at."

Ames closed the sergeant's study manual he was reading and stretched. "If O'Brien did this, surely to God I can."

"O'Brien is smarter than he looks. He's quite a dab hand at the crosswords," Darling said, putting on his hat. The day had become hot, and on the street below people were cowering in the thin line of shade provided by the overhangs and awnings of the shops. Darling had taken his jacket off and slung it over his shoulder in a rare moment, Ames thought, of dapper casualness.

It was nearing four when the maroon Ford pulled up in front of the Van Eyck garage, which was a mile past the Balfour store, perched just above the lake. The policemen got out of the car and went toward the open bay of the garage, where a car was up on a hoist and another had its hood up. Someone in overalls was leaning into the engine and making a clanging sound. "Bloody plugs!"

They were both surprised that the voice was that of a young woman, who stood up and wiped her brow with her forearm, a wrench still in her hand.

"Gentlemen? We're backed up for a couple of days till Friday if you want your car fixed."

Darling shook his head and showed his card. "We're looking for Mr. Van Eyck."

The woman, in her mid-twenties Ames calculated, took the card, looked at it, and then handed it back. "I'm his daughter, Tina. Is this about that Castle kid? I heard he's AWOL."

"Yes, actually. Do you know anything?"

"Nah. He was pretty cut up about getting laid off. Made a big fuss, said it wasn't fair. A bit rude about me. Only fair, I guess. I'm the one who took his job."

"Oh," said Darling. He was surprised Mrs. Castle hadn't mentioned that her son had been let go. "How's that?"

"Simple. I worked as a mechanic in England during the war, and when I should have come home, I stayed on because I was going to get married . . . that was a bust! Anyway, I just got home, and Dad grilled me on my mechanical skills and thought he could save a bit if I did the work instead of someone else he had to hire." She laughed. "Pays me a lot less, I can tell you!"

"When did you last see Mr. Castle?" Ames asked.

"A few days ago, on Friday. He came in for work, and Dad gave him the bad news. Gave him two weeks wages, though. Dad likes the kid, if the truth be known. But Dad has to watch his bottom line. Told him if business picked up, he'd happily hire him back. Suggested Castle should go up to Kaslo. With the mines and the mills there ought to be plenty of automotive work. But the kid wasn't hearing it. It wasn't fair, bloody women taking jobs that belong to men, et cetera, et cetera. Honestly, I did feel bad for him. I think he supports his mom. Anyway, he climbed into that yellow car of his and stormed off. That's the last time I saw him."

"Do you know any of his friends?" Darling asked.

"A kid like that? Nah. Anyway, I've been away. Things went west for me in the old country, so I came home. There ought to be a permanent mark on a man's forehead so you can tell if he's already married!"

Ames bumped the car down the rutted drive to the chicken farm. Mrs. Castle was outside with a bucket and turned to watch them approach. Her anxiety showed on her face.

"Any news?"

"Nothing on our end, I'm afraid. I need to get the licence number of the car, if you've found it. We've been to the garage to make inquiries. Did you know he'd been let go?"

Mrs. Castle put the bucket down. "What? Why would he be let go?"

"Mr. Van Eyck's daughter came home and she's a mechanic. It was cheaper to keep it in the family. I'm now wondering if he simply drove off in search of another job. Maybe he's planning on making a reappearance when he's landed one," Darling said.

"A woman! It's shocking." Mrs. Castle sat heavily on the stairs leading up to her front door. "My poor boy! How can any self-respecting woman put a hard-working man out of a job? I ought to go give her a piece of my mind. It's unnatural."

"I don't think that's a good idea. Let's focus on finding Carl. We'll need to get the licence plate. He's got the car; he's somewhere out on the road. The Mounties are bound to catch sight of it. He has two weeks' pay on him. I expect he didn't want to come home without a job."

"A man shouldn't be put into that situation," Mrs. Castle said angrily. She stood up and said, "Wait here. I found a photo. You can barely see the number. A red plate. Sticks out like a sore thumb on that yellow car." She went into the house and came out with a small black-and-white photo of a man standing beside a car, one hand on the hood. "I had to tear the place apart, but I knew it was in here somewhere. That's Carl. It was taken early this year."

Darling took the picture and looked closely. The licence was just visible, enough of it to give to the RCMP. "Can we keep this? It will help us."

As they gained the main road bound for King's Cove, Darling said speculatively, "I don't know, Amesy. Did you think her protests were a bit much? She didn't seem surprised to know he'd been laid off. Well, no. Maybe that was news, but I have the feeling she no longer thinks he's dead in a ditch."

"No. How can you say that? She seemed upset to me. Anyway, it is a bit weird, sir, you must admit," Ames added.

"No, I don't. What is?"

"It doesn't seem right, a woman being able to take a man's job like that."

"It is 1947, Ames. Women can do all sorts of things. I knew women who flew planes and fixed them. We may have found the source of your problems with women."

"Very funny, sir. But even they don't agree with it. You heard her."

"If that show was genuine, then it's possible Mrs. Castle is bitter because it was her baby boy that got put out of a job. I daresay if she had a daughter she might feel differently. Still, I think you might share your views with Miss Winslow. See what she has to say."

This caused Ames to fall silent.

"Shall we ask her what she thinks?" Darling persisted.

"You wouldn't," Ames said. They'd arrived at the base of the hill up to King's Cove. "Down to the wharf or up to Miss W's?"

"Better go up. She'll have to show us what she's seen." As Ames turned the car at the sharp corner up to King's Cove, Darling continued, "It's interesting that you don't want Miss Winslow to know what you think. It may suggest that you should examine your attitudes. Isn't your Violet doing a job in the bank that men usually do?"

"But a mechanic, sir. It's . . . I don't know . . ."

"Dirty? Unfeminine? You should have seen some of the mechanics I knew! They cleaned up very well. Too bad you were stuck here during the war, Ames. You would have a wider view of the world. Miss Winslow, for example, I have learned, is extraordinarily capable."

Ames thought about Violet in the bank. It had been a man's job. Mostly still was. Violet herself had said she was anxious to marry and quit the job. That was how it ought to be. But his boss was right. Miss Winslow was another kettle of fish altogether. It made him think, that's for sure.

Lane heard the car coming up the road and, assuming it would be them, was ready at the top of her driveway. The evening was still warm, and she was wearing a white cotton shirt and a pair of fern-green shorts. Darling's heart turned over, seeing her standing at her gate, her arms crossed, smiling at them. Her skin was golden from the sun, and her auburn hair was drawn back and tied with a scarf.

Ames shook his head and muttered, "Wow."

"Good evening, gentlemen. Lovely night for the beach. Ames, how are you? Is the inspector treating you well?"

"You know he's not, miss."

"Poor dear." Lane climbed into the back seat. "When we've finished down there you should come over to the post office and see the new puppy before you go. She's absolutely scrumptious. They've called her Alexandra after what Eleanor calls our 'dear king's late grandmum.'"

As Ames backed the car onto the road, Darling said, "Amesy here thinks women ought not to be mechanics."

"Sir! You promised!"

"Did I? I don't think I did. In fact, he's rather against women working at all if they take a man's job. What do you think?" Darling turned and looked back at Lane, resting his eyes on hers, feeling like it was home.

It was difficult, she thought, not to lean forward and kiss him. Instead she sat back and looked out the window. "I think it's a question that should be treated seriously. On the level of the individual cases, a man, who is expected to support his family, needs to have a job. What if he comes home, as so many have, and finds a woman doing that job? Logic says she should leave it, because in the natural order of things, there's a man somewhere who can support her. But what if she has no man? What if she has an old parent to support, or her man was killed, and she has children?"

"Ames?" said Darling, raising his eyebrows at his constable.

"I hate this road," Ames said, beginning the winding, narrow descent to the lake.

"And I think the final question is, what did we learn from the war? Hitler kept most women out of the workplace before the war and made little use of them during it. England on the other hand had every able-bodied woman in a job, and England won. Forget the messy end of the war when an awful lot of women had to leave jobs. I think it might say something about a society where the intelligence, skills, and energies of every citizen are put to the wheel."

"There, Ames. Something to think about, eh?" Darling smiled genially.

"Thank you, sir. We're here." Ames pulled the car up next to the apple shed and jumped out to open Lane's door.

Lane led them down the sandy embankment onto the beach. "I stowed it under here so the children wouldn't get at it. Oh." They had arrived at the base of the wharf, but the boat was, most evidently, nowhere to be seen. "Well, that's funny. I put it right under here. You can see it's been dragged out. The oar is gone as well."

Darling looked out at the lake, as though he expected to see someone rowing away. "Could it have been taken by someone local?" he asked.

"I don't think so. People don't usually swipe other people's boats around here, though I suppose someone could have taken it for a joy ride."

"Not much joy with all that dried blood in it," Ames said. "Look, you can see it's been dragged to the water."

The rowboat had evidently been pulled along under the wharf to the water's edge. The water lapped gently at the dissolving ridge marking the boat's progress in the sand.

"Well," said Darling, walking out from under the wharf into the light, "if it isn't someone helping themselves, then it's someone who wanted the boat back and knew it was here. I bet it's been hidden somewhere along the lake and we'll never find it. Or more likely, it has been burned or scuppered."

"Or what was in it." Lane put her hand to her mouth. "Oh my God. Could someone have followed the boat, or been looking for it, and then watched us pulling that poor man out and sending him to hospital? That means . . ."

"Right again, Miss Winslow. That's exactly what it means. Fast as you like, Ames. We need to get to a phone." Darling ran back up to the wharf and leaped into the car, Ames and Lane behind him. "Come on, Ames, no time to waste. If that man hasn't died of the unnatural cause of being shot, he's very likely still in danger."

LANE'S PHONE BEHAVED and Darling was put through to the hospital.

"That patient is still unconscious, poor kid," the nurse informed him. "But at least he had a visitor. The visitor was asking for Joe Smith, and of course we didn't know what he meant. We don't have a Joe Smith here, but when the visitor described him, I realized who he meant. He didn't stay long. He said he was a cousin of the patient, who had gone missing a couple of days ago, and that was why he was checking the hospitals. Said he'd be back in a couple of days. He's a logger so he doesn't get to town much." The nurse paused. "There was a funny thing. When I came in to check the patient's vitals, the visitor was going through the little drawer by the bed. He said Joe was a fellow logger and had the key to a locker they share. I told him we didn't find any key. I asked him to give me the man's full name. He said it was Joseph P. Smith. He didn't know what the *P* stands for. I've got it on his file, anyway. I was tired of calling him John Doe—that's a name for a dead man. I did ask him how the poor kid got shot."

Darling frowned and looked at Ames and Lane. "What did the visitor say?"

"He said he didn't know. He heard there'd been an argument at a bar. He didn't even know where. He seemed in a hurry to leave. He said he'd come back, but I told him the poor guy has very little hope. He's been going downhill since the surgery."

"Can you tell any visitors that might come again that the patient is too ill to be seen? I'll have a policeman assigned to sit outside the room. Can you do that for me?"

"A policeman! Oh . . . did I do something wrong? He seemed like a nice enough guy. Pretty nicely dressed, for a logger, now I think of it." The nurse sounded worried.

"No. It's all right. Just taking precautions." Darling hung the earpiece on its hook, muttering "Bloody phone" under his breath, and turned to his waiting companions to share what he'd learned.

"Boat taken, well-dressed man going through the drawer. And how did he know the victim was in the hospital with a gunshot wound? He was there, whoever it was, or knows someone who was. What was he looking for? What have we missed?" Ames asked. "Because aside from that letter, I didn't find anything unusual in that horrible bag."

"And on the other hand, we have the missing Carl and his oh-so-protesting mother. Can they truly not be connected?"

"You doubted her?" Lane asked Darling. They had walked out and were standing in the driveway. The golden dying light of the day was showing its final finery on the tops of the trees, but the air still held a close and soothing warmth.

"Inspector Darling thinks she protested a bit too much about her son losing his job to a woman," Ames said, climbing into the driver's seat.

"I can't help feeling she's lying about something," added Darling. "Either she knows he was let go, or maybe she knows for certain he's not dead somewhere, though I must say her distress about his being missing seemed genuine enough."

Lane stood in the driveway, relishing the feel of the slight breeze that moved the warm air soothingly across her bare arms. She listened till she could no longer hear the progress of the police car out of King's Cove. She wondered when she and Darling would feel comfortable in front of Ames during what she suspected would be one of many, many partings. They could be sitting now on the porch watching the light fall behind the far mountains on the other side of the lake, Scotches in hand if . . . if what? They were a normal couple? If they were married? At that thought she felt a surge of almost fear. Wondering at her own response, she turned and walked back to the house.

"You fell in love with a policeman," she reminded herself out loud, and then imagined that instead of Darling, she had a puppy greeting her when she came into the house. Very sweet, and it wouldn't talk nonsense. She'd talked with Darling about getting a dog in the winter. Maybe it was time to act.

EARLY THE NEXT morning, when Angela had given in to the exhortations of her three boys and was lying on the wharf trying to warm up after her early dip in the lake, Philip, playing on the beach with the others, cried out, "Hey, Mom! Look what I found!"

He was holding up a small metal pin, a blue circle with a bright red swastika in the middle.

CHAPTER NINE

LANE SAT ON HER PORCH early the next morning, Thursday. The days of the week had meant nothing during the war, and they meant nothing in particular now, except she wondered if they ought to. A reasonable independent income meant that she did not have to work, but it also meant her time did not have the shape it had had when she worked for intelligence. Though not on a Monday to Friday schedule then, she nevertheless had had furloughs during which she had taken the train to Oxford to visit friends or had gone out at night to noisy, smoky clubs.

Deciding that she could celebrate a day with no pressing obligations by not weeding her garden, she sighed contentedly and sipped the cup of coffee she held in both hands. She looked at her view from the lawn that stretched out below her, across the forest at the edge of her property and out to the lake. She loved to watch the morning move like a sparkling river over the lake and up the mountains on the other side. It was cool still, and she was wearing her green cardigan. Her mind was divided between the knowledge that the crushed shell in the egg cup next to her was the remnant of the last egg she had in the house, and the fate of the young man they'd found on the beach. She wondered if they had let themselves be carried away by the idea that someone would come and try to finish the job.

She opened one of the two books she'd brought out to read. Before leaving England after the war, she'd gone to her favourite bookstore and scooped up armloads of books and packed them into the crates that would be sent on when she had found a home. The crates contained her complete set of PG Wodehouse, her dictionaries of French and Russian, and several novels in each of those languages, including, she'd been unhappy to see when she unpacked them, *Madame Bovary*, which, when she'd read it during the war, she had found tiresome with its powerless, wilting heroine. Perhaps she could give shape to her weeks by rereading *Bovary* and learning to see her in a different light. Lane had spent the time since she'd returned from her latest trip to England pulling the last of the books out of the crates and putting them into her built-in bookshelves. Earlier in June she had gone to be with Darling when he'd been called back to London to account for the wartime crash of his Lancaster, and she'd had a visit with her grandparents in Scotland, where she'd introduced Darling to them. They'd been delighted with him, but she could see they wished she would stay in Scotland. As much as she loved them, she knew she belonged here.

The book arranging had been a firm notice to the universe that she was here to stay. Her trip back to London, a city she adored, had taught her that she had cast her lot with Canada, and she intended to make her life there. She felt a freedom in her new home that she had never felt in London, though she had lived there on her own with no parents to placate. She knew that the limitations she had felt there were caused by her war work, but her return to England had served to show her that she could not shake that feeling of being controlled and overlooked, especially as many of her friends and colleagues had simply continued their work for British intelligence and had switched from fighting the Nazi menace to fighting the communist menace. A brush with her old handler had been the final straw.

She had been stricken when she pulled from the crate a copy of *Winnie-the-Pooh*. She had bought it to give to a friend who had just had a baby girl, but both had died in the bombing in 1942. It reminded her that for some people "back to normal" would never occur again. She had opened the book and seen the inscription she'd written, "To darling little Sally." She had put the book first on the shelf that contained all of her favourite books so that she would never forget.

She had purchased a number of books she thought she ought to read—"duty" books. One of these was on her lap now, Nancy Mitford's *Pursuit of Love*, but instead of reading she was gazing out at the lake. She had hoped the clearly biographical book, with its bevy of girls trying to sort out their lives and find mates, would hold her interest. She turned the corner down on page five, wondering vaguely how she'd read that far and what she'd missed by being distracted, then closed the book and took up *Animal Farm*, another duty book. It looked earnest and took her mind back to the egg problem.

She would go along to the Balfour store and pick some up. She knew that Gladys could supply her eggs, but Fred Bales got his eggs from Mrs. Castle, and in her mood of feeling lucky to be alive, Lane wondered what fears Mrs. Castle must be enduring because her son had disappeared. The sun had completed its work of lighting up the lake, which now sparkled below, and the cardigan, no longer necessary, was left on the chair when Lane went into the kitchen to check her clock. Nearly nine. The store would open at nine.

Fred Bales was sweeping the front steps when she pulled up. His black Lab, which often lay on the road, had stationed itself between the gas pump and the shop door. He pulled himself to a sloppy sitting position and thumped his tail on the ground when he saw Lane, who went over and stroked the top of his head. Maybe she should get one of these, she thought.

"Usually he's lying in the middle of the road," she commented, smiling at Bales.

"Morning, Miss Winslow. That's when the sun gets over there. He should be making himself a nuisance to passing traffic at about noon. I can't seem to break him of the habit. The police nearly ran over him the other morning. They were in a big hurry. I hear there was something at the wharf . . . a young fellow in a rowboat."

Lane knew perfectly well that he had "heard" from Lucy, the girl who worked the telephone exchange out of the back of the store. "Yes. Kenny and Angela and I were fishing when we found him. He was nearly dead, but I hear he's still clinging to this world."

"That's good, anyway." Bales put the broom against the wall. "What can I do for you?"

"I just need some eggs," Lane said.

"Now that's the very thing I don't have. I usually get them from Mrs. Castle down at the farm, but she hasn't got a car since that son of hers drove it off somewhere. I'm supposed to go down to the farm and fetch them, but I haven't had time."

"Oh. Well, I could do it. I need some anyway. I could go down and get some for myself, and bring your supply back here. Two birds." And a third, Lane thought with satisfaction, because now she would get to meet the lady herself.

"Well," said Bales, "if you don't mind. That would be helpful. I've hired a young fellow to pump gas and do the odd job around here, but he's not coming back till next Tuesday. My last one quit and went out to the coast."

Lane, following the instructions Bales gave her, bumped down the road to the chicken farm. A woman, whom Lane assumed was Mrs. Castle, was outside dressed in a coverall with a white scarf wrapped around her hair and tied over her forehead. She had a hammer in her hand and a trio of nails in her mouth. She turned away from the fence she was mending and watched as Lane got out of her car.

"Good morning. I've just been up to the shop for some of your lovely eggs, and Mr. Bales says you haven't been able to deliver them the last few days. I said I'd be happy to take them up the hill to him. After buying some for myself, of course!" She turned on her most engaging smile. If ever a woman needed cheering up, it was this one. Her angular face looked drawn with a permanent cast of worry.

The woman took the nails out of her mouth and put them on top of a post. "Coyotes," she said, indicating the chicken wire she was securing onto the wooden fence. "Crafty beggars. I got eggs boxed up and ready to go, so if you want to take them up there that would be fine. Want to come in for a coffee? I've been at it all morning. I'm Vanessa." She didn't put out a hand but went instead up the stairs into the house.

"I'm Lane Winslow. I live up at King's Cove," Lane offered, following her. The front door issued directly into a cluttered kitchen, every surface of which was piled with crates and cardboard egg boxes. Vanessa Castle cleared a space on her kitchen table and pulled out a chair. The table was by the lakeside window, and a band of sunlight shone across the table's painted lawn-green surface. It would be bright looking, Lane thought, under other circumstances. She waited while her hostess filled two mugs with coffee from the percolator that had been keeping warm on the stove.

"You're not from here," Vanessa said. "I've got no milk, sorry."

"This is fine. No, I'm from London." That was easier than the complicated story that was her life. "I moved here a year or so ago. I love it."

"Is there a Mr. Winslow?"

"No. I was busy working during the war and never got around to it, I'm afraid."

Vanessa stretched her legs out under the table. "There

was a Mr. Castle. Finally died on me. Drink, according to what the doctor said. I wasn't sorry to see him go, and neither was my son. If it weren't for my boy, I would say I was sorry I ever married, but a woman needs a man to look after her, so, there you are."

Unable to think of what to say to that Lane asked instead, "How old is your son? He must be a big help around the farm."

Vanessa's mouth turned down, as if she were holding back feelings. "He's twenty. He did some work here, but he had a good job as a mechanic. Got laid off on account of a woman who got his job at the garage, and he took off. I haven't seen him since last Friday morning, if you want the truth. I told the police, but they don't seem inclined to help. I told them I know something is wrong. He wouldn't go off like that. A woman!"

"How very difficult and worrisome for you." Lane wanted to ask if she had relations he'd go to, or friends, but knew that Darling would already have asked that.

"He's a good boy. He knew what was right. A woman taking a man's job isn't right. And now all these foreigners are coming in, taking our jobs. All these darkies and Japs and the like."

Lane hesitated. Here was a street she didn't want to go down with this bitter woman. "Do you think he went off because he was upset about losing his job?"

"Maybe, at first. But he wouldn't stay away, not without telling me. I'm on the phone here."

"What are you afraid might happen to him?"

This question seemed to flummox the distressed mother.

She leaned back, looked out the window, and shook her head. "This country isn't what it used to be. It used to be a good place for people like you and me. God-fearing Christians. British stock. Now look. Hitler wasn't far wrong, you know."

Lane, who thought Hitler very far wrong, struggled with the logic of this woman's resentment. She'd met her share of people at home who were very keen on winning the war but nevertheless harboured views not unlike this one.

"My son doesn't have the predilection my husband did. But I wouldn't put it past some degenerate to try to get him to drink . . . then . . ."

"You're worried he might have been angry about his job and gone off to drink somewhere?"

"I don't know! I don't know, okay. I just know he's gone. He hasn't called and he isn't with the others up north."

"Others?"

"His friends. Do you want these eggs or don't you? I haven't got all day." Mrs. Castle had stood up and was piling egg cartons onto a wooden flat.

"Of course. Listen, you must have had trouble getting your groceries as well. Why don't we put these in the car, and you let me drive you up to the store. You can deliver them yourself, and then Mr. Bales can pay you. I could bring you and any supplies you need back here."

"I gotta finish this fence," Vanessa said doubtfully.

"Or I could run the eggs up and pick up what you need," Lane offered.

"Well, if you don't mind. Bales knows what I get, it's always the same. Tell him to take it out of what he'll owe me."

Relieved to be driving away from the dark and complicated anger that animated the world view of Mrs. Castle, Lane looked at the gentle slope of land with the rows of trees and the green cover of grasses, already turning to gold with the lack of rain. The peaceful, kindly rural landscape seemed such a contrast to the roiling anger and very justifiable fear Mrs. Castle felt at the unexplained absence of her son.

Pulling up next to the store, Lane noted that the Lab had moved closer to the road, following the sun. Bales came out and took the crate of eggs out of the car and into the shop.

"I've offered to bring her groceries back to her. She says you know what she usually gets," Lane said, once he'd pulled some money from the drawer of the register.

"Her son shouldn't have gone off with her car like that," Bales opined as he put bread, milk, coffee, and an assortment of packages of cereal and cookies on his counter.

"She's worried something's happened to him. She's notified the police, apparently." Lane had, of course, known this before, from the police themselves.

"Has she, now?" Bales said, interested. "Whatever trouble he's in, he got into it honestly. The boy's dad was trouble. He signed up in '16 and came back strange. Vanessa's father was a local politician, you know. The Dominion for the British sort of thing. I never did see what he was on about. Aside from a few harmless tribes and some Doukhobors, it's about as white a country as you can get. I think that's about right," he said, putting a can of Macdonald's Export tobacco into the last remaining corner of the wooden flat Mrs. Castle had sent the eggs up in. "That's two dollars and ten cents."

Lane paid him out of the money he'd given her for the eggs and drove back toward the lake. If Vanessa Castle had been the daughter of a politician, she was used to a better life. More to be pitied than censured? Lane wondered. Circumstances sometimes dictated people's political views, and perhaps the difficult life she now lived had coloured her outlook. Unfortunately, holding repellent views was not a crime. After all, that was what Canada was supposed to be about, Lane thought, the freedom and space to think what you want. She shuddered. It was, she found, hard to accept this easily after the war she'd just been through. Still, Vanessa was harmless enough, she supposed, with her egg farming, far from any danger from the foreign hordes she so feared.

Lane pursed her lips as she took her own groceries out of the car at home. She had had an earful, she thought, and was no closer to understanding where Mrs. Castle's son might be, what with his mother's evasions and Bales's revelation that the boy might be no better than he should be. She could hear her phone ringing as she opened the door. She waited. Two shorts and a long. It was for her. She put her groceries on the floor and pulled the earpiece off the hook. "KC 431, Lane Winslow speaking."

"Oh, Lane, you will never guess what Philip found at the beach today! It—" but the phone went dead. She really would have to get it fixed. She'd put her groceries away and go up to Angela's to find what the heck it was that Philip had found.

CHAPTER TEN

Kootenay Lake, August 1910

ELEANOR SUSKIND SAT IN A rattan chair near a luxuriously laid tea table on what, she thought, must be the most perfect August afternoon. She had been surprised, when she and her aunt were ushered through the house to the back garden, by the display of white lace tablecloths, china, and plates of exquisite sandwiches, biscuits, and cakes. A crowd was already gathered outside, young people standing in clusters holding plates and laughing. A group of people were playing croquet at some remove from the tea tables. Older people were sitting in small groupings of chairs. While the sun was still high, it was filtered through the leaves of weeping willow and birch and evergreen, casting a shower of gold and shadow across the lawn.

"Do sit over here, ladies. I should try to find Mr. Thomas. You will want to meet him," Mrs. Franklin said, and then added, "Ah, Lady Armstrong, you know Miss Suskind of course, and this is her lovely niece Eleanor. She's visiting for the summer. I must find Edward!" Mrs. Franklin looked distractedly around the crowd of guests and then bustled off. A maid wearing a white cap offered them tea, and then Eleanor settled back to gaze at the scene. In a kind of ecstasy at the beauty of the afternoon, she stretched out her legs and waggled her feet.

"I can't help wondering what it's like here in winter. It's so utterly beautiful now. Like an English summer day, but not, if you understand me," she said to Lady Armstrong, who smiled and put her teacup on the little table beside her.

"It *is* a bit of a wilderness, there's no denying it, but with a good stove it has its charms. Piles of puffy snow. Very picturesque. I must say, I don't mind it. There is, as you see"—she indicated the forest that seemed to be pressing in, trying to reclaim the lawn and gardens of this sturdy white house with its defiant and sweeping English garden—"plenty of wood."

"Why did you come out?" Eleanor asked.

"My husband took a diplomatic job in Ottawa. Nothing grand. A sort of Dominion liaison, and it stuck. Society at home can be so stuffy." Lady Armstrong laughed. "Of course, here everyone tries to outdo everyone else in manners. But our children all grow up like barbarians, nevertheless. Look at my boys." She pointed to where a young man of about twenty-two had collapsed into a chair. A younger boy lay spread out on a blanket at his feet. "Kenneth and John. They have run quite wild. It took all my persuasion to get them out of their suspenders and dungarees and into some proper clothes." She smiled at her sons with such evident fondness that Eleanor turned to look at them. It seemed to her that someone who engendered this much love must be wonderful indeed. "The young man over there is my nephew, Robin. He came out to stay with us when his parents died." Robin was talking to two pretty young women that Eleanor deemed to be still in their teens. "You must allow me to invite you and your aunt to come to tea next Saturday. We live, of course, much more humbly, but our view is lovely."

"Kenny, John, this is Miss Suskind, who is visiting for the summer."

Kenneth Armstrong, feeling as though he had been caught staring, turned away in confusion. He had, in truth, been unable to take his eyes off Miss Suskind. She was slender, with an expression of utter sweetness, but she had an underlying look of strength and determination. Her blond hair, rolled into a knot at her neck, escaped in strands from under her hat. When she turned to look at him, her sea-blue eyes sparkled with amusement and he thought, I am lost.

He stood up and bowed, looking only briefly into Eleanor's eyes. His brother, John, shook her hand eagerly. "Topping! How long did it take to get here? I'm dying to go back to the old country!"

"John is always dying to be anywhere else," commented his mother. "Kenneth, on the other hand, is always dying to stay right here and escape any danger of being forced into any enterprise requiring a suit."

Eleanor was about to make a response to John about the length of her trip, and was scheming about how she might engage the handsome and shy Kenneth Armstrong in some conversation when her view was obstructed by the looming figures of Mrs. Franklin and a man, whom she had by the arm as if she were trying to position him in exactly the right location in the tableau that was her garden party.

"Please, meet our young guest," Mrs. Franklin said. "Miss Suskind, this is our local politico, Mr. Edward Thomas. He is our distinguished representative in Victoria."

Mr. Thomas, a handsome man, though perhaps tending to middle-aged stoutness, with sandy hair and blue eyes, attired in an obviously expensive linen suit, bowed and took her hand. "Miss Suskind, how very charming!" A chair was brought and he sat next to her. "Now then, you are here on a visit. What do you think of our little community?"

Eleanor glanced toward Kenneth Armstrong, but he had been diverted by something his mother was saying to him. "It is beautiful. I'm not sure I expected to be sitting in my best clothes drinking tea out of beautiful china. I thought there would be more wilderness."

"But my dear, the wilderness encroaches on us at every moment. We have carved a miracle from it. Mines, timber, orchards even. There has never been such a land of opportunity! I am sure, dear Lady Armstrong, that you must agree with me."

Lady Armstrong inclined her head in his direction and then returned to talking to her boys.

Eleanor wanted to say that he sounded like a travel guide but instead said, "It must be an honour to represent the local area."

"How well you understand me! It is. I feel keenly the responsibility to guide and shape the development of this part of the Dominion. We ought to support the enterprises and the men who build them. I am in a unique position in government to ensure that those who immigrate here are people who will contribute to the growth of the community. Good English stock. Hard workers. People with vision. And we shall need wives for them." Here he smiled broadly at her, in a way that made Eleanor suppress an instinct to recoil. She was saved from the necessity of having to answer by the arrival of a tall woman who was struggling to hold a parasol and a baby dressed in a frilly bonnet and gown who was wiggling and straining in an effort to see everything.

"Edward, do be a dear and fetch the perambulator," the woman said, her face a mask of near disapproval.

"Ah. The wife," Thomas said, winking at Eleanor. "Our daughter." He got up and bowed and followed his wife, who was sweeping off around the side of the house. She apparently had no wish to be introduced to Eleanor.

Lady Armstrong shook her head. "He never stops glad-handing to draw breath. It must be exhausting being him."

"Is he any good at his job?" Eleanor asked. "I expect people vote for him to get him to go away to Victoria."

Lady Armstrong laughed. "He's good enough. He came out here and made a fortune and, though it is churlish to say it, probably supports legislation that is kind toward his business interests. Still, he is right, I suppose. We must build up immigration, develop the land, and whatnot. I find it exhausting to think about all the industry he envisions. I imagine our little community awash with prospectors and sawmill operators, if we aren't careful. We just want to grow fruit and live in peace. I have spent a good deal of time persuading him that prosperity may include agricultural interests as well. He's an ambitious man. And I'm sorry to say he loves someone with a title to an almost intolerable degree."

"I believe he was trying to recruit me to come and be someone's wife. He might have called me 'good British stock' if his wife hadn't come along and asked for the pram."

Lady Armstrong laughed in a way that Eleanor found delightful. It was a laugh full of fun and undisguised mirth. She must, Eleanor thought, have been not only beautiful but also unconventional when she was young. "Yes. He does go on. Very keen. I suspect from this that he lacks the imagination to envision a world that is just left on its own. Still, he works hard. One should give him that. He's been able to have only one child, after, one hears, years of trying. Much to his chagrin, it's a girl. He's the sort of man who no doubt sees a future only in a son. Well, I have an embarrassment of riches, don't I, with two sons. I'd have loved to have a daughter, as jolly as these two are. I don't envy that little girl. I expect he ignores his family in his effort to make himself agreeable to everyone else."

"Oh, how lovely!" Eleanor cried.

Kenneth looked up to see what Eleanor was exclaiming over. Two West Highland terrier puppies had been released from somewhere, and Eleanor was bending to pick one up. "We always had these in my family! Yes, we did," she cooed to the wiggling puppy on her lap. "Do you breed them?" She turned to her hostess, Mrs. Franklin.

"I do, yes. Happy to set you up with one. Got a nice litter. These two little fellows are still looking for homes."

"I wish I could! It wouldn't be fair, though. I'm only here for three months and then I'd have to leave it to go home to finish my studies. Auntie, you wouldn't keep it after I left, would you?"

Eleanor's aunt, a severe and erect specimen in the high-collared fashion of the previous decade, looked over her spectacles with a downturned mouth. "Certainly not. You shouldn't think of doing anything so irresponsible."

Eleanor was undaunted. She glanced up, saw Kenneth looking at her, and winked. "I shall have to be satisfied with a little cuddle now." And then everything changed. Kenneth Armstrong put down his teacup and went to where she was sitting. He stooped next to her and began to play with the second puppy, which was on the grass.

"Maybe you should get one," Eleanor said to the top of his head.

He looked up at her now, his dark hair falling over one eye. "Maybe you should stay here," he said.

LANE ARRIVED AT Angela Bertolli's spectacular cabin to a flurry of barking dogs that, seeing who it was, moderated their vocalizations from a challenging to a welcoming sort of half-bark, and then went to collapse on the shady side of the porch. The cabin may have started out small, but when the Bertollis had moved from New York to start a new life, one where David could focus on music, rather than be made to run his family's business, they had made additions to the little log building. It now had a great, light-filled open sitting room with plenty of windows and space for a grand piano. They had added an open second floor, which the children had the complete run of. Lane knew that David, who taught at the high school in Nelson, was contemplating converting the barn into a studio for Angela.

"Oh, Lane, that phone! Come in. I've made iced tea and set up a couple of chairs under the trees." Angela bustled Lane into the kitchen and then handed her two glasses from out of the dish drainer. Dishes in Angela's house seemed to always be in transit from the sink to the drainer and back. "Here, you take these. Can you believe this weather? The boys want to go back to the beach tonight. Bonfire. What do you say?" They settled back into their canvas chairs. The heavenly sound of ice and tea clinking into glasses seemed to bring the temperature down.

"Never mind all that. What did Philip find?"

"Oh, yes! Philip! Philip, darling, run and get that horrible thing. It's on the living room table," she called out more or less into the ether, as there seemed to be no children in evidence. "They're playing Monopoly in the basement. It's much cooler there. I shouldn't criticize your phone—mine has conked out as well a couple of times, and I think Gwen Hughes was complaining about theirs. I wonder if some squirrel has chewed through the wires. Honestly, we're sitting ducks out here if the phones go! Thank you, darling."

Lane thought about the Hughes ladies, old Gladys and her two daughters in their fifties, in their neat house on the hill above the post office. They were fiercely independent and resourceful with their chickens and pigs and massive gardens, but if Gladys were to become ill or an accident occurred, they would need to have the phone in good nick.

Philip had indeed heard the summons and now stood before them, proudly holding his find. "I'm the only one who saw it. I even would have missed it, because the water was coming over it."

Lane looked at what he held in his hand and almost didn't want to touch it. It was an enamelled metal lapel pin with a red swastika set inside a blue circle. She frowned and reached for it. It looked new, though the pin was a little bent and didn't reach the place where it would be hooked to attach to a garment.

"How clever of you to see it! I'm sure it's important," she said, holding it on her palm.

"It's a German army thing, isn't it?" he asked.

"That it is, though I've never seen one quite like this. Do you mind if I hang on to it? I think Inspector Darling might be interested in it."

"Sure!" said Philip, beaming. "I thought it might be important 'cause of that guy that was hurt."

"That's exactly what I'm thinking," said Lane.

"INSPECTOR," LANE SAID.

"Darling," said the inspector.

"Should you be calling me that during working hours?" asked Lane.

"There's no one here. I can call you what I want. Amesy is off investigating some unsolved burglaries about which we have been getting considerable heat. That way I shall be able to blame him when he makes no progress."

"What sort of robberies?"

"Jewellery, some antiques. It's quite specific. They don't even take cash, or people's gramophones, the sorts of things you'd think robbers would want for easy fencing. But you haven't called to hear about my troubles."

"No, though I must say your troubles are always interesting. I wouldn't have suspected that the area was awash in antiques, except of course the old ladies here have extraordinary things from the old country. Anyway, Angela and her boys were down on the beach today, and the enterprising older boy, Philip, found a swastika pin right near where we pulled the boat up onto the beach. I've never seen a pin like it. A red swastika with a blue surround. It gave me a turn, I can tell you, having to look at one of those in my brand new shiny country."

"Well, isn't that interesting. And we are sure it is related to the boat?"

"Hmm. I should ask him to show me exactly where he found it. I have this idea it could have fallen out when we turned the boat over. Or it could have been there for ages, though it certainly looks in good condition, except for the pin being a little bent. No rust or whatnot, which it might have if it had been lying about. We're going down to the beach tonight for a bonfire and some hot dogs. It doesn't sound like the pin was buried or anything. Are you familiar with this symbol, I mean, aside from the fact that it's a Nazi symbol that we both saw far too much of?"

"I do know it, as a matter of fact. There was an openly Nazi party in this country, emanating from Quebec, and its name was changed to the National Unity Party. Despite the name change, it fooled no one, and the government, in its wisdom, I must say, arrested a number of members and kept them locked up during the war. I believe they're poking around the edges again, looking for credibility. It's amazing to me, especially after this war, how anyone can think Nazis had the right idea," Darling said.

"Now, wait. It's not the first time I've heard that said in the last day. Mrs. Castle said much the same thing to me. 'Hitler had the right idea.' How odd. I thought when I came here that I'd left all that sort of thing behind."

Darling was silent for a beat, and Lane wondered with irritation if her phone had gone dead again, when he spoke. "You've been talking to Mrs. Castle," he said evenly. "Now why am I not surprised? Perhaps you'd better explain."

CHAPTER ELEVEN

May 1927

VANESSA THOMAS TURNED AND LOOKED again, taking up a handful of grain in her gloved hand and letting it slide like a river back into the barrel. They were on the sidewalk outside the feed store; her friends had gone ahead, not realizing she'd stopped. He was there, his blue eyes boring into hers, his lip curled in a slight smile. She could not understand the tremor she felt in her chest at the sight of his bared and sunburned arms, his shirt open because of the heat. "Vanessa! For Pete's sake, we don't have all day!" The sound of her friend, who'd run back to get her, broke the spell, and Vanessa turned away from the young man, who now stood and watched her, pushing his dark hair out of his eyes.

"All right, all right. Keep your hair on. The frocks will still be there." She wanted desperately to turn back, to smile, to indicate in some way the impact he had had.

"Why on earth would you stop at a feed store? Planning to get a horse?" Her friend had taken her arm and was propelling her up the street toward Meyer's haberdashery where the new dresses that so excited her and her friends had come in. Her friend looked back and saw the young man and frowned. She pulled Vanessa to a stop before they caught up with the others.

"That? That's why you stopped there like a kid at a candy store? First of all, he's a nobody, and second of all, I happen to know he's no good. He got . . . he got . . ." her voice fell to an outraged whisper, "he got one of Cynthia's servants in trouble! She had to go back north. She's sixteen! He's at least twenty. And he didn't marry her."

Vanessa shook her head, laughing lightly. "He sounds like a real catch!" But in her heart she felt the beginning of a longing she had never experienced before, and with it a proud conviction. *He would never leave me like that,* she thought.

ROBERT CASTLE HEARD the noise of the bicycle rattling down the rutted road to his farm before he saw it. He was putting up a new shed behind his tiny wood-framed house. Much to his relief the sky was overcast, and it had not been too hot. He might get the shed up by the next afternoon. He put his hammer on top of a post and turned back to see who was coming. He frowned, confused. It was that girl from the other day at the feed store. He looked up the road and then down toward the lake in an unconscious attempt to understand. Her prettiness was heightened by the flush that exercise had given her.

He walked toward her as she stopped and stood, leaning on the handlebars. She wore a skirt that she had hitched the bottom of into her belt, and a blue and white sailor top. She was much younger than she'd seemed outside the store. "You must be very lost," he said.

"I'm not." She said this with a smiling show of defiance.

"Well, then, what are you doing down here? This road only comes here, it doesn't go nowhere else."

"I came to see where you live, Robert Castle."

"And how do you know my name?" He moved closer to her and took the centre of the handlebars, holding the bicycle steady while she got off. Being close to her was intoxicating. The idea that she had found out his name and come all the way here from wherever she lived made his heart beat faster at the wonder of it.

"I went back to the feed store and asked them. I told them I bought something from you and forgot to pay you, so they told me where you live. Do you sell anything I would buy?"

"You can buy a chicken off me in a few weeks. Do I get to know your name?"

"Vanessa Thomas."

The name caused Robert to step back, releasing her handlebars as if they were molten. "Well, then, Miss Thomas. You can get right back on that bike and ride home. You can send your cook to buy a chicken if you still want one." He waved his hand toward the top of the hill and the Nelson road as if he were shooing away a cat.

Vanessa frowned, hurt. "Why are you being like that? I rode all the way out here to see you."

"It beats me why. Go back to your fancy house. I know who your father is, and I've got troubles enough. And anyway, how old are you?" He stepped back, scowling at her.

"I'm seventeen."

And well developed for your age, he thought. "There's my point. I've got work to do and it's going to rain." He turned and walked back to where his hammer lay on the fencepost.

"My chain is broken," she called after him. "You have to give me a ride home."

"Are you kidding me?" He turned, angry now, and then looked up as the first heavy drops began to fall. He strode to the house and threw his hammer onto the porch. "I'm not dragging the horse out into this. You're gonna have to wait till it stops. I'll fix your chain and that's it. You better come in. And your father better not come here looking for you. Did you tell him where you were going?"

"What do you take me for? Of course not!"

"No. I don't suppose it is something you'd tell your old man. Which is another reason it's not all right. Here, let me do that." He took the bike from her as she struggled to get it up his stairs and through the doorway.

In all the years and trials that followed, amid all the anger and recriminations and rages, the drink, the increasingly wretched other women, he never forgot his first taste of her lips, full and wet from the rain, or the puzzling triumph of her response to him.

September 1927

"IT'S ABSOLUTELY OUT of the question. You have a duty to this family," said Edward Thomas, who was pacing angrily in his study.

His daughter, Vanessa, looked at him sullenly. "You don't care about this family. You only care about yourself. Your reputation, your business, your seat in parliament. It's always you. It's no wonder Mother is ill. She's probably trying to die to get away from you!"

Thomas did not move from where he stood. His voice took on an icy tone. "How dare you? You ungrateful little wretch. Is this how you thank us? You've had the best of everything money could buy, a respectable family with the highest standing in the community, and you propose to bring us all into the gutter by tying yourself to this . . . this . . . trash!"

"He's a good, hard-working man. Just because he has a farm you despise him. He's the very 'salt of the earth' you claim to love so much!"

"He's a womanizer and a drunk. I can't believe you haven't got the brains to stay away from this one, for yourself if not for me."

Vanessa shook her head. "You've had him followed, no doubt. Like a gangster who thinks he runs the world. Well, it won't matter. I'm having a baby. His baby. We're getting married and there's nothing you can do to stop us."

Her father, who had turned his attention back to the paperwork on his desk, lifted his gaze, his face unreadable, his eyebrows raised. "That's the lay of the land is it?" His voice was cold and even. He pulled open a side drawer and removed a leather folder. He opened it and took up his fountain pen, unscrewed the cap, placed it carefully on the table. "You will pack your things and go. I don't care where. From this day forward I do not wish to hear of you or from you. I will consider my duty to you expunged with this cheque." He wrote a cheque, tore it carefully from his chequebook, and held it out.

Vanessa stood, unable to move. "You can't dismiss me like some henchman you found stealing the petty cash!"

"Can I not? You have stolen from us. You have stolen our trust, the reputation of this family, indeed, even its future with that bastard child." He put the cheque down and pushed it toward the edge of the desk. "It is a great sorrow to me that we were only able to have one child. I was able to overlook the utter disappointment of your being a girl by taking comfort that you would marry well and our fortunes would be secure in the hands of a responsible man. Please do not look to me ever after for any help. It goes without saying that you will find no succour in my will."

"And yet you are saying it," said his daughter, her own rage burning inside, holding her in her spot.

"And do not importune your mother. She is not well. That will be all." Her father put his chequebook away as if she were already gone. He closed the drawer and, after a moment's thought, removed a key from his waistcoat pocket, locked his desk, and replaced the key, patting his pocket. Pushing himself to a standing position, he walked out of his study without looking at her.

Vanessa turned and watched him. He reached the foyer and she could hear him calling the housekeeper. His voice was decisive, as if, she thought, he had finally gotten rid of a long-term irritant. "Ah, Mrs. Harding. Mrs. Thomas and I will be out this evening. Could you give every assistance to Miss Thomas and then lock up after she leaves?"

"IT'S TRULY NOTHING sinister. I was off getting eggs in Balfour and Bales was out of them, and of course, he gets them from Mrs. Castle, so I offered to pop down to her place and pick them up from her because that son of hers has wandered off with the family car," Lane explained to Darling. She was leaning against the wall by the phone, happy as always to hear the warmth of his voice down the line.

"How thoughtful of you," Darling said.

"No need to take that tone. It's what anyone would have done."

"And as she was handing you the eggs, she was explaining to you how Hitler is just the man."

"Yes," Lane replied. "Something like that. It seems so strangely coincidental. She espouses these repellent views and we find a swastika lying on the beach, which could conceivably have belonged to the wounded man."

"It does seem like a lot of fascism all at once, I grant you, but that wounded boy is not hers. Sometimes things are nothing more than coincidences," Darling said.

"Still, I'm surprised about the whole thing. I suppose I'm simply naive. I wanted all my Nazis parcelled up and put on the shelf of history after all our hard work in the war. I didn't expect to find them here."

"Some comfort can be derived from the fact that the domestic ones have sunk into obscurity, ballot-box wise. I suppose there will always be people who believe their sort of nonsense. But now that you've had that conversation with her, I'm going to have to put it in my notes, aren't I? Just in case. You're a confounded nuisance," Darling said, the warmth in his voice belying his words.

"I'm sorry, darling. Anyway. I'm out of this one. I only do murders, after all."

"That's quite all right. It will be a relief not tripping over you in the middle of this investigation. Nevertheless, if you do find out where that blasted Castle boy has got to, don't hesitate to call." He paused. "When are you going to replace that phone?"

"Never, I've told you. I love it because you talk to me on it. In fact, it's a miracle that it has not gone dead. We've had an awful time with the phones out here. I'd better tell you I love you before it does conk out."

"All right," Darling said.

"All right, what?"

"Tell me you love me. I would tell you, if I were in your shoes."

"I love you. There. Happy?"

"Very. I'd be happier still if I were with you there."

"HELLO, LITTLE ONE!" Lane stooped down to greet the tiny wiggling mass that was Alexandra. "Who's a sweetheart then?" She stood up, holding the puppy in her arms, submitting to having her cheek licked enthusiastically.

"Mind the bowl!" Eleanor said, pointing at the floor where a large rectangular porcelain bowl of Chinese design was parked next to a folded quilt.

Lane put the puppy down, only reluctantly, and then eyed the bowl. "That's never her water dish. She could bathe in that thing!"

"We've always used it for our dogs. My grandmother gave it to me when I came out here. Made me promise I'd use it only for the dogs, as she had. Never had a nick in it. I don't know where she got it. From her grandmother I expect."

"That would place it back in the seventeen hundreds. It's a veritable antique. That grandmother there?" Lane pointed at a small watercolour of a very elderly woman with her head swaddled in a shawl.

"That's the one. Granny Bentley. I believe she was considered eccentric, though I adored her."

"She must have been to water her pups out of a priceless Chinese bowl! Are you sure it will survive Alexandra?"

"It survived all the others," Eleanor said stoutly.

On the shady back porch of the post office, Lane leaned back, looking out over the Armstrong garden. Alexandra had settled on Kenny's lap and was sleeping off her earlier excitement. The garden, a handsome mix of vegetables and flowers, swept out toward the edge of the underbrush. Sweet peas climbed a wooden trellis and fell forward near the top in a profusion of heavy multi-coloured blooms. Eleanor always said she had to keep them picked, which is why everyone in King's Cove went home from the post office with their newspapers, bills, and letters, and a fistful of flowers during the growing season.

"This is the real luxury, isn't it? Just like in the old songs. A cottage, a garden, a puppy, a home built for two. Well, for two and the pesky neighbour who's always over guzzling your food," Lane said.

"You didn't come here to discuss our garden, but you are guzzling our tea, so you'd better cough up," Kenny said.

"Really, Kenny," his wife chided. "Such bully tactics. Leave the girl in peace. She'll cough up when she's good and ready. Well?" She turned to Lane, smiling sweetly. "I believe you said you delivered Mrs. Castle's eggs to Fred Bales. Any news of her missing son?"

"No, alas. But I did learn something about her," said Lane. "Apparently she hasn't always been a farmer. She's the daughter of some local politician. Fred told me that. It made me feel a bit sorry for her. She's so thin and worn down, and there can't be much money in eggs. I imagine she needed the extra income her boy brought in from the garage. Mind you, my sympathy was a bit tempered by her telling me what a great man Hitler was. I'm not even sure I understand what she thinks Hitler could do for her in these circumstances."

Eleanor put her hand to her chin in a thoughtful manner. "Now then, I wonder . . . there was a local scandal in the late twenties. Do you remember, Kenny? That awful blowhard Whatshisname. He was introduced to me, I think, at that tea the day I met you. Goodness! Isn't that funny that we're back at the day we met!"

"That Thomas fellow. Mother despised him. Had a bad end, didn't he? His wife died, he married again, a much younger woman. Wife number two never had children, but he had a daughter from the first wife. There was a rumour he tossed his own daughter out without a farthing. It didn't do him any good. Apparently when he died of a heart attack, the estate was bust. Bad losses in the crash, and then he borrowed heavily on his property without telling that poor chit he married. She got nothing."

"That's right!" said Eleanor eagerly. "There were rumours up and down the lake about that girl. She ran off with someone very unsuitable. Maybe that's why her father disinherited her. I bet that's who Mrs. Castle is."

CHAPTER TWELVE

THE VIGIL AT THE HOSPITAL continued, both for the doctors and for the uniformed policeman who sat outside the patient's door. No other attempts to visit the patient were recorded, and he hung on, barely, to life. Darling did not believe for a minute that he was called Smith, but nevertheless had put Ames onto trying to discover such a person in any community up and down the north end of the lake. On top of that their blight of unsolved burglaries had expanded and now appeared to be moving like a slow wave, out of town and up the lake. He had dispatched people to visit victims at Willow Point and two summerhouses farther north, and take note of what had been lost: an ancestral portrait, a Dutch vase, and a gold watch with a heavy gold fob.

Darling, knowing that Ames was safely away looking for likely Joseph P. Smiths, had his feet on his desk and was wondering where to put his attention. It was hot, and in spite of his having pushed his window right to the top, the air was still and muggy. He looked at the three files neatly spread across the top of his desk, just beyond the reach of his well-polished dark brown, single-tone brogues. He'd bought them in England, eschewing the flashier two-toned variety. He'd admired the double row of stitching and had made the plunge as an affirmation, perhaps, of life, and a bid to get rid of the shoes he'd worn in prison in London. He did not admire them at the moment, though they gleamed at eye level.

It would be splendid if the three cases—the missing Carl, the unidentified man found shot in the boat, and the stolen antiques—were related to one another, he thought. Then evidence in one might illuminate something about the other two. He set himself to imagining how any one could be connected to either of the others. Carl Castle could have taken up stealing antiques and now be on the run. That seemed unlikely. He'd been fired from his job and was in a filthy humour. He'd go on a bender, not go stealing antiques. Carl Castle could have shot the man in the boat and would then have had a reason to go on the run. Darling drew a blank piece of foolscap forward and made a note. Carl Castle could have been "involved," as his mother put it, in an antiques stealing racket and for some reason threatened to expose the other people in it. That should mean he was the one shot, not the alleged Joseph P. Smith. Of course, Castle could be dead, and they just hadn't found him yet.

Darling sat back and shook his head. Trying to squeeze the antiques into the equation felt artificial. And maybe after all, they were three separate matters. Perhaps inspired by the stultifying and unmoving air in his office, which made him think of the doldrums in *The Rime of the Ancient Mariner,* he came up with an inane rhyme.

"Evidence, evidence everywhere, nor any way to think," he muttered. The problem was, he was short of evidence. He'd heard nothing from the Royal Canadian Mounted Police about the yellow car with the red licence plate; there had been nothing of interest in the pockets or bag of the wounded man in the boat, besides the letter fragment, unless the swastika pin was counted, which might or might not be his; and no one who'd been robbed of their precious family antiques could think of how a thief had known precisely what to look for. The one local antique shop had not received any of the stolen items, or so an inventory of their current stock seemed to show.

With decision he picked up the phone, and then with equal decision he put it down again. Lane wouldn't be at home on a day like this. She'd be at the beach, keeping cool. Blasted lucky woman! Well, he was a policeman, and his lot was not a happy one. He reached over, pulled the burglary file toward him, and opened it, hoping for a pattern of some kind to leap out at him.

BUT SHE WASN'T at the beach. She was at the Balfour store again, buying some supplies for Mrs. Castle. Lane was beginning to wonder if perhaps Mrs. Castle did know where her son was, or knew why he'd left. She wasn't sure why, except that she was trying to imagine what she herself would be like if her son were missing. She was certain she'd be sick with fear, unable to sleep, probably bothering the police with desperate demands for action, constantly imagining him at the bottom of a cliff or drowned in the lake. Everyone wears fear differently, Lane thought. Mrs. Castle was a woman who had clearly had a hard life. Perhaps fear for her was an angry, mute, hard knot inside her.

Bales's dog, which evidently had found the sun too much, even for him, was lying in the shade provided by two fruit trees at the side of the store near the gas pump.

"You get a nice breeze up the hill here," Lane said.

"I get a nice breeze from my fan, thank you very much," Bales said, pointing to the ceiling. "Blast. Sorry, I'll attend to this and be back."

A large black car had pulled up to the gas pump, and the driver was honking impatiently. Lane, reluctant to leave the environs of the fan, watched with interest through the window. The car was certainly massive and luxurious. The hood ornament looked a bit like the bombsights she'd seen on planes in hangers. She'd thought the car was the latest model something—she couldn't see the front—but perhaps it had been manufactured during the war. She was about to turn away when she saw the driver. To her surprise, it was the offensive young man Councillor Lorimer had had with him at Lorenzo's restaurant. His secretary, Lorimer had called him. She watched the gasoline bubbling in the pump and wondered what he'd be doing way out here.

"Sorry about that," Bales said, coming back in. "Big man in a hurry."

"He's Councillor Lorimer's secretary, I believe. I wonder why he's all the way up the lake? Do people here vote in the municipal election?"

"Not so far as I know. Maybe he has an old mother he has to visit," Bales said. "Right. Where were we?" He continued to pile things into the box, walking through the shop ticking off things on a list. "That's the lot. You wouldn't mind stopping by with the eggs after you drop this off? I called her and she's got some on hand. Here's the money, minus the groceries. That boy of hers better come back soon. He's left her high and dry. Anyway, okay about the eggs?"

"Perfectly. They're so easy to move around in their cardboard flats."

"Those were invented right here in British Columbia," he said. "Around 1910 or 1911."

"You don't say! That's terribly clever. Imagine even thinking of it. I couldn't invent my way out of a paper bag. I hope the inventor made a million."

"Bet he didn't, though. All the wrong people make the millions. Look at that guy in the car. How does he make all that money being a secretary?"

"You have a point, Mr. Bales. I guess the rest of us will have to be content with a good honest day's work." This was slightly disingenuous on her part Lane realized, as she started down the hill a few minutes later. Mr. Bales, Mrs. Castle, Inspector Darling, and Constable Ames, they all did a good day's work. She wasn't sure what she did, besides write rather indifferent poetry, visit her neighbours, and sit gazing at her view, but the days seemed to race by. Well, she was owed a year, after the war. Maybe this year she'd get down to it and tackle the apples. Robin could help her. She wondered how he'd feel about being asked.

Picking season would be here before she knew it. She tried to imagine asking him and in her head heard his rebuff, which no doubt would be accompanied by a comment about "damn fool women."

Driving around the corner, she saw the turnoff to the Castle farm just up ahead and pulled to a stop, frowning. Coming out of the farm road, and speeding off to Nelson in a cloud of dust, was the same big black car that had been at the gas pump. What did it mean? Whoever it was wouldn't have been there long. Five, ten minutes at the most? Relieved that he wouldn't know her car and would be very unlikely to remember her if he saw her, she waited until he'd gone around a bend, and then she slowly let out the clutch and turned down to Mrs. Castle's.

"AH, AMES. THERE you are. You took your time. Any luck with Joseph P.?"

"No, sir. But I'm happy to confirm that Smith is the most common name in the world."

"And you've—damn!" The phone on his desk rang. "Yes? Darling here."

"Inspector, I'm calling from the hospital. That patient you have here under guard? That Joseph Smith? He's died, I'm afraid. The doctor said I was to ring you right away. The doctor had to go into another surgery, but would you like to talk to him? He could probably see you before he goes home around six."

"Yes. Yes, I'd better talk to him. Thank you for calling." Darling hung up the phone, folded his hands, and looked across at Ames.

"Well, we now have a possible murder. Joseph P. did not make it. I'm going round to the hospital to see the doctor later."

Ames sat down and shook his head. "That's too bad. I was hoping he'd come to and tell us his real name and how he got shot like that."

"So was I, Ames, so was I. You'd better go arrange for him to be transported to the cooler. Gilly can have a look at him, though I imagine I'll get chapter and verse from the doctor." Their pathologist, Ashford Gillingham, affectionately known as Gilly, would perhaps have some insight. Darling realized that much of what Gilly could tell them, time of death, content of stomach, et cetera, et cetera, was moot. The injured man had died in full view of everyone at the hospital moments before. They could sure use some insight, Darling thought glumly. "It'll mean an inquest."

"The strangest thing, sir, about all of this, is that no one has claimed him. You'd think by now some desperate wife or mother would have come out of the woodwork."

"As it happens I was about to say the same thing, Ames. You'll make a heck of a sergeant! I'd better phone Miss Winslow. That old dear of hers, Mrs. Armstrong, will no doubt want to know."

Muttering "Run along" with a shooing motion, Darling dialled Lane's number.

"INSPECTOR, HOW WELL met. I have some news for you, of sorts." Lane wondered if she'd ever break herself of the habit of calling him "Inspector." She recalled couples of her youth who'd called each other "Mrs. Thomas" or "Mr. Dickinson" their whole married lives. She pushed aside the churning anxiety she felt at the thought of marriage.

"Me too, I'm afraid, and you'd better let me go first. The man from the boat has died, I'm assuming of his injuries. I'm seeing the doctor in about an hour. I thought you'd want to know," Darling said.

"Oh, I am sorry," Lane said. She was. She had hoped somehow that because the man had hung on for several days, he might still recover. "Poor Eleanor and Kenny . . . oh, and Angela. Oh my God, and the boys. I shall have to tell them somehow as well."

"That sounds like a job for their mother," Darling suggested gently.

"Yes, of course. You're right. Gosh. It's a murder investigation now, I guess."

"Yes. And I suppose you think you should get involved."

"Don't be silly," Lane said. "Of course not. That poor man. Did no one come to claim him?"

"That's exactly what Ames said. It's like he was all alone in this world."

"I wonder if some clue was left behind wherever it happened. Perhaps he was robbed and someone took his money and threw his billfold away. Oh. You said the wallet was there, with money in it."

"We don't know where it happened," Darling pointed out reasonably.

"What was that you said?" Lane asked, suddenly animated.

"That we don't know where it happened."

"No, before that, something about Ames and being alone."

"That he was all alone in this world?"

"That's it. What if he was all alone in *this* world? What if he was an immigrant, or a refugee, or something? Someone like that might have come without a family. We've just had a war, after all."

Darling made a face. She had a point. "Is this you staying away from my murder investigation? What were you going to tell me, by the way?"

"I had to drop by Mrs. Castle's again today, and I saw Councillor Lorimer's secretary driving what I expect is Lorimer's very expensive black car out onto the Nelson road from Mrs. Castle's driveway."

"I don't even know where to start. First of all, how do you know it was Lorimer's secretary?"

"He came into Lorenzo's with Lorimer to have lunch when I was there with Mrs. Armstrong. He tried to pinch the table Lorenzo had prepared for us. Lorenzo wasn't having it, of course. Happily he didn't hear the imprecation the man muttered on the way past us to another, very inferior table. Very unpleasant man. My question is, what on earth can he have to do with Mrs. Castle?"

"Obviously Mrs. Castle herself didn't tell you while you were on your so-called supply mission?"

"No. She was very vague. I said something about the beautiful car I saw coming away from her place, and she said that since Carl went off with the car, she's had her egg customers coming directly to her some of the time. She seemed . . . I don't know, nervy."

"So, Lorimer has his eggs delivered in a limousine. That is not in itself a crime," Darling said.

"And did I tell you? Mrs. Castle is not just Mrs. Castle. It turns out she is the daughter of a prominent politician from the 1920s. There was some sort of scandal involving an unsuitable liaison . . . with dead Mr. Castle, I assume, and she was disowned."

"Again, not a crime."

"I don't know. I bet you couldn't throw a teenaged girl onto the street nowadays without someone making a fuss. Anyway, I see what you mean about coincidences, but I've got some paper and some good sharp pencils and I'm going to make a few notes, perhaps draw a map of the area, in my usual not-getting-involved way."

During previous cases Darling had been impressed with the clarity these maps of hers had engendered. "Well, if it keeps you from getting underfoot, you carry on. I'm meeting with Gilly in a bit to see what he has to say."

GILLY WAS THOUGHTFUL as he dried his hands. "Unusual situation. Usually I'm investigating cause of death, time, et cetera. No doubt you heard from the hospital. He died of sepsis, consequent upon a gunshot to his midsection causing blood loss, and ultimately infection, possibly from clothing fragments in the wound. He probably didn't have a chance. But that's all a matter of medical record. Anyway, I did see that his hands are very calloused from some labouring work; judging from where the callouses are he's been digging . . . I'd have said farming, except that his hands are full of the small splinters you might get from logging without gloves. These are more recent probably. And it looks like he was in a fight recently. There was swelling and bruising on his knuckles, and he had a bad bruise that was still fading on his left shoulder, as if he'd been hit with something. How was he found again?"

"Miss Winslow," Darling began.

Gilly laughed. "Really?"

"If you let me finish, Miss Winslow was fishing with her neighbours, and one of the children saw a rowboat floating near the base of the point. They heard a groan and found him inside. Would their moving him out of the boat have made the matter worse?"

"It wouldn't have helped, but he died of sepsis—the seeds of that were already planted. With the blood loss it's a miracle he made it as long as he did. Is she worried about that?" Gilly rather liked Miss Winslow for her practical good sense. That's what he told himself, anyway. How beautiful she was had nothing to do with it.

"I think she knew that. He had been in the boat all night and it had taken on a good deal of water, so much of him was submerged. I think they rightly calculated that they ought to get him out to keep him warm, as the ambulance was going to take an hour to get to them."

Gilly nodded. "No idea who he is?"

"Nope. And no one has called for him. You'd better prepare the spare bedroom. He'll be staying awhile."

CHAPTER THIRTEEN

Bohemia, 1938

"MY GOD, WHAT IS IT?" Klaus groaned and turned over, pulling his pillow over his head, refusing to open his eyes.

"Get up! For God's sake." Otto pulled at his roommate. "We have to go, now! They're here! Sylvia saw them driving into town with their beastly flags."

Uttering an oath, Klaus sat up, his heart beating frantically. He reached around on the covers and found his shirt, and then sat on the edge of the bed and pulled on his pants. "How much time do we have?"

Otto was pushing things into a rucksack. "How should I know? Maybe they are going to stand down and drink coffee all morning, but I wouldn't count on it."

Klaus was up, following Otto's example, pushing a pair of pants, socks, and some undershirts into his rucksack. They'd been preparing for this. They'd heard that the Gestapo had gone into other towns and rounded up people like them—members of various Communist workers' parties, union leaders. It was a matter of time, they were told. Hitler already had a starter list and wanted to eliminate every last one of them.

"All right. I don't need the rest of this crap," Klaus said, giving the room one more look.

At the bottom of the back stairs, Klaus opened the gate and looked cautiously into the street. He could hear a rumble in the distance coming from the north. "Let's go," he said.

They ran down the empty street toward the bridge. If they could get over the bridge, they could run across the fields to the junction where Sylvia should be waiting with the car. That was their plan. On the avenue crossing the bridge, traffic was coming toward them, making for the centre. Germans going to welcome the Nazis, flags flying, people shouting out of the backs of trucks. Otto and Klaus walked normally, trying not to attract attention, looking as much as possible like labourers going to their jobs. The noise of honking and shouting picked up.

"Idiots!" muttered Otto.

They had just made the other side of the bridge and were pushing through the oncoming crowds when Klaus cried, "Oh my God! The membership lists! I ran off and left them. If they find them . . ."

"You can't go back!" Otto grabbed Klaus's sleeve. "It's too late. Please, come." He pulled at his friend's arm, willing him to keep going, away from the jubilant crowd and the rumble of the approaching army.

Horror coursing through him, Klaus looked at Otto. "They will have the name of every single person. Julia,

Frank, the children." He turned away and plunged into the crowd, pushing to get ahead, looking like someone eager to welcome the coming plague. He thought he could hear Otto calling his name above the shouting of the crowd.

April 1939

THE TRAIN PULLED to a stop. Klaus looked out the window but could see nothing but snow-covered wilderness. Bending to look out the opposite window, he saw the station platform. It was tiny and looked as if it had been dropped into the middle of a great, vast nowhere.

"This is it?" he asked.

Hans shrugged his shoulders. "This is apparently it."

The two men pulled their bundles off the racks and helped the women who were setting the three children down onto the platform. Some men were dropping heavy wooden boxes onto the platform in a way that suggested they were glad to be rid of them. The silence after the noise of supplies being unloaded was the first thing that struck Klaus. His ears were ringing from the roar of the train, and now there was a long moment when no one spoke. He stood with the others, looking at their new home. It was as lonely a place as he had ever seen. Vast, shrubby, a forest pushing in from one side. And covered in snow. In April! At home in Bohemia it would already be spring; the trees would be garlanded in tiny pale green buds. He thought stupidly for one moment that he could not even tell what was north, or south, and then he saw the sun in the west and tried to orient himself. Nothing in his life equipped him for this. He had been born and brought up in a town. Involuntarily he took in a great draft of air and then realized the Canadian Western Railway agent who had accompanied them was talking loudly.

"This is it. You live here now." Almost shouting and speaking slowly, he pointed out at the landscape. When people turned to look at him he muttered, "Bloody foreigners. Tents! Tools. All right? Tools. You can build." He used his hands to make a house shape in the air.

Hans's wife, Elsa, moved toward Klaus. "Why is he shouting? What is he saying?"

"He says we live here now, here are some tools, build a house."

"But can you ask him where? Are there not others here already? I see no sign of anything."

"Excuse me," Klaus said. He had studied English in school and had been in England at the beginning of his exile, but suddenly he felt awkward in the face of this impatient and shouting man. "Where are we to go?"

Before the man could answer, a loud "Halloo" rang out from behind the station, and they could hear the sound of horses.

"There," said the agent. "They have come for you."

Two great flatbed wagons, drawn by horses snorting steam into the rapidly chilling air, pulled up at the end of the platform.

"Sorry we're late! One of the wagons got stuck. Welcome! Welcome! We had better get you to the settlement. It is no Praga, I warn you, but we can put you up for tonight and put your tents up tomorrow."

Klaus, relieved to be hearing them speak German, stared at the two men who had brought the wagons, and shuddered. They were wearing brown parkas. The hated brown of the Gestapo.

"I'm Willi, this is Leo. I see you looking at these coats. Believe me, we wouldn't wear them if we could avoid it. It's what they give you, and in the middle of winter it's fifty below. Even for a principle I won't freeze to death! Now, it is a long drive back so we should move."

The agent made a cursory show of helping to move things onto the wagons. "Train goes by three days a week."

"What's he saying?" asked Hans.

"The train stops at this paradise three days a week. I don't know why he is telling us this. We cannot leave."

"Oh, it's not so bad as that. Some of us work on the railroad, or on other farmsteads," the man called Leo said.

Klaus nodded and watched the train pulling away. "I gather there will be no use for my electrical training?"

"Electricity! Ha! We don't even have enough kerosene lamps yet! And I hope you brought your own bucket for water. We don't have enough of those either."

The wagons were heavy now with long wooden boxes of tools—like coffins, Klaus thought—three heavy canvas tents, boxes of cans and sacks of flour and sugar, potatoes, cooking tools, and grates for the fire, as well as sacks that were to be filled with straw for bedding.

"We look like a bunch of refugees," said Hans, Elsa's husband.

"We are refugees," Klaus said.

"It's going to be dark soon, and the children are hungry," Elsa said.

"What about money? They said there would be fifteen hundred dollars for a family. We have been given nothing," Hans said.

Willi shrugged. "They tell us that they have the money on account. Everything they give you they take off that amount. No one has any idea how much is there."

"So why can't there be more buckets?" asked Klaus.

"They know better than us. Your English is good. Maybe we send you to negotiate for buckets and all the other things we don't have enough of."

"I'm nineteen years old. No one will listen to me."

"Believe me, kid, they don't listen to any of us very well."

That night, lying in the tent they had set up to protect the supplies because he was the only single man, Klaus stared into the dark, in the unfamiliar silence of the wilderness, longing to hear traffic on the street outside, the sound of people leaving the bar below his apartment. He saw his sister Julia, could hear the last words she ever said to him: "Silly brother. You worry too much. Off you go home and get some sleep or you'll be late for your shift." She had kissed him on the cheek and pushed him gently out the door. He had looked for her among the refugees in England, asked and asked, but no one had heard of her, or her children, or her husband. In his addled state of mind as sleep stole over him, he thought that when he destroyed the lists, he must have made the people all disappear as well.

LANE TOOK OUT a piece of paper and pulled a pencil from the cup she kept next to her typewriter.

"Sorry, little typewriter," she said. "I will get to you, I promise. First rainy day."

She drew an approximation of the shape of King's Cove, rounded it out around the corner past Balfour and on the other side, around and up the lake toward Adderly and Kaslo. Near the point where she and Angela and Kenny had been fishing, she wrote, "Man in boat found." On consideration she also drew a tiny boat out in the space that would be the lake and wrote a question mark above it. It loomed larger now, because it was possible someone had been watching them move the injured man out of the boat. Then around the corner in the approximate location of the Castle farm, she drew a square and wrote, "Castle farm" and then, "Carl Castle missing from here." Then she sat back and gazed at her own bit of the lake framed by her kitchen window. There wasn't enough room to show the whole of the north end of the lake, so she moved a piece of paper next to the first one, drew in the shoreline, and wrote in "Adderly" and "Kaslo." How far could the boat have come? The man had still been alive but barely. She was no doctor, but left any longer, the man surely would have died if they had not found him.

What lay between Adderly and Kaslo? She needed a map, she thought. There should be some sort of detailed map of the lake. An ordnance map of some type perhaps? She would go into town and find one she decided. She looked at the lines she had drawn. She was looking down on King's Cove and the lake from above, the way she'd seen France laid out from the airplanes before she jumped. It suddenly made sense to her that this was how she approached her "connecting" process. The knock on her door interrupted her analysis of her process and the follow-up pleasant thoughts of stopping by the police station in town, and maybe even getting a lunch at Lorenzo's out of the deal.

A man in grey coveralls with a belt full of tools stood at the door. "Ma'am. I'm from the phone company. We're having a look at the wires here. I understand the service has been spotty."

"Oh, good. I meant to call someone, but I see one of my neighbours has. What was your name again?"

"Oh. Eddie Carter, ma'am." He stood expectantly on the doorstep.

Lane glanced past him up to the driveway. A grey van was parked at the gate. "Service certainly has been spotty. Have you found the trouble?"

"We're checking the lines into each house, as well as the main lines. Do you mind if I have a look at your phone?"

Lane recognized the reluctance she had felt on seeing him but dismissed it. She had been so focused on her map that the intrusion had unsettled her. Obviously he was a phone man, with a proper vehicle, and the phone cutting out all the time had become a bloody nuisance. "It's an old thing, but I'm fond of it. I'm glad to hear it's the lines. I thought it might be my phone, though I did hear that a couple of my neighbours have had some trouble as well. Help yourself."

The man came in and then said, "Do you mind if I ask for a drink of water? It's a hot day out there."

"No, of course not. Come on through."

"Thanks, ma'am. I'll just slip off my boots."

Lane went into the kitchen and ran the water, and then set out a couple of glasses.

"You lived here long?" the man asked as he came through the kitchen door. "I notice most of the other people round here are a bit older."

"Just a year. Have you already been to the other houses? Any luck finding out what is wrong?"

"Nice place. You came out from England I'm guessing." The man drank the water down at one go and put his glass down. "Thanks. That really helped. I better have a look at that phone now."

Lane watched him track back through the sitting room door and frowned. He was being evasive about the problem with the phones. She put the glasses in the sink, went into the hall, and watched him pick up the earpiece and jiggle the holder. "Any luck?" she repeated.

"This is a classic. My parents had one of these. But it seems okay. I just have one line to check, connected to the main line down the road. I imagine something is loose there." He leaned over and slipped on his boots, adjusted his belt, and pulled at his cap. "Thanks again, ma'am. I expect we'll have it fixed by day's end."

Lane stood by the door and, as he turned the van, noisily grinding the gears, she could see that there was a phone company logo painted on the side. She could hear the progress of the van as it reached the intersection, slowed, and turned right, its gears grinding some more, and then headed down the hill toward the Nelson road.

Muttering "Hmm," she slipped on her shoes and, closing the door, walked across the little bridge over the gully and made her way to the post office. She didn't doubt that he was a phone man, but she certainly doubted his ability to fix anything.

She met Gwen Hughes from up the hill just leaving. "Morning, Gwen. Lovely day."

"It is. I've left Mother on her knees among the lupines and Mabel putting up some beans."

Lane smiled. She loved the industry of these three women. No doubt bread was rising, and raspberry jam was cooling on a windowsill somewhere. "Have you had the phone man up to yours?"

"Oh, him. Yes. I don't expect he knows his behind from a gatepost. We were in the garden, but he spent ten minutes inside doing things to the phone and then thanked us and left. They never know anything, these fellows."

"Did he say what he thought was wrong?"

"Something about the line connecting us with the post office," Gwen said.

"He was terribly vague with me, as well. I don't hold out much hope. They must have just recruited him. He didn't look like someone with any real technical knowledge." As she said this, Lane realized that was the impression she had been left with. Gwen jerked her head toward the entrance to the post office, where a sudden hoot of laughter from Eleanor emanated. "They've all had him. We can only hope he knows what he's doing."

Lane smiled. "We can indeed. Give my love to your mum and Mabel."

"Come up later. No, wait, I'll call you, so we can see if the phones are working, then you can come up. The bread will be ready, and I've just done some gooseberry jam from our few salvaged bushes. The first since . . . you know."

Lane did know: the complete and utter devastation of the Hughes family, and their root cellar, in the spring, when the bones of a child were discovered buried next to the house. Besides the disruption to their lives the macabre discovery caused, they'd had to tear out all their gooseberry bushes. Some, she recalled, had been recovered and transplanted.

"I would love to. Yum!"

"All right. I'll call you just before three thirty, in time for tea. Mother will be pleased."

Her afternoon comforts thus attended to, Lane went to the post office door as Alice Mather came out. Balancing some sweet peas and some letters in her other hand, she greeted Lane by raising her walking stick in a salute. "Morning," Alice said, and then stopped her progress. "You had that phone man in?"

"Yes. He just left. You?"

"Yup. I didn't like him," Alice said decisively.

"No?" Alice was inclined to dislike most things, Lane thought, even when her mental state was in a positive period. But Lane knew she was shrewd. Behind that slightly mad cloak of weird behaviour, which included some frightening moments for the Cove when she took it into her head to go shooting at imaginary cougars, she was a pretty good judge of character. Lane knew Alice didn't much like her own husband, Reg, and that alone was a sign of good judgment.

"Looked slippery. He fiddled with the phone, asked for a glass of water, and that was it."

The nearness of this description to his behaviour in her own house made Lane frown. "Did he indeed? You know, I'm not sure I don't agree with you. The proof will be in the pudding, I suppose. Let's see if the phones start behaving."

Alice raised her stick one more time and barrelled off up the hill.

"We were just discussing the phone man," Lane said to Eleanor once she was inside the post office. "No one thinks much of him. Is that squeaking noise I hear on the other side Miss Alexandra?" At the sound of her name, Alexandra barked happily, and Eleanor picked her up and handed her through the window to Lane.

"All right, all right. Keep your fur on. Here's your beloved Miss Winslow."

The puppy wiggled ecstatically in Lane's arms and licked her face. "I ought to get one," Lane said. "They could play together so happily."

"Yes, you could. When you've finished messing about come round and tell me about the phone man. Kenny saw him, but he's driven off to Balfour with the truck, so I haven't had a report. And I've got a letter from Scotland for you. And a parcel! From France."

Lane took the puppy outside and put him down on the grass. A parcel from France? It could only be from Yvonne. She heard the post office window slam down and walked around to the kitchen door. Alexandra raced between her legs up the step and bolted into the kitchen, stopping at her water bowl, where she lapped up some water and then bounded, dripping, back to Lane.

Inside, when Alexandra had finally settled, Lane said, "I shouldn't be so suspicious. Just because the phone man put me off and two other people felt the same way, I'm assuming he doesn't know his job. It's not scientific, is it, forming a view simply because a couple of other people agree with a prejudice one has developed oneself."

"Quite. But what matters in the end is, will the phones work?"

"Oh, dear. Speaking of phones. The inspector called, and that poor man has died."

Eleanor sat silently, looking down at Alexandra, who had gone to sleep. She shook her head sadly. "If I'm honest, I don't know how he survived this long. Do they know who he is yet?"

"No. But I can't shake the idea that the whole business is connected to Mrs. Castle, the egg woman."

"You think Mrs. Castle might have shot him?" Eleanor asked. "That would be a surprising turn of events."

"No, maybe not that, though she is a very unhappy and bitter woman. No, I think it's just that her son, Carl, disappeared the day before we found the man in the boat. I wonder if he might have been involved or knew the man. Maybe they got into a drunken fight that went too far, and Carl is trying to disappear."

"You know, I must say, he didn't smell as though he'd been drinking," Eleanor said. "But I see what you mean. One man gets shot, another disappears. It's hard not to want to connect them. Now then. I can see that you want to open that exciting looking parcel at home. Will you call me and tell me what's in it? It'll be a good way to test the phones as well."

CHAPTER FOURTEEN

AT HOME LANE PUT THE parcel and the letter on her table. It was like Christmas. A letter from her grandparents and a parcel. Brown paper and string. There ought to be some ceremony to it. A cup of tea and a biscuit. But she took up the letter first. The parcel was a complete surprise, so it must be left to last. Her grandmother wrote newsily and affectionately about her garden, and how the new black doctor was getting along in the village. "He is the sweetest man, so kind. And he doesn't seem to mind in the least how badly some are behaving. 'They will get over it,' he says. He's been an absolute tonic for your poor Gamph with his sore knees. People are disgraceful." Lane smiled as she got to the end of the letter, bathed in her gran's effusive protestations of love. Now the parcel. She folded the letter and put it back into the envelope and then, after only a second of thought about whether she ought to attempt to undo the knot and save the string, she took up her bread knife and cut it.

There was a note inside the box on top of something wrapped in tissue paper.

"Ma chérie, I had so hoped that I might come out to see you, perhaps in the fall, but I have met someone. No, stop! I can see your face now, full of smiles." Lane's face *was* full of smiles. Like, it seemed to her, most women, Yvonne had had her share of unfortunate love affairs, and she had become exceedingly cautious. If she said she had met someone, then it was big news. "It is too early to drink champagne, my dear. But I like him. He understands horses. He is not too bossy. One will see. But now, you wonder about the package. Don't ask how I got it! I was owed a favour. It is from one of the minor fashion houses and it is from the spring show. I saw it and I thought of you instantly! You will say you have no place to wear such a thing, but you wait; once you have this an occasion will materialize—poof! Like that! It will be something nice to hang next to your wool lumber jackets or whatever you have to wear out there."

Lane put the letter down and pulled the pink tissue paper open, her heart pounding. She knew already that whatever it was would be completely impractical, but at that moment she felt like a young girl again, about to see something beautiful. She gasped. A black satin blouse with a mandarin collar and exquisite cloth-covered buttons lay in the box. She pulled it out and saw that it was tightly fitted at the waist and had perfect cap sleeves. But it was what was under the blouse that took her breath away. A long silk skirt, black, with deep yellow and red oriental designs running up one side. She held it up and then pulled it to herself, feeling tears well up. How extravagant of Yvonne! And of course, she would never be able to wear it. She spread the skirt across the sofa and placed the blouse at the top of it. She had never seen anything like it in her life. The evening gowns from the war were so different. Beautiful, certainly, with their beading and gathered fabric. But this! Sleek, modern.

She ought to get a longer mirror than the one on her dressing table, she thought. She held up her hair and imagined herself at a ball wearing this, her arm linked through Darling's. "Rubbish," she said aloud and dropped her hair. She looked at her watch. She would be late for tea if she didn't step on it. As if it could hear her thoughts, the phone rang. It was Gwen, as promised.

"I can hear you, can you hear me?" Gwen was talking loudly, as if the phone might still be broken.

"Perfectly well. The proof will be if the phone doesn't cut out."

"Mother's ready to pour, so you'd better come up," Gwen said. Lane thanked her, and as she was about to hang up she heard Gwen mutter, "Well, it seems all right to me," as she disconnected at her end. Lane's shorts and white cotton blouse would be more than adequate for tea. Clean white socks and her plimsolls—as formal as it got in her wilderness life, besides the suit she wore to church.

Lane decided to walk up to the Hughes' by the road. The path from the post office was shorter, but she rather liked the grassy rutted road, and Gladys had recently bought a milk cow that she had placed in the fenced field along the edge of it. She spotted the cow munching grass and called out, "Hello, lovely." The cow looked up and watched Lane, and then to her delight sauntered over for a closer look. "Aren't you a treat? What do they call you?" The cow continued to grind on a mouthful of the long dried grass that was the result of what seemed like weeks of no rain.

"What a lovely creature your cow is!" Lane exclaimed to Mabel, who was setting a small tea table under a maple tree. "What do you call her? Hello, you two," she added to the two cocker spaniels that, after a perfunctory "woof," were now sniffing at her shoes.

"Rhoda. Not my idea. Gwen thought it was a dignified name for a cow. I would have gone with Bessie."

"It's a lovely name. What can I do?"

"Sit. Mother's on her way out with the bread and jam and Gwennie's got the tea."

The tea poured and the bread and jam on little blue plates, the three women looked expectantly at Lane.

"The new root cellar looks splendid," she said, "as if it's always been there." The old cellar had been collapsed and covered over with wildflowers, and a small cherry tree had been planted on the site to commemorate the child who had been buried there. The new root cellar had been placed on the other side of the garage, and though the roof was covered with new and growing grass, which the Hughes women were obviously watering, it blended in nicely because of the trees shading it from behind.

"Enough about the root cellar," Gladys said. "What's going on with that fellow you found on the beach?"

Lane put her cup down. "He died, unfortunately." She could see from their expressions that they already knew that.

"But have you made any progress figuring out who he is, how he got there, and who shot him?" Gwen asked.

Lane laughed. "That's a job for the police."

The ladies let that sit, though Gladys emitted the tiniest snort. "He could have lived along the lake. Do you know there are coves up and down the lake? Some of them are along side creeks, and prospectors have set up looking for gold in them. They build little cabins, and grow long beards, and eventually die, having wasted their lives. But some are still there. You can only get to them from the water, some of 'em," Gladys said.

"You think he could have come from one of those? He didn't look like a prospector. Or maybe he was new and hadn't had time to grow the beard. No, wait. Inspector Darling said that, from the state of his hands, it looked like he was working the logging camps."

"Or he could have got like that felling trees for his cabin," Gwen said.

"What if someone tried to steal the gold he'd found, and he tried to fight off the robber and he got shot?" Mabel suggested.

Lane smiled. There's a whole story, already made up to explain the end of the poor man's life. Still. Based on the little they knew, it was as good a story as any. "It's like something from one of those *Boy's Own* magazines: 'Tales of the Dark Wilderness,'" she said. "But, given what we have, it could well have been just like that. Oh, except that they think he was a logger, not a miner."

"You mark my words," Gladys said. "It will be a bad business involving someone with a beard. They lose all sense of civilization, those men, living alone like that in the bush!"

"Do have another slosh of tea," Mabel said happily. Her mother only snorted again, swigging the remainder of her cup down as if she were drinking whisky.

That night, Lane started a new category of notes—"Theories"—and wrote down Mabel's gold-robbery theory. She sat back with her Scotch and an unopened book, and suddenly remembered that Reg Mather had a rowboat. She knew about it because she'd had an appalling morning on a fishing trip with his son Sandy when she had first arrived. She still shuddered at the memory of what she'd naively let herself in for. Well, Sandy was in the penitentiary out on the coast and would be for some time. What she wondered now was, did Reg Mather also have an outboard motor for it? I mean, she thought, what would be the harm in a little trip up the lake? Her last thoughts, as she dropped off to sleep, were of herself in Yvonne's chinois evening gown. It was too bad no one would ever get to see it.

AMES SAT AT the edge of the lake. It was just after six in the morning. He had left home early because he wanted time to clear his head. He'd had a bad night, a circumstance so unusual for him that he had left before his mother was up to make him breakfast. He had woken early, at 3:30, and instead of falling right back to sleep as he usually did, he had been tormented by anxiety. He worried first about the trip to Vancouver and the sergeant's course, and ultimately the exam he had to take. He found himself muddled about whether he was anxious because he wanted to be a sergeant and failing the exam would kill his promotion, or because failing it would mean disappointing Darling. His thoughts about these unresolvable issues were strong enough to wipe away any more positive view of his being very likely to pass, then moved on to Violet, with whom he had had a rather stormy evening.

Now, bleary eyed but relieved that morning had come, he sat looking across at Elephant Mountain, where the golden light of the early sun was stealing along the upper reaches. Ames took a deep breath and relished the cool morning air, fragrant with the smell of trees and water. In a couple of hours the heat would settle in. He hoped that whatever lay in store for the day would take place away from the office. He picked up a pebble and tossed it into the lake. It made a "sploosh" sound and the little waves moved outward in an ever-growing circle. He should not have ignored how he had been feeling on the subject of Violet.

"How long are you planning to keep this up?" she had said. They had been walking along Baker Street, just before climbing Cedar Street toward her house, but now she stopped.

Ames remembered looking around nervously, but no one else was in the street. It was after nine, and the sun had long since vanished, leaving a warm grey evening.

"Cat got your tongue?" she'd continued. "I'll spell it out for you. We've been going out for the better part of a year, and it doesn't seem like you're going to pop the question, does it?"

"I'm . . . I'm not sure I'm ready," he'd managed to stammer.

"You're twenty-five years old. I'm not about to become an old maid because you 'aren't ready.' You better tell me now, is there someone else?"

"No, of course not! The sergeant's exam . . ." He hadn't been able to state the truth: that he did not think they were suited, that their beliefs about what mattered were too different, that he hadn't liked, at a deep and surprising level, what she'd said about the boy caught stealing. Somehow he'd known that saying he didn't believe in beating children would not have sounded convincing to her.

He listened now to the quiet lapping of the tiny waves against the shore. Traffic above him in town was beginning to pick up. He remembered the absolute steel in Violet's voice when she had said, "You're lying," and had turned up Cedar and walked away from him. It came to him clearly, suddenly. It mattered what she thought about the boy, and no doubt there were many other things that would begin to emerge about which her views diverged from his, but more importantly, it was her. She had been angry and hard like that with him a few times, but he had put it down to her fiery temper, something he had admired, if the truth be known, at the beginning. Now he felt he recognized it for what it was: a lack of kindness. He tried to imagine himself talking to her in that way, and he couldn't.

He looked at his watch. The café would be open, and he could use some coffee to wipe the bleariness from his brain, if not his eyes. His jacket slung over his shoulder, he made his way back up the hill, wondering what his world was going to be like now.

"THOUGHT I'D FIND you in here malingering," Darling said, throwing himself down next to Ames. "We're going to have to go up the north arm and visit the logging outfits along there. Joseph P., according to Gilly, has recent splinters. God, you look awful!"

"Thank you, sir."

"Drinking last night?"

Ames looked at him. "Have you met Violet, sir? One beer and that's it. She doesn't hold with drinking."

"I get the feeling she doesn't hold with much," Darling said, raising his hand to get the attention of April behind the counter. "Still, she's sharp."

"As a whip," said Ames glumly.

"You ought to have stuck with this one," Darling said in an unnecessary stage whisper indicating April, who was pouring their coffee at the end of the counter.

Ames ignored his boss's comments on his woeful personal life and said, "We could save a whole lot of time going straight to the watering holes in Kaslo. Where do loggers and miners all go at the end of the day, the lucky bastards? To the bars. If he was working any of those camps, someone will know him."

"The usual, please, thanks, April," Darling said.

"And should I stiff Ames with the bill, as usual?" she said, winking.

"No, not today. I'm in a generous mood, and he's just said something clever." Darling waited till April had gone back to talk to the man at the grill. "See, that's the sort of thing the exam won't pick up, smart insights like that." He lifted his coffee mug in a salute and then glanced at his watch. "I don't guess the staff will be in the bars till about eleven, so let's head out at ten. Oh. Blast. The inquest. We'll have to stay for that. It's at eleven." Still, as inconvenient as it was, it would mean seeing Lane, who would have to testify. He would try not to let Ames see how smug he was feeling.

Ames, cheered by the unusual praise and the fact that between the inquest and the trip up the lake they would be out of the office most of the day, attacked his breakfast with renewed vigour. Knowing Darling was picking up the tab made it taste even better.

CHAPTER FIFTEEN

THE INQUEST WAS HELD IN the legion hall. Lane, who would have to testify along with Kenny and Eleanor Armstrong, was seated in the front row with them. The coroner took his place and adjusted his glasses to better see his notebook in a space that, with its narrow windows set high in the tall brick walls, was gloomy on even the brightest day. Lane turned to see who was coming in to sit in the gallery rows behind them. She was surprised that only a few seats were empty. She hadn't read the papers when the young man had finally died, but the story must have been somewhat sensational to garner this number of people on a Thursday morning. She caught sight of the reporter she'd seen at a previous inquest, and of a number of ladies dressed in suits and hats as if they were going to church. Perhaps it was similar, she thought. Attendance on the dead had a religious feel to it. The ladies sat with their handbags on their laps, whispering or staring silently at the coroner and the witnesses, fearful and hopeful that they would hear something gruesome. A couple of men leaned on the wall by the door smoking. One of them, to Lane's disgust, dropped his cigarette butt on the floor and ground it out with his shoe. He looked familiar. It was a small town. When she came in for supplies, she was beginning to see more and more people she recognized.

There was a stir as Inspector Darling and Constable Ames came in and made their way down to the front. Darling sat down next to Lane. She smiled and said quietly, "You all right?"

"Yes, though I can't answer for Ames. You?"

"Thank you, yes."

Darling leaned across Lane and thanked the Armstrongs for coming into town. The coroner's voice suddenly cut through the hum of the crowd. "What are we still waiting for?" He was looking at his watch and addressing the clerk who would be calling up witnesses and taking notes.

"The, ah, the doctor, sir. A Dr. Robles, I think it is." He pronounced it so that it rhymed with "nobbles."

The coroner looked up across the crowd. "Well, where is he then?"

People in the room looked back toward the door, as if doing so would conjure the doctor into the room. The clerk said something quietly to the coroner and looked fretful in a way that suggested he fully expected to be blamed for the doctor's lateness.

"What's wrong with Ames?" Lane whispered to Darling.

"The usual," Darling replied. "I'm sure he'll give you chapter and verse if you express the slightest sympathy toward him. Ah. Finally."

"Sorry, sir, we had an emergency at the hospital. I came away as soon as I could," Dr. Robles said, as he came toward the front. He took his seat on the other side of Ames.

"Thank you, Dr. Robles. I'm sure we all understand." "Nobbles" again.

"It's Robles, sir."

The coroner frowned. "What's that?"

"My name, sir, it's Robles."

Looking as if this information could not be more inconsequential, the coroner said, "Yes, yes. Very well. Can we get started?" He banged his gavel on the table, unnecessarily, Lane thought, since the crowd was already fully attentive. "Now then. This inquest is to examine the facts about the death of a young man who has been identified as a Joseph P. Smith, who was found, severely wounded, on the nineteenth of July of this year in a rowboat that washed up at King's Cove. Primarily, we ought to determine whether this man's death was the result of misadventure, suicide, or could be placed in the category of a wrongful death. I will now call upon Miss Lane Winslow."

Lane, who had not counted on being called first, felt a stab of anxiety but then reminded herself that what mattered here was the dead man, not her stage fright. Speaking clearly so that all could hear, Lane detailed the events of the morning when the man was found.

"And did you yourself reach any conclusions about how the man might have come to be in this state?"

"I can only say what I observed. That the wound looked very grave and he had lost a good deal of blood."

"And did you not feel some concern that moving the

body might result in his condition worsening?"

Lane looked down and then at the Armstrongs. It was, to her, the one vulnerable point. "I did, we all did, but he was soaked through. Half of his body was submerged, and he was very, very cold to the touch. We thought it best to get him as dry and warm as possible."

Thus acquitting herself, Lane made way for Kenny Armstrong, who merely confirmed her telling of the events, and he in turn made way for Eleanor.

"Mrs. Eleanor Armstrong, your honour," Eleanor said in response to the coroner's request to speak her name slowly for the recorder.

"And you made an attempt to treat this man in some way?" the coroner asked, when Eleanor described how she'd been brought to the scene. "Do you have some experience or qualifications that would allow for such an interference?"

"I was a front-line nursing sister in the Great War. Although it was nearly thirty years ago, during the war I treated many injuries like his. I cut away his clothing and put a dressing on the wound so that the chance of infection would not increase—I felt he was at risk because the sun was getting hotter and he probably had fragments of clothing in that wound. I thought it might be enough to keep him alive until the ambulance arrived."

"And having had a closer look at it, did you have any ideas about that injury and it's possible causes?"

"I did. It looked like a gunshot wound."

"Could it have been self-inflicted?"

"I suppose so, yes, because it seemed to me he was shot at very close range, though I wondered at his being in a boat, a leaky one at that, floating up the lake. If I were going to do away with myself, I'm not sure I would go to such elaborate lengths. It seems to me it must have been the result of an accident. No one would deliberately shoot themselves in the stomach."

"That's as may be, Mrs. Armstrong. No doubt your suppositions will be confirmed by Dr. Ro . . . by the doctor. You may step down."

"If I may," said Eleanor, putting up her gloved hand.

"Yes? You have something to add?" The coroner spoke as if he was used to being obeyed. When he said, "Step down," he expected the witness to step smartly down.

"It's just that I did hear him say something. He seemed aware I was trying to help him. He said, 'Just let me die.'"

This caused a stir among the audience. Several of the ladies gasped, and wooden chairs creaked as people leaned forward.

The coroner dropped his glasses down his nose and looked over them at Eleanor. "You're quite sure that's what he said? 'Just let me die'?"

"Quite sure, yes."

The coroner dismissed her again, and Eleanor sat down and was rewarded by Kenny's warm pat on her hand.

"How did Mr. Smith die in the end, Doctor?" the coroner asked, addressing Dr. Robles where he sat in the front row.

"It was infection. We tried to treat it, but he had already lost a great deal of blood and had little in the way of resources to fight for life."

"I see. And did you form an opinion as to how this person came to be injured?"

"Like Mrs. Armstrong, I thought it appeared to be an injury inflicted with a gun at very close range. There was no trace of the bullet, but it inflicted significant damage to the intestines. It is surprising that the loss of blood did not bring on death more quickly."

Inspector Darling was called up. He explained that Miss Winslow had called him as there were circumstances that suggested a violent attack.

"And what did you learn in your investigation?"

"I should say at the outset that we are doubtful that the man's name was Joseph P. Smith. We at first thought he might be a man who was reported missing earlier the same day we were called to this case, a Carl Castle. However, the mother of Mr. Castle indicated the injured man was not her son."

"Then why do I have the name Smith?"

"It is the one the hospital gave us. During his time at the hospital, the victim was visited by someone who claimed to be the patient's cousin and provided the name Joseph P. Smith. Consequent upon learning of the purported cousin's visit, I set a guard at the patient's door. In addition I asked my constable to search for any record of that name."

"Why did you set the guard?"

"The nurse said that the visitor stayed only a short time and seemed to be searching for something in the bedside drawer in which a patient's possessions are normally kept. We were concerned that if the man had been attacked, someone might have come along to finish the job. No further attempt was made on his life, however. We recovered two things from the boat. A third item was recovered later from the beach itself that may or may not be associated with the incident. Of significance, we recovered the second page of a letter sent to the man by the International Red Cross."

"And were you able to read the contents?"

"We were, what there was of it. The letter was typewritten, so the page we have survived its immersion. I have a photograph here." Darling handed a manila envelope to the clerk. "The gist of that last page is that the Red Cross investigation revealed that Julia Fischer and her family were recorded as having been shipped to the east, and offered its regrets. I assumed from that that the man had asked the Red Cross to initiate a search for this Julia Fischer, and would have learned that she and her family probably died in a death camp of some sort. The signature was unreadable, unfortunately." This elicited a murmuring from the onlookers. The coroner looked at the photograph the clerk had handed him and appeared to read through the letter to verify Inspector Darling's testimony.

"You said you found something else?"

"Yes. A Smith and Wesson revolver."

"And would the bullet have come from that weapon?"

"I'm afraid that without the bullet, we cannot determine absolutely that it came from the gun found in the boat. That is part of our investigation."

"But it would be fair to draw a conclusion of sorts based on the presence of the gun and a gunshot wound?"

"Not one hundred percent, no. But it is certainly a high probability."

This seemed to satisfy the coroner, who wrote some more notes. "Now then, you mentioned something else that was found?"

Darling nodded. "This was a metal pin such as might be worn at a political rally or during an election cycle. The design was of a swastika in red with a blue surround. You will find it in the envelope." This time a gasp and an upsurge of whispering came from the crowd.

"I hasten to add that we have no way of knowing if this pin is connected in any way. It could have washed up on the beach, or been dropped there by a visitor or someone working the steamboat that docks three times a week at the King's Cove dock."

The coroner was holding up the pin and scowling at it. "What is this supposed to be?"

"I believe it is the insignia of a political party called the National Unity Party. It is an organization that was outlawed, for obvious reasons, during the war when it openly called itself a Nazi party and has enjoyed some resurgence since the end of the war in Quebec, Alberta, and even here in British Columbia."

"If there is no more testimony, I will adjourn for one hour," announced the coroner. "I will try to make head or tail of this very unsatisfactory set of findings." With that he slammed his gavel once again, causing Lane to jump.

In the scraping of chairs and the sudden rise of chatter Lane said, "He certainly likes to wield that gavel. Who's for a bite? Can we go to that café by the station? I had a nice piece of pie there once. Have you two been there?" she asked Eleanor and Kenny. "It's just around the corner."

"Why not? It's a great place to watch Ames's life unravel." Darling held the door open for the Armstrongs and Lane.

Lane looked with displeasure at the cigarette, still lying

where the man had ground it out, and then said, "What sort of verdict do you think he's going to bring in? And a follow-up question, why is the coroner always so bad tempered? I seem to recall he was very short with everyone at the last inquest I attended."

"I expect it's that he sees nothing but the seamier side of life. I'd probably be like that too," Kenny said.

"You never would," said Eleanor fondly.

Ames's life withstood any unravelling, and in due course everyone was back in the legion, waiting to hear what the coroner would say.

"It is very tempting in this case to return a verdict of suicide," the coroner began. "The presence of a letter, though incomplete, suggests that Mr. Smith, if that is who he is, received grievous news about a close family member perhaps. Would it have been enough to attempt suicide? I would say yes. And there is the statement by the victim, 'Just let me die.' This too is suggestive of a failed attempt at suicide. However, there is also the circumstance of the victim being adrift in a rowboat. It is possible that the victim wished to take himself away from any populated area, but it seems an unusual course of action. As well there is the question of the obviously bungled shot. One imagines that at night, in a state of despair or even inebriation, near water, the gun could have slipped and misfired. It is more difficult to imagine a scenario where someone else wishes, for whatever reason, to do away with Mr. Smith, misses badly, and then places him in a rowboat and throws the gun in after him. And yet, we have the evidence of someone visiting him in hospital and searching among his effects for something. It is peculiar behaviour for someone who might have cared for Mr. Smith, and it appears that nothing whatever was taken. All these facts are highly equivocal and make a clear verdict difficult to make. I am inclined, by the circumstances, particularly the existence of the letter, to bring forward a verdict of suicide. Because of the inconsistencies, the doubt about the man's identity, I declare this a death by misadventure, either by himself or person or persons unknown."

"I could have told him that," muttered Ames, stretching his long frame. Chairs scraped and people, already talking about other subjects, filed outside.

"Well," said Lane, as they stood about on the sidewalk, "that is inconclusively that. We're off to that nifty supermarket and then away back to King's Cove, so we'll leave you to it."

"I very much doubt your ability to leave anything to us," Darling remarked.

CHAPTER SIXTEEN

LANE WOKE UP WONDERING IF she should try to borrow Mather's boat or visit Mrs. Castle again. The boat would require learning how to use the motor, getting the boat to the lake—and then a whole day of wandering along the shore stopping in at likely coves. In the light of day, the Hughes' theory seemed somewhat fanciful, and she did owe Mrs. Castle a visit to deal with transporting her eggs to the Balfour store. Lane barely disguised from herself that she was in full detective mode. She couldn't bring herself to use the word, so she settled on "curiosity." Her reasons for going were, after all, unassailable. She had become useful to Mrs. Castle's business, and, despite the woman's biting personality, or maybe even because of it, Lane felt sorry for her.

Lane had left the French doors open overnight and now stood leaning on the doorframe, listening to the high, lilting song of some robins, calling out to one another somewhere in the trees below her. Her heart lifted as if, she felt, the song had bypassed even her ears and gone straight to her heart. She was somewhere in her childhood again, on a sunny morning like this one. Then she imagined standing here with Darling, in the quiet of the morning, his arm around her shoulder. Shaking her head, she turned to remove the bubbling coffee pot from the stove. She waited for the gurgling to subside and then filled her mug. It was no good, she thought. They lived in different worlds. She poured cream decisively into the mug, watching it whirl. She ought to stop imagining Darling here, in King's Cove, with her. Waking up with her, going to sleep with her, sitting in the evening over Scotches with her. She hadn't known what love was going to mean when it had happened, but it didn't seem to involve domesticity. It hadn't with Angus during the war, and it didn't now.

VANESSA CASTLE FROWNED when Lane got out of the car. She had been kneeling in the garden and stood, a trowel in her hand, as the car pulled up.

"You don't need to keep doing this," she said. "I'll figure something out."

"Goodness, it's no trouble at all," Lane said. Then she noticed the dark circles under Mrs. Castle's eyes. "Are you all right? You look all in."

The woman put the trowel down on a rock at the edge of the border and sat down on the front stair, in the shade of the overhang. "I just didn't sleep well. I'm fine."

Lane came and sat next to her. "Still nothing from Carl?"

"No. I . . . no. Nothing."

Lane noted that Mrs. Castle said nothing about the police not finding him. She may know he is not dead, but it was clearly the case that he had not contacted her. Not for the first time she wondered about Lorimer's big black car, if it had been Lorimer's. Could he have anything to do with the disappearance? That was absurd on the face of it. Lorimer was a politician who flew in much higher circles than the chicken-farming Castles. Of course Vanessa's father had been a politician, if the rumours were true. She hadn't always been poor.

"Do you have family? Has he contacted any of them?"

"Nope," she said, getting up. Lane didn't know if she meant she had no family or family hadn't contacted her.

"I have a sister whom I never talk to," Lane said, smiling. "It can feel a bit like not having family."

"My . . ." But whatever she was going to say was lost by her turning toward the kitchen door and pulling it open. "We'd better get on with these eggs. I've trespassed enough on your time." She pushed into the kitchen and began to pack the cardboard egg flats into a wooden box.

"What would you like from the shop?"

"I don't need anything. I still have stuff from before. He can pay me later."

"Why don't I pay you now? I've got some money with me, and I'll collect it from Mr. Bales?"

"Sure, that'll save you from having to come back down." Vanessa Castle sounded relieved.

Lane paid for the eggs and followed Vanessa out, holding the door for her. On the way to the car Lane noticed something she hadn't before . . . the grass in front of her own car was squashed down. There'd been someone parked there.

Don't jump to conclusions, Lane told herself. After all,

Mrs. Castle had said that people were driving down to get eggs. She closed the latch on the trunk and, as she was opening the driver's door, she looked up at where Vanessa Castle stood, her arms folded, watching her, waiting for her to drive away.

"Oh my God, I almost forgot. Apparently the young fellow we found up the lake has died. Poor thing. They still don't know who he was."

Vanessa Castle's hand flew to her mouth, and she looked as if she was going to turn away. But she recovered and made as if to speak. There was a beat and then in a hoarse whisper she said, "When?"

"I'm not sure when, exactly. I heard about it yesterday. Infection. They said it was amazing he survived as long as he did." Lane wondered if she was saying too much. Would Mrs. Castle wonder how she knew so much detail? She thought of manufacturing "a friend who knew someone at the hospital," but decided against digging herself in any deeper. "Well, I'd best be off. Oh. Why don't I give you my phone number? That way if you have something you need or eggs ready, you can call me."

Mrs. Castle had not moved from where she stood, so Lane opened her bag, found an envelope, tore a strip off it, and wrote the number. She went around the car and held the slip of paper out to the distraught woman. "KC 431," she said. Vanessa Castle took the piece of paper and looked at it, misery etched on her face. Lane put a sympathetic hand on her arm. "You're worried about Carl, because of what happened with that young man," she said, more of a statement than a question.

"Just leave me alone," Mrs. Castle said, going to where she'd left the trowel.

"Call me if you need anything," Lane said to the woman's back. She got into her car and began to back up the drive to the little flat patch where she could turn the car around. "Well, well," she said. There was a lot to digest.

WHEN SHE GOT home, Lane sat at her table with her pencil and a piece of paper. She wanted to get a handle on what she thought was anomalous about her visit. It wasn't just that the woman seemed distraught—her son was missing, after all. She wrote down the things that struck her as odd:

She seemed to want me to leave, was relieved when I said I'd pay her and collect the money from Bales.

What had she been about to say? "My . . ." what? Son? Family? Father?

Seemed very upset about boat man dying. Why? Because she feared it could be Carl's fate? Seemed more immediate. Does she have some reason to suspect Carl is involved in some way?

Grass was flattened ahead of where I parked. Could be egg buyers . . .

Lane put her pencil down. That last point was silly. What did she imagine? That Carl had driven there and was lurking somewhere waiting for her to go, the car under a canvas in the garage? No. There wasn't a garage there. But it did raise again the question of why the sleek black car had been leaving the farm. Lorimer lived in, or near, town, she guessed, and no doubt had people who went to Liberty, that sleek supermarket in town. She sat and stared at the paper. Too many unconnected ideas. And she shouldn't be sweeping Lorimer into the mystery because she disliked him. Unless there was a political connection of some sort. Vanessa had some fairly fascist views. Did she and Carl belong to some secret organization? Did Lorimer? Now there was something. Lorimer was running for office. If he belonged to a shady organization he might not want the voters to know about it. Well, she could start by writing all this down and looking at it again later to see how it held up.

The phones seemed to be working again. That phone man, as inadequate as he appeared, must have fixed them. Lane learned this when, with some trepidation about being cut off again, she phoned Angela to ask if she'd like to go on an expedition with her in a rowboat.

"That would leave poor David with the children," Angela said in a voice that conveyed both worry and satisfaction.

"Oh, of course, how foolish of me. I hadn't thought of that," Lane said. She was certain she could tootle along the edge of the lake in a boat with an outboard motor and not get lost, but had thought Angela might like the adventure of it.

"The children mostly run themselves up here, but they do suddenly appear from time to time demanding food. David is capable of assembling some peanut butter or bologna sandwiches. I'll make lemonade and leave it in the fridge. All right. I'm your man! Why are we doing this exactly?"

Why indeed? thought Lane. A wilder or goosier chase she could not imagine. "I got the idea from Gladys. She said the lake is full of little coves where would-be prospectors might set up shop. Some of the creeks apparently spit up a bit of gold every now and then."

"You're making me shudder. Why would we want to go and visit probably unwashed and possibly wild-eyed prospectors?"

"You don't know they're unwashed. They could be like our own resident prospector, Glenn Ponting, trained geologists living in comfortable and sanitary cabins. But I see your point. The reason is that I wonder if the poor man we found, whom the police have nicknamed Joseph P. because someone visited him in hospital and claimed he was called Joseph P. Smith, and was seen rummaging through his bedside drawer looking for something, maybe lived in one of the coves himself."

"Wow! I didn't know anyone had been to visit him. Who was it?"

"I don't think the police know. He came once and never came back. It did alarm them and they put a guard on the patient's room in case someone came back to finish him off, but there was never another visit, and then the poor guy died. Anyway, this whole expedition depends on Mather lending me his boat and motor."

"Oof. Good luck with that. Let me know. When are you proposing for this outing?"

"Tomorrow morning, early. I'll make some sandwiches. I don't know how long it will take to get up as far as Kaslo. Right, I'm off to tackle Reg. He still doesn't like me much, I'm afraid."

"He never met a beautiful woman he didn't think would swoon for him. Just turn on that Winslow charm."

LANE SIGHED AS she stood at the turn of the road where Reginald and Alice Mather lived. Since their son had been sent to prison the year before for his part in the death of a man found in the creek that fed Lane's house, Reginald, who had been outgoing and had seen himself as the de facto leader of King's Cove, had become more and more withdrawn and crotchety. Alice, his wife, on the other hand, a woman who had violent swings of mood, had become more visible and sociable of late. Lane wasn't sure she could remember how to "turn on the charm." It was a skill required of her from time to time during the war. She'd had to pretend to be someone else, either German or French, to be light, easy, attractive, to allay any suspicion that she might be anything but an attractive German or French girl. Looking back, that sort of charm seemed to her to be disingenuous and artificial. She was not even sure she could be convincing anymore without seeming insincere. Well, she would try to be ordinarily kind and courteous and see where that got her.

She opened the gate and walked up to the front porch, a long stone-flagged affair across the front of the house, with two chairs that she had never seen anyone sit in, and knocked on the door. She heard a shuffle inside, and a tentative bark. Then Reg was in front of her.

"Yes?" The charm of her smile was evidently not going to work right away.

"Good afternoon, Reg. It's awful cheek of me, I know, but am I right in thinking you have a rowboat?"

"What of it?"

He was not going to make this easy. "It's just that I'd like to go out on the lake for a bit of an explore, and

I rather hoped, if you had a boat, and maybe even an outboard motor, you would lend them to me." She leaned over to pat the dog, which was sniffing at her knees in a friendly manner.

Reginald Mather seemed irritated that his dog was not toeing the party line. "Get off with you!" he said to the dog. "Have you got any way to get it down there? You don't expect me to be hauling it down for you."

Relieved that he appeared inclined to let her have the boat, Lane said, "Good grief, no! It's so kind of you to let me use it at all. I can tie it to the top of the car." She'd never tied a boat to the top of a car, but she figured that between her and Angela they could manage it. In the event, Reginald was willing to help her with that part of it. He opened his gate and had her back up near where his car was parked, and together they lifted the boat out of the garage and up-ended it on top of Lane's car. While he went back into the garage to find rope, Alice came out of the house and leaned on the porch pillar eating a piece of toast. Lane smiled at her and, getting nothing back, opened up both her doors so that the rope could be tied through the car.

Reg came out of the garage with a length of rope and threw it over the boat.

"Careful driving down to the water. I wouldn't trust him to tie his own shoes," Alice remarked.

The boat affixed to the car, Reg went back into the garage and came out with a small outboard motor. It looked fairly beaten up and smelled of oil. "Know how to use one of these things?" he asked.

"Is it complicated?"

"Easy. There's a cord here and you pull it to start the engine. Make sure the propeller end is in the water before you do it. You'll need gas. Put this in the trunk." He handed Lane the motor, which was heavier than she expected, and went back into the garage. Lane put the motor in the trunk, wishing she'd brought a tarpaulin to protect the trunk from leaking gas and oil. Reg returned with a galvanized metal gas can.

Having stowed it next to the motor, Lane wiped her hands on her handkerchief and stood next to the driver's side door. "Thank you, Reg. It's terribly kind of you. I couldn't think who else to ask."

Perhaps it was a sense of having helped a woman in distress, but Reginald Mather suddenly displayed a largesse that had been entirely absent throughout the interaction. "Don't use it much anymore, do I? Glad to see someone get some use out of it."

For reasons of her own, Alice, who was still on the porch, uttered a loud "Ha!" and went back into the house.

Back in her own house, Lane called Angela to say she'd got the boat and arrange for an early morning pickup, and then set about making sandwiches.

CHAPTER SEVENTEEN

May 1939

KLAUS LAZEK PARKED THE TRUCK in front of the Canadian Western Railway building in Dawson Creek, where the administration for the Sudeten refugees was housed. At home he had no difficulty confronting officials. Here he felt he was like a country bumpkin coming hat in hand to some faceless bureaucrat. At home he had a suit, good shoes, and a good education to back him up. Here he was clad in coveralls and wore heavy rubber boots stuffed with cloth to keep his feet warm and out of which he was sure he would never be able to get the mud. He pulled himself straight. The situation was dire. His new friends told him that the winter had been hard, and the spring came late here, and they had not enough equipment for the farming they were expected to do, and were well short of the money they had been promised for basic supplies. Thus, determined by survival if nothing else, he took off his hat, moved his blond hair off his face with a sweep of his hand, and asked to see the person in charge of the German settlement.

"Yes?"

"My name is Klaus Lazek. I am from the settlement of German refugees."

"I can see that. What do you want?" The man behind the desk delivered these words in a perfunctory manner. He was young and smooth. He appeared to be attempting not to smell the man standing in front of him. His hands rested on the desk, his right hand still holding papers as if he had been interrupted in important work. He did not ask Klaus to sit.

"We are doing the best we can to build shelter, but money has been promised and we don't see it. We should buy more materials for building and farming, and we must buy food. With the money we have we cannot do both. Also, we are trying to prepare more ground for planting, but it is very poor."

The man behind the desk rubbed his chin and gave a regretful sigh. "Well, for the moment I'm afraid you'll have to make do. I'm not sure what you mean by 'money that has been promised.' There is no other money. You are settled here solely on the basis of becoming engaged in farming. If you have misrepresented yourselves, well . . . that can have grave consequences."

"We are not farmers. We never said we were. We are grocers and factory workers and electricians. We are grateful to be here, of course, and we will do our best, but we cannot operate without proper equipment and the money that we were promised when we set sail from England. How are we to get the equipment we need?"

"Look, Mr. La . . . whatever it is. There isn't any money. I don't know about equipment. As far as this office is concerned you've been given everything you need. Considering the state of the world at the moment I'm surprised you feel you can come here and complain. Good morning." The man rose and indicated the door.

Lazek looked at him, at his well-tended hand with the heavy gold ring on it.

"You have taken our money!" he said, a sense of outrage building in him. "*You* come out and try to live on that so-called farm land, see how you do!"

"I suggest you remove yourself from my office immediately, or I shall have you removed. You cannot be the recipients of the Dominion of Canada's generosity and then come in here making demands and accusations. It will certainly do your cause no good. I know of no other money, and if I did, at this point I would be inclined to use it for other purposes and not on an ungrateful group of German DPS. We are likely to be at war with Germany soon, and frankly I would mind how you go."

Lazek turned and stormed out the door. "Generosity! Ha!" he said in German.

He stood on the street in front of the truck, trying to calm down. German DPS. It was an insult, he knew. But they were displaced persons. That was the truth of it, and as such apparently they were entitled to no respect here in their new country. The conversation had taken him to a very familiar place. Trying to reason with and get something from the faceless bureaucracy: the factory owner, the government official. They are all the same the world over, he thought.

He looked back at the window of the administrator's office. He could see the man watching him.

I will never forget that face, he thought. Because that one is dishonest as well as being heartless. Lazek decided he would pick up the minimum supplies they needed and could afford, and then he would try to find out who was above this man.

It was not long after that that he, and all the members of the settlement, were told to report to the RCMP.

DARLING HAD FIRMLY resisted looking up toward King's Cove as they passed the turnoff. He did not want any of Ames's backchat. He needn't have worried. Ames was mired in glum anxieties about how to handle the Violet situation. They drove in silence for some minutes. Darling had the window open and was resting his elbow on it and looking out at the passing scenery, enjoying the warmth of the air blowing in. The road between King's Cove and Kaslo was barely twenty years old, he knew, and though it was well used, it still had a raw feel, as though only recently carved out of the cliffs along the lake. Trees had been felled along the route, and their replacements were only starting to grow above the brush that now covered the once naked edges.

"I wonder how long the paddle wheel steamers will continue going up and down the lake?" he mused. "With roads going everywhere, wouldn't it be easier to load your apples or what have you onto a truck and drive them to the station?"

"I couldn't say, sir. I don't have any boxes of apples to move."

"You've got some kind of burden, though. You're not providing much entertainment," Darling observed.

Ames ignored this oblique invitation to share his feelings and slowed the car to negotiate the descending hairpin bend over the wooden bridge at the bottom of the hill, slowing even more as a motorcycle coming the other way passed them at a sharp angle. Ames shook his head, and then geared down to take the rise that would take them along the most terrifying and narrow stretch of road that skirted the very edge of a stark drop to the lake, far below. Darling pulled his elbow back, feeling slightly winded at the sight of the sheer drop immediately next to him, and thought about how near Lane had come to dying at this very spot during the winter.

Ames, hoping they would meet no more cars until the road widened again, said, "It's bad enough in a car. I wouldn't ride the damn thing on a motorcycle."

As the road widened again and was back on what Darling thought of as dry land, his tension eased. "So what is eating you?"

Ames held the steering wheel in both hands, as though trying to steer his own life with more care. Darling had issued a genuine invitation, somewhat at odds with his usual cavalier communications with Ames. Should he take him up on it? It suddenly occurred to Ames that without a father, he had no one to guide his thinking, though who knew if he would have confided in his own father. Maybe people didn't.

"It's Violet, sir. I think I've put my eggs in the wrong basket, as it were. I thought she was pretty and spirited, but more and more I'm finding she's pretty and a little . . . I don't know . . . mean. Mean-spirited covers it. She was pretty angry with me because I haven't asked her to marry me, and I told her I wasn't ready. She was unimpressed. But I suddenly felt that we would be at odds on so many things, especially on how to raise the kids."

Darling sat back and pondered this communication. He wondered if he and Lane would begin to hit bumps of disagreement on the subject of, say, children. They certainly had never talked about children. The first bump might materialize on the subject of even having them. At the moment he couldn't imagine himself with a child. But he could imagine Ames with children.

"I think you're very right, Amesy, to put the brakes on. You were already feeling unsure before, and now you seem more certain. Your dilemma, if I am not talking out of turn, is that you admire Miss Winslow, who is a bit glamorous in her independence, but you would like to marry and settle down and have a family. That may take a more domestic model."

Ames was silent. Finally he said, "You're right there, sir. My big problem right now is that I hope she's broken it off with me, but I'm terrified she's going to call and apologize and want to make up. She can be volatile like that."

"Sooner you than me, Amesy, sooner you than me. In the meantime we have a toothsome little murder to help keep your mind off it."

June 1939

"THIS IS OUTRAGEOUS," Hans said to Klaus. The small room at the RCMP office was crowded and noisy, the settlers all talking with each other, frightened, trying to understand what was happening. "You have to tell them, we are here because we were enemies of the Nazis. How can we now suddenly become enemies of Canada with a piece of paper?"

"I've tried. The man won't listen. We will have to get outside help."

"Quiet! Quiet, please." The loud voice of the RCMP officer startled the settlers, and they stopped talking and looked at him. "Mr. Lazek, you tell them that when they have been issued with papers declaring them enemy aliens, they will not be able to travel about, or take any work. Is that clear?"

"But sir, the ground we have been given produces barely enough. We have many people who work on other farms, or for the railway companies building the routes. If you take this away our families will lose the ability to survive."

"I don't make the rules. I enforce them. When I get an order from above to clear you, then that's what will happen. Till then, you do as you're told."

CHAPTER EIGHTEEN

"DIVINE!" EXCLAIMED ANGELA. SHE WAS leaning back, her face held toward the sun, her dark hair billowing gently, the ends of her fingers trailing in the cool blue-green water. "I don't know why we haven't got a motor for our little boat yet. If I'd known it was this lovely, I would have done it the first summer we were here."

Behind her Lane held tiller and steered the boat along the edge of the lake. She had fumbled initially, getting the motor attached, gassed up, and started. They had bobbed about ten feet from the shore while she made several failed attempts to start the motor, but finally there had been a gratifying roar as the engine sprang to life. Now, tooling along in the sun, she was considering the purchase of a small boat herself. She could go fishing with Darling . . . perhaps he didn't fish . . . picnics in a cove?

"I've driven up and down that beastly road to Adderly, and now I'm wondering why we don't putt along in a boat to get there," Angela called back.

"Because by the time you've wrestled the boat onto your car, messed about with the motor, and wrapped the boys up against the icy cold in the winter, you'll have wished you'd got into your nicely heated car to get there."

"They have boat trailers, you know. I could get one of those. But I see your point."

They travelled in companionable silence for some time, and then Lane pointed to a creek pouring noisily into the lake. "Look, that hairpin turn at the bottom of the road over that wooden bridge. We'll be at the bottom of that horrible great cliff in a moment."

The land gradually rose beside them, the sun seeming to cascade like a waterfall along the stony surface of the cliff. Rocks lay tumbled along the edge, and one or two brave trees clung tenaciously to ledges high above the lake. Lane pressed her lips grimly together. This was the place she might have died. She knew that the car had been pulled free, but she could still hear the sound of it going over, of the explosion. A man had died horribly right here, just this last winter.

"Look," Angela said, "isn't this where—"

But Lane interrupted her. "Yes. We should see Adderly along here soon." She looked firmly forward, turning the throttle on the motor to speed up.

Adderly showed itself with a docking wharf and the hotel standing partway down the treed and pleasant but dilapidated street that descended toward the water's edge.

"I thought you said there were coves all along the lake? What exactly are we looking for?" Angela asked, as they moved on past Adderly.

"I didn't say it. Gladys did. We've passed a couple of creeks, but most of them have been very small. I don't know what I'm looking for, really. At this point just a nice place to have lunch, I think."

Angela glanced at her watch in response to this and retied her hair, much of which had come loose and was blowing in her face.

"Ah!" cried Lane. "That's the sort of thing!" She slowed the boat. They were about twenty minutes past the hot springs and were approaching a wide fan of sand and pebble beach, and as she throttled down, they could hear the burble of a sizeable creek flowing along its stony banks and spreading into the lake. She raced the motor to push the boat toward the beach and pulled it up when the lake bottom looked too near. She heard the prow crunch onto the gravel. "Can you jump out and pull us in?"

Angela stood up, holding the sides of the boat, and climbed out onto the beach. "Well, that's one foot wet." She pulled until the rowboat was halfway onto the beach and then stood up and surveyed their landing spot. A curved line of cottonwoods hugged the edge of the creek a little higher on the beach.

Lane was beside her, holding the haversack with their lunch and a blanket. "Let's find a cool, shady place for this, and then have a bit of an explore."

"This is absolutely lovely!" exclaimed Angela. "So quiet!"

"Well, yes, except for that creek and the birds and whatever that distant roary sound is."

"You know what I mean—nobody here but us kind of quiet. Previously unexplored, undiscovered beauty kind of quiet," Angela said. "And what a lovely smell! It's the cottonwoods I think. It reminds me of a childhood holiday in South Carolina."

"We're not the only people," Lane said, her voice suddenly cautious. She was walking ahead of Angela along the creek. The cottonwoods had given way to a denser cover of mixed evergreen and birch. The shadows seemed deeper against the morning sun. "Look at this."

A circle of stones made a fire pit, and a rusted and burned grate was propped along the edge of the pit. A chipped blue enamelled saucepan lay upended in the pebbles, and there were several discarded empty bean and soup cans.

They walked deeper into the shadow. The land rose in a high canyon, and the roaring sound became more pronounced.

"There's obviously a waterfall up here somewhere," Lane said. "Look, someone's put a rough bridge over the creek here. There seems to be a path—oh!" She stopped. On the other side of the path, tucked behind a fold of land above the creek, was something resembling a shed.

"That looks relatively new. Do you think someone lives here?" Angela asked. "I mean, perhaps we ought to scurry on back to the beach and find somewhere else to lunch."

But Lane was already across the bridge and knocking on the rough door of the shed. "Hello? Hello! Anyone home?" Receiving no answer, she pulled at the door, and it swung out easily on its leather hinges. A quick look inside told her someone had been living there. Running along the edge of the back wall was a pallet on the floor with a rumpled sleeping bag, looking like someone had just got out of it.

A small leather suitcase served as a side table, and on it were two books that looked like they'd travelled a fair bit. A kerosene lamp hung on a hook to the right of the door. An overturned box held a cup with shaving equipment, toothbrush, toothpowder, and a hairbrush.

"Well?" called Angela, outside and reluctant to advance any farther.

"The books are in German," Lane said.

"What books? There are books?" Angela retreated a few more feet. "Really, Lane. I mean, German books. After that swastika pin Phil found. I think we ought to scram."

"Whoever it is hasn't been here for a little while," Lane observed.

"Oh. And how do you know that?"

"The smell, I suppose. Let's go farther up the creek. I bet that sound is a waterfall."

"The smell? I'm not even going to ask. We go look at the waterfall and then we go back to the beach," Angela said, as if she were making a deal with recalcitrant children.

The path became damp in front of them. Rounding a curve, they were hit with a nearly deafening wall of sound and white water crashing and cascading down twenty feet of cliff, sending a fine spray into the air like a halo. Dark green moss clung to the rocks and small ferns grew on the ledges, their fine lacy leaves bobbing with the wind sent up by the cannoning water.

Both women stood silent, mesmerized by the power and beauty of water in this violent form.

"Nice place to live if you're a German spy," Angela said at last.

"We don't know he's a German spy, and it may be nice, but it's not terribly convenient. And in any case, what employment would there be for a German spy? The war is long over. Come, let's see if we can see any other way to get here other than by boat."

"I would just like to sit in the sun and dry off," Angela protested.

They walked out of the dark canyon and back toward the bridge. Their hair was bedewed from the mist of the waterfall. Back in the warmth and quiet, they crossed the bridge and walked in the opposite direction from the shed.

"Look, here!" Angela cried. "This is a path, and it winds along the top of the beach here, and then heads up the hill. Do you think it goes as far as the road?" She was pointing at a dusty path, narrow and rocky in spots and overgrown with yellowing grass in others.

"You know, I should have looked at those books more closely. They might have a name. If I'm right that whoever set up camp here hasn't been back for a while, why? If he had found a better place to live, he'd have come for his things. I'm popping back to have a look." Lane made determinedly toward the bridge.

"I'm 'popping' down to the beach to set up lunch, and then I think we ought to 'pop' back up the lake to the safety of King's Cove."

"I'll be right there," Lane called back, pulling the door of the shed open. She knelt down and took up the books. "Well, well, well," she said softly. "You're not a Nazi then." She flipped open the cover of the first book and saw a name inscribed. "K. Lazek." She saw the same name in the second book and was about to put it down when she realized a page was marked with a bookmark. When she opened the book to the mark, she saw that it was a photograph of a young family taken in the summer in a sunny garden—a lovely young woman holding a baby, a little boy leaning on the arm of her chair and looking shyly at the camera, and a man in another chair, one leg swung casually over the arm. He was raising a glass toward the photographer and laughing. By their clothes the photo looked to be from the early 1930s. She turned the picture over, hoping for some names, but there was only the photographer's stamp. She was about to put the photo back and then she frowned. It wasn't a German name on the stamp. "Foto Novak, 39 U Svoboda, Asch." Novak? Svoboda? Polish, maybe?

She stood up, still holding the book. She realized her temptation to take the books and photo was completely irrational. Whoever owned them was likely to come back and be very upset that so precious a family memory was gone. She put them back on the suitcase, resisting the urge to open that as well, and went outside, just in time to hear Angela calling her.

"Are you coming, or what?"

"On my way!" Lane called.

"He's not a Nazi," Lane said, accepting her wax-paper-wrapped sandwich and plunking down next to Angela on the blanket. "The two books were by German communists. Rosa Luxemburg—she's very famous, and completely illegal in Nazi Germany, of course, and another one I've never read, but it's about a man I know of, Hermann Broch. I expect he was illegal as well."

"Well, that's a relief. He's only a communist then," Angela remarked. "Wine?"

"Wine? You clever girl! I thought we'd be drinking lemonade! Yes, please. Then I think we ought to follow that path up to see if it goes to the road."

"And what if we meet him coming down the road?"

"Then we'll offer him a glass of wine. I don't see that he's been enjoying a lot of creature comforts here."

Angela picked up a pebble and threw it into the lake. "You're incorrigible. Are you forgetting you got locked into our barn for your troubles last time you got too nosey? Not that I mind. The children were thrilled to learn you'd been trapped in there by a bad guy. Though I note that they haven't ventured in there to play much. Anyway, is any of this our business?"

Lane was thoughtful. "You're right. It's none of our business. But in the back of my mind I'm wondering if whoever lived here was our poor man in the boat."

"That's what you had up your sleeve the whole time! I am not in the least bit reassured. What if it was him, and whoever killed him comes here looking for . . . I don't know . . . the gold this guy stole from him?"

"That's exactly what Mabel said. But no one has been down till now. Look. I know I'll be kicking myself if I don't at least go see. You enjoy the sun and the lapping waves, and I'll be back in a jiff."

Lane ran back to the path. Trees kept it shady, a boon, as there was a long steep climb toward the edge of the canyon, and then the path covered the sharp rise in switchbacks. She could hear the falls on her right. Finally she could see ahead to where the trees cleared and the path opened onto a narrow strip of grass, dried and yellowed from the sun, and just beyond, behind a thick growth of thimbleberry, the road, as she'd suspected. She pushed her way through the bushes and walked to the edge of the road, and tried to figure out where it was in relation to Kaslo. She'd only made the trip once, and that was in heavy winter snow. The terrain looked completely different in the dry late summer. Just around the corner from where the path came onto the road, she saw the wooden bridge over the creek. Kaslo is probably less than six miles up the road, she thought.

Really, all this is in aid of nothing in particular. We don't know who was camped down the hill, and it truly is none of our business. A harmless prospector, who, being German, was perhaps unable to get a job during the war? Or Carl Castle? He's disappeared. But no, there is no indication he'd be reading communist literature in the original German. So caught up was she in thinking as she made her way back down the path that she was nearing the bottom before she heard Angela calling her.

"Yup! Coming! All done," she called back, and ran the rest of the way down the path to the beach.

"Finally!" Angela said. "I packed up the boat and went for a walk across the other side of the creek. Perhaps you'd be interested in what I found while you were fooling around doing your imitation of a mountain goat."

Angela led Lane along the beach, where the creek had spread into a small delta, and continued across on dry stones. On the other side the beach curved slightly west. She stopped abruptly and said, "I left it exactly where I found it and have not touched it. I read detective fiction, you know."

There, half in and half out of the water, being gently rocked by the quiet lapping of the lake, lay an oar that looked, Lane thought, the absolute twin of the one in the rowboat.

CHAPTER NINETEEN

September 1941

KLAUS LAZEK STOOD BY THE wagon that was piled with part of the wheat harvest, chewing a blade of dried stalk. "It's not a bad harvest, considering we are a bunch of city people."

"No, indeed. It's too bad those idiots won't give us any place to store it. Have they even been here in the winter with all the snow or in the spring with those floods of rain?"

Lazek shrugged. "They are company men from where? Manitoba? Someplace with no rain. They keep our supply money from us, make us build their railroad for nothing. I think someone has been stealing the money."

"For God's sake, Klaus, don't go shouting that about! We are on thin ice as it is here. I'm sure some of them would love to see us do something wrong. They'd love to throw a German in jail."

Lazek kicked at the wheel of the wagon. "I'm tired of it, Hans. The minute we've built something to store this in,

I'm leaving. I'm going to sign up. Now that they've lifted those ridiculous enemy alien papers from us, I'm going to fight the Nazis."

"Good luck, my friend. Just because they don't call you an enemy anymore doesn't mean they'll let you suit up in one of their uniforms. You're still a German." Hans took a last drag of his damp cigarette and dropped the remainder at his feet, grinding it with his boot toe.

"Precisely, Hansy, precisely. I speak German, and so does the enemy. I could be useful. That has to count for something. Now let's get this lot out of here before it rains again."

AMES'S SUPPOSITION THAT most of the local miners, loggers, and boatmen frequented the hotel pubs proved to be right. His supposition that it was going to yield information was beginning to look futile, however. The silence in the room that accompanied them showing their police identification to the bartender in each of the hotels they entered made Ames suggest, as they walked to the next establishment, that they were all "up to something guilty."

"Keep your focus, Ames," Darling said. Showing the admittedly unattractive picture of a dead man around had so far netted only the shaking of heads. Finally one man had frowned and said, "He does look kinda familiar. He never drank in here though. Try the Nugget up the road."

"Inspector Darling and Constable Ames," Darling said to the bartender at the Nugget. "We're looking for any information you might have about this man."

The bartender glanced at the picture as if he already knew he'd have nothing to say, and then did a double take.

"This guy looks dead."

"He is dead," Darling said. "And we'd like to know who he is."

"May I?" The bartender reached for the picture and held it up to the light provided by the window above his bar.

"I do sort of recognize him. He lives . . . lived out of town somewhere. He didn't come here often, I can tell you, especially after the ruckus. In fact he stopped coming here."

"Ruckus?" asked Ames.

"I never did know what happened. A group of guys took him from the bar here to join them at a table a week or so ago. They were standing him drinks and patting him on the back. It was a busy night . . . a Friday, I'm guessing, and there'd been some sort of meeting a bunch of them had been at, and they all came back here at once. I didn't see the lead-up, but suddenly I heard a chair flying. This guy," the bartender lifted the picture, "was standing and yelling something. He had a pretty thick accent. I couldn't hear what he said. But he slammed out of here yelling something like, 'You're sick. You're all sick.' Someone took off after him, spoiling for a fight, but a couple of the other fellows went after him and held him back. You know what people are. Everyone poured out onto the street to watch, hoping there'd be a fight."

"Was there?"

The bartender shrugged. "I was trying to keep things together here. I couldn't leave, obviously. There was no one else here. It seemed over pretty fast, so I thought those fellows managed to stop it."

"Did you find out what the dispute was about?"

"Nope. I was more concerned with keeping the peace. I told that table they'd better behave or they wouldn't be allowed in again. It was pretty surprising because they were all very lovey dovey when they first came in. When they settled down again they had their heads together. I'd say they looked like people who'd taken someone into their confidence and were angry he wasn't who they thought he was. Or they were trying to play a trick on some poor foreigner sort of thing. Anyway, in a few minutes they were laughing again, and left shortly after, so I figured it was over."

"Did you catch the guy's name?"

"I never asked him, but someone else from another table did go out after him. Looked like he wanted to calm him down, and he didn't come back that night. I'm pretty sure he called him Klaus. That man over there is a friend of his, I think, or was." The bartender pointed at the end of the bar where two men sat talking but watched the police guardedly.

"Is there a room we can use?"

"Sure. There's a ladies lounge behind that door. Nobody in at this time of day."

"HARRY BRONSON. I work at a mill up near Slocan. What's this about?"

"We're trying to find out about an incident you might have witnessed a few days ago."

"Oh, that thing with Klaus. One of those bastards tried to get at him, but Klaus is a big man. He pummelled the man. I had to pull him off."

"The bartender said someone tried to go after him, but his mates held him back?"

"They held one of them back, but not that crazy who got out and tried to start a fight."

"Let's start at the beginning. How do you know Klaus?" Darling asked.

"I don't understand. Has Klaus done something?"

Ames pushed the picture of the dead Klaus forward. "He's dead. We'd like to know why and how."

Harry Bronson frowned. "Those bastards!" He took up the picture and looked at it closely. "That's Lazek, all right. No wonder he hasn't been at work. I thought he'd quit."

"How did you know him?"

"We served in the same unit. He was in weapons training. Never went overseas. But we reconnected after the war, and I said he should come work here. It's mostly mining here, but he didn't want to go underground. I think he knew miners back home. I remember him saying they didn't last long. So he worked in the mill with me. I live south of here about ten miles, and I used to pick him up in my truck. He had a place somewhere along the road, but he never would show me where."

"His last name is Lazek?" Ames asked. He had his little black notebook out and was writing in it.

"Yeah. He was a serious sort of guy. Didn't talk much, but we got along. He told me he used to be an electrician in the old country, but he had to leave because of politics. Ended up in the north somewhere. He never said much about himself. Didn't usually drink either. I'd come in here on a Friday and he'd get himself home. I think he walked.

Or he could have gone back in his little boat. He brought it to town when he wanted supplies."

"What kind of boat?" Ames asked.

"I don't think I ever saw it. Just told me he had one."

"Do you know what kind of politics?" Darling asked.

Bronson shook his head. "You know Europe. It's crazy over there. He did say once that he hated Nazis, and I was a little surprised, because I thought he was German. But of course there must have been plenty of Germans that weren't Nazis."

"So he came from Germany," Ames said, writing.

"No. That's the funny thing. He said he wasn't from Germany. That's what I mean. Europe's kind of mixed up."

"Do you know how he ended up in the bar with that other group that night?" Darling asked.

"I don't. I was surprised. For one thing, those guys work at a mine, at least some of them do. A couple I never saw before. And they're troublemakers. They claim to belong to some secret society, and they swagger around like they own the place. Maybe they thought because he was German he'd go for their crazy ideas. I know at least one of them spent most of the war in prison."

"Were they in the bar just now?"

"No. In fact I haven't seen them either since then. Thank God."

"Did you see where Klaus went on that Friday night?"

"I pulled him off the guy he was beating, and he kind of shrugged me off and started to walk off. I was worried about him, so I offered him a ride back to where I usually dropped him off, but he said to leave him alone. He was going toward the water, so I assumed he was going to his boat. I left him to it. I wanted to get home. Some of the guys were way too drunk that night."

"You mentioned Klaus Lazek stopped working. Did you go look for him when he wasn't there to be picked up?"

"I stopped on the Saturday where I usually pick him up, near Fletcher's Creek there, to see if he was all right, but I couldn't see any place anyone could live. He was pretty secretive, as I said."

"Do you know if he has any relations, wife, parents, siblings?"

"I don't think so. He never talked much about his past. I think he had a sister, but I have a feeling she stayed behind in the old country. He did say he came here as a refugee in 1939. I liked him. He kept to himself, but he was honest and hard working. He trained in weapons when he signed up, and he was posted to train the rest of us. I always wondered if they didn't send him overseas because they couldn't entirely trust him because he was German."

"Do you know the names of any of the miners involved in the incident?" Ames asked, drawing a line under something in his notebook.

"Nah. They aren't my type. There were a couple of people there that I never saw before that night. I don't think they were miners."

"Do you know which mine the others work at?" Darling asked.

"I couldn't say. Barkeep might know."

Darling nodded at Ames, who went back into the main bar.

"Would you be willing to show us where you picked him up every day? We could follow in our car."

"Sure. I want to head out now anyway."

Ames was back. "The Cork, he says."

KENNY ARMSTRONG PULLED his red truck onto the grassy sward by the sloping pasture where he usually parked. The horse that had once pulled his mail wagon trotted to the fence and threw his chin up and down in greeting. Holding Alexandra, Eleanor climbed out of the cab and stretched.

"Hello, old thing," she said stroking the horse's muzzle. "Off you go!" she said to the dog, putting her down. Alexandra ran off toward the house and then stopped, emitting a noise neither Kenny nor Eleanor had ever heard before. The horse flattened his ears and then twitched them, and pawed the ground. Kenny stopped and looked at the dog, putting down the bag of flour he'd been lifting out of the box in the back of the truck.

"What's up with the mutt?" he asked, frowning.

Alexandra had stopped five feet short of the front door. She began to bark softly, punctuating the bark with growls.

"Stay back," Kenny said to his wife as she started toward the dog. "She thinks someone is in there." He moved toward the house. "Okay, old girl. Let's have a look, shall we?" With utmost caution Kenny pulled open the screen door, turned the doorknob, and pushed the kitchen door open. Scooping up the dog, he went cautiously inside.

Eleanor waited for an anxious moment and then, rebelling at the thought of anyone dangerous being in the cottage, she took up the remaining bag of groceries and went determinedly into the kitchen. Putting the bag on the table she called out, "Everything all right?" Alexandra bounded excitedly into the kitchen, wiggling and sniffing. "Investigation complete?" Eleanor asked her.

"I don't know what the fuss was about," Kenny said, coming in from the back of the cottage. "There's no one here but us chickens. Maybe someone stopped by and put their head in the door to look for us and then went off again. I don't reckon we'll be murdered in our beds with her around." He leaned over and ruffled the top of Alexandra's head.

It wasn't until the flour, sugar, salt, and cans of treacle were stowed that Eleanor noticed what was wrong.

"Where's the dog's water bowl gone?" she asked as the phone rang.

"DAMN," LANE SAID. "I wish we had a camera. I don't want to touch anything."

"It's probably been there for ages. It might not even be the other oar. I'm sure it will last till tomorrow. Why don't we get on back and you can let that nice Inspector Darling know?"

"Where would someone who lived here keep a boat?" Lane asked.

"They'd pull it up onto the beach, as we have," suggested Angela.

Lane was dying to take a quick walk along the edge of the beach. If someone was shot here somewhere, there must be some evidence—dried blood, scuffed up ground denoting a struggle—but she resisted the urge to look for it.

She could mess up evidence, if she hadn't already, bounding in and out of the little cabin as she had. She didn't relish Darling's censure.

"Well, it's probably nothing. Abandoned oars must be a dime a dozen along a lake. Look at all the logs and wood that drift onto the beach," Lane said.

In spite of this light talk, the creek and its brooding waterfall cascading in the shadows beyond made the atmosphere sinister. Fighting the urge to nose about, Lane started back toward their boat.

"And you're right. We should get back as soon as we can and phone the police. It may be nothing, but on the other hand, it may be everything."

"HELLO? KC 285, Eleanor Armstrong speaking." Eleanor did not take her eyes off the space where Alexandra's water bowl ought to be.

It was Gladys. "Someone's pinched my silver teapot! It was my grandmother's. And I don't know what else is missing. We've lived here undisturbed for nearly fifty years. Who would have the cheek to rob us?"

Oh, dear, Eleanor thought. "I've just now seen that Alexandra's water bowl has vanished. Oh, wait, Kenny is making some sort of wild signs from the door of the sitting room." She put her hand over the receiver. "What are you dancing around like a dervish for?"

Kenny, who had been making, he thought, perfectly understandable fencing motions, burst out, "Someone's taken my father's sword!"

Her heart sinking, Eleanor got back on the phone.

"Kenny's father's regimental sword is gone as well. Were you out of the house?"

"Of course we were out of the house!" Gladys said impatiently. "We have work to do. The girls were up at the orchard, and I was out in the vegetable garden. The top one." Eleanor knew the Hughes' top garden was well away from the house, screened by a hedge of myrtle and a copse of birch trees.

"We've just been up to town. Anyone could have had a field day. It's outrageous. We never lock anything. Who could it be?"

"Someone who knew exactly where to go," said Gladys. "I'm going back to see what else the swine has swiped."

"I'll get Kenny to check the rest of our things, and I'll phone and see if Reg or Robin has lost anything."

"I bet Reg is fine. That wet blanket Alice never leaves the house. The Bertollis too. The dogs and children would be barking like mad if anyone tried to approach them."

Knowing Gladys was right, Eleanor hung up the phone. Issuing instructions to Kenny to have a closer look around, Eleanor prepared to phone Robin, when the instrument jangled again.

"The phone man." It was Gladys again. "He had time to have a good look around. I didn't think he knew a damn thing about phones."

That was exactly what Kenny had said about the phone man. She began to piece together a possible series of events. "I wonder if he nobbled the phones so he could come around and snoop," she said. "I'm sure he'd have to cut a wire or something. Well, be that as it may, we'll make a thorough list and then call the police."

CHAPTER TWENTY

September 1941

THE TAMENESS OF THE COUNTRYSIDE amazed Klaus. Passing farms and ranches as he moved south on the train filled him with longing. It was beautiful, like the countryside in Bohemia. Accessible. Farmable. Not like the mosquito-infested swampland they'd been sent to. He would go to Vancouver and sign up. There was a war on. They could not fault him for leaving. Anyway, the others were more patient. They had had a good enough harvest in spite of every setback. Perhaps those clowns at the CWR would reward them by giving them everything they were entitled to. Besides, he thought, there is nothing to hold me there. Or anywhere. As he fell into a doze he imagined himself in uniform, fighting in Europe. He imagined a village wrested from the Nazis and in it, surviving still, thin, defiant Julia and the children. The agony of being stuck so far away from what he should be doing was palpable.

DARLING AND AMES waved at Harry Bronson and watched his truck as it turned the corner and disappeared. The two policemen stood in the green silence left by the receding truck and looked around. "Not very promising, sir."

"No, indeed, Ames. Your insight is blinding." They had looked all along the stretch of road where Bronson said he always picked Lazek up for work, and they could not find anything remotely like any kind of dwelling, or even a lane leading to one. A stretch of open land on the west side of the road suggested that the area had once been a field, but now it proved to be a marshy grassland created by the creek backing up.

The sun was hanging low, nearing the mountain ridge to the west, when Darling shook his head. "I don't understand. Did he camp here somewhere? I think we'd better call it a day and come back out tomorrow, or send some of the boys to hack around in the underbrush."

Relieved not to be sent to do the hacking, Ames gratefully hopped into the driver's seat and waited for his boss to have one last look around. Darling took off his jacket and threw it into the back seat with his hat.

"So now we know who he is. But why was he shot and set adrift? Because he was a foreigner? It seems a scant excuse, though I know there's a segment of the populace that doesn't like foreigners. Drink? That group was already drunk and bellicose, and if Bronson is to be believed, Lazek beat one of them badly. That would be enough to at least start another fight, one that a vengeful combatant might bring a gun to. Too many guns still floating around. I wonder if he was beaten badly enough to seek medical attention? Add it to your list, Ames." Darling sat back, gazing at the passing forest and thinking what a perfect time of day it was to be sitting on Lane's back porch. "And while you're at it, where's the boat? Miss Winslow said she pulled it up under the wharf, and someone clearly dragged it away."

Ames too fell into a broody silence. With each mile closer to town, his anxiety about Violet increased. They hadn't formally broken off. He had opined that he wasn't ready for the noose, and she had gone off in a huff. She was prone to going off in huffs, but she usually was amenable to being talked around. If he didn't try to talk her around this time, would that constitute an official end of the whole business? He glanced at Darling and felt a real sense of embarrassment. That, he was certain, was not the way a gentleman would end a relationship. So confused had his musings become that it was with genuine delight that he saw Lane Winslow's car turning up into King's Cove, proceeding very slowly because a rowboat was tied to the top of it.

"Sir, look!" he cried, honking twice. He pulled up behind Lane's car where it had stopped.

"Yes, I see, Ames. No need to wake the dead." Darling got out of the car and walked toward the driver's side of Lane's car, his hands in his pockets.

"What's all this, then?"

"Hello, Inspector."

"Hello, Inspector Darling!" said Angela, leaning forward from the passenger side. "We've been on the lake, and . . . well, you'd better tell him, Lane."

"Tell me what?"

"Look, we can't fill up the front door to King's Cove like this. Why don't you two come up to the house? We could certainly use a drink after the day we've put in. If you have time, I mean. I believe we do have something important to tell you with regard to the poor man we found in the boat."

Darling looked back at Ames, who had gotten out of the car and was smiling cheerfully at Miss Winslow. "Have we got time, Ames? Miss Winslow has something she'd like to say to us about our case. Again." Here Darling threw her a pinched smile and returned to the police car.

Lane parked the car in front of her barn, deciding Reg could wait for his boat until the next morning, and thought about what she had in the house to eat. Ames pulled up into the driveway, and the two policemen got out. Angela stood undecided and then said, "I need to get back. Poor David has had the boys all day. I expect I'll find him in tatters."

"Oh, of course!" Lane said. "Let me run you home. Constable, I'm afraid you'll have to back out so I can take Angela home to her waiting family."

"Nonsense," said Darling. "Ames, be good enough to run Mrs. Bertolli home."

Ames saluted and opened the passenger door gallantly for Angela. If he couldn't break up with Violet like a gentleman, he could at least be one getting Mrs. Bertolli home.

Lane and Darling watched the car back out and trundle up the road.

"I can't decide whether to kiss you now or wait to see what interfering thing you've been up to," Darling said.

"I should get on with it now, because you'll be cross with me about the interfering, and Ames will be back in a minute."

He took her hand and they walked toward the house. The door was open and Darling could see the pool of light in the sitting room.

"It's too bad about Ames," he said, pulling her close.

Lane closed her eyes at the feel of his lips, and agreed that it was a bit of a shame about Ames.

"Are you going to answer that?" Darling whispered, his mouth brushing her cheek as the phone jangled in the hallway.

"Two longs and a short. I suppose I'd better. I mean, it's no good, is it, with Ames popping back any second." She reached up and kissed him again, and went into the hall. "KC 431, Lane Winslow speaking. Oh, hello. No, I've been on the lake with Angela." She listened and then looked down the hall toward her living room, frowning. Darling had gone through and now stood at her front window watching the evening coming on. "Her water bowl? And the sword? Good grief. Anything else? No, of course you must. Inspector Darling and Constable Ames are here right now. No, no, that's quite all right."

The tone of Lane's voice alerted Darling, who now came into the darkening hallway and watched Lane. "And Gladys? All right. I'll certainly tell them, and when there's a complete list they can look at it. I suppose I'd better check my own house, though I've not got much that's stealworthy. Will you be all right?"

Assured that Kenny and Eleanor felt safe, Lane hung the earpiece back on the hook. "Someone has been around stealing things from the Armstrongs' and the Hughes' places. They think it's the phone man. Do you mind? I just want to take a quick look. I've been out all day. The thief could have loaded up a moving van and taken the lot. Though as I told Eleanor, I don't have much of any value."

Darling, wanting to be the one to go through the house in case whoever it was was still inside, followed Lane into the kitchen.

"Everything looks all right. I expect if it was the phone man, he scratched me off the list after his inspection."

"He was here?"

"Of course he was. Allegedly to fix the phone. I didn't pay attention to what he was doing, so he probably did a quick scan to see if there was anything worth taking. Listen to me! Blaming the poor phone man. He's probably innocent."

"Possibly," Darling said cautiously. "But he's the only stranger that's been around and in people's houses. What did he look like?"

"A phone man, really. He had on some sort of coveralls and one of those peaked caps with a phone logo. I did notice that he kept the cap on when he came in. Maybe your height, brown hair. I couldn't have told you about his eyes, as they were sort of in the shadow of the hat."

Ames knocked on the open door at that moment and came in.

"Those dogs bark even when the lady of the house comes home," he commented. Seeing Lane's and Darling's expressions, he added, "What's going on?"

"A couple of people here have reported having things stolen sometime earlier today," Darling said. "Antiques."

"Well, I'll be da . . . I'll be."

"Thank you, Ames. Moderation in all things, including your language. Take your little black notebook and pop over to the Armstrongs', and then up to the Hughes'. They seem to want to wait till they have a full tally, but I'd like to get to this at once."

"Sir," Ames said, resisting an impulse to salute again. He cast one last longing look at the sofa and side table with its promise of a drink.

"There's a good constable. In the meantime, Miss Winslow, you'd better tell me what you've been up to."

Ames left, not in the least bit fooled by that "Miss Winslow" nonsense. Darling and Lane sat in the two easy chairs, which in the winter she had situated in front of her Franklin stove but were now placed facing the window and the view of the lake, with a convenient end table holding a bottle of Scotch and two glasses, between them.

"I DID KNOCK before I went in," Lane said. Darling listened intently and without comment as she reached the part of the story when she and Angela had discovered the shed, and was feeling anxious about the next bit. If it proved to be important, he would probably be cross about her having been in the shed, touching things.

"What did you find?"

"Clearly someone has been living there. There was bedding, a kerosene lamp, a suitcase used as a side table, and a couple of books in German on top."

"Which you can read perfectly, I suppose?"

"Not perfectly, no. I speak better German than I read. They were both classics of socialist thought."

Darling said, "Our dead man turns out to have been German. We were up in Kaslo while you were bumbling around what may well prove to be the crime scene, and we learned a fair bit. His name was Klaus—"

"Lazek!" cried Lane. "That was the name in his books. I mean, not the 'Klaus,' it was just 'K,' but 'Lazek' was the surname."

"All of which goes to explain why we couldn't find hide nor hair of where he lived. He used to get picked up along the road by a fellow worker, but he told us he never saw Klaus's house, and we couldn't find anything to indicate where he might live."

"Oh. I think I can help you there. There's a very rough path up the hill from the beach and it comes out near the road. I didn't go right out to the road because I didn't want to fight through the underbrush, but I'm certain I could find it from up on the road. It's just before a bridge."

"Anything else?"

"There was a photo of a family in one of the books, with a label in maybe Polish, which I thought was odd. Oh, and Angela found the other important thing: the beach sort of curls around toward the northwest. She was exploring while I was going up the path, and she found a single oar sort of floating half in and half out of the water. And before you ask, I realized this might be a crime scene, so tempted though I was, I backed away with a view to calling you about it."

Darling smiled. "It's good to know you are not a stranger to all decency. Of course now I'm going to have to drive all the way back there and have you show me what you found and where the damn place is."

AMES CALLED OUT and then came through the door.

"All done, sir, as far as it goes. I've got a list of items I can check for in the local antique shops tomorrow."

Lane got up, smiling. "Scotch, Constable Ames?"

Though a beer man himself, it had been a long day. However, Darling apparently had no interest in Ames's day ending.

"Not for you, Ames." He stood up and stretched. "You're driving, and we should set a good example. Thank you, Miss Winslow. We'll see you tomorrow at, say, nine? Let's go, Ames. You can tell me what you found out about the thefts, and if you're very good, I'll tell you what Miss Winslow has found for us."

The night was a soft, inky, moonless darkness as Ames turned the car onto the Nelson road. They could see a few lights twinkling along the great curve of the cove. "It would be nice to have a summer home along here," he commented.

"You'd hate it. You're a townie if there ever was one."

"You're right there, sir," Ames said. "It's pretty isolated out here. Take these robberies. None of the victims lock their doors. I'm surprised they haven't been robbed before now."

Darling, who was doing a poor job of ignoring his anxiety about leaving Lane alone in her house, though she had assured him that she would lock all the doors, said, "Well?"

"Well, it's pretty much what Miss Winslow learned from her phone call. Someone broke into—but, that's wrong, isn't it?—walked into the Armstrongs' and the Hughes' and helped themselves to some valuable antiques. I've got a complete list here, but you know the sort of things: Chinese porcelain, silver tea service, regimental sword, some sterling boxes. They're the only two affected. I know this because they called around to the neighbours. But some places had someone home all day, and others didn't have antiques, as such, like the Bertollis'."

"I can't help thinking this must be the same outfit that's been stealing antiques in town. I noticed that they were beginning to move up the lake a bit, but there must be scores of people between the last house they robbed and King's Cove. What made them pick it?"

"I don't know, but they do have a theory about who is behind it . . . the phone man. Apparently there have been some problems with the phones, and a guy in a van with the phone company logo came round and checked everyone's phones, but people weren't very impressed with him. To quote old Mrs. Hughes, 'If he's a phone man, I'm the king of England.'"

"That's what Miss Winslow thought as well. Did the phones start working? I know there was some trouble. I've been cut off a couple of times in conversations with Miss Winslow."

"Yes, sir. It all stopped as mysteriously as it started."

"Any description?" Darling asked, hoping the other victims had had a better look than Lane.

"About forty, medium height, brown hair. Some sort of brown work coveralls and a cap. In short, every second repairman for miles around."

"Wonderful. Let's put O'Brien onto interviewing every man of that description. It'll serve him right," said Darling glumly.

"If I looked like that, I'd embark on a life of crime. It's the perfect disguise."

"Yes, well. It's also a perfect disguise for perfectly law-abiding citizens. I wouldn't recommend a life of crime for you, Amesy. You'd be picked out of a lineup immediately. You look like an over-eager Boy Scout."

CHAPTER TWENTY-ONE

"WHAT'S THIS?" DARLING ASKED CROSSLY as he came into the station the next morning. He was holding an expensive-looking envelope on which his name was written in elaborate script.

"I don't know, sir. It had your name on it so, as tempted as I was to steam it open with the morning's tea kettle, I thought I'd better give it to you," O'Brien said.

"No need for cheek, O'Brien. Ames and I have to go up the lake. Where is he?"

"Gassing up the car, sir. It's a good thing there's no crime in Nelson, the way you two gad about. Are you going to open that envelope or not?"

Darling put his finger under the flap of the envelope and tore it open. Much to his amazement it was an invitation to an "evening" at the home of Councillor Lorimer to celebrate the work and achievements of the distinguished citizens of Nelson. "Feel free to bring a guest. RSVP."

"What's this nonsense?"

"I thought, now that you've opened it, you'd tell me."

"Why am I getting an invite to some sort of do at Lorimer's?"

"You're the inspector?"

"I'm to bring a guest," Darling added.

"Well, that shouldn't be too hard, should it, sir? Ah. Here's Ames. I'll try to stave off the criminal hordes while you're gone."

"You'll do better than that. Find out where a person who was injured in Kaslo would go for treatment, and when you've done that ask them about any man who came in looking like he'd had a beating in the last week or so. Find out if the mine up there has an infirmary, for example, or if the town has a local doctor who goes out. And get the names."

O'Brien, thinking longingly of his quiet days answering the phone and doing the crossword, said, "Sir," and set about finding the pile of local directories the station had.

"I HAVEN'T HEARD a word from her," Ames said, as they were driving down the hill from the Balfour store and gas pump. Darling, who had not asked and had been using the long silence since they had rumbled off the Nelson ferry to think about the missing man, Carl Castle, and whether he might be connected to any of the other crimes they seemed suddenly to be juggling, now raised his eyebrows and looked at Ames.

"By 'her' you mean your Violet?"

"Yes, sir. Sorry, sir. But it's nerve-racking. I feel like a guy who goes into his house having no idea it's been booby trapped with a pail of cold water over the door. She's going to pop out from behind a building somewhere, and I'll have to get into a donnybrook with her."

"You ought to manage your affairs better, Amesy. Break it off, for God's sake. You've already said you have doubts. And at least she doesn't work at the local café, so we won't be subject to her bitterly slinging our cups of coffee at us in the morning."

His boss was right, Ames thought. He should break it off. He should telephone her—no, that would involve the slamming of receivers. He'd much better be a man and ask to meet her. The worst that could happen is she'd flounce off. Or slap him and then flounce off.

"Are you planning to take the corner up to Miss Winslow's at breakneck speed, Ames?" Darling asked. "Or shall we drive on by and go digging around ourselves?"

"Sorry, sir. I was a million miles away," Ames said, slowing precipitously and just managing the sharp corner up to King's Cove. A truck behind them that had not expected this manoeuvre honked loudly.

"Well, get back here, and try not to kill us in a road accident."

A chastened Ames pulled the car up to the gate at Lane's house and waited in the car while Darling went to collect her.

"Good morning, darling," Lane said. "I've not been idle since last night. I've talked to Robin Harris, who asserted that that 'damn fool didn't look like a telephone man' to him, and that the fellow hadn't got past the kitchen because he could see at a glance that Harris would have nothing worth stealing. And Eleanor called and wanted to add a silver frame to the list. She and Kenny are both upset because it contains a picture of John right before he went overseas in '15. You may recall he was killed over there."

"I do, yes. Swine. We've contacted the phone company, and they said they'd had reports of some trouble on the lines up the lake but had not sent anyone out yet. So he wasn't a phone man. I've got someone going around the antique shops to see if any of the things turn up for sale."

"Surely they wouldn't be so foolish as to fence them locally. If it were me, I'd send them all to the coast."

"Happen you're right. I hope you don't take up a life of crime. You're too clever by half."

Lane insisted on the back seat, in no small measure because it was her plan to move to sit behind the driver's seat when they drove the frightening stretch of road just before Adderly so she wouldn't have to look out at the sheer drop.

The road was quiet and the morning fragrant and warm. Lane wondered, not for the first time, if she should be at home husbanding something or other in her garden. She was sure her neighbours would be busy all day digging potatoes or canning corn. Her plan was simply to pick enough peas from her little garden patch for dinner, and not to consider for one minute the full-scale battle plan that must be required to put up a lot of food for the coming winter. Lane rolled down her window so that her hair whipped around her face, and she drank in the scent of the passing forest, warming in the morning sun. She thought about Darling's remark.

"You know," she said, leaning forward, "it makes me wonder. Do you two think criminals are clever? I mean, fiction is full of diabolical and intelligent malefactors who can be stopped only by brilliant Holmesian detection. You have a lot of experience with crime. What do you think?"

The two men considered this. Ames finally said, "I think they think they are smarter than they truly are, some of them. Why else are they committing crimes in the first place? They can't think of legitimate ways to get what they want, or get out of some jam they're in."

Darling opened his mouth to speak, and then Ames went on, "I mean, take what we're dealing with now. We have three different sorts of crime, all committed for different reasons. Someone disguised as a phone man is stealing antiques. Someone has killed this Lazek guy, and that Carl Castle has disappeared. In the case of the antiques, it's sheer burglary to try to make a quick buck. The criminal thinks he's fooled all the victims, and because he hasn't been stopped yet, I bet he feels he's fooled everyone."

"He fooled you," Darling pointed out.

"Yes, but not for long. We're already after him, aren't we? People have seen him, the phone company doesn't own him, it's a matter of time. Someone like that should take the money and run, but he won't. He'll think, I can do this one more time and then I'll clear off, and that's when we'll have him."

"And our murderer?" Lane asked.

"There's a story there, isn't there? The victim was a threat to someone or he made someone mad. Either way, killing him, or trying to, if that's what happened, was the act of someone who was not smart enough to think of another way to handle it. We just have to figure out what the story is."

"You are not buying the coroner's verdict of a possible suicide? I believe our Ames is going to retire and write books like Watson did," said Darling. "I think, in a way, we have the advantage on the criminal. He's busy trying to cover up his crime, now he's had the misfortune to commit it. He was either drunk, or frightened, or angry when he did it. His mind is focused by fear, so he is limited in what he thinks about. We come in—not you, Miss Winslow; I'd like to reduce the amount of involvement you have in police work—and we can look at all the angles and possibilities. We are not limited in our thinking by fear. We are animated by logic."

"At the moment you're animated by the fact that I know where Lazek lived and you don't," Lane pointed out.

July 18

KLAUS WALKED DOWN to the edge of the water, well away from the business of the dock. In the distance someone was shouting instructions, but the voice seemed to lift into the sky and become cloud. The envelope was in his pocket where he had put it when it had been pushed through the post office window at the dry goods store in Kaslo. He went to put his hand in his pocket to pull it out, and then stopped, fearful that his hand would shake and he would not be able to read it. Turning away from the water's edge he sat on a stone. Because he'd brought his boat, he didn't have to worry about getting a ride from Harry, as he did whenever he needed supplies. The Red Cross. After five long years. He felt a sick fear and almost debilitating hope as he thought about what might be in the letter.

"STOP HERE," LANE said. They were about ten feet away from the bridge. "I'm pretty certain I was looking at about this point on the road from behind those bushes. And that bridge was visible." Ames parked the car on the shoulder and they got out. There was a laboured flapping of wings as a raven lifted off from the tree nearest the edge of the road and called out a warning. Lane recalled the Scottish myth that a lone raven is a harbinger of death, and then smiled. This one is warning its comrades about us, she thought.

"This is exactly where we were," Ames said.

"You were looking for a house. You weren't thinking that he might be living in a makeshift shed all the way down the hill near the beach. Let's see. I think about here." Lane had gone along the underbrush at the edge of the road and came to where someone could see, if they knew what to look for, that the bushes hid a slightly worn path across a patch of dried grass and then down into the trees.

"Ames, collect your things and step lively," Darling commanded. He turned to Lane. "Is it dusty?"

"It's a little bit of everything. You're thinking of Ames's nice shoes?"

Darling smiled and Lane felt giddy for a moment. "You ought not to be so heartless. One day you'll be hanging over the edge of a cliff with only Ames to save you, and then what will you do?"

"Remind him where his paycheque comes from. Ready?" Ames, carrying his camera case, had pushed through the sturdy thimbleberry bushes.

Darling stood up at the top of the now-clear descent toward the lake. The roar of the falls was becoming evident on his left. The path was distinct enough that he suspected it had been there long before Lazek decided to build his new home by the creek below. Gold seekers, perhaps from early in the century or late in the previous one, had probably made the path. It was wide enough to accommodate a small wagon drawn by a mule or a horse, but, as was evident from the growth on the path, it had barely been used in many years. They walked in silence, Lane leading, the sound of the waterfall becoming pronounced as the path skirted the canyon, and then receding as the descent became less steep and the path flattened gradually with a turn away from the creek and then back toward the beach.

Lane led them to the fire circle where Lazek had evidently cooked his meals, and then across the rough boards that constituted the bridge over the creek to the cabin.

"Miss Winslow, I'm going to ask you to come with me and give the cabin a quick look around and verify that it looks the same as when you saw it yesterday. As well I'll need to know what you touched. Ames, stand by, ready to take snaps."

"Sir," Ames said, which nearly prompted Lane to say it too.

Darling pulled the door out and in this position Lane could see that the door had a hook on it that could secure it open against the wall. Darling saw this and, with his handkerchief, hooked the latch over the bent nail that had been driven into the outer wall.

"Now, then." He stood back and let Lane look over the room.

It was the loneliness that struck her this time. How long would Lazek have continued squatting down by the creek had he not been shot and died? She saw the books, left where she had placed them, and wondered what companionship and society a German-speaking socialist would find so far from anything he must have been familiar with.

"It is as I left it. I touched the door, of course, and I picked up the two books. That's it, really. There's a photo in one of the books that I handled as well."

"Thank you. Ames, you can step in and take some pictures. Miss Winslow will show me whatever else she found."

Ames nodded and prepared his camera, pushing some flashbulbs into his pockets. Both men had left their jackets in the car, and Ames had already rolled up his sleeves. The sun was full on the beach now, and the heat seemed to emanate even into the shady sections under the trees. Lane waited while Darling finished giving some quiet instructions to his constable, then turned and walked down toward the lake, with the inspector a step behind her. A light gust picked up, and the leaves on the trees shimmered.

"It's a lovely place, I'll grant you that," Darling said. "I suppose a self-sustaining sort of individual could fish and eat berries and whatnot."

"He may have done that, but there were the remains of cans around his fire. Perhaps he wasn't used to roughing it. We know he sensibly brought his supplies in by boat, the distance to Kaslo not being too great. It would be a lot easier than carting heavy things down that hill. In fact, he was doing so that day, wasn't he? All those cans and things in his rucksack. I don't believe he tried to kill himself, however ill the news from the Red Cross was."

"Fair point," Darling said.

They stood at the edge of the water looking out across the lake. They could see to the south that the land across the lake jutted into the water and hid another great section of the lake behind it. They could just make out a smokestack tucked into the trees. They were not much more than a distant carpet of dark green, and it took a moment for Lane to realize how big the stack must be to be visible from all this distance away.

She turned to Darling and pointed across the creek. "Angela crossed over there and went around the bend and found the oar. I encouraged us both to stop and turn back when I saw it, as I suddenly imagined a fight to the death going on right there, and the boat with the unfortunate man being pushed out. I'll sit here while you go have a look."

"Send Ames along when he's done," Darling said, and followed Lane's instructions toward the natural stepping stones across the now-widening creek.

Lane sat on the warm pebbles on the beach and leaned back against a log. She heard Ames crunching down layers of flat pebbles on the beach in his expensive shoes, and directed him to follow the route she'd sent Darling on. She closed her eyes to let the light from the sun warm her face. During the summer, since she had returned from England in mid-July, she had written nearly nothing besides a letter to her grandparents, and she wondered about what poetic approach one could take that would encompass at once a scene of such sensual beauty and the spectre of the dark absence and death of the man who had come to live here. She fixed in her mind her physical sense of this great dichotomy, and then she heard the footsteps of the returning policemen.

"We're going to need to look around in the cabin and collect his few things to take back with us. Can I entrust you with the books, Miss Winslow? You mentioned before that you read German," Darling said.

"I do, though not terrifically well. You don't need to know the content of the books, do you? I can give you the gist because it does suggest what sort of things mattered to him," she answered.

"More in case there is further correspondence under his pillow or in that suitcase."

"Of course. Any luck? Was the oar still there?"

"It was. There is no evidence that it did anything but float there. There's no sign of violence, really, anywhere on that section of beach. No bloodstains or convenient fingerprint-covered weapon discarded nearby. It was Ames who pointed out that if the oar had been used by the man while he was still alive, it could have some bloodstains on it. I've pulled it up onto the beach. I'll get him to carry it back up the hill. Something might be found on it. On the whole, though, I'd say the attack did not take place here. But wherever it did, there must be blood. I can't believe he was shot in the boat. The bullet exited the wound and wasn't in the boat, and didn't put a hole in it."

"So he's shot ham-handedly by someone and he gets into the boat himself, to try to get away . . . but wouldn't the shooter have seen that he'd made a bad job of it and finish it up?"

"Unless he thought he'd succeeded. His victim falls, stunned, and doesn't move. The killer pushes off, and the victim comes to enough to crawl into the boat."

"Or, the victim falls, stunned, but right into the boat, because the shooting happens right beside the boat, and the shooter tosses the gun in and cuts the boat loose," Lane said.

"Do you know, you have a positively ghoulish enthusiasm for this sort of thing that's very unladylike."

"You don't actually think that, do you?"

Darling smiled. "I feel I should, but I don't. I fear it's a flaw in my own character."

"Do you think he got his mail in Kaslo?" Lane asked as they made their way back up the hill. "I mean, maybe he's received a letter or two that might tell us more about him."

Darling looked at her and rolled his eyes. But when they were in the car, he said, "Ames, set a course for Kaslo."

CHAPTER TWENTY-TWO

WITH SOME RELUCTANCE, AND AFTER a close inspection of Darling's warrant card, the woman who handled the mail in the dry goods store handed him one envelope. "It came earlier this week. He never got no mail to speak of. One letter a week or so ago, and now this. It's not even a real letter. It's just a returned letter he sent out. 'Addressee unknown.'"

"Your reward, Miss Winslow, will be to read this letter to us, as I suspect it is in a foreign language." Darling passed the letter back to where she sat in the back seat as they drove out toward the Nelson road. "One thing it may tell us is who else might know him. It's addressed to Hans Bremmer at Tomslake here in British Columbia."

"I think that's up north somewhere, sir," said Ames.

"That narrows it right down, thank you as always," Darling said. "Miss Winslow?"

"German," she said, when she had it open. "It'll take a minute. I'm more used to reading printed German." She read silently for a few moments. "'Dear Hans: Sorry I didn't write before, earlier' . . . something like that. 'I've had no word, or news, of anyone from the old days. I don't even know what happened in the end. Your . . . your' . . . ah . . . 'little ones must be grown up now . . . it has been eight years. I enlisted, as you know and am living in the south now. You would not be . . .' I can't read this word . . . 'proud,' maybe? 'You would not be proud. I live like one of those crazy men in a . . . small hut,' maybe . . . 'by a creek and work in a mill. I don't mind. I am not fit for anything else. It is a kind of . . . banishment? Exile? I will not be free until I know of Julia from the Red Cross. They always told . . . tell . . . told . . . me everything will be fine. If she was in a refugee camp she will be helped. But, Hans, I already feel in my heart she is dead, and the children, her husband. It is my fault, you see. I managed to get to the lists on the papers, but I did not get to the people on time to make them come with me to Poland.' This is sad. Is Julia his sister? The one in the photograph?" Lane asked, rhetorically. "There's one more section. 'Really, I write to tell you that I saw him, our very own local Bahn führer.' That's 'train commander,' I suppose. I think he means more of a dictator, given his communist leanings. 'You won't credit or believe it, Hans, he is a local man. No doubt he took all our money and made himself rich. I accused him to his face. I marched into his office. Like the old days! I confronted him and he kicked me out. I told him I would tell everyone the truth. He could not care less. I am like a fly . . . he pushes . . . swats,' maybe, 'me away. But he will know I don't forget ever what he put us through. Maybe I will come back one day and see you, but I will not lie. I never want to see Peace River again. You know me. I'm a hot head. I'm writing because I want to find out what happened. I want to be fair. Just because he didn't give us what we were promised, I suppose doesn't mean he took it for himself. So maybe in the end you got it all? Please write and tell me. Maybe after all, I won't have to kill him. You see. I still have a sense of humour. Ha ha. Yours, etc., Klaus Lazek.' Well, what is to be made of that?"

"It's most irritating that he hasn't named the man he says he confronted, but I suppose both he and his correspondent knew the name, so he didn't have to bother," Darling said. "Ames, slow down at this corner."

"Sir."

"What do we know about this man, besides that he's nasty?" asked Lane.

"Not enough," Darling said flatly. "Can you make a translation for us? I will leave you with this, and we can arrange for pickup when you're done."

LANE STOOD WATCHING with some regret as Ames and Darling disappeared up the road from her house. She stayed at the top of her drive to listen as the car turned the corner and started down past the church and onto the road to Nelson, and then she turned listlessly toward the house. It was a beautiful afternoon, and the peas were waiting to be picked, after all. But instead, she went to her writing desk where the papers comprising her map were piled. She spread them out in their correct sequence and taped them to the kitchen table. They knew so much more now. The man's name, where he lived, who he travelled with to work.

And this extraordinary letter he sent. Not where he died, or why. As usual she wrote in everything she knew, under the headings of the places where things could reasonably be supposed to have happened. What struck her when she stood over the map, with a cup of tea in hand, was that the locus of all the activity was Kaslo. He must have died there. No doubt Darling and Ames would be concentrating there, interviewing more people. The other thing that caught her attention was that, according to Darling, the man named Bronson had seen the disagreement at the bar, and some other men . . . there were several? Was that right? Or did he say a number? Apparently these men were not part of the usual group there. And that, according to Bronson, some of those miners were part of some secret, or maybe not so secret, fascist society.

Not for the first time, she wondered about Mrs. Castle's son, Carl. He had disappeared right around the time they'd found the body. What if he belonged to this secret whatever it was, and was one of the strangers at the bar that day? This gave rise to other possibilities. He could have killed Klaus Lazek and fled, or he could have seen who killed Lazek and been killed himself. She mentally shook her head. No body. Yet. She made a mark on the map roughly where they had found Lazek's lonely dwelling, and then put the pencil in the jar where she kept her sharpened pencils.

Though the day called out to her, she sat down and translated the letter. What came to her forcibly was that there seemed to be invisible strings connecting dead Klaus, missing Carl, and the local politician and prat. The memory of Lorimer's secretary driving that big car away from the

Castle house came to her suddenly. She shook her head. She could maybe draw a string between Lorimer's secretary and Castle, ostensibly involving the business of picking up eggs. But none of that was of any use. Later, while she was outside picking peas and reflectively eating them before they got into her basket, something scurried forward from the very back of her mind.

February 1939

LANE WINSLOW'S NEW flatmate, Irene, stubbed out a cigarette and brushed the ashes off her flannel nightie. They were both lying in their beds, battling the cold with thick duvets and extra blankets. The blackout curtain helped keep some of the damp cold out, and there was an illusion of warmth from the little lamp between them that threw an orange light over the bedside table. Lane sighed, flipped her book over and lay on her side, her elbow propping up her head, and looked at Irene.

"You ought to give it up. It's smelly and costs money."

"It's terribly sophisticated. Haven't you been to those dances? If you have a ciggy in your hand, fellows leap from all sides wanting to light it for you. Nothing else garners attention like a cigarette. Anyway, it calms me down."

Lane, whose only experience with tobacco had made her feel giddy and light-headed and the very furthest thing from sophisticated, asked, "Why do you need calming down?"

Irene laughed mirthlessly. "Dearie, there's a war on. We all need calming down. And I know I'm not supposed to say anything, but today—"

But Lane stopped her. "Then don't. The war and all that." She didn't know for certain what work Irene did, nor did Irene know hers. That sort of sharing was strictly off limits.

"No, but this is nothing like that. I don't think it's hush hush, and anyway, I was only going to ask a question. If we're at war with Germany, why are we bringing Germans here? That's all I want to know."

Lane frowned. She knew Irene was a German speaker, and she suspected that it was this skill that was being put to use. What did Irene mean, "bringing Germans here"? Lane could think of no operation that involved bringing Germans into the country, though she could imagine that there must be double agents at work for Britain. And she was certain that people passing themselves off as English were in fact Germans and no doubt engaged in espionage. The reverse was certainly true.

"You know, Irene, I don't think you should say anything more. You know the rules."

"I know, but they brought in a boatload the other day. Refugees, they called them. I was sent down to translate. I mean, we already must be knee-deep in German spies, and we have plenty of British sympathizers. Bastards!"

Against her own better judgment Lane said, "Refugees? They're bound to be Jews then."

"Yes, I suppose one or two were, but the rest were Germans, with German names. From Sudetenland. Doesn't that strike you as odd? Hitler goes barrelling over there to liberate the German masses stuck in Czechoslovakia and starts this bloody war, and now suddenly they're swarming over here. I mean, yes, there were women and children, but that's good cover, isn't it? I mean, it's incongruous. They're busy rounding up 'enemy aliens,' like my poor friend Suzy who had the misfortune to come here as a child with her family, and sending them off to Australia in ships. At the same time, in come a whole lot of Germans on other ships."

"Maybe they're planning to send them to the colonies too."

"They better be. Where are they going to stash that lot in this country?"

"GOOD EVENING, INSPECTOR. I've remembered something. In fact, I don't know how I didn't think of it immediately. It was rather a big thing at the time. I say, is Ames all right? He seemed a little distracted today."

"As do you. Any chance you could finish one thought at a time? I should mention, before we go on, that I miss you."

"Nonsense. We saw each other only hours ago," Lane said. "You have a lovely voice, do you know that?" She wondered suddenly what would happen if they ever lived in the same place and she could not hear his voice on the telephone every evening, intimate, resonant.

"I'll not allow you to introduce one more subject into the conversation. I had something to say as well, you know, which I will get to in a minute. Ames is a little distracted. Well spotted, you. Girl trouble. I think he's going to break it off with his current flame, Violet. He will make a hash of it. I'm afraid I can't help him much. I've little experience with such things."

"You've never broken off with anyone?" Lane asked. "Never?"

Darling uncrossed and then recrossed his feet on the ottoman in his sitting room. He felt a bit guilty that he was lounging in comfort on an easy chair with his feet up, gazing out his large window at the twinkling lights of Nelson below him, and she was having to stand in her hallway, leaning on the wall. He wondered momentarily if he should feel guilty about never having told her about the disaster that was Gloria, his very failed wartime romance. Still. She had never given any details about being mixed up with that perfect ass Angus Dunn.

"Well, hardly ever."

"For the record, it is you who has introduced Gilbert and Sullivan. What were you going to tell me?"

"You first," Darling said.

"All right then. I remember now that as the war was starting there were a whole lot of British refugee organizations wanting to help German refugees from Czechoslovakia. It came to me because I was thinking of the words on the back of that photo. I thought they were Polish, but I see now they could have been Czech or Slovak. My roommate in London was complaining about it, asking why all these Germans were coming to England. When Hitler went in to 'liberate' Germans living in that region, he immediately put socialists and trade unionists in his sights. Of course Chamberlain didn't think about those people when he decided to overlook Hitler's annexation. So while I'm not sure how they did it, they managed to get a load of people out through Poland and Sweden and bring them to Britain, and I think some of them ended up here in Canada. Everything points, fairly obviously I now see, to poor Klaus Lazek being one of them. And his reading matter. He must have been one of the socialists that had to flee. And I'm guessing his friend Hans Bremmer was one as well, though he seems also to have left where they were originally made to stay."

"Ah. There should have been something in the papers if they came here. I was in Europe, so I knew nothing. I'll get Ames to go to the library and look at the papers from the early years of the war. It will keep him from thinking about the mess he's about to make."

"You're always so thoughtful. What prompted this breakup, anyway?"

"Well, here I think I have to hand him some credit. Apparently he and Violet had a disagreement about children. She thinks they should get thrashed from time to time, and he is against it. I'm rather inclined to agree with him, I think."

Lane looked down at the patterns on the Persian runner that graced her hallway floor, surprised at the sudden compression in her chest. An unbidden image of herself being held nearly aloft by one arm as her father spanked her. For what? How old could she have been, four? For a second she could remember her own choking fear.

"Darling?" His voice was softer, concerned.

"I was just remembering something. Ames has gone up in my estimation even more. And you know, I'm glad we agree on this. It's important, don't you think? Now then, what did you want to say to me?"

After a beat, Darling said, "I was so taken with Lazek's letter that I forgot to mention this. That's not true—I just didn't want Ames in on the thing. Anyway, I've been given an invitation on expensive stock in overzealous script for an evening with Councillor Lorimer, who wants to celebrate the good works of exemplary citizens. As much as I would like to give it a miss, he will possibly be my boss one day soon, and I wouldn't like to do anything to make our police work any more difficult. What do you think?"

"Indeed. You can inspect him up close in his native habitat before you decide how to vote. How splendid! What will you wear?"

"My only suit, and I was rather hoping, you on my arm. Apparently I can bring a date."

"Funnily enough, I do have something to wear," she said, thinking of her lovely outfit. Yvonne had been right. If she had the dress, the occasion would come.

"Ah. I may be forced to hire proper evening dress. I didn't know you had fancy clothes. It's true that I can get a closer look at him, but I'm planning to use you as a distraction while I sneak into his study and rifle through his papers. I've always been suspicious of his business practices. Then when his henchmen drag me outside for a good hiding, you can scoop me up and take me to hospital. What do you say?"

"Yvonne told me that if I had the outfit, the party would materialize. When is it?"

"On Saturday."

"I suppose I shall have to pack an overnight bag, if I'm to mount a vigil at the hospital by your nearly lifeless form," Lane said, her smile carrying all the way down the line. "Why would you be rifling through Lorimer's papers again?"

"No reason. I just don't like him." Darling was joking, but he couldn't shake the idea that if anyone bore closer investigation, it was a man like Lorimer. How often did businessmen with a high profile and dubious business practices manage to charm their way into public office?

CHAPTER TWENTY-THREE

Friday, July 18, 1947

CARL PULLED THE CHEVY ONTO the grass beside the garage and got out. He wasn't overly enamoured with Fridays. The weekends ought to be restful, but he spent his working on the farm, fixing things and helping out with the deliveries. His mother was none too cheerful. She seemed always to be in a bad mood recently. It was getting to be time to move out, set up on his own, but he could think of no way he was going to be able to leave her to run the farm by herself. He found his time at his own job, away from the house, restful. He was starting to think he should go to more of those meetings. "Morning, Mr. Van Eyck!" he called out.

"Carl, son, come over here." Van Eyck came around from the inside of the garage and gestured for him to come in. "This is my daughter, Tina. Just got home from England."

Carl was going to offer his hand, but Tina, dressed in coveralls and with a scarf holding back her blond hair, was wiping her hands on a greasy rag. He nodded instead. She was pretty, he thought. An oval face and blue eyes. A little older than he was, maybe.

"The thing is, Carl, Tina is an experienced mechanic. She worked over in England during the war. Was going to marry a fellow there . . ." At this, Tina scowled at her father. "All right, all right. The point is that she's going to be working here."

Carl raised his eyebrows. Was there work enough for two mechanics—if she was a real mechanic? He'd probably end up fixing everything she did. "Is—" he began, but he was never able to ask the question.

"I have to think of the bottom line, Carl. I must make enough money to keep us and the business going. Tina isn't going to cost me a thing, so as much as it hurts me, I'm going to have to let you go. I'll give you a good reference, of course. They've got a big outfit in Kaslo, looks after the mining and logging trucks. I bet they can use the help. Look, I feel bad. I've put two weeks' salary in here for you. That should hold you till you get your next job."

When Carl was driving angrily away, he couldn't remember what he'd said. The last thing he heard Van Eyck say was, "Now don't make me regret . . ." Regret what? Carl would never know. He got up onto the main road and paused, the dust from his sudden stop swirling around him, blowing forward on the breeze off the lake. He couldn't go home, that was for damn sure.

"YEAH, WELL, THE war's over, and we need to think about ourselves. What did we fight for if we come back and find the place overrun with Chinks and Jews and women doing men's work?" The speaker put down his beer and wiped his mouth. He took his cigarette out of the ash-tray, knocked the accumulated ash off it, and put it back between his lips.

"Easier said than done. How do you plan to get rid of them?" Carl Castle looked around the hotel bar. He'd had two or three beers; he'd lost count. When he'd first signed up for boot camp with Heppwith, it had been fun. Now Heppwith seemed angry all the time. Maybe something had happened while he'd been overseas. Carl was wondering if he'd made a mistake seeking him out, but Heppwith had sent him a note inviting him to one of his damn meetings he was always going on about. He worked at one of the mines. He might know of some work for him.

Buck Heppwith shook his head. "Things need to get back to normal. You never used to see women poking their heads in where they weren't wanted. Look what's happened to you. When a decent hardworking vet loses his job to some bint, you know things aren't right." He looked at his watch. "Drink up. Time to go. Wait till you meet Gus. He's the real thing, I promise you."

Carl found himself in the sitting room of a boarding house that smelled of sweat and unwashed work clothes. A pall of smoke caught the light of the single bulb and eddied in murky brown swirls. He looked around the room. Which one was Gus? And what made him real? Would this be like that last meeting? There was a man sitting in the front row with a suit on. Was he the one? Men were talking quietly. Someone laughed at a joke and then was silent at the sound of a gavel hitting the wooden table toward which the chairs in the room were turned.

"Good evening, gentlemen. For those who don't know me, I'm Gustav Sadler and I'm with the National Unity Party of Canada. Thank you for coming, and thank you for bringing a friend. We will need every recruit in the coming fight. Now, I want to tell you something. I'm a loyal Canadian. And do you want to know how I can prove that? I spent the war in a prison, right here in this, my, country. Why? Because I dared to defend the values of God, honour, and country. Why, I asked the government, are we going to war with members of the white races, when the creep of coloured and inferior races is right around us here, growing and unchecked? This country was founded by the British, bravely conquered by the British, a wilderness made into a fertile and beautiful land by the British. What was my reward for my loyalty and my love for this great country? To spend the war in a stinking prison. But I wasn't alone. No, no. There were others. Proud members of the party, and now that the war is over, they cannot call us traitors anymore. Right-thinking people like us are in the ascendant, my friends, in the ascendant.

"We need to get back to the real roots of this country, to the loyalty we owe the Gracious Sovereign, to the maintenance of order and unity, to respect for authority. We need to be moved by our faith in God and a spirit of obedience. That is what I am offering, gentlemen. That is what I am offering. Who here would not want our great Dominion to be ruled by these simple and unassailable principles? What we need are members, gentlemen, members who can send a message to Victoria and to the rest of the country. Now, Herbert here has all the paperwork . . ."

Outside, Carl Castle sucked in a great breath of cool, clean night air. It was dark by this time. He had signed up for the National Unity Party, recognizing the truth of good men like him put out of work, and he was disappointed that he did not feel some sense of peace or purpose. If he was to be quizzed on why he'd signed up, he'd have said he needed a job, and one of these fellows could probably help him with that. He was jarred by a sudden pummel on the back from Heppwith.

"What did I tell you? You feel in your bones that he's right. I'm glad you signed on. You won't regret it! Let's get back to the bar. I want a drink to celebrate."

"He sounded a little bit like one of those Nazis. We used to see newsreels of Hitler in the army."

Heppwith laughed. "Want to know a secret? This party started out as a Nazi party in the thirties. Just because we went to war with Germany doesn't mean the Germans were wrong. That's why our leaders were thrown in jail. Obviously we don't use that sort of terminology anymore. It doesn't look well. But the values are the same. Good, strong, Christian, and British values. And we should fight to keep foreigners out of here. They bring their ways here and try to dilute what we have."

Carl nodded. His mother would agree. He felt a start of guilt. His mother. He hadn't gone home after his rage at the garage. He should have gone home, or called her. He felt, he knew, anger and shame, and he just couldn't face her. They were approaching the hotel. Light and noise poured onto the street through the windows and doors, opened to let in the warm night air. The other hotels nearby seemed to be doing a roaring business as well. He'd stay here for a few days. There was bound to be a job between the mines and the mills. Then he'd go home with something to show her.

The bar was loud, and they moved to where some of the other men from the meeting had already gathered at a round table. The man in the suit was at a table near the bar, talking to another man. The speaker, Gustav, approached him, and Carl saw them shake hands. The man in the suit made a gesture and then they all sat down.

"I'll go get them to bring us all another round," Heppwith said, throwing his jacket over the back of a chair.

Carl sat and submitted to being introduced to the other men, whom he'd seen at the meeting. He was worried about money. He'd been given that envelope by Van Eyck at the garage, but he didn't know how long he would need the money in it to last. He looked up at the bar. Heppwith was talking to a man who was sitting on his own. Carl watched as Heppwith gave him a pound on the back and gestured toward the table. The man looked back in their direction and then shrugged.

"Look, everyone, meet Klaus. Join us. I'm pretty sure we have a lot in common!" He winked at his new friend, who did not wink back. A man came into the bar and looked at Klaus, and then shrugged and moved off to sit at the end of the bar alone.

Carl nodded at the newcomer and then turned to the man on his other side, who had asked him a question about what he thought of the meeting and why he'd come. Carl explained that he had come to Kaslo to look for a job, and told the story of his having lost the one he had.

"To a woman?" the man asked incredulously, shaking his head. "Listen, you can be sure that guy is going to be sorry. I don't care if it is his daughter, his business will be under before he can turn around. No woman is going to be a mechanic. The idea is laughable! That's what's wrong with this country. It's only a few of us here, but people will get behind it. Look at that guy, he's from up the lake in Nelson. Came especially to hear Gus talk." The speaker pointed across the table to the man in the suit, who had turned away and was talking animatedly to a man at the table behind him, blowing smoke up into the fug that was beginning to grow thick in the room.

Carl had several more beers, his concern about his money dwindling. He'd not had a meal since breakfast and was feeling the effect of the drinks. When the burst of violence happened it seemed to Carl to come out of nowhere. Suddenly chairs next to him were being flung back, voices raised. Someone with a thick accent was shouting, "You're sick!" and pushing through the crowded room toward the door. The bartender was there suddenly, and Carl felt himself pushed back down into his seat. Frowning, he looked for Heppwith but couldn't see him. A group of men surged toward the windows, and some more stumbled over each other to get out. He heard shouting and staggered to the window, trying to see outside. A crowd had gathered and circled around two men fighting.

"What's going on?"

"Search me. Too much to drink, probably," said a man who was already losing interest and starting back to his table.

"Morons!" Carl heard someone say. He wanted to get out, to see where Heppwith was, but all the traffic was coming back into the bar. Finally he was on the wooden walkway. Heppwith was being helped up, and Carl went down the steps toward him.

"Leave me alone!" Heppwith shouted, shrugging off the help. "I'll kill that guy. Commie bastard!" he shouted down the street toward the waterfront. Carl looked, but the other man was nowhere to be seen.

"Come on, you should get cleaned up, have those wounds looked at," Carl said, but he didn't reach out to help him. The other men who'd tried were already back inside.

"I want my bloody bag! Where is it?"

"Is it inside? I'll go check. Sit here."

"I'm not sitting anywhere. I'm going after him, now get my bag."

Carl hesitated. Heppwith looked murderous. He'd been badly beaten, and he wasn't taking it well.

The men at the table he'd been sitting at looked up when Carl came in. Suddenly he felt sober. "Have you calmed Heppwith down?" one of them asked.

"I don't think so. He's pretty mad. I wouldn't want to be that guy. Is this Heppwith's bag? I'm hoping I can talk him into going home."

Back outside, Carl saw someone leading Heppwith up the road toward the rooming house where the meeting, which now seemed from some distant time past, had been.

Was it the man in the suit? What had happened to the other man, the one called Klaus? Heppwith had been looking down the road toward the lake. There was no moon and the darkness seemed absolute. Carl started down the road, feeling himself almost stumbling forward. The temporary feeling of sobriety had left him, and now he felt only the need for darkness and clean air. He'd never been to the lakeside here. He could see the large pier where a steamer was docked. A few bulbs hanging along the edge of the roof threw a small ring of light at the beginning of the pier. Otherwise it seemed to be unmanned and was encased in darkness. Farther to the right he heard a sound and stopped. He turned toward it and stumbled down an incline to a pebbled beach. His head whirled and he suddenly felt sick.

"Who's there?" Had he said it or had someone else? He was lying on the beach, recovering from vomiting. He thought he could see the outline of the pier.

Carl managed to stagger to his feet. He had been going to walk down toward the man but stopped. Klaus had beaten Heppwith badly. He could see the man moving dimly in the dark. He was leaning down and pushing something into a barely discernible rowboat. He didn't hear the men behind him till he turned and they were right there. A light went on, blinding him so that he turned away.

All he could think later was that he had to run as far away as possible.

KLAUS LEANED OVER and fumbled with the rope, one hand feeling for his ear, where sound boomed and billowed through his head. He reached into his pocket and found his knife and cut the rope, trying to sit up. He let the knife slip through his fingers into the water, feeling the boat under him bob with his movement and begin to drift free. He wondered that he couldn't hear anything but thunder. If he could just lie down and float . . . but he had to get home. Julia was waiting for him. He took up the oars and pulled. It was always much easier to go home with the current. How good it would be! The children would jump on him, laughing. He was so tired. Someone had been angry, he remembered a shot, the force of it tumbling him into the boat. He was glad it had not hit him because she would be inconsolable if something happened to him. She would be surprised to see him coming by water. The streets of their childhood were all rivers now, flowing past the factory, her garden, flowing, gathering into one great current. He closed his eyes to see the streets, but they retreated and all was darkness again. When the rain started he turned his face and felt the drops falling, and he knew water was above him and below him. He could feel it filling him, making his legs heavy. An oar slipped from his hand and he smiled, relieved of the responsibility. The night and the water pulled at him until he felt himself as heavy as the whole world, sinking into shadow. How she would laugh to see him in a boat!

CHAPTER TWENTY-FOUR

"WHAT DO YOU THINK?" LANE was standing doubtfully looking at the blouse and skirt draped across the sofa. She had met Angela at the post office, and her friend was only too thrilled to come over and inspect the new outfit and bubble excitedly about the fact that it came from a Paris fashion house. "Not too . . . I don't know . . ."

"It's not too anything. It's divine! That red will demand an equally red lipstick. And shoes! Have you got shoes?"

Lane, with some embarrassment at her own vanity and extravagance, pulled a pair of black suede open-toed pumps from a bag she'd tucked behind the sofa, and held them up for inspection.

"Well, I need to sit down! It's exactly what I would have expected of you. Stunning beauty and understated elegance!" declared Angela.

"Now you're being ridiculous. I feel I shall have to hide the whole affair under a long black cape to avoid notice. Now let's have a cup of tea and talk about anything else."

She put the shoes down firmly and moved to the kitchen to put on the water.

With their teacups on the veranda, and the lake laid out before them, the two women enjoyed an easy silence. Then Angela spoke. "Lane, there's no getting around it, is there, you and the inspector? No, don't say anything! I can see you love him madly, and if he doesn't already love you beyond redemption, he will be lost when he sees you in that outfit. So what are you going to do? You can't go on having this silly driving back and forth relationship, can you?"

"We don't just drive back and forth. We talk on the telephone every night." She regretted saying it as soon as the words came out of her mouth. She'd never told her friend about those evening calls.

Angela seemed to appreciate the confidence, and looked at her with concern. "You see? You want to be together."

"Angela, you know by now, I could never leave this house. And anyway, you are being a bit previous—he has no intention of marrying me, if that's what you mean by your coy 'being together.' He's something of a lone wolf, and in that regard he is like me. You see? We suit each other down to the ground, he in his territory, I in mine. Anyway, I'm not the marrying type. I'd be hopeless as a wife."

Angela shook her head. "What nonsense! You aren't in a novel, are you? You're real people, and real people, however exotic, follow convention like everyone else. Maybe you don't see it now, but there will come a day when you simply want to wake up with him beside you, you mark my words."

Lane could make no response to this. She could not disguise from herself the multiple times she had imagined the two of them together, unhurried and content in this very house. With a blasted dog. Wanting to change the subject, she said, "That poor fellow Klaus Lazek may have a connection to someone here. He wrote a letter to someone saying he'd seen someone he referred to as a 'dictator.' A businessman of some sort." She sat up excitedly. "If he's a big enough businessman, he'll be at this shindig of Lorimer's, I'll bet you anything!"

"So killing two birds with one stone," Angela said. "Seducing your inspector with that Paris original and spying on Lorimer's guests. I find him kind of smarmy. I'm not sure I'd vote for him. But there's that other guy, Whatshisname."

"That's why Lorimer will win," Lane said. "No one can remember the other candidate's name, which happens to be James Cray, and he is unfortunately the most boring man between here and the Pacific Ocean. Lorimer is ingratiating and smarmy and rich. No one should be fooled by him, but everyone will be. He will be voted in because everyone wants to be him. I hope someone close to him has done something perfectly vile and it will come out before he's elected. Lazek certainly implied that whoever he was writing about had."

"What sort of thing?"

Lane, ruefully conscious of how far away she was being from the British agent who could keep an official secret under any inducement, said, "I probably shouldn't say. I'm simply guessing about the possible connection between them. Darling, I'm sure, wouldn't thank me for gossiping like this!"

"You're no fun at all." Angela stood up and went back into the sitting room to look at the dress. "You watch out. Lorimer has a bit of a reputation. He will be making a play for you, if you're not careful!"

"I'm sure he won't do anything untoward in front of his wife."

LANE'S BAG WAS taken from her at the entrance to the Dade Hotel, and she was ushered to the front desk through a lobby with a once-plush carpet and heavy leather and wood chairs. The room smelled of stale smoke. Her heart sank slightly. The hotel had seen better days. She had thought about staying at a guesthouse, but she liked the freedom from the society of a garrulous landlady.

"You will be in the corner room on the third floor, madam. There is a nice view of the lake. I hope you will have a lovely stay. I have you checking out tomorrow at noon?" The man at the front desk removed the key from a mail slot behind him and signalled for the boy who had brought up her bag to accompany her to the third floor.

It was more than an hour before Darling was scheduled to call for her. She had brought a book to read, and a notebook, no doubt to be ready for the inspiration she was ever hopeful would suddenly seize her for some sort of groundbreaking poetry. Even so, an hour was a long time to live with this awful combination of anxiety and hope. Was it because it was their first real outing together? If they appeared at a "society" event together, it could never be taken back. She felt a little sad that what had seemed theirs alone would take on this more public face. Would it increase the pressure to be more conventional, as Angela had suggested? She pulled the skirt out of her suitcase and hung it in the closet, suddenly regretting the vanity that had led her to bring something so showy. Perhaps her anxieties were exaggerated. Smiling, she remembered what her practical and affectionate grandmother had said once when she was young and had asked desperately, "What will people think?" "Laneke," she had said, "you will soon learn that no one is thinking of you. Everyone is only thinking of themselves. You will feel liberated when you understand this."

So she was going into Nelson society. What constituted "society" in Nelson, anyway? Big business leaders, she supposed, members of the local legion, and Masons, the local gentry like that dog woman in the mansion. Not Lorenzo, she was certain. All people to whom she would be utterly insignificant, and whom she herself could not care less about, though she had rather liked the dog woman . . . Enderby, that was her name.

Feeling slightly more relaxed at the prospect of knowing someone at the fête, Lane ran a bath and laid out her hair brush and pins, and put the new lipstick on the dresser. Darling was most certainly not a member of the upper echelons of local society, and so no one would much care who he brought to the party, she told herself. She had brought the outfit because she rather liked how she looked in it, and Angela had been so enthused. The fashion, according to her and the magazines she showed Lane, was trending toward tight bodices and voluminous skirts, but Lane had loved the sleek, long lines of the silk skirt.

It was simple and unfussy, with just enough extra fabric creating a pleated fall down the back of the skirt to give it a touch of elegance.

Sunk into the bath Lane tried to give herself over to the luxury of hot water and an empty mind, but instead her mind used the opportunity to focus on the lines she was drawing between the people in the case. Reminding herself again not to jump to conclusions, she mulled over this new and unexpected connection between a businessman Lazek had found—according to his letter—to be an old enemy. How threatened or angry would that person have been about the confrontation Lazek described? Enough to kill him, or try to? She sat up, water cascading over the edge of the bath. What if, just what if Lazek had been speaking of Lorimer? She sank down again. That was palpable nonsense. A man like Lorimer would not have something murky in his past and still be running for mayor, and he wouldn't kill anyone. He'd have someone do it. She thought of his vile secretary. Her mind wandered past the mysterious businessman of Lazek's letter, and focused on Lorimer. She'd found him so unpleasant. Did that secretary of his simply drive Lorimer around in the fancy car, or did he have a more sinister job? And this brought her to the Castles. That very same man had visited Mrs. Castle in his fancy car. That was the part Lane couldn't understand. It connected Carl to Lorimer, but how? And why? And where the blazes was he?

When the phone on her bedside table rang, she was ready. She had pinned up her dark auburn hair, and put on the red lipstick Angela had seemed so keen on, and now picked up the receiver with her stomach in an uproar.

"There is an Inspector Darling here for you, madam," said the voice on the other end of the line.

"I'll be right down."

She slipped on the short black velvet cape she had bought in Nelson the day she bought the shoes and, taking a deep breath, made for the elevator. Darling was standing near the front door, not wearing his brown suit but a full suit of evening dress, watching people go by on the street.

"Hello," she said brightly, behind him.

Darling pivoted and saw her, his heart lurching. He took her hand and pressed it and then leaned close to her. "My God," he said. "Let's forget the party, and go back up to your room."

She turned so that her mouth brushed his, and then she smiled and said, "Absolutely out of the question. It took me an hour to assemble this! You polish up nicely yourself. You did hire a dinner jacket."

"There's a lot you don't know about me. For example, I can be reckless. I actually bought this damn thing. I've also just decided to throw my career to the wind and beat Lorimer to within an inch of his life if he tries anything with you." He took her arm, and under the admiring gaze of everyone in the lobby, they went out into the street where the maroon police car was waiting, Ames acting the chauffeur.

"May I say, Miss Winslow," began Ames.

"No, you mayn't," said Darling.

Ames smiled happily and made for the Lorimer mansion.

Lorimer's home was high on the hill above the town, rather appropriately looking down, Lane thought, on the lesser citizens whose more humble houses cascaded below him. Ames pulled the car into the driveway, and Darling got out to hold the door for Lane and then took her by the arm to lead her upstairs to the front door. Ames watched them fondly as they went up the stairs. To see his boss in a black evening suit with a beautiful woman on his arm was to suddenly see him in a new light. It had never dawned on Ames before how handsome Darling was. Momentarily awestruck, Ames put the car in gear and drove down the hill to the station, where he would occupy himself with paperwork until the appointed time for him to return to Lorimer's.

The evening was warm, and Darling and Lane were shown out to the back garden. They passed through a foyer and a sitting room that owed much to the opulence of the late-nineteenth century, all dark panelling and heavy drapes gathered at the sides of long windows. French doors issued onto a generous stone terrace, where the quiet buzz of the great and the good drinking champagne and gossiping filled the air.

The appearance of Lane and Darling caused anyone who saw them to fall silent, and for a brief and agonizing moment it seemed to Lane that every head had turned, and all eyes were on Darling and her. Lorimer peeled himself away from a stout person who looked like a crabby man of business and came to Lane with both hands out.

"Miss Winslow! How absolutely delightful." Lorimer reluctantly let go of Lane to shake Darling's hand. "You must be Inspector Darling, is it? You're a dark horse, aren't you? I'm glad you could tear yourself away from fighting crime and bring this lovely creature to my party.

Drinks over there, and later a light buffet supper and some dancing." He winked at Lane. "You will save me one? Ah. Here's my lovely wife, Linda. Linda, this is Miss Lane Winslow, who lives out . . . Balfour way, is it? And our very own Inspector Darling—the reason we sleep safely in our beds at night."

Linda Lorimer, slender and pale, wore a blue gown that nearly matched the colour of her eyes; those eyes gave her the cold air of someone who was constantly on guard and suspicious, despite her attempt at a smile. Once the formalities were over, Lane and Darling drifted to one end of the terrace and stood looking at the perfect, manicured garden and holding glasses of champagne.

"God, I shouldn't gulp it. I've not eaten much. I'll be tipsy if I'm not careful," Lane said.

"I haven't seen you tipsy. What are you like?" he asked, smiling at her.

"Not at all tidy, I'm afraid. Hopelessly emotional."

"I'm hopelessly emotional already," he said softly.

Lane felt herself flush and then said, "Nice garden. I could only dream of making my wild tangle into something as lovely as this."

"I much prefer your garden, as tangled and wild and mysterious as it is."

"Right, Inspector. That's enough. Look. There's Mrs. Enderby from that Tudor place up the lake. Eleanor's puppy comes from there. Would you like an introduction, or shall I go take refuge with her on my own?"

"You go on. I'd better do the politic thing and get around and press some flesh, and keep an eye out for a dishonest-looking businessman." He took her hand where it hung by her side and gave it a surreptitious squeeze, and then moved off toward the man that Lorimer had been talking to. She watched Darling disappear into the crowd, and wondered if he was, like her, watching Lorimer with some interest. She had asked him in the car on the way up, "What do you make of the possibility of a connection between Lazek and Lorimer?"

"Nothing at all. I am the cautious inspector, you the impulsive amateur sleuth interfering where she doesn't belong. Just because Lazek mentioned a man of business, it does not follow that the man must be a confidant of Lorimer's. So rather than jumping to conclusions, let's both keep our eyes open, shall we?"

"Inspector," she had said, "are you impulsively asking me to help you?"

"No, I am not. But since you're here, I might as well make use of you."

Now Lane approached Mrs. Enderby and was rewarded by that lady turning away from a plump woman encased in pink chiffon whose mouth was permanently set in disapproval. Mrs. Enderby smiled at Lane in delight.

"Mrs. Enderby, how lovely to see you," said Lane, meaning it. The icy reception from the lady of the house had nearly undone her.

"You are a sight for sore eyes, my dear. Look at you! Every woman pales next to you. How is Eleanor's little Alexandra getting along?"

"She's splendid and, surprising for one so young, an excellent little guard dog. She was certain when they came back from somewhere the other day that someone had been in the house. She had her little ears down and was growling ferociously."

"They are very loyal, and quite indomitable, the wee Highlands. And had someone been there?"

Lane frowned. "Yes, unfortunately. While they were away someone had been in and helped themselves to some rather priceless antiques. Priceless in and of themselves, but especially priceless to the Armstrongs."

"Oh, dear, yes! I've heard that's been going on, but I thought it was more at our end, near town. I'd no idea it had gone so far up the lake! I've taken to locking all my doors. I've told William to let no one in we don't know. Have the police been able to do anything?"

"Nothing yet, I'm afraid." Lane looked across the terrace and down the stairs to the well-coiffed garden. "Lorimer got a puppy too. I guess it wasn't invited to this do," she said.

"That was the very thing I was wondering about myself." Mrs. Enderby leaned in and whispered, "I'm not over-fond of the man. Bit of a humbug if you ask me. He wouldn't get my vote, I can tell you."

Lane laughed. "I'm glad to hear it. Those are my sentiments exactly. Look at all these servants. He's got much too much money." Then she frowned. There was a man in the black-and-white uniform worn by all the servants in the house standing at attention by a side table with hors d'oeuvres laid out. He looked familiar. Her brain whirred so that she nearly missed what her companion was saying.

"But he didn't come by it all honestly, you mark my words."

"There does seem rather a lot of it, certainly," Lane said. "Mining or logging interests?"

"And then some, if the rumour is to be believed. He used to work for one of the railway companies before the war. I only get invited to these soirées because I'm a member of the local bourgeoisie. He must know I can't abide him. He'd better be treating that dog properly, that's all I can say."

LATER, SUPPER OVER, Lane was feeling slightly giddy as she watched the couples begin to drift onto the dance floor cleared in the great central hall. A small orchestra at one end of the room had begun playing popular show tunes. Darling, who stood with his arms crossed next to her, leaned in and said, "Shall we?" and offered his hand.

Lane looked at him in surprise and felt her face grow warm. "I didn't know you danced."

"I'm not a complete heathen, you know. I was young once, and at university. Dancing was very de rigueur on Saturday nights." He led her onto the floor and put his arm around her, his open hand warm on her back.

"You trot a pretty good fox," she said. "I don't know if it's you or the champagne, but dancing suddenly feels like the most wonderful thing in the universe."

"It's me," he assured her, pressing her closer.

Lane was readying an answer when she stopped suddenly, holding Darling's hand tightly. "I've remembered. He's over there looking at me."

Darling, alarmed by this sudden change in her tone, searched toward where Lane was looking, but he saw only one of the servants turning away with dishes in his hand. "Who? What have you remembered?"

"He's the phone man. I'm certain of it! And it's just dawned on him as well. He was staring at me as if he were trying to place me."

Darling pulled her to the edge of the dance floor. "Are you—"

"I saw him at the inquest too!" she exclaimed, interrupting him. "I noticed him because he threw his cigarette on the floor and stubbed it out and left it there. I thought what swinish behaviour it was. He was impersonating a phone man and now is impersonating a waiter. Can he be 'casing the joint,' as I've heard it called? Lorimer should know he may have an imposter here eyeing his knick-knacks."

CHAPTER TWENTY-FIVE

"WHY DID YOU PHONE THE police?" Carl's voice down the line sounded desperate, angry. "You've only made everything worse."

Vanessa Castle, who had felt wild with relief at the sound of her son's voice on the phone, now felt growing anxiety. "What was I supposed to do? You disappeared like that . . . I was desperate. I thought you'd had an accident or something. When they took me to see that man who was shot, I was beside myself! I thought . . . where are you?"

"What man? What are you talking about?"

"The police. They found some man who was shot and they thought he might be you. He was in the hospital. Where are you? Why don't you come home? What is going on with you?"

"Then he's not dead—if he dies, I'm done for. Did they say where they found him?" Carl's voice was breathy and he was almost whispering.

"I can't hear you properly. He did die. Carl, do you have anything to do with him? Who is . . . did you . . .?" Vanessa Castle sat down, her words high pitched in her panic. "And that man. A man came in a big expensive car. He was asking for you. He said he wanted to find you because he had a job for you, but I didn't believe him. I told him I don't know where you are. Is someone after you? Carl, what have you done?"

There was a long silence at the other end of the line. Vanessa thought he'd hung up, and was about to call out when he spoke. His voice was calmer, hard. "Listen, Mother, I'm all right. You can stop fussing. I have to go away for a while. I'm sorry about the car. Don't tell anyone, anyone! Do you understand? I didn't call, you don't know where I am. Please say you understand, Mother!"

"I don't understand! If you're in trouble, I can help you. Please, you must come home, then we can do something."

"No one can help me."

Vanessa sat, the receiver in her lap, the loud hum of the phone the only sound after the slamming down of the receiver where Carl was, somewhere, alone and in some sort of trouble. All she could hear, over and over, was her son saying, "If he dies, I'm done for." Vanessa could not remember ever being so sick with fear.

LANE STOOD AT the edge of the whirling couples. The band played a tune from *Oklahoma*. She knew this only because she had seen the production in London earlier in the summer when Darling had miraculously been freed. A man in a white suit sang, "Your hand feels so grand in mine. People will say we're in love . . ." She watched the table where the waiter had been, waiting for him to come back. Darling had disappeared into the crowd in search of Lorimer. Much to her dismay, she saw Lorimer approaching her, no doubt to claim his dance. She took a deep breath. Seeing neither the phone man she was watching for nor Darling, she pasted on a facsimile of a smile.

"You are abandoned, my dear, by your careless companion. I see my chance!" He offered his hand. "What has happened to Inspector Darling?"

"He went off to find you, in fact," Lane said, frowning. "Did he find you?"

"Not yet. I'm sure he'll find me if I'm with you." He smiled ingratiatingly and bowed. "Do you know what about?"

She was tempted to tell him but thought Darling would not necessarily appreciate her interference. "I'm not sure," she said noncommittally.

"Well, then, let's throw caution to the wind until I am clapped in irons!" Lorimer said, offering his hand again.

Surprised that it was not slimy, Lane allowed herself to be escorted into the middle of the throng. She saw Mrs. Lorimer in the arms of an elderly burgher nearby. She had the air of having spent the entire dance trying to keep an eye on her husband, and her face lit with angry triumph on seeing him escort Lane onto the floor.

"Do you know what I find myself wondering?"

Lane had no desire to learn what he was wondering. Lorimer was holding her unnecessarily close, and she could feel his breath on her cheek. "No," she said politely.

"I wonder if you are not a good deal too good for a policeman." His hand curved around her waist. "He's a little man. Provincial. You are surely made for grander things. Now I could . . ."

Lane, her heart pounding with rage, would never hear what he could do—offer himself, a bit on the side? Find her a wealthy friend who could keep her in the style to which she ought to be used?—because one of the expressionless servants in white gloves came across the floor and whispered something in Lorimer's ear.

"My dear, I'm so sorry. This must be the summons from the inspector. Please forgive me. I shall make it up to you."

Over my dead body, she thought, as he led her to a plush seat on the opposite side of the room from where he had collected her. She waited until she had seen him hurry across the floor to the service door through which she had seen the phone man, as she now thought of him, disappear, and then she moved around the room to the place Darling had left her and would expect her to be. She sat with her legs crossed watching the dancing and mused on Lorimer's joke about being clapped in irons. It was a jest made by a powerful man who knew he was immune to such a fate. No. That wasn't fair. It could easily be the joke of a man who was as innocent as a lamb. And then, unbidden, the thought came to her that the phone man-cum-waiter was not a threat to Lorimer at all, but one of his henchmen. All right, "henchman" was a bit strong as well, and it implied that if there was a ring of antiques thieves, Lorimer was in on it. She shook her head. He was smarmy and not her cup of tea, but that didn't make him the boss of a criminal gang.

"Can't even stay put where you're told to," Darling said, interrupting her flow of thought. "I saw you dancing with him looking pleased with yourself. Naturally I felt obliged to interfere."

"I was distracting the host by dancing with him. I need a bath. I hope you riffled through his files. There's bound to be something unsavoury."

"Very funny. He was extremely grateful to hear he might have a criminal in his midst. He hired people for the evening, and Phone Man was among them. Lorimer gave me his name. Harvey Townsend. I left Lorimer on his way to dismiss the fellow and no doubt check the silver."

"I'm glad to hear it. I'm afraid I had the most uncharitable thoughts about Lorimer. I wondered, don't you know, if Townsend was in fact a confederate, I believe it is called, of his. If you hadn't arrived just now, I would have imagined Lorimer in charge of a criminal gang involved in all sorts, including the killing of Lazek."

"That's a bit of a stretch, isn't it? That's why we're the police and you're not. I told Ames to come back at ten. Have we had enough?" Some older couples were making their way to the door where furs were being placed onto the shoulders of the ladies, very unnecessarily, Lane thought, in the middle of a warm August night, and beautifully brushed and rarely aired top hats given to the men. The whole thing had an air of a bygone era of grandeur. The music was picking up, and the room had become suddenly warm and noisy.

"Yes, I think so. You don't need to wait about to arrest Townsend?"

"I shall put Ames on to investigating him in the morning. If he's a seasoned confidence man, I expect he has a rap sheet. With any luck Ames is out front. He's bucking for a promotion, so he won't be late."

When they were on the steps of the curved driveway, they could see Ames waiting in the lineup of cars collecting people. Lane put her hand through Darling's arm, prompting him to look at her.

"You're ridiculously beautiful," he murmured.

"Never mind that," she said. "I've just remembered something. When I was talking to Mrs. Enderby, who doesn't like Lorimer, I might add, she said that he used to work for one of the rail companies."

"And ridiculously annoying. What relevance does that have at this moment?"

Lane leaned close to him so that she could feel the warmth of his skin. She smiled and nodded at a couple finally getting their car. "'Bahn führer' in the letter Lazek sent. 'Train dictator.'"

Darling looked behind them, where through the main entrance he could see the party going on. "You are a heady mix of intelligence and allure. Are you sure I can't come to your hotel? That moves the needle considerably closer to a firm connection between Lazek and Lorimer."

"Under no circumstances. We are not married. The hotel is already struggling. It could not endure such a scandal. Poor Ames, he's still three cars away. I think I was right to be uncharitable about Lorimer. Even if he is not the head of a criminal gang, somewhere in his past he's done something appalling. Maybe he was the one Lazek confronted and possibly threatened."

"Since you will not let me make love to you, I shall get Ames to drop me at the station. I will not sleep tonight, so I might as well go through the files. I shall be arbitrary and imperious and make Ames come to work too, because I know you will feel sorry for him. Finally!"

"Hello, Constable Ames. So nice of you to be on standby like this. I should warn you, the party has not improved the inspector's temper," Lane said sweetly.

"No surprise there, miss. Though if I may say so, I would have thought being with you would have cheered him up."

"You may not," said Darling.

"You see, Constable Ames, he is incorrigible," Lane said, taking Darling's hand in the dark of the back seat, her fingers winding through his.

"The hotel, sir?"

"No. This blasted party has scared up some things that need looking into. Drop me at the station, take Miss Winslow to the hotel, and then join me smartly. We've work to do."

"Sir."

"You can tell Miss Winslow your girl troubles on the drive. It will serve her right."

The street was deserted, the residents of Nelson no doubt turning in after listening to the ten o'clock news on the wireless, when Ames pulled up in front of the station. Darling turned to Lane to say something, but she put her hand on his lips and then kissed him softly. Ames looked doggedly ahead but was warmed by this overt show of their affection. It was a first, and he hoped it would not mean Darling would spend the next days storming about to cover the exposure.

Disarmed by the darkness and her lips, Darling found himself already prepared to punish Ames for his own frustration and sudden vulnerability. "Back here pronto, Ames. We have work to do."

They drove in silence for some moments. Then Lane spoke. "Do you have girl troubles, Constable Ames?"

"I don't suppose they're that bad. His majesty doesn't much like hearing about them. He thinks I'm a lightweight, I expect."

"I don't mind hearing about them at all, if that would help."

"It's just that I thought things were pretty open and shut with Violet, you remember her, miss, from the bank."

"I do, yes. Has something happened?" Lane asked.

"Not really happened. I simply don't know if she's the right one. Mother's taken against her, and while I suppose I should take no notice, I do. She's a good judge of character, my mother." Ames turned down the hill and then pulled around the corner so that he was in front of the hotel.

"What is she concerned about, do you think?"

Ames switched off the engine and turned so that he could face Lane, where she was leaning forward in the back of the car. "I don't know, to be honest, but I'm concerned. It was all about Violet saying it was all right to spank—'thrash' was the word she used—children if they are bad. I don't hold with that. If I married her and we had children . . ." He left the thought hanging.

Lane put her hand on his arm. She felt a wave of affection for him. "Ames, you're absolutely right. I don't hold with those old-fashioned children-thrashing ideas either. I was . . . well. The point is, if you married her and you fell out over how to bring up the children, it would be very painful for you."

"She seems to have given me the bum's rush, anyway, because I told her I wasn't sure I was ready to marry. But I'm a bit scared. She's done it before and then come back all lovey-dovey. I haven't told her I won't ever marry her. In fact till this moment, I don't think I ever told myself for sure."

"Poor Ames. You'll have to break it off properly. Well, if it's any consolation, I am completely in your camp. And I'm afraid Darling is in a mood. But perhaps working all night will help you forget about it for a while. Thank you—oh, blast! I've done something stupid! I've left my bag at the Lorimers'! I'm so sorry. Would you mind if we popped back up?"

Delighted to be of further service to Lane and much uplifted by her support, Ames was happy to oblige. They wheeled around the corner and back up the hill. "Less time to be with him, if he's in a bad mood. What did you two discover that made him want to go back to the office at this time of night?"

"Well, for one thing, remember the phone man we thought might be behind the robberies? His name, apparently, is Harvey Townsend. He was passing himself off as a waiter at the party, so Darling told Lorimer that he might be at the house looking over what he could steal. I must admit, I did wonder if Lorimer doesn't already know that about Townsend and has him on the payroll because of it. But the inspector said Lorimer was grateful to learn he had a possible thief in the house and went off to dismiss him."

"But you suspect Lorimer of something."

"I didn't at first, but a woman I was talking to earlier, from that big Tudor house across the lake, she told me Lorimer used to work for one of the rail companies. Of course, I right away thought of Lazek calling the man he had confronted a 'train dictator.' But then, I'm prepared to believe any ill of Lorimer simply because I don't like him. Not very scientific, I'm afraid. Just pull up here. I'll nip in and pick up the bag. I know where I've left it."

Ames parked to one side, out of the stream of cars, which had died down in any case, as the first wave of guests had left. He could hear the music through his open window. "Boogie Woogie Bugle Boy." He tapped his fingers on the steering wheel and enjoyed this feeling of—dare he call it—*friendship* with Miss Winslow. He began to ruminate on how he might take that final step and break up with Violet, and then he saw he was blocking a car trying to leave. He pulled down the driveway and turned off the engine.

Lane stood for a moment at the threshold of the dance floor. There were fewer people sitting around the edges. Most of the older people seemed to have left, and many more young people were flinging themselves around the dance floor. Smoke nearly obscured the high ceiling, and the heat of the room and the noise of people calling out over the din of the music made Lane pause. Her bag was on the terrace, and she'd have to plow through the gyrating throng to get to it. Then she realized she could go around the outside, just past the driveway. She'd seen a gate into the back garden. As she turned to go back outside, a couple barrelled into her, issuing drunken, laughing apologies. She smiled and lit back out into the hall and down the steps to the driveway. She could see Ames where he had pulled up farther along the lower curve of the driveway to wait for her.

The ornamental gate was a high and elaborate affair made of iron. She hoped it was not locked, but it opened easily and she darted through. The lights on the terrace had taken on a slightly forlorn air, now that the partygoers had gone inside. The path to the terrace was grass, and a high hedge blocked the house. As she approached the terrace she heard voices. Lorimer! She stopped and pulled close to the hedge and stood still in the dark.

"You're a complete incompetent. I asked you to take care of this, but I see now it is yet another thing I'm going to have to do myself."

"No, sir. I have it in hand." The second man was Townsend! Lane held her breath. Lorimer wasn't firing Townsend for being a thief; he was scolding him for . . . what? And what would he have to do on his own? Both men had stopped talking. Had they left?

"You know the saying. It's a fool who gets a dog and then does his own barking. You're my dog, Townsend. I suggest you don't forget it." Footsteps receded across the terrace.

Two sets of footsteps? She waited another long, agonizing moment and then risked inching forward to where she could see the terrace more clearly. Townsend was glaring out at the darkness, his hands in his pockets. Would he never bloody move? Lane could see her bag where she'd left it, under one of the chairs at the edge of the terrace nearest her.

She tried to make herself small and wished she had her watch, because she was sure it had been nearly half an hour since Darling had spoken with Lorimer. One thing was certain. What she had seen was not Townsend getting what Ames would call the bum's rush—it was an unhappy employer dressing down an underling.

Finally Townsend moved and appeared to be about to leave the terrace. He turned toward the path she was cowering on in the dark, as if he were going to skip the increasingly loud dance hall and slip away by the side entrance. Lane looked around in the dark, wondering where she could go, and realized she'd have to run to the end of the hedge and try to get around it before he got there. And then he pulled out a cigarette case and, having tapped the cigarette and lit it, he turned, kicked at a chair, and disappeared into the house, leaving a trail of smoke. On wings, Lane bolted to the terrace, snatched up her bag, and flew out of the garden.

"Let's get out of here," she said to Ames, between gasps for air.

CHAPTER TWENTY-SIX

THE NIGHT MAN AT THE police station expressed no surprise at seeing his boss come in the door looking irritated. He'd seen Darling irritated when he'd been on day shifts as well, though he was surprised to see him in evening dress.

"You look nice, sir. In mufti for some sort of stakeout?"

"Very funny, Officer Paxton. I had a proper invitation to this do, if you must know, and I'm now waiting for Constable Ames to get back here. I'm going up to my office. Send him up when he gets here."

"Sir." The officer, relieved not to have to entertain his boss, went back to his perusal of the back copies of *Popular Science* he got from his cousin, stateside. There was an article about outfitting a station wagon for camping and fishing that had been holding his interest until Darling had appeared.

Feeling ridiculous now in his evening clothes, Darling sat down and switched on his desk lamp. The file on the robberies, the missing Carl Castle, and the dead Klaus Lazek were stacked neatly in the wooden inbox. He pulled the Lazek file out and opened it. He had put Lazek's returned letter into the file, along with Lane's translation. Of course, Lazek had not named the man he had confronted, but the words "railway dictator" stood out. Mrs. Enderby had told Lane she thought Lorimer used to work for the railway. He had certainly been splashing himself about with adverts in the papers and wall posters as the election loomed. It would have been easy for Lazek to know who he was and how he could be got at. Darling took a lined foolscap pad from his desk, uncapped his fountain pen, and began a list.

Find out about Lorimer's past work.

How long had he been established in Nelson? He could not remember him from before the war, but anything could have happened in town while he himself had been away in England fighting.

Find out about Klaus Lazek's background.

Lane had said she remembered something about German refugees from the Sudetenland region of Bohemia in Czechoslovakia. Was he one of these? He added:

Call RCMP at detachment nearest to this Tomslake place.

He wanted to think about what the connection between Lorimer and Lazek might be, but he cautioned himself. There may be no connection at all, in which case he did not want to waste time trying to understand the meaning of such a connection. And even if there were one, it was a long way from implicating a local man of influence, however shady. Darling cautioned himself again that he didn't even have real proof of shadiness, let alone any connection with a sordid and botched up shooting of an immigrant all the way up the lake in Kaslo.

Darling thought again about the mechanics of the shooting. If, as Lane suggested, Lazek had been shot and then fallen into the boat, it would make more sense if he and his killer were standing on a pier of some sort above the boat. Though, he supposed, it could have happened on a beach. Lazek is about to take off in his boat, he's shot, he falls awkwardly into the boat, or is pushed. That would account for the boat being swamped with water. But so would the violent storm that night.

> *Look more closely along the waterfront in Kaslo. The fight was there, likely at night, and so probably was Lazek's killing.*

He put down the pen and looked at his watch. Where the blazes was Ames? He could have been there and back five times by now!

"ARE YOU SURE?" Lane asked. She looked straight ahead. Ames had been taking a circuitous route back toward Baker Street, going downhill and then dodging up the hill, and was now moving north, above the main street.

"Yup. He's about a block and a half behind me. He fell back when we came up here. Too obvious."

"Blast. I don't know where the hotel has parked my car. It must be on the street somewhere, or in the alley. If

I could find it, we could divide up, confuse him. He must have seen me. I saw Lorimer go back into the hall, and then Townsend followed him a few moments later. Townsend must have seen me going past the front entrance to get back to the car. And he must have spotted me at the party when I spotted him. Damn. I wasn't sure that he recognized me. Do you think he knows you're a policeman?"

"Not necessarily."

"Okay, if you can keep this far ahead of him, come down the block and turn so that you're in front of the hotel, and stop before he gets around the corner. I'll crouch down, and when he sees only you he'll think that I've gotten out. Move out slowly to give him time to see you, and you'll see if he continues following you. If it's me he's after, he may stop to think about what he ought to do next."

Ames drove slowly down the street, crossed Baker, and watched the car behind lag a block behind. He'd just have time to go around to the front of the hotel and make a show of saying goodnight. "Okay, now. Down you go. I'm going to open the passenger door so that it looks like you're out, and I'll wave and then close it."

He paused in front of the stairs and reached across to throw open the passenger door, watching in the rear-view mirror. The pursuer came slowly around the corner and stopped. Ames waved and shouted, "Good night!" and then closed the door. He fiddled with his gearshift as though it was stuck and then slowly pulled away, watching the car behind him.

"He's turned off his headlamps," Ames whispered. "It looks like he bought it. I think he's planning to stay put and keep an eye on you."

"Great. Drive up toward the station, only go a block past it to make sure he hasn't decided it's you he wants, and then go around and park at the side. And then let's wait a bit before we get out," Lane said.

Paxton, the night man, was rendered nearly speechless at the sight of Lane in her dazzling party clothes coming through the door. Between the inspector in evening dress and this apparition of loveliness, he could be forgiven for thinking he was suddenly in his very own Ellery Queen novel. He pulled himself together only when he saw that Lane was followed by Constable Ames looking, Paxton thought, a bit smug.

"How do, Paxton. Is the inspector upstairs?"

"Yes, he is. Good evening, miss." Paxton was on his feet.

"This is Miss Winslow, Paxton. It's all right, sit down, we'll show ourselves up."

Paxton did not sit down but went to the bottom of the stairs and watched Ames and Lane till they turned at the top of the stairs, and then shook his head, uttering a silent "Whew!"

Lane threw herself into a chair in front of Darling's desk. "We've solved one question, anyway," she announced to the dumbfounded inspector. "That Townsend man—of course we have no way of knowing that's his real name, but it's a fairly unusual name to come up with on the spur of the moment, so let's say it is—*is* one of Lorimer's henchmen. When I went back for my bag, there they were, as thick as thieves, talking together. Only, of course, the trouble is, I can't go back to the hotel now, which is a shame, because I'd like to go to bed. Oh, but you shouldn't worry. He thinks I'm there."

"You might want to start again at the top. Ames, have you any useful contribution? Because if not get back to your lair and make a list for tomorrow. You can use this as inspiration." Darling handed Ames his own list and then turned back to Lane. "Well? Why can't you go to bed, again?"

Lane told the whole story from the beginning. Darling frowned and leaned back in his chair. "One might almost suppose you'd left your bag behind on purpose," he said.

"Only a suspicious policeman would. I haven't got that much foresight. The point is, we have a situation. Oh, and by the way, any acknowledgement that I was right in my suspicion that Lorimer might have that man in his employ, gratefully-accepted."

"I don't see where we're in a position to be flippant. There's a man of unknown capacity for violence parked outside your hotel. Now what would he think he could do? What would Lorimer have told him to do?" Darling asked.

"Yes, I've been thinking about that. The question is, what is he aware of, and what is he afraid of? He knows you're a policeman, but the only thing he knows for sure that I could tell you is that he is the same man who claimed to be working for the phone company. He sees me come back for my bag, follows me out and sees Ames and not you, and decides to follow to see where I go. He's hardly going to surge up to my room to attack me. That would attract a lot of unnecessary notice. In fact, I'm sure that having assured himself I'm safely in the hotel, he will leave. He and Lorimer will have to get into a scrum tomorrow to decide what, if anything, to do about it. If he's smart, Lorimer, I mean, he won't do anything, because anything he does to try to fix the problem will only draw more attention. I bet the tail has already gone home to bed."

Darling grunted and then shouted, "Ames!"

"Sir?"

"Go back to the hotel and see if the car that followed you is still there. And while you're at it go into the hotel and make sure that there isn't someone in the lobby waiting, and ascertain from the front desk that no one has asked for Miss Winslow."

"I don't like this," Darling said, when Ames had clattered down the stairs.

"I know, darling. But there's nothing to worry about. The car will be gone, you'll drop me off at the hotel, and I'll have a big breakfast in the morning and then drive home unmolested and be out of your hair. I'll get back to my garden and my life at King's Cove with all the old dears. From time to time I'll come into town and you'll take me to lunch at Lorenzo's, as usual."

Darling pulled her hands, which had been resting on the desk, into his. "But things are not as usual, are they? You won't stay out of my hair. You'll find a way to interfere, and we shall have to have words about that. I don't want to argue with someone I love as madly as you. You are nosey and get into trouble, and then I'm forced to come to the rescue, albeit too late, which you don't like."

"Really, Inspector. You're making heavy weather of this. I'm capable of looking after myself, as you well know. I'll stay out of your way, I promise, and I won't need you." They interlaced their fingers, and Lane tried not to feel her heart racing.

"That's a shame. I'd like to be needed. Not to pull you out of burning cars or stop madmen from shooting you, but for the other . . . I keep trying to imagine how it will be when we are married."

Lane withdrew her hands and shifted back in her chair. He wasn't proposing to her; it was a bit of silliness, she knew. I'm supposed to feel elated, she thought, but all she felt was a wave of uncertainty. "Don't be silly. You can't want to marry me. It's . . . well, it's impossible, isn't it? Let's go on as we are, what?"

Darling, suddenly exposed by this easy dismissal of his feelings, stood up and went to the window. "What's keeping Ames?"

Lane watched him, crestfallen. Confused now, and fearful that she had destroyed what she so wanted to keep, she stood up and put her wrap on. "I'm sure he'll be here any moment. I'll pop down and wait for him outside. You both should go home and get some sleep. You've lots to go on with in the case." She turned and went out the door.

Darling followed her a moment later, and they were standing, not talking, when Ames pulled up with the unsurprising news that the car that had followed them was gone, and no inquiry had been made at the hotel about Miss Winslow.

Lane turned to the desk. "Goodnight, Officer Paxton. Inspector." She glanced into Darling's eyes and went out the door.

"Miss Winslow," he returned. "Get on home after this, Ames. I'll see you in the morning."

Ames watched this interaction, his heart sinking. Now what? He could scarcely leave them alone for a minute, he thought, and an arctic front would move in.

Outside the hotel he stopped the car. "Miss Winslow," he said as she went to open the door. She stopped and looked at him. "Miss, there's none better in all the world."

She smiled sadly at him. "I know that, Ames."

AMES WAS MAKING notes as the man on the other end of the phone talked. "Wait," he said suddenly, "can you just go back and read me that last set of names?" He hung up the phone, saying "Aha!" out loud to himself, and made for Darling's office. He was about to knock but then hesitated. Darling was standing at his window with his hands in his pockets, a pose Ames recognized as Darling's lost-in-thought stance.

"I can hear you there, Ames. You'd better come in, and you'd better have something for me." Darling turned, raising his eyebrows in expectation.

Cool customer, Ames thought. He doesn't look as though he's lost a wink of sleep. But this was good. "I think so, sir," he said in a triumphant tone. "I've been on to the RCMP in Dawson Creek, and guess what?"

"Ames!" Darling warned.

"Right, sir. So I initially asked if they had anything on a Hans Bremmer or a Klaus Lazek, but they didn't. However, he said there was a German community there that had come before the war as refugees. He said a lot of them had dispersed, and the program that sponsored them, which was run by the CWR, had terminated and handed the administration to the settlers themselves. He said he'd take a drive out to see if anyone could remember Bremmer or Lazek, and he'll get back to me tomorrow."

"Why would a railway company be running a program for refugees? Did Canada take a lot of refugees during the war?"

"Search me, sir. I could run down to the library and look at pre-war papers to see what was in the news. I honestly don't think so. But that's not the big news."

"Do I look like someone who wants to play games?"

"No, sir," said Ames hastily. "One of the administrators of the program was a man named Lorimer."

"You don't say," Darling said, fully engaged now. "Did the RCMP give any details?"

"No, sir. He was just reading off the names of people involved in the program. I could go down to the library and get into the old papers and see what I can find."

"You do that. And bring me back a sandwich when you're done." Darling watched Ames leave his office, pushing his hat onto his head in what Darling could only describe as a self-satisfied manner. Still. He reluctantly conceded that Ames had a right to a little elation. Lorimer, an administrator in charge of a program for refugees, and Klaus Lazek, one of those self-same refugees. Thinking of Lorimer now, moving smoothly among his guests, charming all and sundry, lying about his connection to Townsend—Bahn führer just about covers it, he thought.

Excited at having retrieved the information that might prove to be critical to the case, and relieved to have something concrete to occupy him, Ames made for the library.

He was a bit unhappy that this moment of triumph was ruined by the spectre of what he had to do later. He'd made a date to meet Violet to settle things once and for all. Even the thought of it made his stomach lurch, and he crossed the street to be as far from the bank where she was working as he could reasonably be.

Darling resisted the temptation to get up and stare out the window again. He had something, and he knew it. He took up the Carl Castle file. Hadn't Lane mentioned that she saw Lorimer's car going to the Castle farm? Ignoring the pang of anxiety he felt at the thought of Lane, he pondered whether this fact was something that might be important. Mrs. Castle had reputedly said Lorimer's driver was there to buy eggs, but that, in the light of this wearisome day, seemed ridiculous. Therefore something was up with Lorimer and the missing Carl. But what? And more importantly, it seemed very possible—no—probable, that something was up with Lorimer and the dead man. Now it was clear that all three cases were probably connected.

The inspector laid the files on his desk so that their corners touched and a triangle formed in the space between them, and then got up and walked around his desk, looking at them, trying to reconfigure all three problems into one. He took a piece of foolscap and on it wrote "Lazek's death" and plunked it in the space. Could they all be connected over the worst event? He sat down and swore under his breath, gathering the files into a pile. The connection between Lorimer and the man who might have been stealing antiques seemed much clearer, though Darling could not believe that even Lorimer would engage in something so petty as filching old people's antiques, but the connection between Lorimer and the missing Carl was so tenuous as to be ephemera that he could scarcely get hold of.

CHAPTER TWENTY-SEVEN

ANGELA WATCHED HER FRIEND QUIETLY. The morning was shimmering, and they sat on the beach keeping an eye on the children playing. "You can't mean that," she said finally.

"I do. I'm almost ashamed that I allowed myself to be drawn this far along in the first place. It was wrong, and now I've hurt him."

"You haven't been 'drawn along,' whatever that is supposed to mean. You fell in love with a wonderful man. Something many people would envy, a once-in-a-lifetime chance at real love."

"It's not for me. I'll make a hash of it. I'm not like you, uncomplicated and cheerful."

"Thank you very much. You make me sound like a collie puppy."

"Would that be so bad? Look, it's no good, Angela. I have a past lover for one thing, and men don't like that sort of thing. He'd only come to resent it."

"Because a man who fought overseas for seven years wouldn't also have one. Anyway, he's not 'men.' He's Inspector Darling. He is not the sort of man who gives his heart easily. Besides, doesn't he already know that?"

"Yes, but—"

"No buts about it. You're making stuff up now. Come on. What's eating you?"

Lane sat silently, picking up a handful of sand and letting it fall through her fingers. What was eating her? She tried to examine her own feelings. The feeling was very familiar to her. Fear. It was the same thing she'd felt right before jumping out of a plane or approaching a safe house in France, especially after a terrible botched connection once in which she'd found that the people she was meant to meet had been shot.

"I think I'm afraid," she admitted simply.

"Hmm," Angela said. "Or excited," she suggested suddenly. "I can hardly tell the difference myself sometimes. You don't want to make a mistake, Lane. He's deep. And he's terribly kind. You should have seen how he was with the children in the winter when he had to ask them about that poor sap who died at Adderly. I nearly wept."

"That only makes it worse."

"You're an idiot, you know that? Rolfie! Where do you think you're going?"

Lane lay back on the blanket and closed her eyes, letting the sun warm her face. Was Angela right? Maybe what she felt was excitement, or something like it. It occurred to her suddenly that she wouldn't have spent the entire war doing dangerous work if the only thing she had felt was fear. She sighed, tuned in to the sound of the children splashing and shouting, the feel of the sun and the fresh cool smell of the lake. Angela was right about one thing. She was an idiot. What she knew for sure was that she loved Frederick Darling. Perhaps, after all, that would be enough.

DARLING, HAVING SENT Ames off to look at back copies of newspapers, decided to take on the job of finding out if Harvey Townsend was a real name, and if the man attached to it had, as Darling hoped, a nice long rap sheet. He tried to ignore the sadness that enveloped him. While he waited on the trunk call to Vancouver, he replayed in his mind his remark about their being married, and each time he felt a wave of embarrassment, and then anger at himself. It was Gloria all over again, wasn't it? He, unguarded, too eager, she, well . . . saw their relationship completely differently. He was too much in love to see the lay of the land. Then, in a moment of mutiny, he thought, dammit, why shouldn't I be in love with Lane?

"Yes, hello? Yes, I've got a pen, thanks." He made notes as the police officer in Vancouver read things to him. "And does he have a regular fence?" He listened and wrote. It would explain why the antiques didn't appear locally, anyway. "Great, thanks very much for your help."

LORIMER RAN HIS tongue over his teeth and thought. He was sitting on his terrace with a cup of coffee. His West Highland puppy, whom he'd called Wolf as a little joke, was by his side chewing a leather bone. Lorimer was prey to a lively anxiety. It had been a near thing. He was certain he'd convinced bloody Darling, but then that woman—and here he could not repress a sigh of longing—had possibly caught sight of them together. But what did that mean? Nothing, really. What it meant was that Townsend was becoming a liability. He'd been useful and had put some prime pieces into his hands, certainly, but he couldn't afford to have a whiff of scandal if he was to succeed in the election. He'd have to cut Townsend loose. Carefully. One last job and he would be out. He'd had to deal with the first crisis himself. You couldn't trust people. That was the problem. Lorimer had thought of putting his secretary on the job, but he'd proved useless in an earlier matter. He was a good driver and a decent clerk, and he dressed well, but he wasn't smart enough to tackle anything too complex or legally delicate, so Lorimer had foolishly trusted Townsend instead, because he had the sort of background that would be useful to him from time to time. But it always came to the same thing. If you want something done right, you had better do it yourself.

He tousled Wolf's furry head. The only problem he needed to focus on now was finding a way to divest himself of Townsend. This resolve to fix the problem provided Lorimer with some relief, and from relief it was only a short road to reminding himself that he had a firm hold on the election, as Cray, his opponent, was a complete nonentity. Feeling much improved, Lorimer went off to see how the cleaning up was getting on. It had been, he was sure of it, the event of the season, and he had made very good use of it, buttering up the local movers and shakers. He was sure he'd have a brilliant brainwave about that one loose end.

AMES BOUNDED UP the stairs two at a time, making Darling's temples threaten to produce a full-blown headache. His constable appeared in his doorway holding a paper bag out in front of him. "Lunch, sir."

"You sound like a bloody moose coming up the stairs. What did you get me?"

Ames opened the bag and began to disgorge its contents onto Darling's desk. "Ham and cheese and a Coke. For both of us."

"At the library, Ames," Darling said with exaggerated patience, but still reached over to retrieve his lunch.

"Oh, right. It was very interesting. The papers in 1939 had articles saying that German refugee farmers were settling in the Peace River area here and in Alberta and over in Saskatchewan, under the CWR immigration and settlement department, and then in the next year the papers seemed to turn on them, and there began to be articles criticizing the refugees for complaining about mistreatment and having their money withheld, and that they had no right to, I guess, look a gift horse in the mouth. I'm hoping the call I get from Dawson Creek later today or tomorrow will fill me in a bit. Apparently they weren't really farmers. I'll tell you something, if you dropped me on a farm in the north and told me to get on with it, I'd be hopeless."

"You're pretty hopeless right here. Still, you managed, somehow, to get something useful. I, in the meantime have learned that Harvey Townsend is a real person, and he's an extremely dubious 'export import' man who deals mainly in antiques. He's been operating for a while, and the police in Vancouver haven't been able to get anything to stick."

Ames went into his own office, rummaged around in a drawer, and returned with a bottle opener. He popped the caps on both sodas and handed a bottle to Darling. "But why would Lorimer saddle himself with a dubious specimen like that? Lorimer's supposed to be an upstanding member of the community. Good for business, et cetera. At least that's the platform he's running on."

"Either he doesn't know about Townsend's past, or he does and simply doesn't care. Don't forget, Lorimer may be the very businessman Lazek confronted, and now he's dead. I see a third option: Lorimer's not too fussy about where and how he gets help to get elected. I wonder who else is helping him now?" Darling mused.

"I don't follow. What do you mean?"

"I mean, Ames, is he getting money from other crooks, or being supported by shady organizations that are more secretive than the Masons? I was quite interested, as I went around chatting with people last night, by how few people seemed to like him."

"Shouldn't you have been dancing with Miss Winslow last night?"

Darling's eyes darkened. "Ames!" he said gruffly. His warning was clear.

Ames got up, swept his crumbs off his boss's desk, and then backed up as far as the door. "I must say something, sir, with all due respect."

"No, you mustn't."

"Sir, you're making a mistake. You shouldn't fall out with her like this. Someone else could . . . anyway, she loves you. She told me."

"Just because you share your repellent girl troubles with me does not give you any right to discuss my business. Now get out!" Darling was on his feet and moving angrily toward the door.

Ames ducked out and hurried into his own office, where he stood listening anxiously to see if Darling would pursue him further, but he heard Darling's office door slam and breathed a slight sigh of relief. Darling could have accused him of not being able to handle his own life, and he'd have been right. Had he told Darling an untruth? Had Miss Winslow said she loved him? Not exactly, but he was certain that there was no other meaning to be put on the words she said to him as she got out of the car when he dropped her at the hotel.

O'Brien called up the stairs, "There's a call for the inspector. Can he take it? He seems in a bit of a mood."

"Put it through, and good luck to whoever it is!"

"INSPECTOR DARLING? THIS is Harry Bronson. You remember? From Kaslo. I used to pick Klaus up for work."

"Yes, of course. What can I do for you?" Darling did not stop to analyze the peculiar mix of relief and disappointment he felt that it was not Lane.

"I don't know if this has any bearing on Klaus's death, but I happened to be talking to one of the men who was at the table where all the trouble started. They were all at that meeting beforehand, it turns out."

"What sort of meeting was it?" Darling asked.

"Someone from an outfit called the National Unity Party gave a talk and was trying to get people to sign up. Well, not to put too fine a point on it, but they're practically Nazis. I can see why Klaus got into a big fight with them. He hated Nazis. He was a refugee because of them. They don't even do much to hide it. They have this little blue and red swastika symbol they use."

Darling glanced at the file on his desk. The swastika pin found on the beach. He would have to think through why an avowed Nazi hater would have one in the boat with him.

"Do you think you could identify the men who were at the table the night of the fight?"

"I don't think so. I don't work with those guys, and I don't drink with them. The best I could tell you is that I've seen them around town. And there were a couple of outsiders that night as well, I guess on account of the meeting."

"Thanks, Mr. Bronson. Is there a way I can get hold of you in case I have more questions?" Darling asked.

"I don't have a telephone, but I work at Green Point Mill, so you could find me there most days."

THE MID-AUGUST DAY had turned hot and felt dry. Lane had come home after the morning by the lake determined to do something completely distracting. The Armstrongs had told her ages ago that she could go through Lady Armstrong's box of things if it would amuse her. She might do that. When she had hung her bathing costume on the rail of her balcony and shaken the sand out of her blanket, she went up the stairs to the attic. The stairs creaked in their familiar way, and she felt momentarily comforted by the sound, and then saddened, because she had imagined being here with Darling in this beloved house, and she knew it was never to be. She'd put paid to that with her little outburst the night before. Best get on, she told herself primly.

The attic was a big open room with windows on all sides, and space under the slanting roof where wooden boxes and crates, both her own and those of Lady Armstrong, had been pushed. She had intended to open all the windows to try to pick up a cross breeze, but smiled when she found two of them already open. Lady Armstrong again, her benign window-opening ghost. But the day was so still that even with every window open wide, the room had simply collected heat. It was impossible to do anything in it.

She went back downstairs and stood in the shade cast by the blue spruce that grew by her front door. What would others be doing? Not moping about, that was for sure. She looked at her watch. Two thirty. Not quite teatime. She knew the Hughes ladies had a lie-down in the afternoons, and she envied them. If she gave in to the desire to nap, she would wake groggy and bad tempered, and it would steal any possibility of sleeping at night. At the moment she didn't think she could bear a long sleepless night of fear and guilt, or worse, an attack of panic and the shakes that had visited her from time to time since the end of the war. She tried to imagine reading or writing and could not. She felt profoundly listless. She could hear Robin Harris's tractor coming from above the Hughes' lower orchard.

On a whim she went to the intersection he would go through on his way home. The noise of his rattling old tractor increased as it approached her. He bumped up and down on the metal seat, a damp hand-rolled cigarette between his lips.

He stopped the tractor and looked down at her. "Well?" he said, as if she'd put herself into the intersection on purpose to stop him.

She smiled. "Hello, Robin. I was just out for a walk, but I'm beginning to think it was a mistake. It's hotter than blazes. How are you?"

"I'll do."

"Why don't you come to the house? I'll make us a cup of tea. You're on your way home for yours now, aren't you?" The rashness of this invitation struck her forcefully. Robin never "visited" the way other people did, and he hadn't been in her house since the summer before when they'd found the body in their creek.

"Do you have any biscuits?"

"Yes," Lane said. "I have a few from Eleanor and I have some chocolate bourbons."

"That'll do." He put the machine into gear and turned slowly down toward Lane's driveway. Lane, amazed by this turn of events, walked beside the tractor and waited while he parked it outside her gate and turned it off. The sudden silence lifted her mood a little.

Robin washed his hands in her kitchen sink and then sat at her small wooden table and picked a strand of tobacco off his lip. "You found another dead man," he said.

Lane smiled involuntarily at his characteristic brusqueness. "He wasn't dead when we found him. He died later in hospital. He'd been shot in the abdomen."

"I heard the coroner said he'd likely shot himself. Yes, please," he said to the offer of sugar. "What do you think?"

"I don't think anything. Thank heavens I'm not involved.

How's the crop looking this year?"

"Humph! That's a first. And since when do you care about the crop? You do bugger all about yours. You should have pruned those trees last year."

Lane felt a twinge of guilt. She had the vestiges of an orchard on the part of her land that was adjacent to his, and, aside from picking apples for herself, she had let the bears get the bulk of the takings. What to do about the orchard had begun to prey on her mind. It was a shame to let it fall into ruin, but she couldn't see herself becoming a farmer. "Robin, why don't you throw my lot in with yours? You're right that I can't let the orchard fall into ruin, but I don't—"

Robin shook his head. "You don't want to do the work. Typical. Apparently I don't have enough to do working the Hughes' crop and my own." He reached disapprovingly for a handful of chocolate bourbons.

"No, of course not. I'll pick them and box them, but you just sell them with yours. I don't really need the money." Ideal, she suddenly thought. I won't have to think about Darling at all if I'm up a ladder for the next while.

"I don't even know if what you have is worth selling. That orchard's been neglected since the old lady died."

"Why don't we go out and have a look when you've finished your tea? What I don't know about apples is just about everything."

Looking reluctantly pleased, he slurped the last of his tea and put his cup down.

He'd pulled out his tin of hand-rolled cigarettes and lit one up as they left the house, and now stood with it in his lips at the upper edge of her barn looking across at her small stand of apple trees. The grass had grown tall between them, standing like a golden sea, unmoving in the windless air. She saw the thing through his eyes. On the other side of the far fence in his orchard, the grass between the trees had been kept short and the ripening apples gleamed on the branches. By contrast hers looked like part of an unkempt and abandoned farmstead, which in fairness, it was.

"You haven't sprayed them. You'll have maggots and moths and all sorts eating them." He strode through the high grass, stopped at the first tree, and looked up. "See? You can see them at it already." He picked an apple and pulled a pocket knife out of his overalls and sliced it in half, revealing a green worm wriggling frantically at the sudden exposure.

"Oh. Do you mean I'd have to spray that smelly yellow stuff you put on yours?"

"Look, Miss Winslow. I haven't got time for this. Scale, mildew, insects of every kind—that's what you're producing in this mess. I suggest you give it up as a bad job if you're too namby pamby to spray and look after them properly. Thank you for the tea." He turned and plowed back through the grass and went around the front of her barn to the road, where his tractor waited.

Blimey, she thought, watching him bump noisily up the road. I can't seem to put a foot right with poor Robin. She turned and walked back toward the house. He was right. She was too namby pamby to spray whatever it was on her trees. If it killed fruit-boring insects, it no doubt killed other insects as well. Her feelings of guilt over letting the orchard decay into a memory notwithstanding, she began to picture herself as a sort of bohemian spinster. She would wear turbans and long flowing robes and let nature have its way, tangling and growing up around her and her house. Perhaps she could paint, or take up pottery. Angela painted, and beautifully at that. All right, pottery then, she thought defiantly. Her career as a writer had certainly not progressed.

She put the tea things into the sink and noted with amusement that somehow Robin had got through half a packet of the bourbons. Then she saw herself as she must look to people like Robin, or even the Hughes. She'd moved into an industrious farming community and could swan about not doing anything useful because she had independent means. Everyone was doing something useful. The Hughes ladies were part of the apple economy and grew all their own food, practically working like ants all summer to put things up for the winter. The Armstrongs ran the local post office. Angela brought up the boys and David taught and wrote music. Even Reginald Mather grew a garden and planned appalling sawmills that never materialized. All up and down the lake people did good honest work. Look at poor Vanessa Castle, coping with her egg business without her son, running herself ragged.

Looking at her watch, Lane felt a surge of determination. She could at least jolly well help in that department. She closed the box of cookies, suddenly imagining insects getting into them as well, and got ready to drive to the Castles' place.

CHAPTER TWENTY-EIGHT

"I'VE HAD THE CALL FROM Dawson Creek already, sir. Both Lazek and Bremmer were part of a group that arrived there in the spring of 1939 or '40. Bremmer was there till 1942, and then he moved off, they thought down east somewhere. Lazek was young, maybe nineteen. He came on his own. They remembered him as being fairly unhappy. He worked hard but didn't like it, and apparently he had family back home he was always worried about. As far as anyone knew, he signed up after the enemy aliens designation was dropped." Ames was holding his notes, standing in Darling's doorway.

Darling frowned. "I thought you said they were refugees. How did they become enemy aliens?"

Ames shrugged. "I asked about that. They were refugees all right, but I guess someone got all excited about the fact that they were German and hardly knew English, so the RCMP registered them as enemy aliens. They made a fuss, and someone must have gone to bat for them, because that designation was dropped not too long after. A few of the men signed up. They weren't much for the farming, though there's a lively little community there now, with a school and so on, so it must have worked out for some of them."

"And where did they come from originally?"

Ames consulted his notes. "Bohemia—Czechoslovakia now. As Miss Winslow suspected. They ran off when Hitler came in. He had it in for them because they were communists or something. I picked up some of that in the newspaper articles. The RCMP officer I spoke to said they were decent people, but early on they made themselves pretty unpopular because they thought there was supposed to be money given to them to settle, but the money was handled by the CWR, and the settlers complained pretty loudly that they were being swindled and demanded to know what happened to the money. It doesn't sound like it was very well handled. The officer I talked to said that he was surprised by how little the people were given for their settlement. On top of that, they were given old horses, broken wagons, used tools."

"So someone might think that the railway was creaming off the money. Did they speak English?"

"Oh, yes," Ames said, "Lazek was one who spoke English. They often sent him to negotiate at the CWR office. Someone mentioned how angry he would get. He called them fascists more than once."

"Aha. He had form confronting people. How much do you want to bet Lorimer was the very man he confronted back then? Anything else?" Darling asked.

"That's pretty well the lot, sir. What now?"

"I've just had a call myself. Mr. Bronson up in Kaslo just telephoned to say he happened to be talking to someone and found out what kind of meeting was going on the night of the fight, the night Lazek was shot. The National Unity Party. One small name change away from being Nazis. It's no wonder Lazek got into a fight. Now, did one of them shoot him?"

Ames pushed himself off the door jamb and looked at his watch. "It will be quitting time in about an hour. We could go up to Kaslo and interview some of those people the barkeep said were at the table when the fight broke out. By the way, before you ask, O'Brien did call around to any place that would fix up a man with injuries, but no one saw any sign of a badly beaten man. That wouldn't be unusual, though. Apparently there are plenty of fights and people simply let nature take its course."

"Charming. Right, go start the car. And while we're there, let's explore the waterfront. If he was shot down there, there might still be traces of it."

LANE PULLED UP to the front of the Balfour store. The black Lab peeled himself off the grass and came to say hello, his tail wagging lazily.

"Too hot for the road today?" Lane asked, rubbing behind his ears, and then gave Bales a wave as he came out. "I've just stopped by on my way to Vanessa's. Is there anything I can take her?"

"Now that's funny. She's usually called me by now. I've kind of added her in to my deliveries since that boy went off with her car. I haven't had time to check back.

Better take her some milk at least. And I could use some eggs if she's got them. Let me give you some cardboard flats." He turned and went back into the shop while Lane waited. The gas in the pump gleamed a red-gold colour in the sun. The smell reminded her of the airplane hangers during the war, and even further back, of her father's car in the garage. Just when it was occurring to her that smelling gas, however nostalgic, was no more healthy than smelling sulphur insecticide, Fred came out with a pile of flats. Lane opened the door and he piled them on the seat next to her.

"I'm a bit worried about her," Lane said. "She's having to cope all on her own. The last time I saw her she looked exhausted."

"She ought to hire someone to help her. I'd like to give that boy of hers a piece of my mind."

"Well, we don't know if he ran off or if he met with an accident somewhere. I know she's having a dreadful time because she doesn't know."

Fred nodded and shrugged. "Fair point. But he'd been getting . . . I don't know what you'd call it . . . too big for his boots, maybe, lately. He tried to throw his weight around in here one time, implying I was shortchanging them. I was pretty surprised. It wasn't like him."

"How recently was that?" Lane asked.

"Just in these last three months. I got the feeling he'd fallen in with some new people. He never used to be like that. Nice boy, a bit shy even. I don't say anything to her, of course, but that's why I don't think anything has happened to him."

This matched the direction of Lane's thoughts. On the way down the hill she reviewed her own suspicions that Vanessa either knew where he was or at least knew he wasn't dead in a ditch somewhere.

"What do you want?" Vanessa offered this with no preliminaries. She looked awful, Lane thought. Gaunt, hair unbrushed, her eyes shadowed with exhaustion. She was standing on the top step by the front door, and when Lane came forward she sat down abruptly, as if she could no longer hold herself up.

Lane put the egg cartons she was carrying on the roof of her car and hurried to where Vanessa sat, her face in her hands.

"Goodness, Mrs. Castle! Can you get up? Let's get you inside." Lane supported her to rise, feeling how close to the surface her ribs were, and led her inside the house. Surprisingly the kitchen was not a mess, but then Lane realized that it was probably because Vanessa was making no effort to eat. The stove was out, and Lane contemplated having to collect kindling and wood to get it going for the cup of tea that seemed so desperately required here.

"Listen, why don't you come along to mine? You can have a nice hot bath and I can make you a meal," Lane said.

For the first time, Vanessa looked up at her, her eyes wide. "No! No! I . . . I have to stay here . . . I shouldn't leave."

Lane sat down and took Vanessa's hands. "What's going on? I know you've been terribly worried, but you've been coping. Have you heard something about Carl?"

Vanessa snatched her hands back. "No! Why do you say that? No. Of course not."

She's lying, Lane thought, and she's frightened. "Why don't you tell me what's happened," she said gently.

Vanessa looked out the window and angrily wiped away a tear with the back of her hand. "My father was a big-shot politician," she said, surprising Lane with this turn in the conversation. "Men like that think they can control everything. They've been on top so long it doesn't even occur to them that they can't. But he couldn't control me, no sir. I was seventeen and I was going to do what I wanted. He couldn't think of a way to get me back in the harness, so rather than try and lose, he wiped me off the face of the earth. But it didn't matter to me. I was in love, and I made Robert love me." She laughed without mirth. "See. A chip off the old block. I thought I could control everyone too. I thought when I left my father's house I was free from everything I despised. His hypocrisy, his control. I was on fire with happiness. But you know, it was awful almost from the beginning, only I was never going to admit it. I would never have given my father the satisfaction. Then I had Carl. Probably the only real happiness I've known. When Robert died I felt peace for the first time. I thought I had finally made it. Just me and Carl. Do you understand what I'm saying?"

Lane nodded. "I think so. Vanessa, you know where he is, don't you. Something's happened."

Vanessa turned away and then got up, went to the sink, and began to run water, and then turned it off and looked at Lane. "That two-bit henchman of Lorimer's has been around asking for him. Is that who Carl got mixed up with? I don't know where he is. He won't tell me. But he's done something terrible."

THE BARTENDER AT the hotel where Darling and Ames had met Bronson leaned over and indicated with a nod of his head the men who had been present the night of the fight. "That's the usual group. They've started drifting back here. There were more there that night. Some out-of-towners who haven't been back since. I think they must have been part of the meeting. You know, I can see men meeting to get a union going. Lord knows, they could use one, but—"

Darling wasn't interested in his views on working conditions. "Can we use the ladies' lounge to talk to these people again?"

"Go right ahead."

Darling thanked him and nodded at Ames, who approached the table. The men had long since stopped talking and had been watching the two policemen warily. One of them made to leave. Ames pulled out his card. "Constable Ames, Nelson police. Would you mind sitting down, sir? We need to ask you all a few questions about an incident here a couple of weeks ago. Inspector Darling is in the ladies' lounge. Sir, will you go along? I'll sit here and keep you two company." He smiled genially. "Shouldn't take long. Routine questions."

The man he'd indicated stood up reluctantly. He looked at his two companions, perhaps for support, but both had their hands around their mugs of beer and were looking down.

"Well, now," Ames said. "Were you two here the night of the fight?"

The two men looked at each other now, as if they had both realized their dilemma at once. They did not know what their companion was saying to Darling in the other room. The outside door of the bar opened, and two men in coveralls came in and made straight for the bar, cursing good-naturedly about the heat of the day. Ames's companions watched them and then looked down again.

"It's best if you tell me. We're investigating a murder, and we suspect that fight had something to do with it. We don't have a suspect yet, so you look as good as any." One of the men looked up sharply, his face red.

"What do you mean, a murder? No one died in that fight."

"Ah," Ames said. "Good. Why don't you tell me about it." He took out his notebook and smiled. "Your name?"

"Weaver. This is Heppwith. Nothing to do with us."

"Excellent. First name, Mr. Weaver?"

"Tim."

"Good. Now, tell me about that night." Ames sat coolly poised with his notebook in hand. "Did you attend the meeting?"

Weaver snorted. "We did. A load of nonsense. I was overseas fighting bastards like that. I looked around and I couldn't believe how people were sucking it up. We all came back here after, and these two other fellows sat at our table and kept up the propaganda. I'd had about enough and was going to put up an argument, when Heppwith here called over a man who was just coming in. What did you call him? Something with a K. 'Hey, come over here. You're German, you should join us.'"

"Did you know this man, Mr. Heppwith?" Ames asked.

Heppwith looked toward the door, shifting his chair, as if he were going to leave. "Klaus? Sort of. That speaker was talking sense," Heppwith added, looking disdainfully at his companion. "I was overseas too, and Canada wasn't the same place when we got back."

"And what made you think Klaus would be interested?" Ames asked.

"He was German. Of course he would be. At least I thought so. But he went crazy. He pushed me nearly off my chair, told me I was sick, and stormed off. Now if you don't mind, I don't have time for this." He stood up and started toward the door.

Ames was up in a flash. "Sit down, Mr. Heppwith. I see you have the remains of a bruise on your cheek. Did you get that in the fight?"

Heppwith scowled, and Weaver looked at him and seemed to signal him with his eyebrows. Ames waited.

Weaver finally spoke. "You gotta tell them sometime." He turned to Ames. "He got beat up pretty bad. That Klaus guy was bloody crazy. I told him not to go after him."

They were interrupted by the return of Darling and the man he'd been speaking to. "Who's next?" Darling asked.

"I think we'd better speak to Mr. Heppwith here, sir. He seems to be in a hurry to leave. He's the one who got into the fight with our victim."

"Excellent. Would you be good enough to wait?" Darling said to the other man. "If you'll come with me, Mr. Heppwith, and you can join us, Constable."

"I'll tell you something, Constable," Weaver said, as Ames was about to follow Darling, "I went home after that fight. It's ridiculous that we just fought a war against fascism, and now we got people fighting over the same rubbish right here on our streets."

"Why do you still drink with them?" Ames asked.

"Aw . . . Heppwith is a good man. He's frustrated and unhappy. Wife left him, he's not crazy about the work. He feels like he fought hard and works hard and has nothing to show for it. He got a head wound at Dieppe and lost a lot of buddies. He's been a little short-tempered since then. He simply wants to blame someone. He's been more down than usual lately. These guys from the meeting are blowhards. I can't believe anyone is going to take them seriously. I surely don't want to be one more person who abandons him."

"Do you think Heppwith went looking for Klaus Lazek after being beaten so badly, later on, say?"

Weaver shook his head. "That's what I don't know. Something happened, and no one's talking. Heppwith has clammed up tight. I don't think he'd ever kill anyone, so I'm hoping he'll come clean. I'll tell you something. He wouldn't have a chance against that Klaus."

"Does he own a revolver?"

"Heppwith? I sure don't think so. I'd be afraid if he did, because he'd use it on himself first and foremost."

"Do you have anything more to add?"

"I don't think so. Do you still want me to wait?"

"Just give me your contact details then, and I'll catch up with you if I need to."

AMES JOINED DARLING with an apology. He was sitting with Heppwith at a table against the wall. "Ah, Ames. Mr. Heppwith was about to fill in what happened that night after the initial fight. Please go ahead. I'll have the constable take a few notes, if you don't mind."

Heppwith was somewhere on a continuum between frightened and resigned. "I swear, I didn't know the guy was hurt, let alone dead."

"Let's take it from the top. Tell me what happened after the fight."

"I think I came back in. I was pretty drunk, and he'd worked me over. I remember someone talking to me . . . that fellow from somewhere . . . maybe Nelson. Next thing I know we're going down toward the lake, where I guess that Klaus must have gone."

"When you say 'we,' who do you mean?" Darling asked.

"That Nelson guy."

"What's 'Nelson guy's' name?" asked Ames.

"I couldn't tell you. He was at the meeting. I think he came with the speaker. He was sitting to one side like . . . like a guard or something. I remember him watching us. I don't know much else. It was dark. I think we ran into someone. The guy took the gun, I know that."

Darling leaned forward. "You had a gun? Can you tell me what kind please?"

Heppwith seemed to realize he was in a corner. "Well, it wasn't mine, really."

"Then whose was it?"

"Look, I can't remember. Can I go now?"

"I think, on the whole, Mr. Heppwith, I'll have to take you in. It is likely you'll be charged with the murder of Klaus Lazek. And I'll just have you show us where it happened."

CHAPTER TWENTY-NINE

LANE WAS DOGGEDLY READING *The Grapes of Wrath*, a present from Angela, and was unhappily conscious that she would have been enjoying it, but for the misery she felt over Darling. She put the book face down on the floor beside her chair and stared at her feet, propped on the unlit Franklin. She was being, what? She couldn't even think of an adequate word for it. And she wanted to be a writer! It amazed her how little she could understand herself. Her whole life she had wanted to be logical and strong, to show her father, whose voice still lived in her head somewhere saying, "You're a little coward," that he was wrong. Now she seemed unable to muster one cogent thought about her condition. She got up impatiently and strode to the kitchen and stared around it as if it would provide the order she needed. But even the kitchen betrayed her. It showed her all too clearly that she lived like someone who would at any moment be on the move. Look at her meals. Toast and jam, omelettes, beans on toast. The only decent meals she got were when she went out to other people's houses.

The whole point of being here was that she wanted to settle, but after more than a year, she saw herself as she truly was, always poised to leave. No. She shook her head. That was unfair. But she was running from something in herself. Some psychotherapist could no doubt untangle her state of mind, but, she thought rebelliously, he needn't sweep her lousy meals in with his diagnosis—she was simply a bad cook. Feeling that the fresh evening air might knock the cobwebs out, she went to stand on the veranda. The air was not so much fresh as hot and thick, but sweet with the smell of drying grass at the edge of her lawn. The lake lay impassively before her, as if certain of itself, comfortable with its own depths. What she suffered from more than anything was a longing for Darling. She had run from him, afraid in the last moment. That's what her invented trick cyclist would say, that she'd had a bad time with her father and compounded the problem by picking that ass Angus, and so she was afraid of loving any man.

But it was no good. She did love Darling, and she knew he was not either of those men. He was Darling. Oh my God, she thought, I'm going to cry. She put her hand on her mouth, willing herself not to, but she could not stop the tears. She loved Darling, she had ruined it, and it was too late. Thank heaven, she thought ruefully, I'm alone. For her, misery loved only solitude.

She thought of the sweep of her lawn, the woods below it, and the lake in the distance, where even now, the shadow of a cloud changed the colour of the water as it passed overhead. She needed to break out, somehow, so she turned back into the kitchen, sat at her typewriter, and wrote:

Here it is greens mostly,
And beyond the names
We find for them, they are layers
Of infinite colours made by shadows
and slants of light
Glittering wittering let's call
Them fern, apple, forest, moss
Because we have no other way
To call them to heart
They are like the layers
Inside me liquid, unbounded
Greys mostly like this sky,
Simmering withering let's call
Them longing and loss

By the time the phone rang she was on the ascent again, trying to imagine what she should do to settle into her new life. Paint the house. Take the orchard seriously. Get on with the bed she had made. The call was for her.

"KC 431, Lane Winslow speaking."

"Miss Winslow, I need your help, please." It was Vanessa Castle. That "please" was drawn out, desperate.

Lane, after a start of guilt because she had intended to go and help Vanessa with her eggs and groceries, was instantly alert. "Of course, Mrs. Castle. What can I do?" She was already eyeing her shoes by the door, the car keys on the hook.

"Carl needs help. He's been hiding, you see, and he's out of food and gas and money. I ought to go to him. Please can you take me? I couldn't think of anyone else to call."

"Of course. I'll be there as quick as I can. Put something together for him and we'll go." After she hung up she realized that she hadn't asked Vanessa where Carl was. How far would she have to drive? He could be anywhere. Nightfall was two hours away, but she grabbed her cardigan in case they were late, though she certainly didn't need it now. The day was still stifling, in that dry August way.

She looked at her gas gauge as she approached Balfour. Half a tank. Maybe. The gauge had been wrong before. It was maddening now that she didn't know where Carl was. She pulled up to the gas station and Bales came out.

"Miss Winslow," he greeted her.

"Hello, Fred, could you fill it, please? I . . ." She couldn't say that she was in a hurry, that Vanessa knew where Carl was. "I have to go into town and I'm not sure I have enough."

Bales went about the business of unhooking the hose and undoing the gas cap. "Warm afternoon," he commented.

"Yes," Lane said, trying to be patient with this small talk. It wasn't slowing down the filling after all. "I hope it won't be muggy all night."

"There you go. Three gallons. You were nearly empty. Seventy-nine cents please."

Lane rummaged in her purse and found a dollar. "Here. I'm running a bit late. I'll pick up the change another time."

Relieved to be on the road again, she sped down the hill toward the turnoff to Vanessa's. She had only just thought, with a guilty start, that perhaps she ought to have telephoned Darling or Ames—Carl was their lost man, after all—when she pulled off onto the shoulder of the road and stopped. A strange car was turning out onto the road, going north, the direction Lane had just come from. As the car sped by, she saw with a shock that Townsend was driving and Vanessa was in the front seat. For a brief moment Vanessa looked back, saw Lane, and opened her eyes wide, terrified, pleading, and then it was over.

Had Townsend seen her? Lane prayed not. She waited until the car was about to crest the hill toward the store, and then she turned the car, skidding, raising a cloud of dust, and set out in pursuit.

At the crest of the hill she slowed and watched the car she was following descend. She swerved into the gas lane at the store and was relieved to see Fred Bales still outside. "Fred, call the Nelson police—get inspector Darling, if you can, or Constable Ames. Tell them I am following a car heading in the direction of Adderly or maybe Kaslo, and they are to come as soon as they can. Do you understand?" She didn't wait to hear his reply but crossed her fingers, hoping that she could follow a car on this lonely road without being seen.

AMES THREW HIS notebook on the desk and barely stopped himself from putting his feet up on the passenger side of Darling's desk. "He's still saying he didn't do it, and he's still saying the gun wasn't his, and he's still saying he doesn't know the name of the man he was with."

"Okay, let's try to piece together what he has said. He went to a meeting where the speaker was someone from this fascist party. He doesn't remember the name of the speaker. He was with his mates, and when it was over people were signing up, and everyone was given one of these natty little things." Darling tossed the swastika pin onto the desk between them. "They go back to the hotel to drink and talk. There is one person at the table who he doesn't know and who was at the meeting, and he isn't introduced. He thinks he has something to do with the speaker. He's wearing a swastika pin, and at the meeting he's been sitting behind the speaker looking at the audience. Back at the bar Heppwith is fired up by the fine message of the speaker and sees Klaus and brings him over, thinking it's too bad he missed the meeting, he would have enjoyed it. Klaus is in a mood, but when Heppwith tells him what the meeting is about, Klaus is outraged, pushes him hard, and makes to leave. Heppwith admits he sees red and goes after him, only to be beaten to within an inch of his life.

"So then what? He is brought back into the bar by his friends, but they can't calm him down. Then the man he doesn't know starts talking to him, telling him what? He shouldn't let some commie beat him up? He knows a way he can settle it once and for all? And then it goes blurry, but Heppwith remembers going down to the waterfront where they saw Klaus going. Heppwith remembers having the gun in his hand but doesn't know how it got there. He also remembers bumping into someone in the dark. He thought it might have been Carl. He assumed Carl was part of the hunting party. He remembers the flashlight falling into the water, and trying to aim, and then—and this is critical—he feels the gun taken from him, and then a tussle, a cry, a gun firing at close range. He remembers wanting to run, the gun being in his hand again, and throwing it, he thinks in the lake, but he hears the gun hit the boat. They run from along the wooden pier and then they stop. The other man seems upset about Carl, shouts at him that they'll come looking for him. He's surprised, because he thought Carl was right there."

"And, unfortunately for Heppwith," says Ames, "for all he claims he didn't fire, the fingerprints on the gun are his. And, though it looks like someone's tried to scrape it clean, there are still traces of blood visible on the pier."

"Right. He has a motive, he has a gun, he has the right sort of fingerprints, and we have a dead man. That ought to be the end of it. But I can't quite square it. For one thing, he's so very insistent, and for another, Carl disappears, but why? Does he do the shooting after all? Or does Mr. X shoot Klaus and think Carl has seen him?" Darling picks up the swastika pin. "Why is this in the boat?"

"Maybe in the tussle Klaus pulls it off Mr. X. Maybe he thinks, when they find me this will be a clue."

"Ah, Amesy, if only people about to be fatally shot in the confusion of a dark night had such perspicacity, but as usual you may have stumbled clumsily—yes?" Darling picked up the phone on the first ring.

"Inspector Darling? This is Fred Bales, from the Balfour store and gas station at the top of the hill here."

"What can I do for you?"

"I hope you won't think me odd, but Miss Winslow, from up King's Cove way, whizzed by here and told me to phone you and to say, and I'll try to get this right, that she is following a car going north toward Adderly or Kaslo and you're to come as soon as you can."

Darling was on his feet, reaching for his hat, signalling frantically to Ames. "Did she say who was in the car?"

"No, but I happened to see because I was outside repairing the air hose. The car right before her was a brown late model sedan, Chevy maybe, and I didn't recognize the driver, but it was most certainly Vanessa Castle in the passenger seat, and he was driving like a bat out of hell."

"Blasted woman!" Darling said, slamming down the phone. "She's following a car north along the lake, and she wants us there. How much do you want to bet," he said, when they were speeding toward the Nelson ferry, "that it's Mr. X?"

CURSING HERSELF FOR not telling Bales whom she was following, Lane hoped that the urgency was evident and that Darling knew enough about her to know she would not call him out idly. Following people in a car was no picnic, she decided. It always sounded so easy in books, but look at the night of the party. Ames had picked up almost immediately that they were being followed. She tried to keep far enough behind so that she would not raise the alarm. The curvy road was both a curse and a blessing. The bends obscured her from her target, but she had to pray at every moment that they would not disappear up a side road she didn't know existed. She watched the brown car slow down to take the turn over the bridge at the bottom of the sharp bend and then climb the other side. How far back should she stay? The open side of the road was virtually treeless. She stopped. She would wait till they were almost completely up the other side and traversing the dangerous part of the road that hung over the lake. She could linger behind the curve until they had completed that.

As she drove into Adderly she slowed, looking down toward the hotel, and up toward the hot springs parking area. No sign of the car. They must have moved on. After a few miles she became seriously alarmed. She had not seen the car for some time. Had it stopped, or sped up, heading toward Kaslo or some point beyond? Good grief . . . New Denver . . . and from there they could go all the way west. She sped up and was turning onto the bridge at the creek with the waterfall, when she looked ahead. No dust. No car had been by to raise dust. She stopped and looked behind her. Where could they have gone? She turned awkwardly in the road and drove slowly back to the bridge and over it, looking right and left in the underbrush. Could they have stopped here? She wished she'd not let them get so far ahead. Then she saw it. The brown car was backed into the thick cover of bushes. It would be invisible coming the other way. That's how she'd missed it.

In the silence that descended when she turned off the car, she sat for a moment. How long were Darling and Ames likely to be, even if Bales had got hold of them? She leaned out her window and listened intently for any sound of voices. Nothing. Why were they even here? This was where Klaus had put up his shack. Is this where Carl was? She got out of the car and gingerly closed the door. Was Carl's yellow car here? She went swiftly across the road and looked into the window of the brown car, and then ventured farther along into the underbrush. There was no sign of Carl's Chevy, but this brown car was certainly the car she'd been following. For some reason Townsend had brought Vanessa here. Vanessa had been frantic. Had he offered to take her to Carl, and she was so frightened she didn't wait for Lane? No. Vanessa had looked terrified, Lane was sure of it. She looked at her watch. Forty minutes now since she'd asked Bales to phone. They'd be at least thirty minutes away still, but they would stop when they saw her car. Could she wait? Would Vanessa be safe?

A shot plundered the silence and sent a scattering of birds noisily out of the trees. Lane knew she couldn't wait.

CHAPTER THIRTY

THE EXPLOSION OF THE GUN had been so loud that it took a moment for Lane to realize she'd also heard a scream, short and strangled. Had Vanessa been shot? Whatever had happened, it had happened close by, near the top of the winding path down to the water. Lane tried to remember the layout even as she sped forward, keeping low and trying not to make noise. She could feel her whole being poised, focused, every nerve tingling in a kind of synchronicity utterly familiar to her. She stopped, her hearing concentrated. Voices, and nearby, but slightly obscured, as if around a curve in the path. If they were too far down, she would have no cover. She moved forward, crouching by the edge of the path. They were not visible. She would have to risk going into the open. Thank God for the grass verge, she thought. It muffled her progress. Once onto the path she moved slowly to the first bend, created by a hill of land sloping down toward the path. They were there! Three of them, standing on the edge of the path nearest the top of the waterfall. Just there, the sound of the water cascading over the edge and crashing into the creek below was the loudest.

She stopped and watched. Townsend had his back to her, one arm holding Vanessa so that she was facing away from him and toward a young man who looked terrified and had his hands partially raised, either in submission or supplication. Townsend's other hand held the gun, which he was pointing at Vanessa's head. Townsend was saying something, but Lane couldn't hear what. Very cautiously, terrified of raising the alarm with her movement, she backed away so that she was again hidden by the curve of the hill. No one was dead yet. Some bargaining was going on. But what? Townsend clearly was threatening Carl with that gun at his mother's head. Lane looked swiftly around her for a weapon. Useless against a gun, but with the element of surprise . . . she picked up a heavy branch as strong and as thick as her arm. It would have to do. Taking in a deep breath, she darted forward as quietly as she could.

The three people had advanced closer to the edge of the path. Lane knew what could happen next. Townsend would not shoot anyone unless he had to. He was trying to force Carl and Vanessa off the edge. She sprang forward. She could see everything happening at once. Carl saw her, and Townsend turned sharply to see what he was looking at. He turned back, crying out in anger and pain as Vanessa bit down on his arm, and Lane hit him as hard as she could across the back of his knees. Townsend went down and his gun clattered onto the path and slid away from him on a patch of shale. Vanessa, freed, rushed toward Carl.

Still holding her weapon, Lane skirted cautiously behind Townsend, who was beginning to try to get up, cursing aloud. He looked toward where his gun had come to rest and lunged for it. Lane swatted at his outstretched arm with the branch, causing him to cry out and collapse where he was. She snatched up the gun, dropped the branch, and pointed the weapon at him. Vanessa and Carl had backed a little way up the hill, onto the other side of the path from the drop to the falls.

"You broke my bloody arm, you bitch!" Townsend groaned. He lay back now, the upper part of his body partially raised by the rise of ground on that side of the path. He was holding his right arm gingerly with his left and glaring at her.

"That's nothing on what I'll do to you if you move. The police are on their way."

"You're bluffing. You don't even know what you've walked into. That man killed somebody, and I was bringing him in. Now look what you've done! What are you going to do now, eh?"

"I'm not bluffing for a start." Without looking away from Townsend, she added, "Carl, did you kill someone? Is that why you ran away?"

"No! I . . . saw two men. One of them shot someone in Kaslo—he said he'd kill me . . ."

"I wasn't even there that night . . ." Townsend seemed to realize he should probably stop talking.

"LANE'S CAR!" DARLING said, pointing. He was already opening the door before Ames pulled the maroon police car to a stop. "If it's Townsend she's been following, he's probably armed." He reached into his pocket and readied his own weapon, and then raced through the underbrush.

Ames glanced at the car that had been hidden in the bushes. He didn't recognize it. He sprang after his boss, who had rounded the corner, and nearly ran into him. He stifled a bark of laughter that bubbled, unbidden, from inside him, and managed to convert it into an ear-to-ear smile of delight. Even Darling was rendered momentarily speechless.

There before them was Lane Winslow, revolver in hand, her focus trained on Townsend, who was sitting awkwardly and angrily on the path, holding his arm and scowling. Mrs. Castle and the young man that both policemen presumed to be her son were sitting on a log, he with his arm around her.

"Ah," said Lane, without looking away from her prisoner. "It took you long enough." She lowered the weapon and held it out to Ames. "This is Mr. Townsend, the phone man. You remember, Inspector. I expect he was about to force Mrs. Castle and her son, Carl, off the edge here so that their deaths would look accidental. Carl, this is Inspector Darling and Constable Ames. They will be very interested in your story. In fact," she added crossly, "if you had gone to them in the first place, all of this could have been avoided."

"I'M SORRY I'M late, Violet. We had to arrest a man all the way up toward Kaslo." Ames sat down with a thump at the table. She barely looked at him but concentrated instead on the lights of the cars coming around the corner into town. They were in the little restaurant near the hospital where they'd agreed to meet.

"What are we doing here?" she asked, finally turning to him. Her hair was in an unyielding roll off her face, allowing the little angled tilt of her hat that he had always found so attractive. Looking at her now, he suddenly saw all this perfect coiffing as unbending. "If you've come to apologize, it's a bit late," she said, lifting her chin.

"You know I'm going away," he said, faltering.

"For a couple of months. That's hardly a death sentence. Look at all the other men. They went to war, for God's sake. Their girlfriends and wives didn't desert them. I don't intend to either, whatever you say."

Ames rubbed his hands over his eyes and then had to look at the waitress who had appeared by their table. "What would you like, Vi?" he asked.

"Just a coffee."

"Two coffees, please," he said quietly. When the waitress was out of earshot he spoke again. "Look, Vi, it's not only about me going away. I'm . . . I simply don't think it's going to work. We're too different."

"I'm not different. I haven't changed in the least. But I don't even think I know you anymore." She paused, opened her handbag, and took out a compact, which she opened and then closed without really looking at it. She dropped it into her bag, which she snapped shut. "I assume there's someone else. There always is in these cases."

Ames wasn't sure what to say. He expected she would like to hear there was someone else, because she wouldn't be able to accept that he'd leave her simply because he didn't want to be with her.

"Well? Who is it?"

"It isn't anyone, Vi. It's what I said before. I don't think I'm ready." That wasn't true, and he regretted the evasion it represented. "Look, I don't think we'd agree on much. How to bring up children and that. And my job . . . you know what the hours can be like."

"Not agreeing on children? That's what this is about? You're the man. Obviously we'd do what you wanted. I wouldn't agree with it, mind. I don't believe in bringing up spoiled brats, but that's what being married is about, isn't it? 'Love, honour, and obey.'"

The bleakness of this future she outlined for them came to him forcefully. He guessed that it must be right that men were supposed to be in charge, but suddenly he had no appetite for it. He wasn't even sure he believed in it. His father had supposedly been in charge, but, looking back now on the bitter figure that had been his father, it seemed to Ames that it would have been more true to say that his mother had had to take care of his father, as if he were a barely functioning child.

"I don't want to be in charge like that. I want . . . I don't know . . . to feel like we agreed on things and would decide together about things."

The coffee arrived, and Violet stirred some cream into hers and then put the spoon down without drinking. "You know what? I guess you're right. I certainly wouldn't want a man who waffles around like you do. I want a man to be in charge. When my dad was alive he was in charge, and we were all the better for it. That's how things are supposed to be. I don't want a man my children can't look up to."

Ames had no response to this. He sat looking miserably down at his coffee. He would have liked to heap the three spoons of sugar into it that he usually took, but he suddenly saw this through her eyes. It would no doubt be unmanly as well.

"So, this is it then, is it?" Violet asked.

Ames looked down.

"Oh, for God's sake, just say it! I don't even know how you do your job as a so-called policeman. You're pathetic." She turned her little chin away from him, staring again out the window into the dark.

Ames felt something inside him harden. "Yes, okay, Violet. This is it. I don't want the kind of life you're describing. Maybe you're right to say the things you do. I don't know. But your version of what a man is isn't mine." My version of a man, he thought, is Inspector Darling. Honest, imperfect, able to love someone who was as strong as he was. He smiled—nay, stronger.

"What are you smiling at? Is this fun for you? Because I'll tell you something for nothing, I'm not enjoying it."

"No, Vi. It's the furthest thing from fun. I'm sorry it turned out like this. I hope we can be friends after this."

"Really? 'Let's be friends'? I wouldn't be friends with you if you were the last man on earth! You have to at least like someone to be friends with them, and I surely don't like you!" She stood up and smoothed down her dress, and then walked out without another word.

Ames collapsed back on his chair breathing a sigh of relief, and reached for the sugar bowl.

DARLING, UP THE hill in his house, had, if he but knew it, the opposite problem. He had managed, without wanting it, to divest himself of the woman he loved. He stood at his window, which he had flung open, with an untouched Scotch in his hand, listening to the sounds of Nelson below him slowly calming for the night. He wondered at his own . . . impetuousness, perhaps, so at odds with the dour inspector image he portrayed. No, he didn't just portray it. It was real. He was dour in some ways. Nothing in the war had improved his view of humanity, and nothing in his experience of the perennial sordidness and lack of imagination of the people he had to deal with in his job allowed for anything but a grim view of things. Why did he allow himself to commit so wholly to something as unstable and buoyant as love?

He thought of his father—distant, almost unconscious of his own misanthropic wry humour. Had he ever loved his wife? Had he been young and optimistic and willing to give himself entirely to love until Vimy and his wife's death beat it out of him? Darling felt a welling of pain. His mother had been gentle and intelligent, had read to her sons and walked with them. He had loved her in the blind way children have of believing their mothers will be there forever.

A car coming up the hill suddenly faltered and then revved up with a grinding of gears. Darling turned away from the window, as if the truth of a sudden realization would be confirmed in the quiet darkness of the room behind him. He saw himself now in contrast to his father. He had lost his mother, he had fought a war, but he loved someone. He loved her and nothing in his life had diminished his capacity to love this person. Surely his mother would say, right now, "How wonderful that you are able to love."

CHAPTER THIRTY-ONE

DARLING WOKE GROGGY AND THICK headed, as though he'd had too much to drink, something he hadn't done since before he signed up. It was, he knew, the tossing and turning, imagining over and over calling Lane, saying what to her? Apologizing? For what? For being a fool, for assuming too much? Finding the kitchen in his small house as telling as Lane had found hers, with its lack of creature comforts, including breakfast, he took up his jacket, slammed on his hat, and made for the café. Ames was already there, moodily eating scrambled eggs.

"What's eating you?" Darling asked.

Ames thought, I might say the same thing, sir. You look awful. But his boss wasn't much for cheek first thing in the morning. "Sorry, sir. I needed some coffee." He watched Darling order a plate of toast and some coffee and then said, "But it's a big day, sir. We found Carl, and we have the two men involved in the shooting of Lazek."

Darling sighed wearily. "We didn't find him, Ames.

Miss Winslow, our eager Girl Scout helper, found him. And we don't have much. Heppwith and Townsend are both protesting loudly that they had nothing to do with the shooting of Lazek, and Carl will be in to give a full statement today, but he said he couldn't see anyone properly in the dark, and he disappeared because whoever it was threatened him."

"Has Heppwith seen Townsend yet?" Ames asked.

"No, they're in separate cells. Why? Thank you." Darling reached eagerly for the coffee he'd been provided. It had better do the trick. He couldn't go into the day in this state. Confounded bloody woman. That's what Townsend had said, and Darling could almost agree with him in that moment.

"Well, sir, Heppwith says he didn't do the shooting. He said that the man gave him the gun, but when they got to the pier he found he couldn't shoot Lazek, and used the dark as an excuse. The man took the gun, shot it, and then handed it back, telling Heppwith to get rid of it. If we take him at his word, we could simply ask him to identify the man he was with, which we assume is Townsend. With both of them there, we'll get at the truth, all right."

"This isn't a melodrama, Ames. Proper police interviews, if you please. But you have a point. We do need to establish properly that it was the two of them."

Heppwith, as it turned out, was not in the least bit helpful. He was sitting in the interview room with his hands cuffed behind him when Townsend was brought in. He looked at Darling, perplexed.

"Mr. Heppwith. Is this the man you were with on the night Lazek was shot?" Ames asked.

"I've never seen this man before in my life," Heppwith said.

LANE, WHO ALSO had not slept particularly well, was savagely ripping at some weeds in the garden. Darling was insufferable. "Thank you, Miss Winslow, we'll take it from here." She said these words out loud now, remembering how they'd been delivered in that official police-y way of his. Darling and Ames had bundled their prisoner into the police car, and Darling had not even looked back. A wink and a smile from Ames was all the thanks she got. She smiled briefly. Good old Ames. How *did* he work for that prig? She sat back, holding a weed that dropped dirt from its roots onto her crossed legs. She looked at it and frowned. What if this was some important bloom put in by Gladys Hughes when they'd planted her garden? With a twinge of guilt she went back on her knees and dug around the hole she'd pulled the weed from and tried to put it back in. The plant, she couldn't help noticing, was already beginning to droop in the morning heat. "You can blame Inspector Darling," she said to the plant and stood up, brushing off her legs. She clearly didn't know what she was doing, in spite of Gladys's best efforts. How could she be such a dead loss with a grandmother like hers, who could be head gardener for the king?

She had dropped Vanessa Castle and Carl off at their farm the evening before, promising to pick them up in the morning to drive them into town, where he would make his statement to the police, and then take Carl and a can of gas to wherever it was he had abandoned his car. She looked at her watch and sighed. Nine thirty. She'd barely have time to get dressed and pick them up by ten.

Lane pulled a summer dress off the hanger where it was hanging in her cupboard next to the skirt Yvonne had sent her. She wouldn't have occasion to wear that again, she thought. She saw herself as she had been that night, drinking champagne on the terrace, dancing with Darling, dancing with Lorimer, hiding in the underbrush listening to Lorimer and Townsend. She stopped and frowned. What had he said? Something like "Do I have to do everything myself?" Or "Do I have to do it myself, again?" She shook her head, wishing she could remember exactly. By the time she had put her handkerchief in her handbag and closed the front door, she was very certain that what he had said implied he'd already had to do something himself. What? Was he in on the robberies, or was it something more sinister? He'd certainly been confronted by Lazek. Was Lorimer guilty of something that Lazek knew about from the past? Is that why Lazek had to die? She had told herself earlier that Lorimer wouldn't do any killing himself; he'd send an underling. But the underling they'd arrested yesterday had sworn he had nothing to do with Klaus's killing. There was that other man, Lorimer's repellent secretary. He could have done it. And he wasn't arrested, and neither was Lorimer. How long would it take for Lorimer to find out Townsend hadn't succeeded in getting rid of Carl?

Spurred by this new anxiety, Lane hurried down the hill to the main road and tore off toward Balfour, only to find Carl and his mother looking very relaxed, waiting at the top of the lane down to their farm. Vanessa looked more at ease and happy than Lane had ever seen her.

"Good morning. You look wonderful, Vanessa. How are you both feeling?"

Carl nodded and smiled slightly. Vanessa said, "I think I slept for the first time since he left, even though I kept waking up to remind myself that it was true, that my Carl was asleep in the next room. He's told me everything. I think he feels a bit foolish now." She smiled fondly at her son.

"I'm not sure you have to feel foolish, Carl," said Lane, as she drove onto the main road. "It sounds like you were threatened, you said yesterday. I'd want to run off as well."

Carl was sitting in the back seat, his head leaning against the window frame, the breeze coming in the open window lifting his hair off his forehead. "It's not that; it's the whole thing. That stupid meeting, signing up. I was mad about losing my job, and I'd had too much to drink, and I felt that Heppwith was on to something. He's a bit all in with this nationalism thing, and I see some of his points. Anyway, I signed up that night, got my little pin, and then the whole thing unravelled with that fight. I could see that Heppwith wanted to kill that guy, and I got scared. I wanted to leave, but I suddenly felt I couldn't let it happen, so I went down to where I saw Lazek go towards the water to warn him to get out."

"Did you know the man Heppwith was talking with?" Lane knew she ought to leave the questions to the police.

"No. Never seen him before. He was at the meeting, looking like he owned the place. I don't know if I missed the introductions or what. Besides the speaker, he was the only one in a suit. I've tried and tried to remember what I saw that night, but I can't. I only know Heppwith was there because I recognized his voice. I just don't know about the second guy."

Lane hesitated, and then said, "Carl, when you're talking to the police, tell them as much as you can about everything you remember. Any little thing could be important."

"Yes, ma'am. I will."

They drove in silence for some miles, each lost in their own preoccupations, which in Lane's case was how to avoid seeing Darling. She could drop them off at the front of the station and meet them somewhere else, at the café maybe. They were rounding the long curve that led past the beautiful faux Tudor house where Lane had taken Eleanor to pick up Alexandra—Lane remembered the puppies squirming and wiggling winningly—when the rest of that visit came into sudden focus. She'd been put off by Lorimer's smooth presentation right from the beginning, but then she had pointed out to Eleanor that for a man of such pretensions, he had threads pulled out of his jacket lapel.

"Carl, do you still have that little pin they gave you?" she asked.

"Yeah, why?"

"There was one in the boat with the man who was shot. I wondered if it was yours, but it must have been his."

"I doubt that. He was hot about the whole business, called them Nazis and fascists."

"Was Heppwith wearing his, do you remember?"

Carl shook his head in the back seat. "I can't fully remember. He was wearing blue coveralls and they were kind of loose, so even if he put it on, I might not have seen it. But the other guy was. The guy that was talking to Heppwith after the fight. He had that nice suit on and the swastika pin stood out."

"Carl, this is important. Is it possible that that man went after Lazek with Heppwith?" Lane asked.

"That's what I don't know," Carl exclaimed, sounding miserable. "I was drunk, and it was so dark. I thought it might be the guy from yesterday, because he seemed to want to kill us, but I didn't recognize his voice. I wish I could remember!"

They pulled up in front of the station and Lane stopped the car, her hand resting on the gearshift. She had to tell Darling. It wasn't like evidence, she knew. More of a guess. A hunch. After all, here was Carl with real first-hand evidence, such as he could remember. She should leave it. But she couldn't. She felt the bubble of certainty that she could not ignore.

"I'll come in with you. I have to see the inspector for a moment. Then I'll wait downstairs for you, all right?"

Vanessa leaned over toward Lane and put her gloved hand on Lane's arm. Carl had gotten out of the back seat and was standing waiting for them. "Miss Winslow, I don't know how to thank you. I've been so dreadful to you. But you've found my Carl, you've saved our lives, even."

"Call me Lane, please. You shouldn't blame yourself for one minute. I thought you were heroic, all the way through it. I couldn't have coped under similar circumstances, I can tell you." She laughed. "Especially heroic biting that man's arm like that. What presence of mind!"

Vanessa smiled. "It was disgusting, actually!"

Inside, Lane said, "Good morning, Sergeant O'Brien. This is Mrs. Castle and her son, Carl. They are here to see the inspector. And I wonder if I could see him for a moment ahead of them?"

"Go on up, Miss Winslow. I'll tell him you're on your way. If you two would like to take a seat, please."

Lane went up the stairs two at a time, wanting to get it over with, wanting them to know what she was certain of, now that she knew. At the top of the stairs she paused, and then made for his office, but he was at the door before she got there.

"Lane. Miss Winslow. You wanted to see me." His face wore its official expression, but his charcoal eyes looked sad in the shadows of the hallway.

"Yes, Inspector. I . . ." Suddenly, in the station, surrounded by the hard craft of the law, the gathering of evidence, the witnesses waiting downstairs, the men in the cells, her ideas seemed wild to her, suppositions out of nothing.

"Come in here. Do you have something? Should Ames be here?" Ames had heard Lane's voice in the hall and had wanted to come out of his office, but he thought he'd better let them get on with it. His only concession to the situation was that he was crossing his fingers tightly.

"No. Poor Ames. No. Look, Inspector, I had this idea, it's so strong, that Lorimer is the one. You see, when I overheard him talking to Townsend the other night, he said he didn't want to have to take care of things himself again. That 'again' made me wonder. What had he done the first time? What had Townsend failed to do? Had someone made an attempt on Lazek's life before? And then I saw the loose threads on his, I mean Lorimer's, jacket. I wondered at it because he's such a fussy dresser. He was wearing an ascot that day I met him, and I thought it incongruous."

Darling was looking thoughtful and had sat on the corner of his desk, with his arms crossed. "How is the business of the loose threads significant?"

Lane smiled ruefully. "Yes, I know, it sounds ridiculous in the light of day, doesn't it? But there's the swastika pin that was in the boat. What if in the struggle Lazek grabbed the lapel of the man who shot him and pulled the pin off. No, before you say anything, Carl says that there was a man in a suit at the meeting, and he was wearing one of those pins."

Darling thought for a moment, his mouth working. "The thing, Miss Winslow, and by the way, Ames painted the exact same scenario with Lazek pulling the pin off his attacker's lapel, is that the only fingerprints on that gun are Heppwith's. Lorimer could have been shooting people all over Kaslo, but the law can never get him without better evidence."

"Damn," said Lane, deflated. "I didn't know about the fingerprints. It does seem open and shut, doesn't it? I suppose it was Townsend with him after all. He certainly showed himself to be of a murderous turn of mind yesterday. I wish we knew if there'd been any other attempt on Lazek's life."

"Miss Winslow, thank you again for yesterday, but I wonder now if we might get on with the interviews we have to do. Police work, and all that."

"Yes, of course. I am sorry. If it's all right, I've said I'll wait for them, but I can wait next door if you'd prefer." Had his voice softened briefly?

Oh, the things I'd prefer, he thought. "I'll tell you one thing. After this morning we are fairly certain it wasn't Townsend. Heppwith doesn't recognize him. There now, Miss Winslow. Make of that what you will." He stood up and waited for her to turn and leave his office.

But she stood looking at him. "You know," she said, "I . . ."

"Yes. All right. It's fine," he said gently. It wasn't. He didn't even know what she was about to say. That she was sorry, he supposed.

Ames uncrossed his fingers.

CHAPTER THIRTY-TWO

"CARL, WHY WERE YOU AT the creek in the first place?" Lane was driving Carl and his mother to where he had left his car behind an abandoned cabin up a lonely road near Kaslo. They had taken a gas can and Carl had filled it. Vanessa was already in the car, but Lane and Carl were standing outside.

"I'd heard Lazek had lived there. When I heard he'd died I got frightened, but I also wanted to see if he'd left anything there that said whether he had any family. I thought they should know. But anything he had was gone, except his bedding. I stayed there one night, but I was out of money and was hungry. I'd been hiding in an old abandoned cabin, and I couldn't stand it anymore. I walked back out and hitchhiked to Kaslo to telephone Mother. I was terrified one of them would see me, so I hurried back to the creek to wait. Mother wasn't sure how she could get there, but she said she knew someone she could phone, so I waited by the side of the road. I thought the guy was some friend of hers, but then he pulled a gun. That's about when you came in."

"And you thought it was the man who threatened you that night?" Lane asked.

"I did at first. But then I was surprised because I didn't recognize his voice. He was waving a gun at us. I was terrified. I kept thinking that someone had been sent to find me and that we were done for."

"Listen, Carl," Lane spoke quietly so that Vanessa wouldn't hear. "If that's not the man who killed Lazek, then whoever did is still out there. You need to be careful. Stick to home a bit more. I don't want to alarm you. I think the police will have it sorted, but—"

"Oh, don't worry, Miss Winslow. I will be sticking to home. Poor Mum has tried to cope on her own. It's funny, you think you want to get away so badly, and then when you can't go home, you miss it more than anything in the world."

DARLING AND AMES sat in the café. It was late enough that a booth in the corner was free. April was charm itself and recommended, as she supplied them with plates of sandwiches, that they give the apple pie a go for dessert.

"Lane, Miss Winslow, thinks it's Lorimer. It is, if you will, a hunch. But it's a hunch built on a couple of good solid facts. She believes, based on what she heard the night of the party, that another failed attempt must have been made on Lazek, and that Lorimer had gone to Kaslo to finish the job himself. I had a look at this Gustav character from the so-called Unity Party. He made a substantial donation to

Lorimer's campaign. No surprise there. On the one hand that explains Lorimer being in Kaslo on the night of the shooting, to attend the meeting. On the other hand, it gives him opportunity. Did he know Lazek worked there? I bet he did. I bet he sent Townsend to fix him, and when he failed Lorimer thought he'd go along himself and wait for the opportunity. She also said she saw threads pulled out on the lapel of his expensive jacket and, like you, she postulated that in the struggle Lazek had pulled off the swastika pin and it fell into the boat."

"Great minds, sir."

"Quite. But you see the problem. We don't have proof."

"I must say, it's an awful risk to take. What did Lazek have on him? It must have been big to need him out of the way. And what happens if he finds out the man he thinks saw him is still alive?"

"We've locked up his henchman and the man Lorimer evidently set up to carry the can, but Lorimer's election is coming up soon. Surely he wouldn't go about shooting any more people. It would draw the wrong kind of attention," Darling pointed out. "But he can't afford to have Carl out there in the long run. For now Lorimer doesn't know we've foiled his plan and have Townsend in jail. If we can't find a way to nab him, Carl may have to change his name and leave town. Give them a call and tell them to lie low."

Back in the office Ames tried to call the Castles' number. "There's no answer, sir!" he called out from his office. But his boss didn't hear him, because a call had been put through to him.

"Darling."

"Inspector. I'm worried about them. I know Lorimer may not know yet that Townsend failed, but when he doesn't hear from Townsend he'll know something's wrong. I wanted to let you know I've taken Carl and his mother to the little store in Balfour. Mr. Bales can put them up for a bit. But you'll have to find out who the real killer is, or they'll never be safe."

A number of sarcastic replies hung about Darling's lips, but uppermost in his mind was the relief that she had not been mad enough to put them up at her house. "What a good idea, Miss Winslow. Putting them in hiding and suggesting what our next move ought to be. I'll just go along and tell the lads here that we'd better catch the real killer, then, shall I?" All right, so he'd been unequal to the temptation.

"And when you've done that, you might hop to it and find the Armstrong and Hughes antiques."

So had she. Darling hung up the phone, smiling.

"AMES, YOU'LL BE happy to know Carl and his mother are safe. Miss Winslow has stashed them in that store in Balfour."

"Wow, she—"

"Please don't, Ames. Of course, she couldn't resist telling us our job. She'd like us to hurry up and find the real killer, and the antiques. Yes, what is it?"

O'Brien had come upstairs and found Darling and Ames in the hall. "There's a gentleman here to see you, sir. That Mr. Lorimer. Shall I send him up?"

"Now what's he up to?" Darling wondered.

A Month Earlier

"SHALL I SHOW him in?" The receptionist, who was new at her job, sounded uncertain on the intercom. This had freed up his more experienced secretary to do work outside of the office. Lorimer had been charmed by this new girl's lack of confidence. He'd bring her around. She was blond, pretty, and personable. Just what a man needed at the front desk.

"Did he give his name?"

"No, sir."

"Could you ask him, please?" Lorimer leaned into the intercom, lending the request a slightly sarcastic tone. She was a looker, but this was a little too much.

"I did, sir. He wouldn't say."

This put Lorimer on alert. The visitor wasn't a citizen looking for help from a councillor. The councillor was irritated. He'd already made it clear that his "field men," as he liked to think of them, should not approach him through the office. "Better show him in," he said curtly, pulling his finger away from the intercom button and clasping his hands tightly.

The door opened and the receptionist stepped in and let a tall, gaunt man in an ill-fitting suit walk through, and then she hesitated, looking at Lorimer. She wanted to ask if there was anything else, but the expressions on the faces of both men made her feel that she was in unknown territory. Lorimer unclasped his hands and waved one at her impatiently so that she backed out hurriedly and closed the door.

The man stood with his hands in his pockets contemplating Lorimer and then sat down and crossed his legs.

He did not remove his hat. Lorimer frowned, feeling a kind of fury building from somewhere inside. Where were they getting these men? He'd have to have a word.

"What have you got for me?" he asked. He wanted to say, "How dare you sit without being asked?" He had a precise view of hierarchy and what was owed to whom.

The man did not speak for a long moment. He used the time to look around the walls of the office, and then back at Lorimer. "Nice office, but small. When you are mayor you will have that big one down the hall. I see the picture of King George. Did you always have that?" The man had an accent of some sort. He stood up suddenly and made for an elaborately framed document on the opposite wall. "Ah. You have a law degree. That is fortunate, is it not? It will make everything easier. The printing is very good too, considering it is from . . . where? Ah, Manitoba. I had a friend who was a printer. Perhaps you remember him. Hans Bremmer."

Lorimer's outrage had reached a fever pitch. His hand began to move toward the intercom button. The visitor caught the movement and returned to his chair, his hand raised.

"I see that you do not appear to know me. Please. There is no need to raise the alarm. I am quite harmless. If I were not, I expect you and I would both have been dead long ago."

Lorimer found this statement far from reassuring. He was frantically thinking about how he could alert his receptionist to bring in the security man from the front door of city hall, but he feared the reaction of this man to any move to push the button to get her attention.

"You know, your question to me was something like, 'What have you got for me?' But I think you will see on consideration that that should be my question. Don't you agree?"

It was only now that Lorimer began to home in on the accent. Very pronounced. Russian was it? Dutch? He tried to remember the people he had dealt with over the years. German. The man spoke a little like the Mennonite farmers Lorimer had heard as a child when his mother had taken him to buy cheese at a local farm. And then he knew . . . the wave of fear started somewhere in his depths and he could feel it threatening to overwhelm him.

"Ah. I see it is beginning to dawn on you, yes? I have waited a long time, Councillor Lorimer." He emphasized *councillor*. "In fact I never thought I'd see the day, except I saw your picture in the paper. 'Notable businessman,' it said. You are running for mayor. That's nice, yes?" The man smiled suddenly, incongruously and frighteningly.

"How dare you come in here!" sputtered Lorimer. "Get out!"

"Ah, that's more like the old Lorimer I knew, eh? I come asking for something, and you tell me to get out. And I will, in just a moment. You owe me, and my people for that matter, a lot of money. I checked, after the war. Oh. Did I tell you I enlisted? I was trained in small arms work. Anyway. I never went back to Peace River because the land you provided, even you will admit, was garbage, no? But I asked my friend there and you know, they never did see all the money they were promised. I checked with the railway company you worked for as well, but they said everything they'd been given was passed on to the administrators of the so-called program. To you, in fact. Actually, I don't need the money. I have a job, and most of my friends probably have made out okay." The visitor paused, waved his hand to encompass the plush office with the dark panelling and brass ink stand. "And obviously you've put the money to good use. But if I think about what would be best, I think you should step down and give up your campaign to be mayor. I'm not committed to that, though. If you give back the money to the community, I could overlook this mayor business. Some of the children have grown up and would like to go to university. The money would help them. They had a hard childhood, you know, limited food, poor housing, lousy crops. It would be such a good thing for them at last."

This speech over, Lorimer stood up and leaned forward on the desk. "Blackmail is a crime and I'll have the law on you. Now leave!"

The visitor stood up. "Ah, yes. Your degree. Of course, you know the law." He seized Lorimer's pen and dipped it in ink, took an envelope that still lay on Lorimer's desk, and wrote something. "I don't know it like you do, of course, but I'm sure a criminal shouldn't be running for mayor. Here is the company I work for. When you have come back to your senses you can contact me here and we can make arrangements, no? After all, for all I know, you will make a good mayor. You know how to run what I have heard is called a 'tight ship.'"

"MAY I SMOKE?" Lorimer was languidly reaching into his jacket for his cigarettes. He was seated in an unfamiliar position for him, on the other side of a desk, and was making a champion effort to portray the man who is most anxious to help the police with their inquiries.

"I'd sooner you didn't," Darling said with a faint smile.

"Quite right," Lorimer agreed good-naturedly. "It's stuffy enough in this office." He sat back and waited, as if indulging a child.

"Now then, what can I do for you?"

"I came to tell you that you were right. Townsend is a thief. I shudder to think what he would have carried off if you hadn't alerted me. I didn't let on, of course, when I let him go that night. Just said he wasn't needed any longer. I didn't want a scene."

"I see. How did you discover this?"

"It's the damnedest thing, but he actually had the face to turn up yesterday, offering to sell me this. He said it belonged to his wife, but they were short of money and he was hoping to unload it. Says it's from the early Q'ing dynasty. I wouldn't know one dynasty from another, frankly, but I'm willing to bet this is on the inventory of things that have been stolen." He pulled out a rectangular Chinese porcelain bowl and put it on Darling's desk.

Darling looked at it and tented his hands under his chin. So he was right. Lorimer had no idea Townsend had already been arrested. What was his game? He assumes he's in the clear, that Carl is dead. Of course. Townsend was arrested before he had an opportunity to call his boss and tell him he failed. He wants Townsend out of the way, Darling thought. He thinks Townsend won't betray him because it would mean a charge of murder. This way it will be a theft charge instead.

He stood up and put his head out the door. "Ames, could you take this down to O'Brien and have him go through that list of antiques and see if anything like this appears on it, and then could you pop in here? Mr. Lorimer is here to help us with the investigation."

Ames looked at the bowl he'd been given. "It actually looks like something I added to the list myself, from the Armstrongs. I'll get it downstairs and be right back."

Back in his office, the inspector found Lorimer playing restively with his cigarette case. Perhaps he should let him smoke. Relax him. Darling went round and pushed the window wide open. "Go ahead. It should be fine."

"But surely we're done here, once you've confirmed that thing's one of the stolen items?"

"We'd like to get the case as tight as possible. With a good case and a conviction he could go to prison for a considerable time out on the coast at the provincial penitentiary."

"Ah. I see." Lorimer sat back, took out a cigarette, and lit it. Was that a look of relief on his face at the news of Townsend being out of the way? Darling took an ashtray out of his bottom drawer and placed it in front of Lorimer.

Ames came in with his notebook and sat in the back corner by the window, smiling genially.

"Now then," began Darling, "can you tell me about your relationship with Harvey Townsend?"

"I beg your pardon? Really, Inspector, you of all people ought to know I have no relationship with him whatsoever. You yourself warned me about his proclivities. I let him go on the spot."

"But that's not quite true, is it? The two of you were seen sometime later the same evening in an argument. You were heard to tell Townsend he was a complete incompetent and that this was something else you'd have to do yourself. I think you'll agree that this sounds more like something a person would say to a man who is permanently in his employ."

"It's perfectly possible that I was arguing with one of my men. I have a number of staff at the mansion. Whoever overheard this could have heard me speaking to any of them. I don't know where this is going, but I haven't got all day. The election is in two short weeks. In fact," he said, consulting his watch, "my wife and I have a luncheon with the Ladies' Recital Society in an hour."

"I'll be as quick as I can. I should clarify that the witness saw you speaking with Townsend specifically, on the terrace."

"That's ridiculous. It was dark. They could not have seen me speaking with Townsend. He wasn't there, I told you."

Darling glanced at Ames and saw him raise his eyebrows and scribble away in his book.

"Perhaps you're right. Now can I ask you if you are familiar with any of these people? Carl Castle?"

"Never heard of him."

"Buck Heppwith?"

Lorimer frowned. "Look, Inspector. I don't know what this is in aid of, but I've had enough." He stubbed out his cigarette angrily.

"Klaus Lazek? Only he's dead. He was shot and died of his injuries a few days later. He was a refugee from Sudetenland. I believe you worked for the CWR prior to the war and were one of the administrators of the program those refugees came in under. We are investigating his murder, so we're hopeful that with your prior knowledge of him, you might be able to help us track down anyone who might have had it in for him."

"Can't help you, I'm afraid. I did work for the railway in the thirties. My resumé is no secret. There were hundreds of refugees, and I was a minor official. I scarcely had contact. Didn't even speak English, most of 'em. Anything else, Inspector? My wife will be waiting for me to pick her up for the luncheon."

"Yes, just one more thing. Are you familiar with Gustav Sadler? Only I see he's given a substantial donation to your campaign."

"Yes. I do know him, and I don't see, at this point, what business it is of yours. He's been very supportive."

"You are aware he spent most of the war in jail because he openly espoused Nazi propaganda?"

"He is the leader of a perfectly respectable local branch of the Unity Party. I know nothing of this so-called Nazi business."

Darling opened his desk drawer and pulled out the swastika pin. "Really? Because this is the official pin of the Unity Party."

Lorimer was standing. "If that's the case, I suppose I will have to vet my support more carefully. If you've nothing further, good day."

"I may need to contact you if I have more questions," Darling said, also standing. "I'll walk you downstairs."

Lorimer strode briskly away from the station, crossed the street, and walked toward city hall. When he was in his office he closed the door and sat down heavily. He had covered every angle. He'd had the boat destroyed. He'd been sure there'd be a verdict of suicide, because they'd never connect the killing to Heppwith. But if they did, he'd pay a lawyer to defend him, knowing those prints on the gun would be enough to convict him. He'd sent his secretary to the hospital to make sure. The man had been dying, so there was nothing to worry about. He told himself this firmly, but his hand was shaking as he reached into his desk drawer for the Scotch. It was the shock of seeing that damn pin. He poured a drink. He had to watch it—there was still the bloody ladies' luncheon. His heart, under the influence of good sense, slowed down. Of course, it wasn't his pin, they were a dime a dozen, and no one could pin that one on him. He chuckled mirthlessly at his little joke, and stood up, ready to face the ladies, ready to face, more exactly, his own lady.

"HEY!" EXCLAIMED HEPPWITH, who was having breakfast in his cell and had been given a copy of yesterday's paper to while away the time. "Hey, guard! This is the guy! This is the guy who gave me the gun." He was pointing at a half-page ad by the committee to elect Lorimer, with a large photograph of the candidate himself.

CHAPTER THIRTY-THREE

LINDA LORIMER STOOD LOOKING OUT at the stone terrace, light reflecting on it from the window. All her life she'd wanted this. A beautiful house with a stone terrace onto the garden. She'd fixated on the terrace when she was young and stuck in the tiny rooms upstairs in a dilapidated shanty in East Vancouver. A great solid stone base upon which her whole life could unfold in beauty and plenty. She could scarcely think how she'd gotten here, or what here was, after all. It was people who are fickle and unstable, she thought. It was a wonder to her that after her experience with her mother's drunken fragility and her father's disappearance, she didn't remember this when she'd cast her lot with Lorimer. Whatever happens, she thought, I'm keeping the terrace.

She turned and went down the long hallway to her husband's office, her fingers trailing lightly on the panelling, as if to mark it as hers. Her husband wasn't there. It wasn't a woman this time. He'd stormed angrily out of the house after waiting most of the day for a phone call, muttering, "Where the bloody hell is he?" He was sinking, and she sensed it with a cool inner triumph. She pushed open the door and went to his desk and reached into the back of the third drawer, where she found the key in the tiny secret inner drawer. She took the key, as she'd done many times before, and went to the cabinet where he kept first editions. She opened one of the books, revealing that it was a secret document box. She sorted swiftly through the papers, stopping when she heard a sound outside the door, her heart beating faster. But it was only the butler turning down the lights in the hallway. Finding what she wanted, she closed the book and then the cupboard, locked it, and replaced the key.

She looked at the clock in the hallway. Someone would be at the police station. Now that she had it, she wanted it out of the house and in the hands of the police. With it safe in her handbag she went out to the foyer, slipped on her light summer coat, and then went around to the garage, where the chauffeur was doing something to one of the cars. She looked at him appraisingly before he turned and saw her. I'll keep him, and the cars, she thought.

When the chauffeur pulled up in front of the station, she got out of the car and then looked in the passenger-side window. "I'll be only a few minutes. Will you wait?"

"Madam." He'd lost sleep over her more than once.

Inside, Linda Lorimer approached the night man, who could scarcely conceal his delight that yet again, on one of his shifts a beautiful woman had come into the station, and said, "I have something for Inspector Darling. Will you see he gets it?"

THUNDER RUMBLED ACROSS the sky, making a sound like someone in the attic moving Lady Armstrong's boxes. Lane had been upstairs to make sure the windows were closed. Lady Armstrong's ghost had opened the windows in storms before. There was another crash of thunder, and she waited, counting. It was close, but she could probably dart to the Armstrongs' without being incinerated. She slipped into her wellies, pulled her yellow storm jacket on, and went out the door. Rain was pelting down, making the delicate arched boughs of the weeping willow dip. She stood out in the deluge, her face turned up to the roiling granite sky. Only another roll of thunder ended this symbolic and largely unsuccessful washing away of sadness, and she sloshed hurriedly across her little gully and made for the post office. She pulled open the door and shook off the rain, and found Gwen Hughes leaning on the post office window. She turned when Lane came in.

"Finally, eh? Mother's worried the blooms will be knocked off what's left of the lupines, but the pigs are in heaven! By the way, she'd like to thank you for recovering our things. Come up for a proper lunch after church tomorrow. We have a lovely bit of beef."

"I'm afraid I had nothing to do with the recovery. All good police work, but I can't resist a lovely bit of beef. What can I bring? Anyway, I should be thanking you. My garden has been lovely. Fresh carrots. An absolute luxury!"

"Bring nothing at all . . . unless you have something to drink. You know what the vicar's like."

LANE, DIVESTED OF her boots and wet jacket, stood in the parlour with Eleanor and Kenny Armstrong. Alexandra, who had hoped for some new adventure when everyone trooped into the usually closed sitting room, had given up and was sitting alertly on the window seat looking out at the rain cascading onto the now-spent raspberry and current bushes at the side of the house. The humans were looking at the silver-framed picture of John Armstrong, still and forever captured standing loosely at attention in his uniform, his face held for that moment between a shy seriousness and a smile. He looked so young, Lane thought, and so innocent of all that was to come.

"Good to have him back. I missed him," Kenny said, a slight catch in his throat. "I miss him." He turned and walked to where his father's sword hung on the wall next to the cabinet with myriad porcelain knick-knacks and the photo of Eleanor with her nursing sisters. "And as for this regimental sword, it is worse than useless as a defence of this cottage."

Alexandra, seeing action, leaped off the bench and came to stand with them. "But that's your job, isn't it?" Eleanor said, bending over to ruffle Alexandra's ears.

"Ha! Fat lot of good she did!" Kenny said affectionately. "Tea, Mother. What do you say?"

Back in the kitchen, tea and seed cake laid out, Eleanor said, "Alexandra is thrilled to have her water bowl back. Now, what's that inspector up to?"

"Haven't the foggiest," Lane said, biting into a slice of buttered cake. "You must teach me to make this. I've never had anything like it. The seed cake we ate during the war was always dried out."

"I soak the dried fruit overnight in tea. A mix of pekoe and a smoky lapsang, and you know perfectly well what I mean."

It had been a week and a half since Lane had phoned the police station. The election was in a few days, and she'd read in the papers that Lorimer had pulled out, so the election of the blameless but boring Mr. Cray would be a mere formality. She had no idea what had happened with the other principals in the affair. And she didn't want to know, she thought firmly and dishonestly. "I imagine the inspector is busy. He has two people in custody and is likely trying to build a case against the third, that prat Lorimer."

"But what does he say in his evening calls?" Eleanor asked, her face a perfect study in inquisitive innocence.

Lane was silent, occupying herself with a close scan of King George V. He didn't look as unpleasant as she had heard he was.

"What have you done?" Eleanor asked gently.

"Nothing really," Lane said finally. "It's just . . . I think we're better off as friends. It's all so awkward, isn't it? Anyway, he wants me to stay out of his business, and I can hardly blame him. I know he'd prefer we simply maintain cordial and distant relations."

Kenny was sitting back, his slippered feet up on the edge of the stove, his arms crossed, looking up at the chimney pipe.

"What absolute rubbish you do talk!" Eleanor said, dropping a piece of cake for Alexandra. "I've seen the way he looks at you. He's too far gone to pull back now. What are you playing at?"

Lane looked up in surprise. It was certainly the first time she'd been chastised by Eleanor Armstrong.

"I'm not playing at anything. If you must know, he mentioned marriage. Obviously that's out of the question. I thought I'd better put a bit of distance between us."

"It's not so obvious to me. Why should it be out of the question?"

"I . . . I don't know . . . I'm not marriage material, am I?"

Kenny came to life, and his feet dropped off the grate. "I don't know about that. I'd marry you in a jiffy if I were forty years younger. I'll have another slug of that tea, Mother."

"And unencumbered," pointed out Eleanor, pouring. "The point is, why can't you marry? Do you not love him?"

Lane was silent.

"I thought so. You're being foolish, my dear. Kenny and I have been married since after the Great War. At our age we know how short life is. Of course, I understand, the modern girl and all that. Fine then, but you should not throw him over. Men like that don't come along every day. Kind, decent men who admire the women they love." She reached out for Kenny's hand. "And they're sitting ducks if they love you, believe me. Strike, my dear, strike. The iron will never be any hotter."

Nor could my face, Lane thought, as she went back into the rain, now a fine mist. There was a small opening in the heavy charcoal clouds in the east, and the orange light of the setting sun was casting across a growing patch of blue. The smell of the ground, soaked after its long drought, filled her senses. She knew that she was already preparing to cope with the nightly disappointment of there being no phone call from Darling. She struck off up the road to the path that led to the old school. A brisk walk would tire her, and then she would have a bath, read, go to bed early and have a good rest, and try not to long for the time when she hadn't known him and her heart was still her own.

IT WAS DARK when she pushed open the door, kicked off her boots, hung her jacket on the hook by the door, and then nearly jumped out of her skin.

"I've told you before about leaving your door unlocked. Anyone could wander in." Darling, holding a Scotch, was leaning against the door into the sitting room. "I've lit the fire, I hope you don't mind, and helped myself to a drink. Can I get you one?"

"Yes, all right. I've been to the Armstrongs' and I've been getting an earful from them, and then had a long wet walk. I could use a drink."

He poured a Scotch and handed it to her where she'd collapsed on her easy chair in front of the Franklin. "I've stopped by to tell you some news," he said.

That you love me? Lane thought, and then slapped the thought away. "About the case? Lorimer has been overcome by the Holy Ghost and confessed?"

"Not exactly, but close. His wife, Linda, you remember her?"

"The Ice Queen, yes. She didn't think much of me, I'm afraid."

"She doesn't think much of him, either. She turned up at the station yesterday evening with a document showing the gun we have from the scene as registered to him. I gather he's put himself about a bit too much over the years, and she's tired of it. She said she saw him leave with it on the Friday Lazek was shot. It turns out she kept a close eye on his movements. Her one comment was, 'He thinks I'm stupid.' She also, much to my amazement, doesn't care much for his fascist friends. We may have enough now."

"That's brilliant. I love it when the deserving meet a just fate! What I haven't been able to make out is why he went after Carl, but not Heppwith."

"I think because he thought Carl saw him. He didn't realize Carl couldn't see in the dark and was too drunk to make sense of things. He was hoping he could get Heppwith, who is a bit of a lunatic, to do the shooting, but when he wouldn't Lorimer did the work himself. But he was wearing gloves and Heppwith wasn't, so the prints on the gun were enough to keep Heppwith in the frame."

"Poor Klaus Lazek. Misfortune heaped upon misfortune. A refugee, then his family goes into the maw of Hitler's camps, then he's murdered. Why isn't life more like an Agatha Christie novel, where only the repellent meet untimely ends?"

Darling leaned forward, looking into his glass. "Because, I suppose, life is more complicated. You take an action because of something in yourself, and you don't know how the other fellow is going to react. Take Lazek. He was infuriated to see a man he believed had siphoned off money meant for refugees becoming a big political figure, and couldn't help confronting him. Although clearly Lorimer was already a hard and unyielding man when Lazek first met him, he couldn't have known that Lorimer now has too much to lose and has reached that stage of being powerful enough that he truly believed he could get away with it. And like so many people who think like that, he went in for a spot of lily gilding. He knew all about Townsend's antique business. In fact, he allowed Townsend to store his collection in one of his warehouses, and popped down now and again to help himself before they were shipped off. Lorimer came in with Mrs. Armstrong's Chinese dish claiming Townsend had tried to sell it to him. He didn't realize we already had Townsend under lock and key. So if we can't get Lorimer for the murder, we will certainly have him for receiving stolen goods. In any case his political career is over. More?" He held out the bottle.

"You're being fast and loose with my Scotch. Had we better think of something to eat instead?"

"I have thought of that. In your fridge you will find two steaks and a lettuce, and there's a bottle of wine on the counter."

As they moved to the kitchen, Darling asked, "Why were you being lectured by Mrs. Armstrong?"

"She thinks I'm a fool."

"You are, of course, but you write rather well. I like this." He picked up the poem she had left by her typewriter.

"You can put that down smartly." She walked over and took it out of his hand and pushed it into the drawer. His nearness confused her. He took her gently by the arm. "A sad poem. I too feel a sense of yearning and loss, only I wouldn't have said it as beautifully as you." He put both his arms around her, and she leaned into him, feeling in danger of losing herself all over again.

"Should we go on pretending?" she asked into his shoulder.

Darling shook his head. "That's always been my trouble. I can't pretend. I love you. I haven't been able to sleep or eat, and Ames is looking at me as if I kicked his favourite puppy. I can't pretend I don't love you. And I can't pretend I don't want to marry you, especially here, in this beautiful place with you. And if you don't want to marry, fine, but please don't send me away."

LATER, THEIR STEAKS finished, they stretched out in front of the fire, holding hands across the gap between the chairs.

"I've never been proposed to before. Is that how it's normally done?" Lane asked.

"Perhaps I should ask Ames. I imagine he's always proposing."

"No, he's not. He threw Violet over because he wouldn't."

Darling stood and drew her up and took her hands. "Miss Winslow, will you . . .?"

"I'm seeing the vicar at lunch tomorrow, should I have a word? Something for after Ames gets back? Oh, and after the apple harvest. I promised Robin I'd look after my apples this year."

He pulled her close and kissed her. "Never mind the damned apples. Will Ames make a hash of being a best man, I wonder?" he asked.

ACKNOWLEDGMENTS

WHO HAS A KINDER, MORE generous, or more supportive publishing team than I do? Thanks to Taryn, whose belief in my books makes it possible to write them; Renée and her team of editors who briskly and kindly whip my words into shape; Colin, who beautifully designs the cover and interior; Margaret, who creates stunning cover illustrations; and Tori, who works, apparently tirelessly, to connect Lane Winslow and me to the world and an ever-expanding readership through social media and good old-fashioned sweat.

I would like, as ever, to thank my doughty readers, Sasha Bley-Vroman and Gerald Miller. Their close reading, suggestions, and, most of all, encouragement have helped me immeasurably to make this a story worth reading. I am happy to welcome some medical expertise to my team in the person of Dr. Jeff Fine, who has been thoughtful and helpful on the subject of reliably lethal wounds.

I'd also like to thank all the reviewers for their support and for bringing readers to the Lane Winslow mysteries—and you, dear readers, for all your personal notes to me. When confidence starts to flag and I begin to think I would better serve the world by just sitting on the deck with a cup of tea, the personal outreach of readers lifts my spirits and sends me back to work with new enthusiasm.

Finally, I thank my family, whose genuine delight in finding they are related to a mystery writer has given me wings.

And, of course, to my dearest daily companion, idea tester, nonsense deflator, offerer of wisdom and unabashed support, a special gratitude. Thank you, Terry.

PHOTO BY ANICK VIOLETTE

IONA WHISHAW was born in British Columbia. After living her early years in the Kootenays, she spent her formative years living and learning in Mexico, Nicaragua, and the US. She travelled extensively for pleasure and education before settling in the Vancouver area. Throughout her roles as youth worker, social worker, teacher, and award-winning high school principal, her love of writing remained consistent, and compelled her to obtain her master's in creative writing from the University of British Columbia. Iona has published short fiction, poetry, poetry translation, and one children's book, *Henry and the Cow Problem*. *A Killer in King's Cove* was her first adult novel. Her heroine, Lane Winslow, was inspired by Iona's mother who, like her father before her, was a wartime spy. Book #7 in the series, *A Match Made for Murder*, won the Bony Blithe Light Mystery Award. Visit ionawhishaw.com to find out more.

THE LANE WINSLOW MYSTERY SERIES